Sentinel Flame Book 1

Hyroc

A journey of survival for a boy robbed of his home and forced into a world full of dangers and unknowns

By Adam Freestone
Alaskan Writer of Imaginative Creativity

PUBLICATION
CONSULTANTS
We Believe In The Power Of Authors

PO Box 221974 Anchorage, Alaska 99522-1974
books@publicationconsultants.com—www.publicationconsultants.com

ISBN: 978-1-59433-837-3
eISBN: 978-1-59433-838-0

Library of Congress Catalog Card Number: 2019910278

Cover design by Judith Nicolas

Manufactured in the United States of America.

Contents

CHAPTER 1

Black Sheep

Warm rays of sunlight shone through wide gaps between cottony clouds dotting the afternoon sky and a calm breeze kept the air comfortably cool. It was the best kind of day to be outside. Especially for the group of young boys playing a rowdy game near one of the well-groomed trees adorning the grounds of their school. It was considered a test of bravery by some to come this close to the tree. Not that the tree was intimidating. In fact, it looked quite plain as far as trees go. None of its leaf covered branches were twisted in strange ways and its trunk was unmarked by unusual looking knots. And there were no stories where bad things had once happened beneath its shade. By all its qualities it was nearly identical to the other trees scattered throughout the school grounds. Save for one.

That one quality made teachers who were tasked with watching students pay extra attention to the boys playing near it and some older students who occasionally glanced toward the tree. The quality was hard to see, but every so often, a small shift of movement and the faint glint of two sapphire eyes would reveal it. Everyone thought the thing those eyes belonged to was evil, some harbinger of ill fortune. A thing to bring a curse upon them. Why else would it stay hidden if it wasn't planning something dreadful? Only evil things with a hatred for sunlight would cling to the shadows. Why such a thing was allowed to be here none of the onlookers could answer. Most thought things like this only existed in far-off places, or in dark stories. Yet, here it was. Maybe a fit of madness had driven the person who had found the thing to believe it belonged in such a place. Or maybe it possessed powers of enchantment over the mind allowing it to make others think it was harmless.

But despite the rampant and varied opinions about the nature of the thing those eyes were a part of, none were the least bit accurate. The thing possessed no abilities to control others, it had never harmed anyone and it frankly never wished to. It knew harming others was wrong. In many ways it was not dissimilar from the onlookers. But it was still different enough. The thing didn't understand why it's differences made everyone so uncomfortable. And when people were uncomfortable it didn't like how they acted. They would raise their voices and sometimes even hurt the thing. No lasting harm would come from this, but the thing always felt as if it had done something it shouldn't have. Then there was the staring.

It hated being stared at. All those eyes from every direction looking at it. It made the thing want to hide. And it's favorite hiding spot was this tree. Behind the trunk and beneath the cool shadow of its branches the thing could only be seen if people tried hard to spot it. It made the thing feel safe, as if nothing could harm it. But as secure as the thing felt here, it was not content. What it really wanted was out in the bright sunlight, away from the tree. What it wanted was relatively simple. Something a child would want. It wanted to join the group of boys who played in front of it. Even if it had to venture out into sight, where it would be stared at. If it could join the group then being stared at might not be so bad. The thing was sure even with its differences, it wouldn't have any advantage over the boys, it would be a fair game. Though the most pressing issue would be for them to let him join their game. They had never let him no matter how hard he tried. It was aggravating they wouldn't.

With a displeased sigh, Hyroc settled down into a sitting position in a space between two winding roots, putting his back to the group. There wasn't any point in watching them any longer; it would just make him want to join them even more. He rested his head against the tree's trunk, using his hand to smooth out a patch of his fur sticking up uncomfortably against the bark. Why his body was covered in a black layer of it with two dark brown stripes running from his eyes over the back of his head no one could answer. Along with why he had a whiskerless snout and why his head greatly resembled a wolverine's. Hyroc used his fingers to feel along his snout down to his nose, as he absentmindedly stared at the stones of the moss strewn wall surrounding the school. He didn't think it made him look scary like everyone seemed to act. Once his fingers found the end of his nose he moved them down to his mouth and touched the ends of his teeth. It could have been his teeth, they were sharper than everyone else's, but dogs also had those and no one seemed to mind. Hyroc lowered his hand to his neck to feel along the brass chain of a necklace he wore, stopping at a disc of silver attached to the end with the visage of a bear etched into the front. He dropped his hands into his lap and blew out a breath. It really didn't matter why; those boys were never going to let him join their game.

He picked up a twig lying on the ground and began spinning it around in his fingers. A moment later, the boys began yelling excitedly. His conviction to ignore the group dissolved at the sound and he was once again standing against the tree's trunk watching them with his white hand-claws resting against the bark. Being alone wasn't any fun, maybe today would be different; maybe today they would finally let him play with them. He brushed the dirt from his pants and blue gray school robe. Gathering his courage with a deep breath, he stepped toward the group.

His shoe had scarcely touched the ground when he became aware of someone standing behind him. Turning his head, he got a start, memories of pain flashed through his body when he saw Billy Mason leaning against the tree's trunk staring down at him.

Billy was a heavyset boy, three years older than Hyroc, with greasy black hair. Two other boys; Hurly and Phil, emerged from the other side of the tree behind Hyroc, arraying themselves to block any escape attempt.

Hyroc silently chided himself for not keeping an eye out for these three boys. How could he have forgotten? They were always looking for him!

"I thought we were all friends, Scatt," Billy said, walking toward Hyroc. "You ran away yesterday and ruined all our *fun*, Scatt."

Hyroc restrained himself from yelling back the reason; it would only make the beating worse. It would hurt less if he kept quiet.

"Billy, Billy, I came up with another name for Scatt," Hurly said with an evil grin. He lowered his voice. "It's – it's got a *swear word* in it."

Billy turned his head toward Hurly. "What is it?"

Snickering, Hurly said, "Bastard Bear." The three of them burst into laughter. Hyroc flushed, feeling suddenly warm in the face. That was a very bad thing to be called, especially for him.

"That's pretty good. Bastard Bear. I like it."

"Bastard," Phil said chortling.

"What do you think of the name *Bastard Bear*?"

Hyroc's face turned hot. He knew it would make them hurt him more but he couldn't stop himself from speaking. "*My name is Hyroc!*" Hyroc growled.

Billy grinned broadly. "What's that *Bastard Bear*?"

"*Stop* calling me that!"

"I think we hurt his feelings," Phil said feigning sympathy.

Billy stepped up to Hyroc. "What did you say *Bastard Bear*?" He shoved Hyroc sideways away from the tree's trunk. Barely maintaining his balance, Hyroc stumbled over the root riddled ground. "Did we hurt your feelings, *Bastard Bear*?" Billy shoved him much harder. The back of Hyroc's foot caught on a root as he stumbled backward, causing him to fall and hit his head on the ground. "Your mother was a *witch* and she deserved to die." Hyroc's expression hardened and he shot Billy a volcanic glare as he rose to his feet.

"*Don't* talk about my mother that way," Hyroc bellowed.

Billy smiled derisively. "And how are you going to make me, *Bastard Bear*? You're a coward, that's why you run away all the time, and cowards don't fight back, Bastard Bear."

Hyroc clenched his fists. "*Stop* calling me that!" he snapped back.

Billy's smile broadened. "Make me, B–"

Something inside Hyroc snapped. With a primal yell, Hyroc tackled Billy as he uttered the first syllable of the name. Billy hit the ground and Hyroc rammed his fist into the side of the bully's jaw. Billy took a wild swing at his attacker; Hyroc dodged out of the way and using both fists one after another laid into the boy's face. Blood quickly began streaming out of Billy's nose. Alarmed yells of teachers filled the air, but they sounded distant to Hyroc. By the time a teacher finally wrenched him off Billy; the bully's face was purple with bruises and sticky with blood. Hurly and Phil stared at Hyroc with their mouths agape in complete shock. The group of playing boys stopped and stared in amazement at the spectacle.

Hyroc's rage fizzled out when he recognized the teacher as Miss Duncan. If he could imagine anyone as a witch, it was she. She was an old gray-haired woman, with a withering gaze. She punished him for even the slightest infraction, things other teachers would rarely bother with. She raised her hand and struck Hyroc in the side of the face. His nostrils stung as he felt a warm streamer of blood run out of his nose.

"Fighting another student!" she said coolly. "The headmaster will hear of this." She grabbed Hyroc's arm in a painful vice like grip. He gritted his teeth as she dragged him to the headmaster's office.

The headmaster looked up from a piece of parchment laid across his desk, a writing quill in hand, as Hyroc and Miss Duncan burst through the door. The headmaster was a man of average height and build, in his early forties, with brown hair showing thin strips of gray in places across his head. His face was unmarked, with the discerning look of intelligence from long years of study and his eyes were both stern and perceptive.

Bookshelves and glass cabinets covered most of the room's wall space. A large pane glass window sat directly behind the headmaster, with a single door to the right and a fireplace set into the wall on the left.

The headmaster's eyes focused on Hyroc, a flash of irritation showing. He placed his quill in a half-full ink well before it could drip and stain the immaculate polished surface of his desk.

"Yes, Miss Duncan?" the headmaster said, sounding subtly annoyed.

She looked down at Hyroc. "This, *student*," Miss Duncan said as if the mere thought caused her discomfort. "Was caught fighting on the school grounds." The headmaster sighed. "And *he* seriously injured another student."

"Thank you for bringing this to my attention. I'll take care of it." She nodded curtly, releasing her grip. Yanking his arm free, Hyroc rubbed his throbbing arm as she swept out of the room, closing the door behind her. The headmaster stood up from his desk and walked over to look out the window; his arms folded behind his back.

"Is what she said true?" the headmaster said in a stern tone.

"Yes," Hyroc grumbled.

"Who was it?"

"It was Billy."

"Billy Mason?"

"Yes."

The headmaster shrugged. "Who threw the first punch?"

Hyroc glowered but remained silent. He was in trouble now. He shouldn't have done that.

The headmaster turned, giving Hyroc a severe look. "*Who threw the first punch?*"

"I did," Hyroc admitted grudgingly. He didn't want to say it, but lying would get him into even more trouble.

The headmaster narrowed his eyes. "You, what!"

Hyroc spoke in a rapid irritated tone. "He and his friends called me a – a – a 'Bastard Bear'. And they said *things* about – about *my mother*!"

The headmaster shook his head dismissively. "Just because someone says something you don't like, doesn't give you the right to beat them bloody."

"Then *why* is everyone else allowed to?" Hyroc blurted out before he knew he was saying it.

Caught slightly off-guard the headmaster shrugged, his expression softening. He walked over to Hyroc. "Do you remember what I told you about The Ministry trying to take you away from me when you were a baby?"

The man was more than a person in charge to Hyroc, he was his father and his name was Marcus. For as long as Hyroc could remember, he had known something was wrong. The most obvious sign was he looked nothing like his father. When he had asked Marcus about this, knowing the futility of trying to hide the blatantly obvious, he told

Hyroc the truth, at least the little truth he knew. Hyroc had been found in the arms of his dead mother – who bore his matching features – and Marcus had adopted him, raising him as if he were his own. Despite an initial storm of confusion this knowledge brought, beyond no longer referring to him as father, the bond between them remained strong. Marcus then gave Hyroc a necklace that had been around his neck when he was found. The trinket was his only link to his real parents, who he knew nothing about. He often thought about what they might have been like and tried to think back to the time when his mother was still alive. Frustratingly, he could never remember anything before Marcus, just a strange sense of cold that made a patch of frostbitten skin on his ear prickle.

"Yes." Hyroc responded.

"The Ministry is looking for *any* reason to take you away," Marcus said.

Hyroc felt a bolt of fear shot through him. He didn't want to go with them, something bad would happen to him if he did. "I'm sorry; I didn't mean to get in a fight with Billy."

Marcus gave him a dismissive wave. "I know."

"Don't let them take me away, I don't want to go, I want to stay with you and June, I promise I'll do better," Hyroc pleaded.

"I know you do."

"Why do they hate me so much?"

Marcus smiled half humoredly. "They don't *hate* you, they're just scared. You're different and people around here aren't used to seeing things that are different. That's why it's so important for you to avoid fighting."

"And I will."

Marcus affectionately patted him on the shoulder. "I know you will."

Marcus walked back over to his desk, removing a large wooden paddle. Hyroc stiffened at the sight of the paddle taking an instinctual step backward and giving Marcus a horrified look. Marcus had never used the paddle on him, but he had heard disturbing stories of how much pain a strike on the rear from it caused. He stared at Marcus with pleading eyes as he approached. Marcus set the paddle on the cushion of a nearby chair then began watching a space below the door to his office. Hyroc's eyes darted between Marcus' face and the paddle in a mixture of puzzlement and absolute terror. Marcus put a finger to his lips, signaling for Hyroc to remain quiet.

He came up close to Hyroc. "Miss Duncan's listening," he whispered. "I know you didn't do anything worthy of the paddle, if anyone should be punished it's Billy. But she won't be satisfied until I use it on you." Marcus indicated the chair the paddle sat in. "I'm going to hit the chair with the paddle, and when I do, I want you to yell out as if I hit you. Got it?" Hyroc nodded, breathing a sigh of relief. "Make sure those are convincing yells." Marcus walked back over to the chair, picking up the paddle. He glanced back toward Hyroc. Hyroc nodded. Marcus raised the paddle and hit the chair cushion. Hyroc wailed out in simulated pain. The two of them repeated the process four more times. Just after the last strike, a thin shadow slid across the opening beneath the door and the fading sound of footsteps radiated into the office. The two of them studied the door until the sound had died away.

Marcus nodded approvingly, set the paddle back behind his desk and walked back over to Hyroc. "I wouldn't worry too much about bullies bothering you until the end of summer after the beating you must have given Billy. But don't think what you did was okay. Next time I might not be so understanding. Got it?" Hyroc nodded enthusiastically. "Good. Now off you go; it won't do either of us any good for you to miss any more of your class." Marcus made to stand then paused. His eyes narrowed as he noticed blood-soaked fur beneath Hyroc's nose. Anger flared in Marcus' eyes, but it was gone so fast Hyroc wasn't sure it was what he had seen. Marcus pulled a handkerchief from his pocket and handed it to Hyroc. Wordlessly, Hyroc took the proffered handkerchief and began wiping the blood away as he made for the door.

Hyroc had four classes; Reading and Witch Studies came before lunch, then scribing and arithmetic. It was now past lunch, so he made his way to his scribing class.

When he came through the door into the well-lit room. The students were already seated at a long table scratching words into their pieces of parchment with writing quills. The teacher, a tall, brown haired, clean-shaven man, a few years younger than Marcus, looked up from the work of a student he was overseeing. He was strict, and although he kept a close eye on Hyroc, he treated him close enough to the other students to avoid making the classroom overly uncomfortable.

"You're late," the teacher said in a cool tone. "Class started more than fifteen minutes ago."

"I was with the headmaster," Hyroc replied.

The teacher gave an uncaring nod. He indicated a pile of scrolls sitting on his desk. "Read then copy down what is written on the scroll. You will lose points for sloppy or illegible writing."

Hyroc nodded and the teacher returned his attention to the student he was helping. Hyroc collected a scroll from the pile, a blank piece of parchment stacked beside them, a glass ink well, and a writing quill. Carefully balancing his supplies in his arms, he walked over and laid them on the table, then seated himself. As he unrolled the scroll, out of the corner of his eye he saw several students steal a quick, nervous glance at him. He was accustomed to those kinds of looks, but those students seemed more afraid of him than usual, which made him uncomfortable. Doing his best to ignore them, he began copying the words from the scroll onto his parchment. As Hyroc worked, the teacher moved from student to student, eventually finding his way to him. The teacher looked over Hyroc's shoulder, sharply pointed out some flaws with what he had written before moving on.

At the end of class, Hyroc made his way to his final class of the day. All he ever did in arithmetic class was solve various equations and learn to count exact amounts of coin. He found the whole exercise incredibly boring and felt it a complete waste of his time, but Marcus had insisted it was important, so he did his best not to let his annoyance show.

After class, he and the other students were free to do whatever they wanted until dinner. Many of the students gathered with friends at this time, but since Hyroc had none, he simply returned to Marcus' office to read a book. About an hour later, he made his way to the dining hall for dinner.

Streamers of dimming evening light reached into the hall through windows lining the walls; mingled with lit candles atop stands throughout the room. Two large parallel tables laden with bowls and utensils ran half the length of the room. A single closed-door on the rightmost wall, just before the first window, led into the kitchen. Past the tables, two steps led up to a short platform with a wooden podium. Close to the hall's end-wall, running perpendicular to the tables, sat a third table that seated the school's staff.

Hyroc seated himself at the furthest end of the rightmost table where Marcus could more easily keep an eye on him from his seat at the staff table. He watched the other boys hopefully, but as usual, none of them sat within arm's reach of him. Hyroc quickly picked Billy Mason out at the opposite end of the table. His bruised face and a bloodstained wad of cloth protruding from his nostrils made him easy to identify. Billy met Hyroc's gaze with a contemptuous glare. Though Marcus disapproved of the beating, Hyroc felt satisfaction when he looked at Billy. He hadn't thought he had done much damage to the older boy's face. Maybe now he would think twice about calling people names and insulting their mothers.

The cooks emerged from the kitchen carrying steaming soup pots, which they sat on each table. The meal consisted of a stew made with carrots, leeks, potatoes, and some kind of unknown meat, and served with a piece of tasteless bread. After dinner, Hyroc made his way back to Marcus' office where he continued reading until Marcus told him it was time for bed. Hyroc marked the page, closed the book and set it back on its shelf before heading through the door right of the window where the headmaster's sleeping quarter were.

The sleeping quarter was a small room. Marcus' bed sat in the middle of the room against the wall, with a window flanked with red curtains on the left wall. A small table with a lit candle and two chairs were tucked away in the corner, and a washbasin sat near the head of the bed. Hyroc slept on a soft mattress filled with hay, laid at the foot of the bed. Originally, he had slept in the same bed as Marcus, but shortly after he began attending the school, feeling somewhat embarrassed by this arrangement, Hyroc requested that he have his own bed and his father happily obliged.

"Beyond that *incident* earlier, how was your day?" Marcus asked, after he had dressed into a night robe and began helping Hyroc into his pajamas.

Hyroc shrugged his shoulders. "Good I guess," he replied.

"Learn anything interesting?"

"Not really." He couldn't understand why Marcus always asked that question. Nothing he ever learned at the school was particularly interesting.

Frowning slightly, Marcus shook his head in disbelief. Hyroc walked over to the washbasin, opened up a small wooden box containing his boar hair toothbrush, dipped its bristles in the water, and began scrubbing his teeth.

Marcus pulled the window curtains closed. "Did you have any more problems today?"

Hyroc turned toward Marcus with the wooden toothbrush handle sticking out of his mouth. "No, but everyone seems more afraid of me now," Hyroc said humorlessly, careful not to spit out foamed saliva as he spoke.

Marcus gave him a sympathetic look. "Don't worry I'm sure that'll fade. Besides, you're almost done with school until next fall. I'm sure nobody will remember what you did by then."

I've still got almost three weeks here, Hyroc thought unpleasantly. 'almost done' seemed like it should be something a lot shorter. Marcus made it sound as if school was already over.

Hyroc washed his toothbrush off, placed it back in its holder and closed the box.

"Let me see those teeth," Marcus said. Rolling his eyes, Hyroc opened his long mouth, exposing every one of his teeth. He knew how to brush his teeth. Marcus studied them a moment then nodded his approval. Hyroc closed his mouth and climbed into his bed. Marcus crouched down beside him and tucked him in. "I love you." Marcus moved to kiss him on the head but Hyroc recoiled.

"Do you *have* to do that?" Hyroc asked annoyed. He was eight years old, why did Marcus have to keep doing that? He wasn't a baby anymore.

"I'm your father, so, yes," Marcus said, before kissing Hyroc on the top of the head. Hyroc sighed. When Marcus pulled away, he frowned. He opened his mouth, reached inside with two fingers and removed a single black hair. Hyroc laughed. Maybe getting hairs in his mouth would make him stop. Marcus studied the hair then, smiling said, "I guess I deserved that." Fluttering his fingers Marcus shed the hair. He walked over to the table and blew out the lit candle, darkening the room. Carefully he made his way to his own bed and climbed in.

"Good night," Marcus said.

"Night."

The next morning Hyroc was thrust awake when Marcus opened the curtains, letting a flood of bright morning sunlight into the room. Hyroc groaned unhappily, pulling the cover over his head. It seemed impossible it was morning already! How could adults stand to get up earlier than this.

"Come on," Marcus said. "You need to get up and get dressed, or you're going to miss breakfast. And I know how cranky you get when that happens." Hyroc continued to groan, hoping his sounds of misery were enough for Marcus to let him go back to sleep. "Every student in the school does the same thing every morning, and you're not exempt just because you're the headmaster's son." Hyroc groaned even louder. It seemed to be working. "Fine, I guess I'll just have to get the bucket." No, it wasn't. Hyroc immediately threw the cover off, sat up, rubbed the sleep from his eyes, and began getting dressed. Marcus smiled.

Once fully clothed in his school garb, Hyroc walked over to the washbasin. He wetted his head and began combing the unsightly fur all over it. He always hated doing this, he felt like a little girl fussing over her hair. Or at least it was something he assumed little girls did with their hair; he had never actually met one and June had always seemed more finicky with her hair than both he and Marcus. But Marcus told him it was important he look prim to show people he was just as capable of looking nice as everyone else. Now properly groomed, Hyroc headed toward the door.

"You did that kind of fast," Marcus said, stopping him at the door. "Let me see those fingernails?" Hyroc sighed and held his hands up for inspection. Marcus frowned. "They still look sharp. Go back and file them. You won't like it very much if you accidentally cut yourself on them." With an annoyed huff Hyroc turned back, retrieved the nail file and got to work on his claws. He had never cut himself on his claws and he couldn't imagine how he would.

"Much better," Marcus said, when Hyroc had finished.

Breakfast consisted of a gray unsweetened porridge, a single piece of toast and some jam. Hyroc stared into his bowl wishing he had some honey to add to it, before digging in. After breakfast, he and the other students dispersed to their respective classes.

His first class of the day was reading which was by far his favorite. Even if it was still boring. But compared to the other boring things he did at the school, it wasn't quite as bad. Unfortunately, he hated the one after, Witch Studies.

The subject matter entailed long-winded lectures, but what he truly loathed about it was Miss Duncan was the teacher. If at any point in the lesson the subject matter dealt with the creations of witches or anything with some vague physical relation to Hyroc – as it often did – she would always call upon him. And if he or any student got an answer wrong, they would receive a sharp smack with a willow rod. Early on, Hyroc had brought this painful matter to Marcus' attention. Due to the extremely sensitive nature of the subject matter, Marcus could do nothing to make Miss Duncan alter her teaching methods without potentially bringing the wrath of The Ministry down upon the school.

Hyroc was seated closest to the teacher with about five feet between him and the nearest student. Miss Duncan closed the door to the classroom behind the final student.

"Today we will be learning about the Druadic Witch's that assisted Feygratha in overthrowing the King." Miss Duncan said. She opened a large book on her desk and set it in front of Hyroc. "Hyroc, read the description of what powers they possessed, the first paragraph from the top of the first page."

And here it was again. What was going to happen to him today? "The Druadic Witches –" Hyroc began.

"Speak louder," Miss Duncan intoned. "Don't mumble."

"The Druadic Witches," he continued, hiding his irritation as he spoke in a much louder voice, "are witches that draw power from animals. By drawing upon the power of an animal, they obtain its strengths and its physical abilities. But both their physical appearance and mind becomes more like the animal they are drawing upon. This makes Druadic witches incredibly unpredictable and extremely dangerous. Due to the nature of the changes to their bodies, if a Druadic Witch that has drawn upon an animal's strength bears children, their physical alterations will be transferred to their offspring, creating what is commonly known as a half-breed."

Hyroc paused, suddenly realizing what he was reading about sounded frighteningly close to how he looked. Miss Duncan stared down at him with a cold disdainful look. Hyroc stole a quick glance at the students around him. They all stared at him with a mixture of apprehension and fear, which only made him feel like a monster.

"Please continue," Miss Duncan said coldly.

Hating her, Hyroc continued reading aloud, doing his best not to pay attention to the numerous eyes staring at him. "The offspring of a Druadic Witch will inherit both the human and animal features of their parents, giving them a hideously twisted form neither of a man nor of a beast. Their mind is also in a mirrored condition to their bodies', making them even more unstable than their parents."

"Thank you," Miss Duncan said, but her words were full of ice. She took the book from Hyroc, giving it to another student.

The students stared at Hyroc more intensely, and he could hear some of them whispering things to each other. He now felt like some hideously deformed creature deserving only death; he just wanted to curl up into a ball and disappear from the world. He bolted for the door.

"Where are you going?" Miss Duncan said, satisfaction sounding in her voice. "Class is not over." Ignoring her, Hyroc wrenched the door open, quickly making his way to Marcus' office. Tears had begun streaming down his face, dampening the fur below his eyes as he entered the headmaster's office.

Marcus was at his desk working as usual. He shot Hyroc a puzzled look as the boy stormed across the room toward his desk. Marcus' expression rapidly turned to concern.

"Are you, all right?" Marcus said, getting up from his chair.

"I'm – I'm a monster aren't I," Hyroc said, his voice shuddering. Why else would everyone treat him the way they did. They thought he was going to hurt them.

"You're *not* a monster. Who told you that?"

"Today in Miss Duncan's class we learned about Druadic Witches," Hyroc said sniffling.

Marcus frowned. "I don't know much about your mother, but I know she was *not* a Druadic Witch. And neither are you."

"Then why do I look like *this*?"

"I wish I knew, but if you were the son of a Druadic Witch you wouldn't look the way you do. To put it simply, even though you look different, you act just like a normal person and are shaped too correctly to be one of those. When those witches draw upon an animal, their bodies do not uniformly change, which is another way of saying they look like monsters. And trust me, I understand all too well what I'm saying. It was once part of my job to do so. And when those witches have children, their children look even more so."

"You didn't see their faces, how they looked at me. They saw me as some unclean creature, a –a half-breed."

"I don't care what they think; you are *not* one of those creatures!"

"But if I'm not one of those *then what am I*?"

"I don't know, and I wish I could tell you, but you're my son and I love you. It doesn't matter what you look like, all that matters is what's in here." Marcus touched the side of Hyroc's chest where his heart was. Marcus began wiping the tears from Hyroc's eyes. "I had this dog when I was about your age. He was one of the ugliest and meanest looking mutts you had ever seen, but he was the kindest dog a boy could ever have. You see, looks are not always everything."

Hyroc took a breath, some of his sadness melting away. "Do you think I'm ugly?"

"Of course not, but you're definitely warmer in the winter because of the way you look." Hyroc smiled, which seemed to subdue the horrible memory of Miss Duncan's class just moments ago. "I bet the other students wish their hands were furry too; do you know how useful that would be on cold winter days? I know I'd like that. I'm stuck with shoddy gloves that hardly keep the cold out while your gloves come already attached. You see, you're different but because you're different, you can do some things better than a normal person."

"Is that why Miss Duncan hates me?"

Marcus' face softened with sadness. "She doesn't hate you, you just remind her of something bad. And sometimes when something reminds someone of pain, they lash out at it. Do you hate Billy or any of the other boys for what they did to you?"

Hyroc stopped to ponder the question. His feelings toward the boy seemed pretty close to what he thought was hate, but it still seemed far enough from it. "I don't hate them, but I hate what they do."

"Exactly. It's kind of the same thing with Miss Duncan. When she was a young woman, a witch killed her whole family. Ever since then, she's hated anything or anyone associated with their art."

"But I'm not a witch."

"I know you're not, but she doesn't see it the same way. She thinks you're a danger to the other students and in a way, she's just trying to protect them. Just like how I try to protect you."

"Is it because of what I did to Billy yesterday?"

"To be honest, that probably didn't help, but she had already made her mind up about you."

Hyroc shot him a puzzled look. "I don't understand?"

Marcus shrugged. "It's complicated. I don't completely understand it myself either. All you can do is try your hardest to prove to her you're just like everyone else and do your best to move on. You're a good boy and don't let anybody tell you otherwise."

Hyroc didn't really understand, but he felt better and nodded anyway.

CHAPTER 2

Pest

Hyroc sat on the grassy shore of a creek beneath the cool shade of an oak tree's canopy, with a fishing pole in hand. Resting the side of his head on the knuckles of his free hand, he watched the faded brown bobber attached to his line float on the calm water's surface. He gently waved his pole from side to side, slowly dragging his hook through the water, hoping to attract the attention of a fish. He liked fishing; he just hated how much waiting it involved. Sometimes hours would pass without a single bite. Hours filled with nothing more than the sleepy murmur of the creek, the occasional chirp of birds or the chittering of an angry squirrel. It was easy for his concentration to wane at those times, but he knew he could get a bite at any moment and if he wasn't paying attention, the fish would escape. And those hours of boredom would have been spent in vain. Still, fishing, even with all the waiting, was more enjoyable than sitting around and listening to his teachers talk all day.

The boarding school had closed down for the summer two weeks ago. Just as Marcus had said, Hyroc had no other incidents with a bully. But that was about the only good thing regarding his lashing out at Billy. Miss Duncan had continued her practice of indirectly pointing out through her lessons Hyroc was a dangerous monster. This made his fellow students distrust him even more. Whenever he sat down at a table, the gap between him and the nearest student seemed to grow. Then there were the looks he started getting. These weren't the gawking looks of curiosity mixed with a subtle amount of fear he had become accustomed to, there was something new in them. He couldn't identify what the new thing was, but whatever it was made him incredibly uncomfortable. Knowing the behavior was unlikely to disappear, he eventually learned to ignore it, though sometimes it proved impossible to do so. Thankfully, his first year at the school had ended not long afterward and he was free of it for a time.

The bobber dunked down into the water and Hyroc felt a sharp pull on his line. He set the hook then began dragging the fish in. After a brief struggle, he landed a small trout. He held the slippery fish onto the ground with his foot until it stopped breathing. Once he was sure his catch would remain on dry land, he tossed the fish behind him, then baited his hook with another worm stored in a mud filled wooden cup beside him and cast his line. Almost an hour later, when he began contemplating heading home, he got another bite. This fish put up more of a fight, but he still landed it relatively easy.

When it too stopped moving, he tied his line around both fish, then slung his pole over his shoulder and headed up a trail past the oak tree. The trail entered a thin stand of trees, terminating into a gently sloping broad grassy hill.

Marcus' house sat near the top of the hill. It was a medium-sized, two-story building, crafted from light brown brick with a dark gray thatched roof and two chimneys at the center of the structure. A fenced off garden sat at the back containing neat groupings of cabbage, carrots, parsley, rosemary, radishes, potatoes, three strawberry plants, a well, a single alder with branches that hung over the fence and a crabapple tree. Sunflowers, red lupine, foxglove, and grass punctuated with clover patches surrounded the house.

Hyroc walked through the garden gate, closed it behind him, then careful not to step on any of the garden plants, made his way to the open backdoor that lead into the kitchen. After kicking mud interlaced with smashed grass from his shoes, he took them off and stepped inside.

A finely polished oak table sat to Hyroc's right, with a light-colored cabinet toward the end opposite him and a stepped doorway leading into the living room. To his left a black wooden counter ran the length of the wall, curving around an adjacent corner of the room ending at a brick hearth. Cupboards separated by shelves covered with glass jars containing herbs sat above the counter. A bundle of sage, parsley, a garland of garlic, and various cook wares hung from the hearth.

Stepping into the living room, Hyroc found Marcus at his desk in the back corner of the room beneath a window, thoughtfully looking over scrolls scattered across it.

"Did you catch anything?" Marcus said, without looking up from his desk.

"I did," Hyroc said, proudly holding up his two fish. Usually he only caught one.

Marcus looked up from his desk to see Hyroc's catch. A smile crested his lips. "Glad to hear it, we can have those for lunch. Just take them back into the kitchen and give me a few more minutes to finish these."

Hyroc nodded, then went back into the kitchen. Untying the fish, he set them on the counter. After waiting for what Hyroc thought was far longer than a few minutes, Marcus entered the kitchen. He pulled a stool up to the counter and bade Hyroc to sit on it. Once Hyroc had taken his seat, Marcus placed a scale-removing tool in front of himself and slid another in front of Hyroc before placing a fish in front of him. When Marcus began scaling his fish so did Hyroc.

"Make sure you get all of them," Marcus said.

"I will," Hyroc promised, remembering how a scale had cut into his gums when he bit into a piece of fish with one.

"Did you lose any?"

"Not today."

Marcus nodded approvingly. "See, you're getting better at it."

When they finished scaling and gutting their fish, Marcus placed a fresh piece of wood inside the hearth and using a tinderbox, got a fire going. He put a grate over the fire, then put a pan on it. When the pan reached a proper cooking temperature, he carefully placed each fish on the hot metal. The fish erupted into popping and sizzling, sending a delicious aroma wafting through the room. When the fish had finished cooking, using a thickly padded cooking glove Marcus removed the pan and shook each fish onto a waiting plate. He set the pan on a flat stone at the other end of the counter and removed his glove. Marcus added salt and herbs to the fish, then set the plates on the table. Once their meal had cooled, they ate.

"Now, let's take care of the garden," Marcus said. Hyroc groaned unhappily. Digging in the dirt was the last thing he wanted to do. He despised the dry scratchy sensation of dirt scraping between his skin and the underside of his claws. "I let you go fishing this morning instead of working in the garden because I was busy. But now that I've got everything done, we have time."

Grumbling in annoyance Hyroc walked into the garden. This didn't seem like much of a reward for his catching lunch. Marcus handed him a hand spade and Hyroc reluctantly got to work weeding the garden. When he had finally finished his work, to his dismay, it was too late in the day for him to do much of anything else.

"But I'm not even tired," Hyroc protested.

"You need to sleep," Marcus said obstinately. "Now get yourself ready for bed, I'll be up to tuck you in, in a minute."

With a shrug, Hyroc headed up the house's staircase to the hall leading to his room. There were three rooms in the hall; the first was aunt June's, but she had taken a trip to a neighboring town and would not be back for several days. She didn't talk to him as much as Marcus, but he really didn't mind it, and she never seemed overly concerned with his behavior. And he couldn't help missing her a little for it. The second room was his and the last was Marcus'. Hyroc opened the door to his room and went inside. His bed sat in the corner of the room, with a small dresser beside it, and a single window overlooked the garden.

He dressed into his pajamas and climbed into bed. Marcus arrived just as he laid his head on his feather stuffed pillow. Marcus tucked him into bed, told him good night, then blew out a candle and made his way to his own room. Not long afterward, Hyroc was fast asleep.

He reentered consciousness when a diffused shaft of morning sunlight full of particles of dust flitting in and out of existence like tiny fireflies, shone through his window. Sitting up, he rubbed his eyes, then climbed out of bed and began getting into his day clothes. As he dressed, he saw Marcus walking through the garden in a displeased manner. Hyroc racked his memory from the day before for anything that might get him a scolding this morning. Nothing came to mind; he hoped it meant he was in the clear. He made his way to the garden to see what was going on. When Marcus saw him, he waved him over. Hyroc cautiously made his way over. He had to have done something he wasn't supposed to do?

Marcus indicated one of the strawberry plants. "Were you out here playing yesterday?" Marcus said. Hyroc shook his head. "Did you leave the gate open when you came back from fishing?" Hyroc shook his head again. Marcus studied Hyroc's face a moment then nodded. "Then I think something got in here last night. Take a look at this." Marcus crouched down beside one of the strawberry plants. Moving closer, Hyroc saw with dismay its stalk had been severed just above the ground and the upper part lay limply across the soil. He felt a twinge of anger as he looked upon the doomed plant. Whatever had gotten into the garden had decided upon killing the plant with the tastiest things in the yard.

"Probably a rabbit," Marcus said, as he stood up. "I might be able to get another strawberry plant in town from a gardener friend of mine. There's not much we can do about it right now but keep an eye out for any pests wandering around out here. Anyway, I should get started on breakfast before it gets too late."

Marcus made two acorn pancakes and a few strips of crispy bacon. Afterwards Hyroc was forced to work in the garden and sweep out both the hearth and fireplace before he could do anything else. It was after lunch when he finished all his chores and was free to go fishing. He got several bites, but caught nothing.

Hyroc awoke that night to a faint scraping noise coming from outside. Silver shafts of moonlight lit the room, bleaching everything an eerie white. Bleary-eyed, he walked to the window. In the garden, he saw the glint of white fur. Focusing on the shape, he saw a rabbit. *So, you're the thief* Hyroc thought to himself. He slipped on his shoes, then careful not to make any noise, made his way to the back door. Heart thumping with excitement, he quietly propped the door open a crack. After a moment of searching, he spotted the long eared sneak. He walked away from the door, and silently grabbed a knife. With his weapon in hand, he crept out the door. He made it no more than three steps from the door when the rabbit's ears shot into the air, and the hare darted into the shadows. Hyroc heard the rustling of leaves, then silence. Disappointed with himself, he went back inside.

At breakfast, he was just about to tell Marcus about his nighttime discovery, but at the last moment decided against it. He wanted to be the one who caught the rabbit. He could imagine how grateful and proud Marcus would be if he was the one who caught it. Maybe he wouldn't have to work in the garden anymore.

That night, Hyroc waited impatiently at the window for any sign of his quarry. Once the fullness of night had descended, he saw the rabbit in the garden. He went into the kitchen, collected a knife and stealthily headed out into the garden trying much harder to remain undetected. Despite his best efforts, just like the night before, the rabbit fled before he could even get close. The third night was no different. He then decided his current strategy was seriously flawed.

The day after his third failure, he began searching the fence surrounding the garden for any possible entry points. To his astonishment, he found none. *Was this a flying rabbit*, he thought, suppressing a smile at the idea when he imagined it jumping on Miss Duncan's face. Confounded, he double-checked the fence, but he still found nothing. As he considered admitting defeat and telling Marcus, he noticed the low hanging branches of the alder. He had completely forgotten to check under there. After an initial struggle with the flimsy woody branches trying to snap back into position, he found a small space at the base of one of the fence posts where something had dug under it.

He had found the entry point, but he was unsure how this information could help him. Marcus called out lunch was ready. Still pondering a solution, Hyroc stepped away from the shrub, brushed the dirt from his clothing and went inside. Just as he finished his meal, it began to rain. Irritated by the uncooperative weather disrupting his investigation, he made his way into the living room. He grabbed a book he had started reading from off the top of Marcus' desk, sat down in front of the room's fireplace and began reading.

The next few hours passed in this manner and the rain showed no sign of stopping anytime soon. As Hyroc read, he came across a story in his book where a boy was trying to get rid of a troublesome mouse. No matter what the boy tried, the mouse would still manage to nip some cheese from his grandfather's cellar. Eventually the boy outsmarted the clever mouse by using a trap baited with the very cheese the rodent was stealing.

A sudden inspired thought entered Hyroc mind, filling him with a pleasant warm feeling. The rabbit was too fast for him to get to, so he needed to set a trap for it. Other than Marcus teaching him some basic knot tying techniques, he knew nothing about trap making. Closing the book, he rushed over to a nearby bookshelf and fervently began searching for the book Marcus had used to teach him those knots. He found the book and began pouring over the various knots contained within its pages. Toward the end of the book, he found a brief section detailing the construction of two simple types of snares. Searching through the house, Hyroc found a length of the twine Marcus used to make his fishing line.

By now the rain had stopped. With the book and supplies in hand, Hyroc went back under the alder, and following the books instructions, carefully set up his trap. It took him several attempts before he finally made the snare into something similar to what the book described as a snare. Excited by the prospect of finally capturing his strawberry destroying foe, he had trouble sleeping when his bedtime arrived.

The following morning, after quickly getting dressed, he flew down the stairs and out the back door to check his traps. To his utter disappointment, the trap had come apart. Annoyed with himself, he reset the trap and waited for another agonizing day. The next morning he was frustrated yet again. The rabbit had tripped the trap, but the snare loop had closed incorrectly, creating enough slack for the rabbit to escape. The next morning was also a failure, as were the next three. But from each failure, he learned something new, slowly getting better at making his trap. After about another week of failure, he was suddenly thrust awake one night by a horrendous rabbit scream emanating from the garden. When he entered the hallway, a sleepy eyed, somewhat alarmed Marcus stuck his head out his bedroom door.

"What is *that*?" Marcus said. "It sounds like a dying rabbit."

Hyroc smiled eagerly. "I sure hope so," he said excitedly, before rushing down the stairs. He found the rabbit thrashing beneath the alder branches with a loop of twine wrapped firmly around its back legs.

Marcus arrived a moment later. He turned toward Hyroc with a curious look in his eyes. "Did you do that?" Marcus said, pointing toward the struggling hare. Hyroc nodded happily. A proud smile spread across Marcus' mouth. "Great job." He affectionately ruffled the hair on top of Hyroc's head. Another high-pitched scream shattered the happy moment. Gritting his teeth, Marcus said, "why don't we get him out of there, I don't want to listen to *that* all-night." He grasped the rabbit by the back of the neck, while Hyroc untied its foot. "Could you get me a knife?" Hyroc nodded and brought Marcus the sharpest knife he could find. Marcus walked away from the house, before slitting the throat of the troublesome animal. Hyroc felt a strange sadness as he watched. After having been bested by the hare for nearly two weeks he felt an odd sort of attachment to his opponent for outsmarting him for so long. Once the blood stopped flowing, Marcus shook the rabbit, then made his way back to the house.

"We can have him for lunch tomorrow," Marcus said, holding up the rabbit.

"I've been trying to get him since I found him," Hyroc said gleefully.

Marcus paused, some of the happiness drained from his expression. "*You're grounded!*"

"WHAT!" Hyroc yelled. "*But I got the rabbit.*"

"Of course I'm thankful for *that*, but I lost two cabbage plants because you never told me you had found where the pest was getting in. So you're grounded for a week."

"But –"

Marcus turned toward Hyroc. "Do you want it to be two weeks?"

"No," Hyroc said in a subdued tone.

"Good. Now go back to bed."

CHAPTER 3

Duck Hunting

Hyroc awoke with a sense of relief; the week of his grounding had finally ended. He had not been allowed to go fishing, and every day Marcus had made him come up with one merit regarding the importance of honesty before he could eat breakfast. Then to make his grounding even more painful, Marcus made him replace the board in the fence where the rabbit had gained entry and made him weed the entire garden without offering any assistance. It still didn't seem fair for him to be punished so severely after all the hard work he put into catching the rabbit. He hadn't meant for it to destroy those cabbage plants. If he had just kept his mouth shut, none of that would have happened. Marcus would have given him the praise he deserved instead of making him do chores all day and preventing him from doing anything fun. But, mercifully, he could now do whatever he wanted.

He got dressed and eagerly headed down for breakfast. Marcus was already at the table with a steaming bowl of porridge in front of him as he read a scroll. Another bowl sat on the other side of the table waiting for Hyroc. Hyroc watched Marcus warily as he approached his seat, unsure if his father would punish him with one final honesty merit. Other than a slight twitch of his eyes in Hyroc's direction, Marcus gave no signs of doing so. Breathing a silent sigh of relief, Hyroc seated himself at the table. From a wooden container at the center of the table, he added a drizzle of dark yellow honey onto the porridge and started blowing on his first spoonful.

"I need to head into town to get some things this morning," Marcus said.

Hyroc stopped mid-bite, staring at Marcus with disbelief. He had suffered for a week and Marcus wished to prolong his discomfort by making him go into town! There were always more eyes on him there than at the boarding school. Even the way people stared at him felt worse there. It felt like he was naked and every inch of his body was being examined. Out of the corners of his eyes, he often saw people craning their necks to get a better look at him. It made him extremely uncomfortable seeing those people trying so hard to stare at him. The stares were then accompanied with pointing and people speaking in hushed tones. Passerby's gave him a wide birth, but what bothered him the most was how the people who had children with them reacted. Mothers and fathers pulled their children close to them as if shielding them from an imminent animal attack. It made him feel like he was the monster Miss Duncan always made him out to be.

Hyroc irritably dropped his spoon back into his bowl, folded his arms and began staring sourly at the tabletop.

"Don't be like that," Marcus said, turning his eyes from the scroll to Hyroc.

"I don't like going there," Hyroc glowered. And why Marcus thought he should when it was clear how much he hated it was beyond him.

"Sometimes we have to do things we don't like."

"I'm not supposed to be grounded anymore; I was going to go fishing! This isn't fair."

Marcus sighed half humoredly. "And you still *can* when we get back, this won't take very long." He paused. "And if you're good, there's a surprise waiting for you."

Hyroc perked up at the mention of a surprise. He felt a streak of excitement as he wondered what the surprise might be. Then his euphoria faded substantially when he remembered what he would soon be enduring in the town. Deflated, he forcefully slunk down into his chair, it seemed impossible any surprise would be worth that.

Marcus shrugged. "Now eat your porridge before it gets cold."

Hyroc quietly grumbled to himself how mean Marcus was being and continued eating. After consuming his breakfast as slowly as he could manage without getting into trouble, he and Marcus slipped on their jackets and boots. Hyroc pulled his jacket's hood over his head. The hood didn't do much to keep his appearance concealed since the end of his nose poked out of it, and anyone close by would easily see how he looked, but the stares never felt quite as bad while he wore it.

"Going with the hood today?" Marcus said, as he secured a coin pouch to his belt. Hyroc gave him a perplexed glare. Marcus nodded his understanding then the two of them stepped outside and made their way down the road into town.

A steady flow of townsfolk trickled in and out of the gate. Hyroc bowed his head instinctively to keep his face concealed as long as possible as he and Marcus passed through the entrance. The first few people seemed to take no notice of him, but not long afterward, he felt the steadily growing discomfort of being watched. A group of teenage boys on the opposite side of the cobblestone street spotted him and began pointing. This rapidly attracted the attention of anyone close by. Hyroc grabbed his hood and made sure it was pulled as far forward as it would go. He felt Marcus place a reassuring hand on his shoulder. This seemed to give him strength and the town didn't seem quite as bad. Determinedly, he lifted his head back into the air. They could look all they wanted; it wasn't going to bother him.

Rounding a corner leading to the town center, Hyroc and Marcus came face to face with two men on horseback. Marcus yanked Hyroc out of the way of the horses and held him close. The men wore dark brown leather frocks tinged with patches of red. A sword hung from one man's hip, and a cudgel from his companion's. Hyroc felt a wave of fear when he saw above each man's shoulder the embroidering of a silver raven holding a scythe in its talons. They were Witch Hunters.

Which Hunters were those who hunted down witches and anyone or anything that used black magic. Even though through their work they offered a great boon to those they served, Marcus had warned Hyroc never to go anywhere near them. This had confused Hyroc, because it made no sense how someone doing something good for others would be dangerous. His confusion had only lasted up until he had seen one in person. The Witch Hunter looked at him with a disgusted; menacing glare and the man's whole body seemed to radiate hostility. There was no doubt the man would harm him if given the chance. This had frightened Hyroc and he never remembered being more grateful Marcus was there with him.

The two men stared down at Hyroc with, cold, uncaring glares, as they trotted their horse's past. The two men looked away from Hyroc shaking their heads disappointedly. Marcus and Hyroc watched the two men intently for several paces of their horses. Hyroc let out a breath he didn't know he was holding as Marcus relaxed his grip. Marcus gave him a reassuring look and they continued on their way.

Marcus led Hyroc to the shop of the town's bow maker. Wide varieties of finely crafted bows, quivers, and many kinds of arrows fletched with an array of colorful feathers were on display throughout the shop. The shopkeeper gave Hyroc a quick wary glance before enthusiastically welcoming Marcus. They engaged into a brief conversation Hyroc paid little attention to as he studied a bow with what appeared to be animals carved in the wood. He wondered how much work the maker of the bow had put into creating such elaborate designs and if it were possible for him to ever learn to do the same.

"Hyroc, I'll be right back," Marcus said. "This will only take a moment. Don't leave the shop and don't touch anything."

Hyroc nodded his acknowledgment. The shopkeeper led Marcus into a back room. While Hyroc looked through the shop's wears – restraining the strong urge to touch something – he heard the shouting and laughter of children playing outside. Walking back toward the half open door of the shop, he saw a group of three boys about his age, playing a game he had never seen before. They had a small ball made from sackcloth and the boys were taking turns bouncing it off their feet trying to keep it from falling to the ground. Hyroc watched them with growing intrigue. The boys at the school wouldn't play with him, but maybe these three would. While bouncing the ball, one of the boys lost their balance, and the ball fell to the ground. As the next boy bent down to pick up the ball, he started slightly when he noticed Hyroc watching them through the shop's door. Hyroc gave the boy a friendly wave. The boy studied Hyroc with an odd look on his face, but he showed no sign of annoyance like the group at the boarding school he had tried so hard to be part of. Excitement shot through Hyroc as he wondered if the boy was about to invite him to join the game. He had taken one eager step toward the group, when one of the other two children pointed at him, said something he couldn't hear and the group burst into jeering and laughing. Hyroc sighed irritably, feeling some warmth spread across his face. He put his back to the group, folded his arms and kicked at a thin patch of dirt on the floor. Those boys weren't any different. Marcus emerged from the back room holding a rectangular box beneath one arm.

"Are you all right?" Marcus said, with a concerned frown.

"I'm fine," Hyroc replied sharply. Marcus' eyes narrowed when he spotted the group of boys outside the shop laughing. The boy's laughter immediately ceased and with an alarmed expression on each of their faces, the group scattered. Hyroc felt a little better seeing the group flee in terror.

Marcus patted the box with his other hand. "This will probably make you feel better when we get home," he said smiling. All Hyroc wanted to do was play a game with someone his age; it seemed unlikely the contents of the box could ever give him that kind of enjoyment.

Marcus bought some meat, then they made their way to the leather working shop near the edge of town then headed back to the house.

"There's something I want to show you," Marcus said eagerly, after entering the living room. Curious about what could excite Marcus; Hyroc followed him over to the fireplace. Marcus set the box down on the floor. "Open it."

Hyroc did as instructed. Inside he found a small caringly polished child's bow. "I used to be quite the duck hunter in years past," Marcus said. He indicated his bow that hung above the fireplace. "Recently I've been thinking of renewing my trips to the pond. But hunting alone just isn't as fun." He paused, smiling. "And now that you have a bow, the two of us can hunt fowl together." Hyroc beamed, forgetting all the unpleasantness of the day. "Unfortunately the proper duck hunting season isn't until fall. But that's okay, because we have all summer to get ready for it." Hyroc rushed over and hugged Marcus so hard he nearly knocked him over. Marcus smiled broadly. "I take it you like it." Pulling away from Marcus Hyroc nodded energetically.

After lunch, Marcus showed him how to shoot a bow then they spent the rest of the day punching holes in a target with their arrows. The next morning, Marcus had a few errands to attend to at the school. He offered for Hyroc to come with him, but Hyroc promptly declined. Marcus instructed him to weed the ground around the new strawberry plant and not to try shooting arrows without him. Hyroc quickly did his chores. Disobeying Marcus' instructions to practice his archery was a strong temptation, but after overhearing two men talking in town yesterday about how many Flecks they made while trapping, he was eager to begin experimenting with it.

After collecting as much fishing line as he could find around the house, he headed into the thicket not far behind the house. Remembering how he had caught the pesky garden rabbit with his trap at the fence, he searched for similar natural chokepoints. He placed a trap between two birches growing close together on the sides of a hollow, then one in a space between two patches of thick bushes and a similar divide in a patch of tall grass. Then just as he had done with the thief-rabbit in the garden, he would check the traps in the morning. He arrived back at the house just as Marcus had returned. The two of them spent the rest of the day practicing their archery.

When Hyroc checked his traps the next day, he found a large black rat caught in the one he placed between the thick bushes. Though he was still uncertain what animals were of worth, he was certain nobody would pay anything for the ugly rodent. Seeing no real reason to kill it, he slipped on a pair of gloves and reached over to release it. The rat hissed when his hands drew close, giving him a slight start.

"I'm *trying* to let you go," Hyroc snapped. "Do you want me to leave you there for a cat?" In response, the rat rapidly fluttered its whiskers while staring at him with its beady black eyes. Taking a breath, Hyroc grabbed the rat by the mid-section. It ferociously bit at his fingers, but he only felt a mild pinch through the leather of his gloves. Once he had freed the rat, he released his grip and it darted out of view.

Over the next two weeks, he made minor adjustments to his traps until; to his satisfaction, he finally caught a rabbit. After dispatching the animal in the same way he had seen Marcus do it to the garden thief, he realized he didn't know what to do with the rabbit. He remembered seeing animal skins hanging outside the leather working shop and decided skinning the rabbit was the best course of action. When he had finished, he had completely mangled the pelt and it was difficult to tell what animal it had originally come from. Undeterred, he continued trapping. He mangled each animal skin he got a hold of, but just as with his first traps, he got better with each mistake. About a month after his first caught rabbit, he successfully skinned one properly. As he proudly held the pelt up to examine his handiwork, the hair began to fall off in large clumps. By the time he made it to the house, all the hair was missing, leaving only an ugly gray dermis. Confused, he disposed of the skin among the trees, and continued trapping.

A few days later, he was surprised to find a cat snagged in the trap between the two trees near the hollow. The cat hissed and spat wildly the moment he came into view. A wave of fear washed over Hyroc when it occurred to him this cat could belong to somebody. Marcus might not look kindly upon his trapping in secret, but if he found one of the neighbor's cats caught in it, Hyroc could only imagine how much trouble he would get into. He needed to free the enraged feline before that happened. He took a calming breath, then put his gloves on. When he reached for the back of the cat's neck, it hissed again and made a violent flailing movement. Hyroc yanked his hand back. He watched the cat with a growing sense of dread. How was he going to free it without bleeding? Maybe he had no choice but to tell Marcus.

He dismissed the thought with the shake of his head. Marcus didn't need to know, he was positive he could figure this out on his own; it was only a house cat. Gathering his courage, he threw his hand around the scruff of the cat's neck. The cat erupted into hissing and resumed its flailing. It took all of his strength to prevent the struggling animal from breaking free of his grip as he worked to release it. The snare had barely been removed when he lost his hold on the cat. Faster than he could react, the cat flipped over onto its back, swatted at the top of his wrist and raked one of its claws across his skin. Growling savagely, the cat tore out of view. Hyroc looked at his wrist and saw blood oozing out of the injury. Grimacing, he pressed the cloth of his shirt on to the wound.

As soon as he stopped bleeding, driven by a gnawing fear Marcus would find out about his activities, he quickly set about dismantling his traps. If he got rid of them, there was no chance of Marcus discovering their existence and he couldn't get into trouble.

When he had finished with his traps, with the materials in hand, he rushed back to the house. He peeked through the back door into the kitchen and saw Marcus standing at the hearth. He had his back to the door and appeared to be cooking lunch. Hyroc had gotten most of the fishing twine from Marcus' room, so he crept around the front of the house to see if he could sneak in there. He peered through the keyhole, but Marcus wasn't in sight. Silently he opened and closed the door before stealthily making his way upstairs into Marcus' room. He deposited the twine where he had found it then quickly left. Just as he came through the doorway, he started when he spotted Marcus coming up the stairs. Heart thumping, Hyroc darted across the hall to the doorway of his own room, turning so it appeared he was leaving it.

"There you are," Marcus said, as he came to the top of the stairs. "I've been looking all over for you, lunch is almost ready." Breathing a silent sigh of relief, Hyroc nodded and walked toward Marcus. "I wanted to ask you something."

A bolt of fear shot through Hyroc. What was the something! Had he been caught? Barely maintaining his composure, speaking in the most casual tone he could muster, he said, "what is it Marcus?"

"Do you remember where I put the fishing twine? I can't seem to find it anywhere."

Hyroc breathed a silent sigh of relief. His secret was still safe. "I thought you kept that in your room."

Marcus rubbed his chin thoughtfully. "I swear I already looked in there." He waved his hand dismissively. "Bah, I'm sure it'll turn up, probably just misplaced it." He paused. "What happened to your arm?"

Hyroc subdued a sense of dread and calmly lifted his arm up as if he were not aware of the claw marks. "It's just a scratch."

Marcus nodded. "You should be more careful then."

Repressing a smile Hyroc said, "I will."

CHAPTER 4

Claws

Hyroc scanned the reedy shore of the pond, searching for any signs of the fowl he was hunting. A wavy sheet of gray clouds covered the sky and intermittent raindrops struck the surface of the pond, sending out thin circles of ripples as they landed. It was now a year since his first hunting trip with Marcus. The trips were the only times in his life he could remember feeling like he belonged somewhere. The ducks treated him no differently than Marcus, fleeing whenever they spotted either one of them and sometimes he was able to forget he was different for a little while.

A faint quack emanated from a patch of reeds farther down the shore and Hyroc made his way toward it. He found a single duck resting among the vegetation. Carefully he approached his quarry from behind. It was an easy shot and he quickly dispatched his target with no difficulty. After collecting the lifeless bird, he made his way back to Marcus. Marcus was crouched amongst a patch of tall reeds observing a group of ducks paddling across a small indent in the shore.

Silently Hyroc set the duck down beside Marcus in a pile of three other birds they had downed earlier in the day. Marcus turned his head slightly in Hyroc's direction. He noted the fresh fowl, giving Hyroc a proud nod and turned back toward the ducks. A moment of silence passed between them as they watched their quarry. Marcus leaned back toward Hyroc.

"That's the perfect place for an ambush," Marcus whispered, pointing toward the shore of the indent. "I want you to circle around to the other side and take a shot. That way, when they take flight they'll have to fly past me and I'll have a perfect shot. That sound good to you?"

Hyroc nodded, then stealthily made his way to the other side of the indent. Once in position, Marcus raised a hand above the reeds signaling for him to take a shot. Hyroc quickly loosed an arrow. The arrow whistled through the air, striking the nearest duck. In a frantic flurry of wing beats the rest of the group took flight in Marcus' direction. A single arrow shot out of the reeds surrounding Marcus and a duck tumbled into the water with a splash. Marcus stood, a proud smile on his face, and cheered.

"Great job!" he yelled excitedly at Hyroc.

Hyroc smiled proudly. The two of them collected their prizes before making their way to the boarding school.

This was about the only downside toward their hunting trips, the first two months of the school year coincided with the duck season. And although Marcus only took Hyroc hunting on the weekends, many of the teachers, with Miss Duncan being the most concerned, thought he was neglecting his duties as headmaster. Then just as Hyroc thought his favorite activity would slip away from him, Marcus swiftly put the teachers concerns to rest by donating any fowl the two of them killed to the school meals, thus making the trips a service to the school. This arrangement had annoyed Hyroc, because the other students got to eat his fowl when none of them had contributed anything toward acquiring the birds, but if that's what had to be done, then he supposed he really didn't mind. Eating them wasn't the fun part. Though the kitchen staff never seemed capable of making the ducks taste as good as Marcus could.

As the two of them made their way to the kitchen Marcus began to cough.

"Are you all right?" Hyroc asked, suppressing a yawn. The coughs sounded particularly uncomfortable.

"I'm fine," Marcus said, with a dismissive wave. He cleared his throat. "My throat is just a little dry this morning, I just need to drink something." Hyroc nodded.

After dropping off the six fowl, the two of them returned to the headmaster's office to dress into their formal clothing, before separating for breakfast. As Hyroc made his way toward his usual spot at the table, he noticed a brown haired boy about his own age showing an unusual amount of interest in him. He recognized the boy as one of the new students that had arrived near the start of this school year. The only students who ever paid that much attention to him were always the ones feeling the need to do something unpleasant to him. His bullying problem didn't seem quite as bad anymore, but the beatings were hard to forget. He was safe in the dining hall; none of his bullies had ever been brave enough to attempt pestering him with so many teachers around.

Throughout the meal, the boy stole glances in his direction. When breakfast was finished, as the boy filed out of the dining hall he turned away from the door and studied Hyroc for an uncomfortable moment before continuing on his way. The boy was definitely a bully. He was probably trying to figure out the best way to harm him. Concerned by the prospect of an ambush at the door, Hyroc stayed in the dining hall until Marcus forced him to leave.

During the lunchtime break, Hyroc spotted the boy shadowing him down the hall leading to the library. Hyroc rounded a corner and darted outside through a side door. He ran along the side of the building keeping his head below any windows. When he arrived at the nearest corner of the building, he stopped and watched for his pursuer. A few minutes passed and the boy had yet to appear. Breathing a sigh of relief, Hyroc reentered the school from the other side. Keeping a careful eye out for the new bully, he made his way to the safety of Marcus' office and stayed there until dinner.

Hyroc sat barefoot on the limb of an apple tree near the back of the school with his legs laid across the branch and his back against its trunk. Three apples lay at the base of the tree and small brown worms absentmindedly devoured the remaining flesh of the bruised fruit. All the lower branches of the tree had been removed, as was the practice for any trees on the school grounds, preventing students from climbing them. Or it seemed to stop every student except for him. He had discovered this fact by accident shortly after beginning his second year at the school. A group of bullies had been pursuing him across the campus, eventually cornering him at one of the trees. And of course, wishing to avoid the accompanying pain of such situations, he kicked off his shoes, exposing the claws on his feet through a hole he had torn in the ends of his socks, and tried climbing the tree.

The claws on his feet were duller than the ones on his hands, and therefore did not often need to be filed. His shoes were safe from their rubbing against the inside of them, but even with their relative lack of sharpness, his foot claws still tended to snag on his socks. Which was why, whenever he got a new pair of socks he would always tear a hole in the end of them at the first opportunity. Unfortunately, the destruction of a perfectly good pairs of socks was a constant source of contention between him and Marcus. Even if he couldn't understand why.

When Hyroc managed to climb his first tree, without any handholds or claws of their own, the bullies pursuing him were unable to reach him with more than insults and eventually gave up. Because of this discovery, Hyroc often spent his afternoon breaks in the safety of a tree.

The apple tree was his favorite. It was the tallest tree on the school grounds and it sat near the back of the school where students only seldom passed by and he never felt there were many eyes on him while he was in it. Then there were also the apples. The tree only ever produced a handful of apples in a year and because the lower branches of the tree had been removed, anyone wishing to partake of its bounty had to wait until it fell to the ground. So, if he got to the apples before then, they wouldn't get bruised and he had them all to himself.

Hyroc reached into his pocket and removed the carved figure of a wooden bear. He set the bear down in front of him on the branch, trying to imagine the inanimate beast moving on its own. He wished he was big and strong, and fearless like a bear. He could do whatever he wanted and never feel afraid of anything. Maybe then being watched wouldn't bother him anymore. A bear would never let something so trivial frighten them. And none of his bullies would be brave enough to ever heckle him again.

Marcus had given him the bear as a present on his sixth birthday. Then he learned his hands were not the first to glean enjoyment from it. The bear had once belonged to Marcus' son Charlie. It always made Hyroc sad hearing about Charlie and seeing the pain in Marcus' eyes whenever he talked about anything relating to his son. Charlie had been eight years old when he had gotten sick and died. Then Marcus' wife Sarah followed shortly afterwards. Hyroc couldn't stand the thought of playing with the bear once he learned this. Marcus had then subdued his reluctance by insisting he wanted Hyroc to have the bear and that Charlie would have wanted it to be played with.

Hyroc often wondered if he and Charlie could have been friends if they would have had the chance to meet one another. He liked to think so. From what Marcus told him about Charlie, the two of them had a lot in common. There would have been so many things for them to do around the house and chores could have gotten done so much faster. And with them watching each other's backs at the school, bullies would have thought twice about messing with either one of them. But it wasn't meant to be.

He grabbed the bear and began making it walk across the branch toward him, supplying his own growls for the wooden animal. Halfway through its march across an imaginary cliff face the branch acted as, something thumped against the tree's trunk. Putting both his hands against the trunk, Hyroc peered around it toward the other side of the tree where the impact had originated. On the ground, he saw the same brown-haired boy who had been following him the day before, accompanied by two other students. One of the other students reached down, picking up a rock. The boy studied the branches of the tree a moment, then chucked the stone at it. The rock thumped against the trunk, bouncing off the bark at a shallow angle. Looking up where the boy seemed to be aiming, Hyroc spotted two of the tree's three remaining apples. He frowned, realizing they were trying to knock the fruit down with the rocks. The rocks would accomplish that but they would also badly bruise them.

Hyroc felt conflicted about this. The boys didn't seem to know he was there and if the one with brown hair was a bully, those rocks might be suddenly aimed at him if he said anything. But he was a little higher up than the apples and with as much trouble as they were having hitting those, it seemed unlikely they could hit him even if they tried. There didn't seem to be any danger posed to him if he spoke to them.

"You're going to bruise the apples that way," Hyroc called out. The three boys gave him a surprised look. The brown haired boy's companions gave an irritated wave in Hyroc's direction, then turned and headed off. Keeping his eyes fixed on Hyroc; the brown haired boy took two steps backward and stopped.

He studied Hyroc a moment before speaking. "How would you get the apples down?"

Hyroc gave the boy a puzzled look; why was a bully responding to his question and in such a conversation manner? This had never happened before. They usually only called him names. Was this some strange new tactic? How talking to him could be part of a plan to hurt him didn't seem to make any sense. Maybe this was something else, maybe the boy wasn't a bully at all. Continuing their conversation seemed the best way to find out.

"Like this," Hyroc said. He stuck the wooden bear in his pocket and carefully climbed through the branches over to where the two apples hung. He plucked down both apples. He studied one apple thoughtfully glancing between it and the boy below. If the boy wasn't a bully, then giving him an apple might be a good start to being liked by somebody. He held the apple out in offer to the boy. The boy stepped beneath the pro-offered apple and caught it when Hyroc dropped it. Settling into a sitting position with his legs hanging over the branch, he began eating the apple he had kept for himself.

After shining the apple on his shirt, the boy took a bite "Do you really eat those ducks you kill, raw?" the boy said.

Hyroc narrowed his eyes. That was a ridiculous question. Nobody ate raw duck, that was disgusting. Maybe getting the boy to like him wasn't such a good idea after all. "No, *I* do not," he said coolly. "Do you eat *your* meat raw?"

Taken aback, the student shook his head. "That's what the other boys say you do."

"Well, since Marcus and I donate any fowl we get to the schools dinners, I wouldn't believe everything you hear."

"You really do that?"

Hyroc cocked his eyebrow, wondering why what he did seemed so unusual. "Yes."

"Everyone says you're actually a ferocious animal a witch turned into a boy."

"I don't think that's what I am," Hyroc said. He paused a moment in contemplation. "But if that's what people say about me then why weren't you afraid to stay and talk with me?"

"I wanted to see if the rumors were true," the student said proudly. "I've never seen an enchanted animal before."

"What do you think of me now?"

The student paused. "You don't look like everyone else that's for sure, but you don't seem to act much differently." The boy paused. "My name's Thomas."

"I'm Hyroc."

"That's a funny name."

Hyroc shrugged. "Well that's what it is."

"It's nice to meet you, Hyroc." Thomas indicated Hyroc's face with his hand. "Did a witch do that to you?"

"No, I was born this way."

"Everyone says that's what your mother was."

Hyroc gave him a hard glare. He didn't want to be liked by somebody who said bad things about his mother. "I don't like people talking about her that way."

Thomas gave him a startled look. "S – sorry, I wasn't trying to talk bad about her." the boy added quickly. Hyroc gave Thomas a surprised look; no student had ever apologized for talking ill of his mother. "But, if you're not an enchanted animal, then what are you?"

Hyroc sighed. Not even Marcus could come up with a definitive answer. He only seemed to know what he wasn't. "I wish I knew."

Thomas studied him thoughtfully. "Why were you avoiding me yesterday?"

"I thought you wanted to beat me up."

Thomas gave him a strange look. "You get beat up?"

"Yeah, why do you think I'm in this tree?" It seemed a little strange Thomas didn't know that. He thought his differences would make his reason pretty obvious. "What's so unusual about that?"

"Because I would be afraid to try and beat you up." Hyroc shrugged, wishing that were true. His life would be a lot easier. "Did you really beat up Billy Mason?" Hyroc nodded, smirking a little as he remembered what he had done to the older boy. Surprise and admiration lit Thomas' eyes. "Wow, you must be a really good fighter to beat someone *that much older*."

"I'm not, he just had a big mouth and it made me want to hit him."

Thomas nodded. "Well, it was nice talking to you –" Thomas held up his half eating apple "– and thank you for the apple."

"You're welcome."

"I'll be seeing you." Hyroc nodded. Thomas turned and headed off. Hyroc watched the boy until he disappeared around the side of the school. Maybe it wasn't so bad being liked by him.

At dinner, Hyroc sat alone in his usual spot at the end of the table waiting for the meal to be served. When Thomas entered the hall, Hyroc watched the boy hopefully, but expected to remain alone for dinner as always. Thomas noticed him and to Hyroc's surprise, the boy made his way over to him.

"I was wondering," Thomas said, settling into a seat beside Hyroc. "How good can you see in the dark?"

Hyroc had never really been out after dark so he had never thought about it. He shrugged his shoulders. "I never thought to check," he said, curiosity piquing his interest.

"Okay, stay awake until it's completely dark tonight and you'll be able to check."

"Why do you care if I can see in the dark? No one else does."

"I'm just curious. Not to be rude but you look like an animal and well, I want to know if you can see in the dark like a cat. I thought it would be interesting if you could is all."

"I'll give it a try and tell you at breakfast tomorrow."

"Thanks."

Dinner was served a short while later. Hyroc and Thomas spent the remainder of their time in the dinner hall talking about their classes and anything else they could think of until they were forced to separate for the night.

"So," Marcus said as he and Hyroc got ready for bed. "Who was your friend I saw you talking with at dinner?"

"His name's Thomas," Hyroc said happily. It was nice to have somebody else to talk with besides Marcus.

"See what I told you," Marcus said smugly. "People just needed a little time to get use to you." He affectionately ruffled the hair on Hyroc's head. Marcus opened his mouth to say something but a cough interrupted his statement. He pounded his chest with a fist and cleared his throat. "Great," he said mildly irritated. "I just forgot what I was going to say. Oh well, I'm sure I'll suddenly remember it in the middle of the night." He helped Hyroc finish getting into bed, extinguished the room's candles, and climbed into bed.

"Good night," Marcus said.

"Night," Hyroc replied.

Hyroc waited until the fullness of night had entered his room and he was positive Marcuse was sound asleep, before climbing out from under his covers. The shadows obscured the finer details of the objects around the room, but Hyroc could still tell what he was looking at. It had never occurred to him he might actually see things at night differently than everyone else. He crept over to the mirror above the washbasin to see how well he could see his reflection. His reflection had the same appearance as everything else in the room, but his dark fur made him blend into the shadows more and he saw a very faint glow coming from his eyes. When he moved his head closer to the mirror, pulling his eyelid up with a finger, he could definitely see his eyes glowing. Marcus and June had always said that's what his eyes did in the dark, but this was the first time he had seen it for himself. He started, nearly tripping over a stool in front of the basin when Marcus coughed loudly. As Hyroc took a deep calming breath, he thought he smelled something. It was a subtle indescribable odor and there was something unnerving about it. Curious, he moved closer to Marcus and sniffed. He found the odor again.

He pulled away from Marcus puzzling over the unknown smell. He reached up and began feeling his nose and along the sides of his snout. *If I can see in the dark, then maybe I can smell better too,* he thought to himself. *I've never actually sniffed Marcus so maybe this scent is just the way he smells.* Hyroc yawned. Knowing he had studies to get to in the morning, he climbed back into bed and went to sleep.

CHAPTER 5

Window Sneak

A cacophony of voices surrounded Hyroc as he opened the door to Miss Duncan's dreaded class. He seated himself as usual at one of the front desks intentionally set apart from the others. Miss Duncan seemed to think he would attack anyone who came within his reach. How she had come to this conclusion was beyond him. She had to know none of his other teachers had any of the problems with him she seemed to expect. Considering the scolding he received whenever he acted out, there wasn't an incentive for him to be anything but a good student. There just didn't seem to be anything he could do to convince his teacher that none of her expectations held true. He hated her thinking such absurd things about him. The only thing he could do was keep it from bothering him and trudge through this class.

With a sigh, he propped his head up on one of his knuckles and doing his best to ignore the sidelong glances from the teacher, he watched his fellow students file into the class. Most of them acted as if he weren't even there and the few who seemed to actually take notice of his presence, watched him warily all the way to their seat and whispered cautiously to one another.

Thomas entered the room with the last few students. He looked around the room, showing a subtle hint of the nervousness new students often displayed, eventually settling his gaze on Hyroc. After a moment of contemplation, he walked over to Hyroc's desk. Hyroc dropped his hand down to the desk, giving Thomas a look of surprise. This was the first time another student had dared enter the forbidden moat of empty space surrounding his desk. Why did this boy act so differently with him? Not that it was in any way a bad thing. Marcus and June treated him good, so it probably made sense there were others like them.

Thomas made to say something discreetly but was interrupted by Miss Duncan. "Thomas, that seat is clearly taken," Miss Duncan said pointedly, quickly taking notice of the boy's close proximity to Hyroc. "There are plenty of empty desks near the other students, take one of those."

Thomas shrugged, giving Hyroc an apologetic look before he headed off toward the nearest seat. Hyroc felt himself smiling a little. His smile vanished when he saw Miss Duncan glaring unhappily at him. He diverted his gaze down toward the dull brown wood of his desk. The displeased look on her face gave him a strange sense of satisfaction. He definitely liked Thomas.

Pulling her gaze from Hyroc, she picked up a large book from her desk at the front of the room. "Today we will be learning about Life Sapping Witches," Miss Duncan said. She walked toward the other students and set the book on Thomas' desk. "Thomas read the first paragraph."

"Life Sapping Witches," Thomas read. "Are witches that drain the life force of people or animals and use this life force. Most commonly, witches use this life force to gain strength, vitality, reverse their age or vainly increase their beauty. When the victim is drained of their life force, they suffer greatly and always die in agony. Due to the nature of the utilization of life force, any beneficial effects are temporary and in order for the witch to maintain their abilities they are required to frequently harvest life force."

"Thank you, Thomas," Miss Duncan said, picking up the book. She walked to the front of the room as she prepared to continue reading. She glanced in Hyroc's direction and in that tiny movement he knew something bad was coming. She was about to read something to make everybody think he was a monster. Taking a breath, he braced himself for what lay next. "The life force of the victim can also be used by the witch to sculpt their features into whatever shape they wish. Although primarily used in beautification, some witches instead use it to give themselves monstrous features." She paused, glancing in Hyroc's direction. "These features include a tail, claws, predatory teeth, fur, horns, and any number of such unnatural and abhorrent features."

And there it was. Out of the corner of his eye, Hyroc saw most of the class now focusing their attention much more closely on him. He blew out an exasperated breath. His day had been looking like it would be somewhat enjoyable, until now. For the rest of the day and likely the next week, he could look forward to many more eyes scrutinizing his features. Everyone would be searching for evidence of him having a tail and horns. He was thankful he didn't have a tail. As many times as his extra appendage would get yanked on, it would be a miracle if it didn't get ripped off.

Thomas' hand slowly rose into the air. "Yes Thomas?" Miss Duncan said.

"When they cover themselves in fur," Thomas said. "Does it help them stay warm?"

Miss Duncan shot him a look of disbelief. "It may but considering the suffering another living thing would endure for the witch to acquire that extra hair, a coat would accomplish the same thing just as well. And wearing a coat would not harm anyone." She made to call on another student when Thomas spoke again.

"Could they do that to someone instead of themselves?"

"Yes."

"So that person wouldn't have hurt anyone."

"That's unlikely."

"What if it's really cold out, like during a winter night, and that witch was trying to help someone?"

She gave him a stunned look. "Witches care nothing for others and do not help anyone but themselves," she said pointedly.

Thomas expression turned puzzled. "But I heard a story where a witch healed someone."

Miss Duncan's expression hardened. "These are lies; falsehoods meant to soften our hearts toward their evil ways."

"How can doing something good be bad?"

"Your story probably did not explain how the person was healed. Do you know what innocent person paid the price for that person's restoration?"

"No."

"Then your story was a lie and you would do well not to spread it. Feygratha was known to use such deceptions during his rise to power."

Thomas flushed with frustration. "Hyroc's mother was a witch and she protected him!" Hyroc shot Thomas a dumbfounded look. Challenging Miss Duncan never ended well for anyone.

A shadow passed over Miss Duncan's face. "*Thomas that's enough*, we've wasted enough time today on this subject."

Thomas gave her a hard glare. "And Hyroc's nice; he gave me an apple the other day. He's not a monster, he's just like everyone else!"

With a thunderous look in her eyes, Miss Duncan slammed her book down on her desk. "*That's enough!* I will not tolerate you mouthing off to me in my own class." She thrust a finger at the door. "Go to the headmaster's office."

"But I –"

"NOW," she growled.

Thomas stood, sparing a glance in Hyroc's direction before heading out the door. Hyroc made sure he was staring down at his desk before Miss Duncan turned to face him. Her eyes bore into the side of his head and he felt as if he might burst into flames. She scoured the room with her gaze for other, rebellious students. After an uncomfortable moment, she regained most of her usual calm demeaning composure and continued with her lesson. While she read from her book, taking her eyes off Hyroc, he couldn't help smiling. It felt good seeing someone make his teacher uncomfortable for once.

At lunch, Hyroc spotted Thomas walking with a mild limp and rubbing his rear. It was obvious Marcus had used the paddle on him. Hyroc frowned feeling a surge of irritation toward his father. Thomas had been asking a simple question and did not deserve to be punished because Miss Duncan didn't like what he said.

"He used the paddle on you didn't he," Hyroc said angrily, as Thomas seated himself.

Thomas looked around, then an odd smile crept across his mouth. "He didn't use it on me."

Hyroc cocked an eyebrow. "Then why were you limping and rubbing your butt?"

"When I told him what happened, he didn't want to punish me for standing up for you. So, he told me to pretend like he had paddled me. But after that he warned me not to make a habit of it or I would be hurting."

Hyroc smirked. That sounded more like Marcus. "In the class, why did you say those things?"

Thomas shrugged. "She was making me angry and, well, I didn't like how she treated you like you were a –" he paused, giving Hyroc an uncertain look.

"*Like a monster?*" Hyroc interjected.

Thomas nodded. "Yeah, like that."

"Thanks."

"Sorry for calling your mother a witch."

"It's okay, I know what you meant. It was a lot better than how people usually talk about her."

Thomas paused before speaking. "I'm glad we're friends."

Hyroc gave him a look of surprise. He had almost forgotten friend was a word. "Really, you're – you're *my* friend?"

"Why wouldn't I?"

"Nobody else has ever wanted to be my friend."

"Well, they're stupid."

Hyroc arose eagerly the next morning. The school week had ended and not only was he free from the torment of his classes for the next two days, he was going hunting. He quickly dressed out of his pajamas and into his hunting clothes. Marcus was just sitting up as Hyroc pulled the door to the sleeping quarters open. Hyroc stopped when a coughing fit struck Marcus. His cough sounded a little worse than it had the day before. Still holding the door handle, Hyroc gave Marcus a concerned look.

Finishing his fit with a hard cough, Marcus gave Hyroc a reassuring smile. "Don't worry I'm just feeling a little under the weather," Marcus said. "It's nothing for you to worry about. Go ahead without me, I'll be right there."

Hyroc nodded and pushed through the door. Some part of him felt he should stay with Marcus, but Marcus said he was fine. If anyone could tell there was something wrong with them, it was Marcus. Pushing the urge aside, Hyroc continued onward to the dining hall.

Students were already trickling into the space for breakfast when he arrived. A handful of boys stood looking out the windows on the rightmost wall as they talked to one another about their plans for the day. Hyroc couldn't help smirking. What he was doing today could easily surpass whatever plans those boys could come up with. Looking toward his usual spot at the table, he was surprised to see Thomas resting his forehead on the tabletop.

"Morning," Hyroc said to the side of his friend's head, as he sat down.

Thomas turned his head to look at Hyroc and gave a sleepy nod. "I can't believe they *still* want us to get up this early when there aren't even any classes." Thomas said, yawning.

"I guess it's just easier this way," Hyroc said.

"*For them* maybe." Thomas narrowed his eyes and began studying Hyroc's hunting clothing curiously. "Why are you dressed like that?"

Hyroc smirked happily. "Marcus is taking me duck hunting."

"Is it really that fun?"

Hyroc gave him a stunned look. "Of course, it is!"

"How can standing around doing nothing for hours be any fun?"

"We *don't* stand around for hours doing nothing. We're doing something the whole time. You have to make sure the ducks don't see you or hear you coming while you get into position for a shot. Otherwise they fly off and you don't get anything."

"Still doesn't sound like anything *that* exciting?"

Hyroc threw his hands out in complete disbelief. How could that possibly not sound exciting? "There's plenty of *excitement* when you hit a duck midair. Do you know how hard it is to do that?"

"No."

"Well – well, it's hard."

Marcus entered the room walking with an unusual sluggishness and his face seemed more worn than it had looked earlier. He coughed twice as he made his way to his seat at the far end of the hall. Hyroc felt a subtle wave of renewed concern as he watched Marcus pass, but pushed it aside, reassuring himself with Marcus' words. There was nothing to be worried about.

After breakfast Hyroc went back to Marcus' office and removed his bow and quiver from a box beneath Marcus' bed. He laid them out on the floor in front of Marcus' oak desk in the other room and started examining his arrows for any signs of damage that would alter their flight through the air. Marcus entered the room, coughed, and put a teakettle on a hook in the fireplace. He turned toward Hyroc with an unhappy look on his face.

"Hyroc I'm sorry to have to do this," Marcus said. "But I'm not feeling up to taking you hunting today; we'll have to cancel the trip."

Hyroc stared at Marcus with a crushed look in his eyes. For a moment, he thought Marcus was being unfair and nearly started arguing with him, but as he looked at Marcus' warn face, he knew it would be selfish to do so. People got sick. This wasn't anybody's fault, it just happened sometimes. When it happened, people couldn't always do the things they wanted to and it was wrong to be upset with them because of it. Hyroc sighed quietly then reluctantly nodded his understanding.

"I'm glad you understand," Marcus said sympathetically. He coughed. "I know how much these trips mean to you and you know I wouldn't cancel them unless I had a very good reason right?" Hyroc nodded again though he didn't want to. The teakettle began to scream at a steadily increasing volume. Marcus pulled it from the fireplace and poured the steaming water into a waiting cup. He turned his head as he coughed, then set the kettle beside the fireplace and added some Yarrow to his cup.

Irritated by the situation, Hyroc gathered his equipment, replaced them into the box beneath Marcus' bed, dressed out of his hunting clothing and back into his school uniform. He left the room in search of Thomas. He found his friend in the library, between two aisles searching for a book.

Thomas gave Hyroc a questioning look. "I thought you were going hunting," he said puzzled.

Hyroc sighed. "Marcus isn't feeling very good."

Thomas nodded. "What are you going to do since you're not going?"

Hyroc stared thoughtfully at the floor a moment. "Do you like to fish?"

"That's even worse than duck hunting," Thomas said, frowning.

Hyroc shrugged. His friend had a point, fishing was kind of boring, especially when nothing got caught. "Well, what do you want to do? I really don't want to sit around here reading all day."

"Can I see your bow?"

Hyroc raised an eyebrow and stepped closer to Thomas. "I'm only allowed to have it when I'm with Marcus," he said quietly. "I can get in a lot of trouble if someone sees me with it."

"But we've got nothing else to do for the rest of the day. Does he lock it up or anything?"

Hyroc gave him a look of astonishment. "Are you *crazy*? I am *not* sneaking it out of his office. He's never used the paddle on me, but I know he will if he catches me doing *that*." Even Marcus had his limits on leniency.

"Does he keep it near his desk or beside his bed?"

"Underneath his bed."

"Does that room have a window?"

"Yes."

"Then you can just open the window and hand it to me outside."

Hyroc studied Thomas' face weighing his options. That wasn't an altogether terrible plan. Maybe there was some merit to this. It would give them something to do. "That might work. But if I get in trouble for doing this I'm blaming *everything* on you."

"We won't get caught. It'll just be for a little bit."

"Okay," Hyroc said. Thomas smiled appreciatively. "But this will only work if he didn't latch the window this morning and if he isn't laying down in the room."

Thomas shot him an annoyed glance. "Of course I'm not going to make you do it if he's in the room, I'm not stupid."

"Alright."

Making sure they weren't being watched, they snuck out of the library and around the outside of the building to the window of Marcus' sleeping quarters. Stealing a quick glance into the room, Hyroc found it empty, with the door closed. He slowly pushed on the window and it opened. Thomas looked at him excitedly which seemed to give him a sudden burst of courage. Taking a breath, Hyroc slipped into the room. He stepped over to the bed and silently slid the box out from under it, listening intently for the sound of approaching footsteps. His heart thumped furiously and he felt as if he might explode if he didn't leave the room soon. He removed the bow and his quiver full of arrows. Careful not to scrape anything against the windowsill, he passed his equipment out to Thomas's waiting arms. When the transfer was complete, Hyroc closed the box, slid it back into its spot beneath the bed then stepped outside. He closed the window behind him and relieved Thomas of his bow. The two of them dashed toward the wall, throwing the bow and quiver over the mossy stonework before scrambling over it. They peeked over the stonework for anyone pursuing them. Finding nobody, the two of them darted into the woods not far away. Once safely in cover beneath the mottled shade of the trees, the two of them burst out laughing from the exhilaration of what they just did.

A chickadee alighted onto a branch in front of them. Thomas pointed at the tiny bird. "Do you think you can hit that from here," he asked.

Hyroc raised an eyebrow. "I'm not going to eat that," he said.

Thomas gave him an odd look. "Why would you want to eat *that?*"

Hyroc smiled half humoredly. "No, *I don't* want to eat that. Marcus told me to only kill something if I was going to eat it or if it wants to attack me. It's wasteful otherwise."

"Oh all right," he said with a sigh. The chickadee took to the air, disappearing farther into the trees. "What about leaves, can you kill those?"

Hyroc rolled his eyes. He picked up a strip of leather that acted as an arm guard against the painful rebound of the bowstring and wrapped it onto his arm. Selecting a leaf from the same tree where they had seen the chickadee, Hyroc nocked an arrow, aimed, and let it fly. It whizzed through the air, striking the leaf with a papery clack.

"Can I try?" Thomas asked.

"Sure," Hyroc said. Thomas pulled his sleeve up and accepted the bow. Hyroc gave Thomas a quick rundown on the basics of bow shooting Marcus had taught him.

Hyroc pointed to a nearby tree. "Aim for the middle of the trunk." Thomas nodded eagerly, nocked an arrow, carefully and slowly drew the bowstring back, then let it fly. The arrow glanced off the bark of the tree, landing a few feet away.

Thomas dropped the bow, his face flushed red with pain and he clenched his teeth. Hyroc stared at him in a mix of alarm and complete confusion. It didn't make any sense how Thomas could have possibly gotten hurt just from shooting the bow. He caught sight of the leather arm guard tied to his own arm and realized he had forgotten to give it to Thomas.

"Thomas I'm sorry, I forgot to give you the arm guard," Hyroc yelled mortified. "Are you okay?"

"Yeah I'm fine," Thomas said through clenched teeth. "That really hurt."

"I told you this was a bad idea. If either Marcus or June sees that mark on your arm we'll both be in a lot of trouble."

"Don't worry about that." Grimacing, Thomas pulled his sleeve over the angry red mark on his arm. "I can just keep it covered with my sleeve."

"Make sure you do. We should get this stuff back where it belongs before somebody notices that we're gone." Thomas nodded his agreement. "Help me collect the arrows."

The two of them gathered the arrows and rushed back to the school. Entering through the window, Hyroc replaced the bow and quiver back in the box. He got a start when he heard Marcus' voice emanating from the other room. Panic gripped him as he stared at the door, expecting it to fly open. When it didn't after a tense moment, he took a deep breath. Just as he was turning toward the window, he heard the door leading from the hall into Marcus' office open, followed by Marcus welcoming someone into the room. Marcus used a name Hyroc didn't recognize. Curious, he crept over to the closed-door, ensuring his shadow didn't pass over the opening beneath it and pressed his ear against the wood.

"*What are you doing?*" Thomas said in a loud whisper. "Get out of there!"

Glaring irritably at his friend, Hyroc raised his hand pointedly, telling him to be quiet. Thomas threw his hand up in frustration but didn't say anything. Hyroc returned his attention to listening to the conversation in the other room.

"…I wish you would have sent for me sooner," a man said.

"Well, I didn't think it was anything I needed to be concerned about until this morning," Marcus said. "I thought I was just pushing myself to hard."

"That's a common enough mistake, but no matter, I should have you feeling good as new in no time. Now let me have a look at you."

"Do you want me to lay down?"

"You should be fine where you're at." There was a long pause. "You're a little warm to the touch, so you're experiencing a slight imbalance of humors."

Hyroc racked his brain trying to remember what humors were. He had overheard Marcus discussing them with a teacher once. He had mentioned something about the four elements and how they were concentrated in a person's body. These concentrations were something called humors. If there was an imbalance in any of them, they would make a person sick. This imbalance could then be treated with things with opposite qualities to the imbalanced humors. If a person was feverish and hot to the touch, they should eat cold food and if they were cold, they should eat hot food.

"Slight?" Marcus said with a questioning tone. "I almost couldn't get out of bed this morning. That seems a little more than *a slight* imbalance."

"A slight imbalance of any of the humors can still have drastic effects on your strength. Everybody's different."

There was a pause. "What are you prescribing for it?"

"Make sure you get plenty of rest of course and eat plenty of cold things. I've also got a regiment of herbs you should take that should help."

"I appreciate this, Robert."

There was a pause. "I'll be back tomorrow to check on your progress."

"Thank you again for this…"

Hyroc pulled away from the door and crept back toward the open window. He climbed through and closed the window behind him just as the door opened. In a wave of panic, he threw himself sideways below the window. Thomas shot him a fearful glare. Moving on their hands and knees, the two of them headed away from the view of the window. When they were safe, the two of them collectively took a deep breath.

Thomas punched Hyroc in the shoulder. "What was that for?" Hyroc said indignantly.

"You almost got us caught!" Thomas said pointedly.

Hyroc rubbed the spot where Thomas had hit him. "Sorry."

Thomas shrugged. "What was so important that you needed to hear?"

Hyroc's expression brightened. "Marcus was meeting with a healer."

"Is he okay?"

Hyroc nodded. "That healer sounded like he was good at it and he'll get Marcus fixed up fast."

"That's good." He paused. "So now what?"

Hyroc shrugged his shoulders. "I don't know what do you want to do?"

CHAPTER 6

Sticks

"That one kind of looks like a bird," Hyroc said, pointing toward a cloud overhead as he laid on the grass a few steps from the school's apple tree. It was a sunny day, but a fragmented cloud front was steadily drifting in from the east. If the disjointed front coalesced into a solid mass, there was a likelihood of rain the next day.

Lying beside Hyroc, Thomas squinted as he focused on the indicated cloud. "It does a little bit I guess," the boy said.

"Your turn," Hyroc said.

There was a pause. "This is kind of boring."

Hyroc sighed in agreement. This had seemed like a much better idea before they had actually started doing it. He sat up. "What do you want to do?" Thomas shrugged his shoulders. Hyroc removed the wooden bear from his pocket and held it in front of his friend. "Do you have an animal; we could make them have wars?"

"No, not yet."

Hyroc shrugged and stuck the bear back in his pocket. Beyond reading, there didn't seem to be a whole lot for the two of them to do for fun. If Marcus wasn't better by the end of the next week, then the boredom of the last two days was what he had to look forward to.

Thomas sat up and began staring off into space with a thoughtful expression on his face. "Did you think of something?" Hyroc asked hopefully. Anything would work at this point.

Thomas was quite a moment. "We could go out into the woods where we went yesterday."

Hyroc shot him a look of disbelief. What was his friend thinking, their plan had almost ended badly! "You want to do that *again*? We almost got caught!"

"No, *you* almost got us caught."

Hyroc narrowed his eyes at Thomas. "Well, I'm not sneaking my bow out again, that was too close. Besides, Marcus is in there with the healer."

"That's not what I'm talking about."

Hyroc's expression turned puzzled. "It's not? What else can we do out in those woods?"

Thomas grinned enthusiastically. "There's sticks out there, I saw lots of them yesterday."

Hyroc gave him an even more puzzled look. "You usually find sticks around trees, that's where they come from. What's so good about that?"

Thomas shot him an odd look. "We can use the sticks as swords and we can fight each other."

Thomas' words stirred up a long forgotten memory inside of Hyroc. He remembered seeing boys playing a game where they fought each other with sticks on a few occasions when Marcus brought him into town. It had looked like a lot of fun, but as with every game, none of the boys would let him join them.

Hyroc smiled excitedly. "You'll really do that with me?"

"Yeah. You've never done that before?"

Hyroc shrugged. "No. Other than Marcus, you're the first friend I've ever had and even with him we never did anything like that."

"It's a lot of fun. We just have to go get some sticks."

Hyroc's smile faded a little. "Won't we get in trouble?"

Thomas smirked mischievously. "Only if we get caught. But this isn't like what we did yesterday. We're not taking anything with us, so we can't get into trouble that way. And it's not like we're going to be gone all day. We'll be back before anyone even knows we're gone. And what else are we going to do?"

Hyroc sighed, he had a point there. With an agreeing nod, the two of them got to their feet. Sweeping their eyes around, there wasn't anybody in sight. They walked behind the trunk of the apple tree. Stealing another quick glance around the tree, they climbed over the cold stones of the wall and hurried off into the woods. The two of them then began their search for sticks. Hyroc spotted a promising stick half buried beneath a pile of dry leaves; but when he pulled it free, it was covered in centipedes. With a startled yelp, he threw it to the ground and rapidly moved away. The next stick he came across was lying in the crotch of a tree. Shaking off a brown spider, he found no other creatures calling it home. The stick curved awkwardly at the middle making it a little unwieldy. With the stick in hand, he made his way back to Thomas.

He frowned when he saw the weapon his friend had discovered. Beyond a bumpy knot a third of the way from its end, Thomas' stick was almost completely straight. Glancing toward his own stick, Hyroc sighed.

"So, when do we –" Hyroc said, before Thomas lunged forward and jabbed him in the shoulder. "HEY, I wasn't ready," Hyroc yelled, as he lurched backwards. Thomas laughed then poked at him again. Hyroc deflected the strike with a quick swing of his stick. He found himself grinning gleefully. "I'll get you back for that!" He took a fast step toward Thomas and struck toward his friend's shoulder. Thomas blocked the attack then took a step backward. Closing the distance between them, Hyroc took a hard jab at Thomas. Thomas sidestepped the attack, narrowly avoiding a hit to his chest, and tagged Hyroc in the back as he passed.

"Got you again," Thomas said with a smile.

Hyroc turned and gave him a malevolent glare. He had an idea how he could even the score. Grasping his stick with both hands, he raised it above his head. With an exaggerated yell, he ran forward. Thomas yelped excitedly as he tore away from his pursuer. He darted behind a tree. Hoping to surprise him, Hyroc dashed toward the opposite side of the tree where Thomas had gone. The boy emerged in the hoped direction, but he was looking over his shoulder and Hyroc tagged him in the arm without any resistance.

"Got you," Hyroc said smugly.

Thomas jumped away and brought his stick up to hit Hyroc. Hyroc blocked the strike. The two of them exchanged a series of blows with neither managing a strike on the other.

"You're pretty good at this," Thomas said, as he jerked his upper body out of the way of an oncoming jab.

"Thanks," Hyroc said, stepping in a circular motion away from his friend.

"This is a lot more fun than looking at clouds isn't it?"

Hyroc nodded before taking a hard swing at Thomas. Thomas blocked the strike, but the force of it wrenched his stick far enough sideways to leave an opening. Seeing this, Hyroc made a twisting motion into the opening with his stick and poked Thomas in the shoulder.

Hyroc smiled. "Now, we're even," he said.

Thomas sighed. Glancing through his surroundings, he saw a short incline beside him and jumped onto it. Using his height advantage, Thomas struck at Hyroc. Hyroc parried the blow, retaliating with several strikes in rapid succession. He struck so fast Thomas had no time to counter as he barely managed to stave off the flurry of strikes. Thomas was steadily driven to the top of the incline. He held his hand up, signaling his request for a break. Panting a little, Hyroc lowered his stick and took a step backward.

"Where did you learn to do that?" Thomas said breathlessly.

Hyroc shrugged his shoulders. "Nowhere, it just seemed like a good thing to do there," he said. Thomas nodded his understanding. A moment later, he reentered a combat stance and Hyroc did the same. "Are you ready?" Thomas nodded.

Hyroc jerked forward, coming in for a strike. Thomas stepped back, but his foot landed on nothing and he stumbled. Realizing what was happening, Hyroc rushed forward, stretching his hand out to catch Thomas. He was too far away and couldn't reach his friend in time. Thomas began tumbling down the incline. Feeling a thrill of fear,

Hyroc rushed after him. Thomas' stick flew from his hand as he came to a stop a short distance later and lay in a heap at the bottom. Hyroc called out, but Thomas gave no response. Fearing his friend may be seriously injured, he moved even faster toward the bottom.

"Thomas, Thomas, are you all right," Hyroc said, as he reached down to shake his friend's shoulder. Right before his fingertips made contact, Thomas rolled onto his back and lightly poked Hyroc on the shoulder with a tiny stick he had in his sleeve

"That's three," Thomas said with a smile.

Hyroc rolled his eyes, putting his hand down. "I thought you were hurt dummy."

Now smiling, Thomas sat up. "That little fall didn't hurt me."

Hyroc shook his head and stood up. Glancing through their surroundings, he was a little surprised to find they had ventured far enough into the woods that the boarding school was no longer visible through the trees. He spotted a trial of smoke rising above the trees not far away and figured it was coming from the school. Then he began to wonder if they had been gone long enough for someone to notice their absence. They hadn't snuck anything out of the school, but they weren't supposed to be out here and they could still get into trouble if someone discovered their absence.

He turned back toward Thomas, who was already standing and brushing himself off. "Thomas, maybe we should –" he stopped talking when he saw something moving through the trees in front of him. The thing resolved into four shapes that walked on four legs. As they drew closer, he realized they were dogs. Three of the dogs flanked a bigger dark-colored one with patches of ugly matted hair. A ring-shaped bite scar marred the side of its snout and half of one ear looked like it had been bitten off.

Thomas turned to see what he was looking at. His eyes widened excitedly. "Hyroc look *dogs*," he said eagerly. He began patting his leg and calling out to them in a friendly voice.

Hyroc felt a wrongness with the way the dogs were acting. They weren't barking. Whenever he had seen a dog, they were always barking. He had never liked those beasts because of those annoying noises. Cats had been much more pleasant animals to be around because they didn't make any noise unless he tried getting close to them. At which point they often made some terrifying noises and acted as if they were preparing to rip into his face. He didn't understand why the lack of such aggravating noises from the dogs would bother him. Then he saw the look in their eyes. It was even more disconcerting than the dog's silence. They were looking at him like; like he was a piece of meat. He felt a thrill of fear. These were feral dogs. He and Thomas needed to get away from them!

"Thomas, I think they're feral," he said out of the corner of his mouth.

The excitement faded from Thomas' face and he shot Hyroc a frightened look. "What should we do?" he said in a fearful tone.

Hyroc's first instinct was to tell Thomas they needed to run, but he didn't because he knew running was probably the worst thing they could do. Marcus had explained to him once if a dangerous dog ever cornered him, he should not run away from it. "Dogs love to chase things and if you run, they will probably chase you and you will get bitten because dogs can run faster than you can. You slowly walk away from them without exposing your back."

"Okay, Thomas –" Hyroc barely managed to say before Thomas turned and took off running. The big dog immediately bolted after him. Hyroc darted into the path of the dogs and slammed his stick into the big dog's head. With a yelp, the hound jumped sideways. All four dogs abandoned their pursuit of Thomas, turning their attention on Hyroc. They moved into a half circle around him, bearing their teeth and growling savagely. Hyroc swatted his stick from side to side across the ground, throwing up some of the leaf litter as he began yelling. Two of the dogs lurched away in a startled motion. The remaining dog lunged at him from the direction of his offhand. Before he could bring the stick up to whack his attacker, the dog bit into his arm. Its teeth tore through his clothing and sank into his skin. Gritting his teeth, Hyroc rammed the stick into the dog's head. The dog yelped, releasing its hold and springing backward. Hyroc could now feel hot blood trickling down his arm. The big dog rushed toward him. Hyroc lifted the stick over his head and brought it down as hard as he could on top of the big dog's head. The dog grunted as it staggered sideways from the force of the blow. Hyroc then kicked it in the nose. With a yelp, the dog jumped back to join its companions. The three smaller dogs began edging forward. Hyroc growled and began flinging the stick from side to side. The three dogs shied away. Hyroc felt as if he were a bear fighting off a pack of wolves. He was too big and strong for them to have any hope of defeating.

The big dog's tail drooped down as it turned and began heading off. The three smaller dogs gave Hyroc an uncertain look, before following after the larger dog. Arms burning and breathing heavily, Hyroc brought his arms to rest beside him. He grimaced as pain flared through the bite in his arm. When the dogs disappeared from view, he dropped the stick and rolled his sleeve back so he could get a good look at his injury. Despite the amount of blood coming out of it, it didn't seem to him like it was a serious bite.

"Are you all right," Thomas' voice said from behind.

Hyroc glanced over his shoulder and held up his injured arm as he spoke. "I'm fine," he said. "One of them bit me." The casualness of his reaction surprised him. He had expected getting a bleeding hole bitten into his arm by a dangerous animal would bother him a lot more.

Thomas came up beside him and grimaced as he got a closer look at Hyroc's arm. "I can't believe you fought them off all by yourself. Why did you do that? Weren't you scared?"

Hyroc shrugged. He wasn't entirely sure why he had done it either. "I don't know why I did that, it just sort of happened. I saw them running after you and – and I knew they were going to hurt you, so I attacked them."

"That's the bravest thing I've ever seen anybody do."

Hyroc smiled. It felt good hearing that. "We're friends, and we're supposed to look out for each other." He grimaced again as his injury reminded him it was still there. He flicked the blood from his fingers onto the ground.

"I know how to help with that. Follow me." Hyroc followed his friend as he searched for something around the trees. He uprooted a green plant with tiny white flowers, snapped the part with the flowers off and held it out to Hyroc. "Put this on your bite."

Hyroc gave Thomas an uncertain look, but took the flowers and pressed it against his injury. "What is this?"

"It's Yarrow. My father uses it whenever I cut myself at my house. It helps to stop bleeding."

"I thought that was only used for tea."

Thomas gave him a surprised look. "Really, you can drink this?"

"Well, only if you're sick, but it's really nasty." Thomas gave him a look of agreement. Hyroc paused. "Let's get back to the school before anything else happens."

Thomas nodded. "I don't want to run into those dogs again either."

They snuck back onto the school grounds, coming over the wall near the apple tree. Blood had soaked through the Yarrow and Hyroc began bleeding again. He needed to get something else to staunch the flow and he knew the safest place to find something to do so with was Marcus' office. The two of them then separated – so Hyroc was the only one who risked getting into trouble if he got caught – before he made his way to Marcus' office. Rounding the corner of the hallway leading to the headmaster's office, he found June coming out the door. She was three years younger than Marcus, with auburn hair and stood just shy an inch of her brother. Hyroc spun around on his heel but June saw him and called his name before he could step out of sight.

"Where have you been?" she said.

Hyroc turned toward her, making sure to keep his hurt arm behind him and out of sight. "Nowhere," Hyroc said innocently.

"I've been trying to find you for the last hour." Her eyes narrowed as she focused on something on the floor. "Hyroc, let me see your arm." Feeling a wave of panic, he held up his uninjured arm, hoping it was the one she wanted.

"No, the other one." Hyroc sighed and held his other arm up. He was caught. June's expression turned shocked and she began examining his injury.

"I fell," he added quickly. She might believe that. People fell hard enough to bleed all the time.

She cocked an eyebrow. "You fell?" Hyroc nodded. She spoke with a disbelieving tone. "Did you fall on something with teeth? You went outside the wall didn't you?"

"I'm sorry, please don't tell Marcus," he pleaded.

June sighed. "I'm not going to tell Marcus, he shouldn't be bothered with this right now." Hyroc breathed a sigh of relief. "But we need to get that arm taken care of; we can't have you bleeding all over the place. Come with me." She headed back into the office and he followed. Once inside, she scrounged through the drawers behind Marcus' desk, removing a handkerchief from one of them. She held it out to Hyroc. "Keep that pressed down onto your wound." Hyroc took it and did as instructed. June pointed toward the bench beside the fireplace. "Sit there, I'll be right back." She turned and headed out, returning with a damp rag and a bandage. After using the rag to clean the bloodied fur around his injury, she began wrapping on the bandage.

"Did you at least learn not to do whatever you were doing that caused you to get hurt?" she said, without taking her eyes off his arm.

"I did," he answered. He wasn't going to do anything like that again no matter how bored he got.

Hyroc sat on the bench in Marcus' office reading a book. Over the top of it, he saw a small dark mass emerging slowly from under the door to the sleeping quarters. He recognized it as a leech. When he had went in to check on his father not long ago, the healer had a jar full of the blood-sucking slugs sitting on the small table. Marcus had explained they would help make him better. It seemed strange to Hyroc something so repulsive could accomplish anything good. He had had frequent encounters with them crawling into his boots and latching onto his legs, but if Marcus said they would help, then he had no reason to doubt their usefulness. And if they could help Marcus, then the healer probably couldn't afford to lose a single one.

He set the book down beside him on the bench and got to his feet. After identifying which part of the leech had the mouth, he picked up the slippery creature by the back end. The leech doubled back on itself and tried to grab onto the fingers holding it. Hyroc shook his hand, dislodging the leech's mouth before it could stick to his skin. He had to continue doing so as he opened the door. Marcus was lying in bed with his shirt off and several leeches were spread across his chest, their long bodies pulsating as they fed. His face was flushed and he still looked as pale as he did the day before. The healer was reaching in the leech-jar with a pair of wooden tongs as Hyroc pushed the door open.

"Hyroc I told you to stay out there," Marcus said sternly.

Hyroc held up the leech and shook it as it tried to drink his blood. "I found a leech on the floor," he said proudly.

Marcus smiled. "I see that and thank you very much." Hyroc returned the smile. Marcus pointed to the jar. "Go ahead and put it in the jar then."

The healer gave Hyroc an uncertain look before carefully sliding the jar closer. Standing on the tip of his toes, Hyroc reached over the jar and dropped the leech into the wriggling mass of blood hungry black bodies within. The healer nodded thankfully as he moved the jar back into position.

Hyroc turned toward Marcus, trying not to look at the swollen leeches on his chest. "Are they helping?" Hyroc said.

Marcus looked down thoughtfully at the leeches. "I believe they're doing their job quite well," he said. "It doesn't feel very good having them on me and knowing that they're drinking my blood, but it's not so bad when you know they're taking the bad blood away." Hyroc nodded happily. That was a good thing. "I'm glad you brought the leech back. Now, please go back out and sit."

CHAPTER 7

Apple in the Rain

Hyroc awoke to the sound of hushed voices. When he opened his eyes, standing beside Marcus' bed he saw the healer talking quietly with his father. Hyroc stretched and rubbed the sleep from his eyes before climbing out of bed. Marcus opened his mouth to say something to the healer when a coughing fit struck him. His coughs sounded even worse. Hyroc winced as he caught a whiff of the strange unnerving scent he had been smelling on Marcus ever since he had gotten sick. The scent seemed much stronger now and Hyroc could barely keep himself from coughing on it. That smell was worrying him, it made him feel like something was wrong; something the healer wasn't seeing. He forced the feeling aside. Marcus wouldn't be saying he felt better if he didn't actually feel better. The person who was sick could tell the most about such things.

Sparing a look in Hyroc's direction, the healer took a cup of water from the table and held it up to Marcus' mouth. Marcus took a drink and his fit subsided.

"Your fever seems to have gone down," the healer said, replacing the cup on the table.

Marcus nodded. "That's good," he said weakly. Marcus looked toward Hyroc. "You hear that, we still might be able to get in one more hunt before the season ends." Hyroc smiled gratefully. It seemed his next weekend wouldn't be boring as he had feared. "Now, get yourself ready for the day. Just because I'm still sick doesn't mean you can skip out on your schoolwork." Hyroc sighed, and turned away to start getting himself ready.

"How's your dad?" Thomas said at breakfast.

"He's doing better," Hyroc replied. "The healer says his fever has gone down."

"That's good isn't it?"

Hyroc nodded. He paused a moment uncertain if he wanted to say more. "But his cough sounds worse."

"I'm sure he's fine. The healer would know if he's not getting better."

Hyroc gave him a thankful look, but his friend's reassurance did not seem to make him feel any better. He still couldn't shake the feeling something was very wrong this morning.

In his first and most disliked class of the day, he seemed incapable of focusing on the lesson more so than usual. His thoughts kept drifting back to Marcus. It seemed the only thing that mattered to him today. He sat at his desk staring out the window as raindrops plinked against the glass. He got a start when something smacked down hard on his hand. Wrenching his hand back from the pain of the strike, he found Miss Duncan standing in front of his desk with a willow rod in hand and a wrathful expression on her face. Hyroc now had a vague recollection of someone saying something to him. He realized with dismay that that someone was probably Miss Duncan asking him a question about the lesson. Ignoring her questions was sure to incur a swat from her rod and often resulted in a more unpleasant lesson for him.

"Was I boring you?" Miss Duncan said crossly.

"No, no ma'am," Hyroc said quickly. He had an urge to explain he had been thinking about Marcus but refrained from doing so as Miss Duncan would likely think he was lying to her, resulting in him receiving additional punishment. It would just be better to take whatever discipline she dished out.

She smiled derisively. "No? There must be something outside more deserving of your attention than my lesson."

"No, ma'am, just rain. I – I was thinking."

"Oh, you were *thinking*. That's something very important to do. Were you by chance thinking about the consequences of your actions?"

Hyroc repressed a grimace. "No, ma'am."

"Hold out your hand." With a slight tip of her head, she indicated his hand she had already hit. Hyroc unwillingly held his hand out, bracing himself for imminent pain. Miss Duncan struck him in the hand with the willow rod. Hyroc's hand stung, but he did his best to keep his expression impassive.

"Since the rain was so much more interesting, you will spend the remainder of class standing at the window. That should give you plenty of time to *think*."

Hyroc breathed a silent sigh as he got up from his desk and walked over to the window. Compared to the willow rod, looking out a window wasn't bad at all. He leaned forward, resting one of his elbows on the sill. A swift smack on his rear made him stand straight.

"And don't slouch," Miss Duncan said sharply.

He gazed absentmindedly at the streaks of rain running down the window. Miss Duncan's voice sounded in the background but she sounded far away as his thoughts drifted back to Marcus. It felt as if there was something he needed to be doing, but he couldn't think of a single thing. Why did everything feel so wrong? Both Marcus and the healer seemed confident the sickness was going away. Marcus' fever had gone down, that was a good thing. Why should a good thing make him feel like something was wrong? It wasn't as if Witch Hunters were involved here. Maybe he was just worried about Marcus. There wasn't anything wrong with that. Marcus was sick, it seemed like a normal thing to be worried when the man was so uncomfortable. Still, it felt like there was something he could do he wasn't doing, something much more important than schoolwork. And definitely more important than this window.

Through the downpour, he picked out the dark shape of one of the trees on the grounds. As he studied its outline, his thoughts turned toward the apple tree. An idea slowly crept into his mind. The last time he had been near the tree he remembered seeing it still held a single apple. He could give it to Marcus. There was no doubt Marcus would be grateful for the gift, especially after some of the foods full of unpleasant smelling herbs he had been eating. A sweet apple would be a welcome relief.

The only problem was the rain. Hyroc didn't mind going through the discomfort of getting soaked by the cold rain to do something for Marcus, but he would get into a lot of trouble for walking through the halls sopping wet. He turned his gaze toward the clouds. The sky overhead was dark, flanked by a lighter patch of clouds. There seemed a chance the rain could stop by the time his lunch break came.

He then spent the rest of his time at the window mentally going through his plan. His hopes began to dwindle as his class ended and the rain still showed no signs of stopping. Then as he finished eating lunch, the rains slowed to a sprinkle. Fearing the reprieve would only last mere minutes, Hyroc rushed outside, dashing across the soggy grass over to the apple tree. He was relieved to see the apple still hanging from its branch. After kicking off his shoes and stuffing his socks inside of those to keep them dry, he began climbing the tree. With the bark still slippery from rain, he was forced to grip the trunk a lot harder than usual. The base of his claws hurt, but pushing through the pain, he continued his assent. When he reached his designated branch, his arms burned from the exertion and the base of his claws ached. He stuck the apple in his pocket and started back down. The pain was now worse on his foot claws. Gritting his teeth, he descended, fueled by the knowledge he was doing this for Marcus. About a third of the way from the bottom, one of his feet slipped, sending him plummeting to the bottom. He gasped as his tailbone smacked one of the waiting roots at the base of the tree. Glowering, he got to his feet. His tailbone throbbed, but it didn't seem to be broken. He sighed with relief. Breaking his tailbone would not have accomplished anything useful. Marcus would not have wanted him hurting himself, just to give him an apple.

Hyroc was a few steps from the door when the rain broke back into a downpour. Luckily, he was back inside before he could get wet enough for anybody to notice. Smiling, he made his way to Marcus' office. The door to the sleeping quarter was closed and the muffled sound of voices was emanating through it. Hyroc pulled out the apple and began shining it with his shirt. When he was satisfied with its appearance, he pushed the sleeping quarter's door open.

He held the apple out in front of him as he spoke. "Marcus I —" he stopped talking abruptly and his eyes widened with horror. The healer sat on a stool beside Marcus' bed with a blood covered knife in one hand. In the healer's other hand, he held a bowl and was catching blood running down Marcus' arm from two thin slices in his skin. June stood nearby with a concerned look on her face as she watched.

"*What are you doing?*" Hyroc yelled out. June, the healer and Marcus stared at Hyroc in astonishment.

"You shouldn't be in here," June said, as she rushed over to him. She grabbed him by the arm and pulled him out of the room, closing the door behind her.

Hyroc fought to push past her back into the room, but she prevented him from doing so. "He's hurting him!" Hyroc called out.

"Hyroc, *stop*," she said sternly. "He is *not* hurting him."

Hyroc stopped struggling and gave her a baffled look. If anything qualified as hurting someone, slicing into them with a knife should. "He's cutting Marcus!" June nodded calmly, which only furthered his puzzlement. It seemed crazy she should be fine with what the healer was doing.

"You remember the leeches you saw the healer using yesterday?"

"Yes."

"Well, what the healer is doing now is sort of like what he was doing with the leeches. He's making a few little cuts in Marcus' arm so he can help thin out some of the bad blood that's making Marcus sick."

"Why can't the healer just use the leeches, they don't hurt when they bite."

She sighed uncertainly. "The healer was worried that using too many leeches could make Marcus' condition even worse, and since they weren't working, he's letting the blood out himself."

Hyroc stared at her thoughtfully a moment before speaking. "But he's getting better?"

June glanced toward the door. "The healer believes he is, so yes." Hyroc breathed a sigh of relief. It really didn't make sense to him how cutting someone could help cure sickness, but the healer wouldn't be doing it unless it worked. "Why did you come in there in the first place?" She looked at the apple in his hand.

Hyroc smiled and held the apple out. "I wanted to give Marcus an apple. I thought he would like something nice like this after all the nasty food he's been eating."

June returned his smile. "That's very thoughtful of you." She picked the apple up. "I'll make sure he gets it." Hyroc nodded happily. "Now off you go, lunch is almost over." Hyroc turned and headed out the door.

The strange feeling of wrongness vanished as he walked through the hall and without its distraction, he found himself strangely focused on his schoolwork during his next class. He was so much so, he managed to finish copying his scroll before any of the other students had. After making sure he had done all his assignment, he handed it in to the teacher. Looking somewhat surprised, the teach took his work and began going over it.

"Very good," the teacher said. Hyroc nodded his thanks and moved back toward his seat at the table. "Hold up." Hyroc sighed, turning to the teacher. It seemed too good to be true for him to get through his work so fast without doing something wrong. "Since you got your work done early and will be sitting there with nothing to do, I've got something for you." The teacher walked behind his desk with Hyroc following. From a drawer the teacher removed a small piece of parchment with writing scrawled across it. "One of the cooks down in the kitchen needs this recipe for rhubarb pie," the teacher said, holding the parchment out to Hyroc. "Take it to them." Hyroc nodded. The teacher grabbed his shoulder as he turned to leave. "And if tomorrow I learn it never got there, then you will be in for a world of trouble. Got it?" Hyroc nodded again. He had no intentions of disobedience. "Good." The teacher released his shoulder, letting him leave. Hyroc made his way straight to the kitchen.

Within he found two of the kitchen staff preparing a stew for the school's dinner. One was chopping vegetables on a long counter near the door while the other was busy stirring a steaming pot.

"Good afternoon, Hyroc," the woman at the counter said with a smile.

She was an older woman with thin streaks of white running through her silver hair. The two of them had gotten to know a little about each other when Hyroc had begun bringing the ducks Marcus and he had downed during their hunts. At first, she had treated him with the same mistrust everyone else at the school had, but for some reason she hadn't done that for long. She had started having conversations with him about how his trips had gone and she spoke kindly whenever she did so. Then to make his kitchen deliveries even better, occasionally she would slip him a honey pastry when nobody was looking. He had actually found himself looking forward to coming to school on those days because of her.

"How's my favorite fuzz ball doing today? We haven't seen you in here for a while, have those fowl been giving you trouble?"

Hyroc shook his head. "No, Marcus has been sick and we haven't been able to go to the pond ever since."

She nodded sympathetically. "I heard about that. How's he doing?"

"The healer says he's doing better."

"Well that's good to hear." Hyroc nodded in agreement. "Did the healer have to use leeches? I saw him bringing in a jar full of them the other morning."

"He did."

She shook her head. "Disgusting creatures those are. How they can help anybody is beyond me."

"I don't understand either," Hyroc said in agreement. "And earlier I was bringing Marcus an apple from the apple tree –" he paused "– and the healer was cutting him."

She gave him a look of surprise. "Really?" He nodded. "Bloodletting, that's something else I'll never understand." A long pause passed between them. "So, what have you got there?"

Hyroc stared at her blankly a moment before he remembered why he had been sent to the kitchen in the first place. He held the piece of parchment out to her as he spoke. "My scribing teacher told me to bring this to the kitchen."

She accepted the parchment and gave it a quick look over. "Oh yes, his recipe for rhubarb pie. I've been dying to try making this."

Hyroc gave her a questioning look. "You can make rhubarb into a pie?"

"Apparently so. Thank you love."

"You're welcome."

She glanced warily at the other cook who had their back to them. She snatched a warm honey pastry off a nearby table and held it out to Hyroc. She winked as he took it from her.

"Now off with you, I don't want to make you late for class with my gabbing."

Hyroc nodded happily before making his way out of the kitchen and heading toward his arithmetic class. Unlike what had happened with his work in the scribing class, he felt no urge to complete his assignment. He wondered how adding up the prices of imaginary bags of grain could teach him anything. With a shrug, he began slogging through his work. Near the end of class, when he was close to finishing his assignment, June entered the room. She wore a grave expression on her face. She glanced toward Hyroc and the look in her eyes told him something was very wrong. The teacher got up from his desk and made his way over to her. They talked quietly to one another. The teacher shook his head unhappily and used his hand to gesture toward Hyroc.

"What's wrong," Hyroc said, fear seeping into his voice as he stood.

She shook her head, tears glazing her eyes. "Just – just come with me." She put her hand on his shoulder and guided him out of the room and to Marcus' office.

Marcus was lying in his bed with the healer standing over him. Marcus was paler than he was earlier, with dark exhausted eyes and his whole appearance radiated a complete lack of strength. When he saw Hyroc entering the room with June, he dismissed the healer. The man had a gloomy resigned look in his eyes as he left. Marcus motioned for Hyroc to come closer and Hyroc did so without hesitation.

"There's something I need to tell you," Marcus said in a frighteningly weak gravelly voice. "Hyroc, I'm very sick." A knot formed in Hyroc's stomach at the words and he felt the chill of dread run across his body.

"But you're going to be all right?" Hyroc said tentatively.

Marcus shrugged. "I wish I could say that; I'm dying." Marcus began coughing.

"Don't say that," Hyroc pleaded, tears starting to run down his face, darkening the fur below his eyes. "The healer said you were getting better and your fever had gone down and – and – and that we could go duck hunting next week."

"Healers don't always know what will happen. He truly thought I was going to be fine and did everything in his power to ensure that. But when a man's end draws near he can feel it and I feel mine approaching. I'm sorry I have to leave you." He coughed as he finished speaking.

"I don't want you to leave. You have to stay, I want you to stay. Please, stay."

"Hyroc I wish more than anything in the world that I could have more time with you. But I'm afraid fate has decided against my wishes."

"No, don't say that."

"June's going to take good care of you. You may not have been of my blood, but I still loved you as a son. Hold out your necklace." With a sniffle, Hyroc slowly pulled off his necklace. His body didn't seem to want to move. "Look at the back of the medallion." Hyroc turned the medallion over. Intricately etched into the metal was the name Foxclaw above a badger, a fox and a claw symbol. "From what I've been able to figure, that is your true family's name, Foxclaw. From now on I want you to use it as your last name instead of Burk, my last name." Hyroc somberly nodded his agreement then slipped the necklace back around his neck.

"Others may fear you, but never let their fear drive you into despair or hatred. Constantly strive to show them their fear is needless. *Never forget* only you can decide if you are good or if you are evil no matter what others say or how they treat you. You are the master of your own fate. One day you will find the answers I was unable to give you." Marcus lifted his hand and wiped away the tears running down Hyroc's face. "I deeply cherished every moment I spent with you. I would have very much liked to have seen you grow up as would have your mother." Marcus smiled. "She loved you more than life itself." A deep sadness seeped into his expression. It was an expression of regret. Regret at not doing more and trying harder to find answers. "I'm so sorry I didn't do more." Tears began welling up in Marcus' eyes. "There were so many things I should have done and I regret not having done them. I hope you can forgive me for that one day."

Hyroc gave him a sad smile. There wasn't anything to forgive. He knew Marcus was trying. "You took me duck hunting."

Marcus smiled weakly as his eyes began to close. "And a fine hunter you became. There is always light in the dark." Marcus' eyes closed. His chest rose and fell with one final ragged breath.

A torrent of hot tears began pouring out of the corners of Hyroc's eyes. "No," Hyroc cried out, burying his head in the bed blanket. "No." He felt June's hand settle on his shoulder.

"He's gone," she said in a sorrowful but gentle tone.

"No." Hyroc cried out turning and burying his head into the folds of her dress. June held him, trying her best to sooth him, but there was no comfort to be had. Hyroc knew he was now more alone than he had ever been.

CHAPTER 8

Forlorn

Hyroc watched indifferently as the procession of students, teachers and large numbers of people he had never met, move across the lawn of Marcus' home toward the gravesite. Gray clouds pockmarked by openings letting through small amounts of sunlight, drifted slowly overhead. A light cool wind stirred the leaves of the surrounding trees in erratic spurts, giving the air an unwelcomed chill. Hyroc barely even noticed; every part of him had felt cold ever since...ever since he had gone into that room. He thrust his thoughts from the memory. He couldn't bear to even think about it.

June was at his side wearing a solid black dress and a dark veil over her face. The two of them stood behind the open coffin containing Marcus' body. Marcus lay within with his arms neatly folded across his chest. He was dressed in an immaculate dark green and white robe bearing the embroidering of the raven that signified The Ministry. His eyes were closed and his face bore a serene expression. Whenever Hyroc looked at him, for the briefest of moments he could think Marcus was sleeping, but then the harsh reality would quickly crush his spirit back down.

Hyroc stiffened, drawing closer to June when he saw several ministry officials approaching the grave. They were garbed in robes colored in their customary red and black.

"It's all right," June said in a reassuring whisper. "There's nothing to worry about; I wouldn't let them take you. You're safe."

The officials reverently studied Marcus' lifeless face, showing subtle amounts of sadness on their expressions. Their eyes slowly drifted up until they were staring at Hyroc. Most of their number only looked at him with a passing interest, but one or two of them watched him in frightening and very disconcerting manners. After what felt like an eternity under their hostile gazes, the group stepped off to the side, allowing others to pay their respects. The other attendees stared at Hyroc showing mixtures of curiosity, fear and disgust. Thankfully, the majority were people who had seen him on a regular basis and excluding Thomas, only occasionally gave him an uncomfortable glance.

Two men approached the coffin and carefully secured the lid on top of it, then they began lowering it into the grave. Cold dread washed over Hyroc as it slid out of view into the darkness. Deep down he knew Marcus was gone, but he kept the thought at the back of his mind in the hopes that denying it would prevent it from becoming a reality. Now Marcus' death was final and inescapable. There would be no more duck hunts; only an empty void nothing could fill. Hyroc's eyes burned as tears rolled out of them. June's hand came to rest comfortingly on his shoulder. He leaned into her arm as she began leading him away.

"It is unfortunate," a harsh man's voice said from behind. The two of them paused and turned to face the speaker. A bolt of fear shot through Hyroc as he recognized the man as Keller. Hyroc knew from the story Marcus had told him when he was younger, Keller was the man who had tried to take him away and would have killed him.

"One such as he could have fallen so far," Keller continued, shaking his head as he gazed toward Marcus' tombstone. "He did so much good once. But his is the fate of all who fall from the light to embrace darkness." He turned to face them, affixing Hyroc with a dangerous gaze. Hyroc sidled behind June, never taking his eyes off Keller. He had never been so thankful for her presence.

"You are *not* welcome here," June said in a threatening tone. "Leave!"

"As you wish." June reached behind her and held Hyroc protectively as Keller passed. He paused a few paces from them. "Without his blind commitment and cunning mind, it is only a matter of time before *that thing* by your side is just another forgotten memory. It may take me years still, but mark my words, I will eventually make others see what I see. And on that day there will be no place where you can hide that aberration." With that, he headed off. June held Hyroc's shoulder, never taking her eyes off Keller until the man disappeared from sight.

"Don't let what he said frighten you," she said, looking down at Hyroc with caring eyes. "I might not be as good with words or laws as my brother, but I won't let that man hurt you. Marcus had friends who respected him and they won't soon forget their loyalty to him or me, even if they didn't always agree with him." She reached down and wiped the tears from Hyroc's eyes. "Now, why don't we head inside and see what food everyone brought." Hyroc nodded somberly and the two of them made their way inside the house.

They passed empty stagecoaches, with their drivers milling around silently and staring dumbstruck at Hyroc when they spotted him. Taking notice of their unblinking eyes, June hurried Hyroc to the front door. Stepping through the threshold, Hyroc found the living room full of people. As June pulled the door closed behind them, several of the attendees made their way over to the two of them. They offered their heartfelt condolences to June, but they spoke without seeming to take any notice of Hyroc. His eyes began to fill with tears as they did so. He didn't understand why their behavior stung him so much suddenly. He had grown to expect such behaviors and had even learned to ignore them. Why should they bother him now?

"Hyroc," June said gently, her expression showing hints of frustration, frustration directed at her guests. For some reason her frustration melted away some of his sadness. It made him feel better to see someone unhappy with how he was being treated. "Why don't you head into the kitchen to get yourself something to eat? Okay."

Blinking away his tears, Hyroc nodded and walked into the kitchen. On the table and lining the counters, he found cheese wheels, fresh bread, different types of cooked or smoked meat and kippers, pastries with either jam or cream oozing out of them, and a cake. He slid a wedge of cheese onto his plate, then some of the meat, a cream filled pastry and a piece of the cake. With no room to sit at the table, he stepped out the back door. Outside he found a group of three women talking quietly as they ate. Their conversation stopped abruptly as they took notice of him and they began staring intently at him. Repressing another wave of tears, he went back into the kitchen. All he wanted to do now was be alone; he didn't want to be around these strangers anymore. He didn't want to feel their eyes on him. He hurried through the numerous watching eyes and up the stairs to his room, glad to see the hall there empty.

Closing the door tightly behind him, he made his way over to the window overlooking the garden and sat, before taking a bite of the cheese wedge on his plate. His mood lightened a little as he did so, but the sadness of the day prevented him from feeling much at all. Without Marcus, nothing would ever be the same. Tears began streaming out of his eyes and his breathes shuddered with sorrow. He didn't want it to be true. With all his strength, he wished it to be false, though he knew what the truth was and there was nothing he could do to change it no matter how much he wanted to. He was alone.

A knock came at his room door, slightly pulling him away from his pain. He was silent a long moment before he mustered the strength to answer. "Go away," he said sharply in a strangled voice.

"It's Thomas," Thomas said, his voice muffled.

Hyroc wiped his eyes on his sleeve. He didn't want his friend to go away. "C – come in."

Thomas stepped into the room holding a half-eaten pastry with its jelly filled innards exposed. "These are delicious," Thomas said, holding up the pastry. Hyroc nodded absentmindedly and returned to looking out the window. Thomas sat down beside him. "You doing okay?" Thinking that an odd question to ask on such a dark day, he responded with a sigh. "I didn't know him as well as you did, but he seemed like a good person." Hyroc nodded appreciatively. There was a pause. "There's something I wanted to show you." Thomas stuck the remainder of the pastry into his mouth and reaching in his pocket; removed a small polished stone with a greenish tint to its surface. Etched into the center on one side was a symbol Hyroc didn't recognize. Thomas handed it to Hyroc. Accepting the stone, Hyroc ran his thumb across its cool smooth surface.

"That symbol in the middle, it stands for courage. After what I saw you do with those dogs, I thought you would like it."

Hyroc gave him a gladdened look. "You got this for me?" Thomas nodded. "It's – it's really nice."

"I don't think I could ever be brave like you."

"Don't say that, you're not a coward."

Thomas shrugged. "I got scared and ran off and you had to save me. I'm a coward."

"I run all the time and hide in trees. So, if you're a coward then I am too. And a coward wouldn't have smacked that dog in the head. You're not a coward. Besides, you were brave enough to come and talk with me." Thomas smiled thankfully.

"Be careful with that!" June snapped. Her anger was directed at two men who carried the last remaining cabinet from Marcus' office. "That's made from oak and it's a family heirloom over a hundred years old." The men nodded their apologies, then in a more cautious manner continued on their way.

Hyroc turned his attention back to the bookshelf June had instructed him to empty, grabbed a book and placed it in a waiting box at his feet. It had now been two long days since the funeral. The bite of Marcus' death had diminished somewhat, allowing him to again glean some small amounts of enjoyment out of his days. Even so, the loss of Marcus still haunted his every thought, preventing him from escaping the cold emptiness of sorrow for long. He and June were now clearing out Marcus' office in preparation for the new headmaster, who was scheduled to arrive in a week's time, at which point the school would resume. Hyroc was hardly ready to continue with his studies, but it seemed he had little choice.

"When you're done over there," June said. "Go ahead and get the blankets off the bed in the other room."

Hyroc nodded. He finished with the last book a moment later and headed into the sleeping quarter, hesitating briefly at the door. He slid the pillows onto the floor, and carefully began removing the covers from the bed. As he finished rolling them up, he noticed the two boxes containing Marcus and his hunting bows. Kneeling, Hyroc pulled out the smallest box and opened it, revealing his own bow. A single tear rolled out of his eye as the memory of his first hunting trip flashed into his mind. It still felt like those trips had only happened days ago. Before all happiness had been drained from him. He didn't expect to ever be happy again. Wiping away the tear, he closed the box, rose to his feet and continued working on the bed.

It was well past midday by the time the two of them had finished with the room. Hyroc stopped at the door to look back into the now bare room feeling a pang of sadness. He had had many good memories in this room, but now darkened and devoid of all of its familiar decorations, it felt like those things had happened in another place far away. Memories like those would never again happen to him in this room. He lingered at the door a long moment before turning and leaving.

A week later, June woke Hyroc earlier than he had ever been on a school day. He groggily got ready, then he and June headed out into the cool darkness, illuminated only by the rising dome of the sun on the horizon. At the dining hall, a tall man with black hair and a graying beard of the same color stepped up to the podium. He introduced himself as the new headmaster and briefly laid out his vision for the school, which seemed to Hyroc as the exact things Marcus had been doing, just worded differently.

As Hyroc followed the throng of students heading off to their classes, one of the prefects informed him the headmaster needed to see him. Disconcerted by the new headmaster summoning him when he hadn't done anything, Hyroc made his way to the headmaster's office. He was surprised by the change the room had undergone. Adorning the walls, he found numerous paintings depicting scenes of men in battle armor fighting hideous shadow demons wreathed in clouds of darkness. A chill ran down Hyroc's back when he saw the painting of a silver raven perched on a scythe atop a stony precipice, overlooking a field surrounded by rolling hills. Several new immaculately polished cabinets, with still bare shelves had been moved into the room. An orange rug with yellow embroidery in the shape of wheat stalks along its edges ran from the door all the way to the desk at the window.

The headmaster stood left of the window putting books on a bookshelf. When Hyroc closed the door behind him, the headmaster turned to face him. He pointed at the chairs in front of the desk. "Have a seat," he said. Hyroc sat. "You're probably wondering why I asked to see you," the headmaster said, seating himself at his desk. He interlaced his fingers and affixed a piercing gaze upon Hyroc. "There are a few things I need to make clear to you. I've heard concerns expressed about your presence here, but to be frank, if you were a danger to the students I wouldn't expect that my predecessor would have allowed you to be here in the first place. And as such I see no reason to change this. But keep in mind, unlike my predecessor, I have no binding agreement to keep you here and if you should do anything to make me think you are a threat to the other students, you will be gone without question and in whatever manner deemed necessary. Is this understood?"

"Yes headmaster," Hyroc said.

"Good. And do not make the mistake of thinking just because my predecessor was also your parent you will be afforded any special privileges. To me you are just another student and you'll be treated as such –" the headmaster's eyes flickered intentionally to the paddle resting against the leg of his desk "– even in punishment." He paused, letting his words sink in. "You will be housed in a dorm like the rest of the students." The headmaster paused, thinking a moment. "Has everything been understood?"

"Yes headmaster."

"I hope indeed it has. That will be all then. You may go." Hyroc stood and eagerly made his way out the door.

After dinner, a teacher led Hyroc to one of the student dorms and left him at the door holding a pillow stacked on top of a blanket. He felt a surge of apprehension as he stared at the closed door. He had never spent a night with so many people around him. And it disturbed him to even think about it. He liked being alone at night, not crammed into a room like dead fish in a barrel. He wasn't going to like this. But he had to do it anyway. Gathering his courage, he pushed through the door.

As soon as he came through, the room fell silent and every student inside stared at him. He very much wanted to dart back into the hall. Subduing the urge; he took a deep breath and walked farther into the room. Whenever he came to an unoccupied bunk, a student would slide into it and say it was taken. Just as he began fearing he would be spending his nights on the hard floor, he found a bed at the end of the room. By now, most of the students had tired of looking at him, but he still felt an uncomfortable amount of eyes watching him, and he heard the other boys whispering about him as he made his bed.

"This where you're going to be?" a familiar voice said. Hyroc turned to see Thomas leaning against the bunk's bedpost. Hyroc felt a wave of relief. At least there seemed one good thing about his predicament. "It looks like we're going to be bunk mates then."

"You're on top?"

Thomas nodded. He shot Hyroc a mischievous smile. "And don't worry, I don't wet the bed."

Hyroc smirked. "You had *better not*, because I don't think we could be friends if you peed on me."

Thomas repressed a laugh. "I know it's probably not as comfortable as the bed in your room, but they're still soft enough to sleep on."

"That's good."

"Anyway, I've got some studying to get done for Miss Duncan's class."

Hyroc frowned ruefully. "Yeah it's a bad idea to fall behind with her."

That night it took Hyroc what felt like hours to eventually fall asleep in the unfamiliar surroundings of the dorm. He was violently shaken awake as he began drifting into sleep. When his eyes focused, he saw an older boy who he recognized as the head prefect, Simon, holding him down. Behind Simon were three boys a few years younger than he was. The prefect released his grip, pulling back slightly, then the other boys moved closer.

"You don't belong here," Simon said coldly. Hyroc could smell his breath as he spoke.

"This is where they told me to go," Hyroc said confused, trying his best not to sound intimidated. Showing weakness would only make them think he was an easy target.

"Look at his eyes," another student said. "He looks scared."

Simon grinned. "And he should be. Do you know what The Ministry does to freaks like you? They burn them alive. But in your case, I bet they would burn your fur off to see what was underneath. Then they would skin you like a rabbit and then –"

"Leave him alone!" Thomas said from above Hyroc.

Simon scowled at the interruption. "Shut up Thomas," he glowered, smacking the side of the bed frame. "Anyone who shows sympathy to deviants like him will share in the punishment."

"Will you shut up," another student growled from a nearby bunk. "I'm trying to sleep here."

"You're not welcome here and you never will be," Simon hissed. He hovered menacingly over Hyroc a moment, before shoving off from his bed and heading away with the other three boys following.

"Are you all right?" Thomas whispered, sticking his head over the side of the bunk.

"I'm fine," Hyroc lied. Those four boys had frightened him much more than he was willing to admit. He was afraid if he showed any signs of fright, it might encourage others to harass him. He knew it would be better just to feign bravery, even to Thomas.

"Don't let what those idiots said bother you. No one in town would ever do that."

"I know." Hyroc wasn't convinced it was true even as he spoke. He knew there were people who would.

"You're sure you're okay."

"Yeah."

"Okay." Thomas pulled his head back up.

A tear ran down Hyroc's face. He missed Marcus now more than ever. He began to sob silently. Remembering the wooden bear he had placed in his pillowcase, he pulled it out. He clutched it tightly with both hands. Holding the bear made him feel better and he was able to make himself stop crying. *This will do me no good,* Hyroc thought to himself. *Marcus is gone but I need to be strong, strong like a bear. They want me to cry. If I cry, it will tell them they've beaten me. Marcus would not have wanted them to beat me and I will not let them. From now on, I will be strong and not cry ever again.* Hyroc closed his eyes and with his newfound strength, went to sleep with the bear still in his hand.

• • •

CHAPTER 9

"Your request is denied!"

"Denied?" Keller said, his expression turning to a scowl. His request had seemed relatively straight forward and easily carried out. He wasn't expecting any resistance toward it. In fact, he had thought many would be relieved by it. He had believed safety would be of a much greater concern.

"Yes, we see no evidence at this time for such actions," the ministry official said from the other side of their desk.

Keller stared in disbelief at the man. He couldn't believe what he was hearing. How could there be no evidence for his proposed actions.

"No evidence! I should think the mere presence of such a creature near civilians should be reason enough."

The man interlaced his fingers, giving Keller a look of mild irritation. "We have been closely monitoring the creature for any signs of danger and it has yet to manifest anything of concern."

Keller shook his head. "And what of the report where the creature injured a boy? Surely that should qualify as a danger."

The man repressed a laugh. "*Injured* is hardly the term I would use for that incident. All the boy came away with was a bloody nose and a black eye. No lasting harm came to him. And the situation was swiftly dealt with and nothing has occurred like that since."

"No lasting harm came to the boy *this time*, but how do you know it won't be worse for the next person that sets it off? How do we know that boy didn't just get lucky?"

The man shook his head dismissively. "You make it sound as if we are dealing with Feygratha himself? It seems doubtful after only a single mild disturbance the creature's ferocity would increase to such a level without us recognizing the signs first."

"I thought it was our duty and that of The Ministry to ensure the darkness of such creatures is never allowed to do harm to others, no matter how small of a possibility that may be?"

"Your examinations of both Marcus and the creature failed to reveal any evidence either possessed any traces of witchcraft. I may agree that the creature's appearance is baffling considering that, but as I already indicated, I am certain it does not pose a danger to the students at the school. And if it'll put your mind at ease, the new headmaster has been apprised of the situation and will be on the lookout for such dangers should the creature begin showing any troublesome behaviors. The students will be safe under his vigil."

"Safe?" Keller scoffed, a sharpness seeping into his voice. How could this man possibly believe such preposterous things? "No one at that school has been safe since that fool Marcus decided to bring such an aberration there."

The man's expression turned stormy. He spoke with a biting tone. "I would watch what you say about Marcus in my presence, Keller. Have you forgotten how much of his work we still utilize? He knew more about the darkness of witchcraft than both of us combined. Yes, I agree his decisions regarding the creature were unusual, but if anyone knew how to handle that creature it was he. And if I understand correctly, under his guidance the creature had even begun providing a service to the school. If such a creature could be made to lighten the burden of others, I must agree with his judgment.

"That should then make clear to you why your proposal was denied." The man's expression darkened further. "And I would warn you against anything that could be construed as an attempt to sully the reputation of a good man or harassment upon his remaining family during this time of mourning." Glowering, Keller nodded. "Good. You are dismissed."

Keller rose to his feet, gave a respectful bow to the man and left the room. The other man's thoughts were absurd, but unless he wished to risk his position and his ability to successfully deal with threats directed at innocents, he had to obey his superiors. It would not be on his head when the Hyroc creature inevitably showed its true dark nature. And when it did, he would finally remove its threat once and for all.

• • •

CHAPTER 10

Hanging Tree

Hyroc was thrust awake in the darkened boy's dorm when a hand pressed down hard on his chest while another closed over his mouth. He tried yelling but his call only came out as a muffled groan. Thrashing to free himself, he made a fist and punched toward the outline of his attacker's head. Another hand caught his arm before it could make contact, forcing it down to his side. More hands grabbed his arms and legs to restrain him, then a loop of rope was cinched tight around his snout. Unable to offer any meaningful resistance, he was dragged out of bed in nothing more than his breeches and hauled through the dorm's door. His assailants carried him through the dark halls of the school, eventually stopping outside in the chilly autumn night air. Hyroc shivered as they set him on his feet. His fur lessened the bite of the air, but enough of the cold still reached his skin for it to affect him.

A single torch illuminated the faces of his kidnappers. Among them, Hyroc recognized the head prefect and several other students he had seen in the dorm. He tried bolting away from the group, but one of the nearest boys grabbed him and struck him in the stomach before he made it more than two steps. With a gasp, he doubled over, clutching his abdomen.

ADAM FREESTONE

"Hold him," Simon snarled. "We can't let him go free." Two boys grabbed Hyroc by the shoulders and stood him up straight. Simon motioned for everyone to follow him and the two boys forced Hyroc to obey. They led him to one of the school's trees near the corner of the wall behind the dining hall. One of the boys threw a long length of rope over the branch of the tree into Simon's waiting arms on the other side. The two boys pushed Hyroc toward the tree. Hyroc realized with horror the group planned on using the rope to hang him from the tree.

Digging his feet into the ground, he struggled to stay in place to no avail. He watched helplessly as a boy tied the rope to his ankles. Then with a hard yank the ground and black sky, lurched together in a dizzying clash as Hyroc was pulled off his feet. His necklace slipped from his neck. He reached out to catch it, but in the chaotic swirl of motion, he missed. The world slowly calmed, settling upside down. Simon scooped up the necklace. Hyroc groaned angrily, trying to tell the prefect to give it back, along with something more vulgar.

Simon examined the necklace and grinned up at Hyroc. "This is nice, I think I'll keep it as a souvenir; something to remember you by." Hyroc scrabbled furiously at Simon's face, wishing very much to do something harmful to the older boy. Simon stuffed the necklace into his pocket. He turned halfway toward the group of boys. "I think we've upset him." The group laughed mockingly. Simon shrugged his shoulders. "I don't know why, I heard he liked being in trees." The group laughed again. Simon paused, his expression turning thoughtful. "Maybe this has gone too far, maybe we should let him down." Hyroc gave Simon a perplexed look. After everything they had just done, why would they let him down? Simon looked up at him with sincerity. "Do you want to come down?" Hyroc nodded eagerly. As confusing as this was, he still wanted down. "Ask nicely and we'll let you down." Hyroc did his best to speak his request though his words only came out as differently toned moans. Simon shook his head. "I didn't catch that." Using two of his fingers, Simon pushed on the back of his ear to show he was listening closely. Hyroc tried speaking more clearly through his closed mouth, but his efforts didn't seem to make much of a difference. Simon shrugged his shoulders, turning toward the group. "I guess he wants to stay there." The group laughed. "It would be rude of me to make him leave, so I'll give him what he wants."

Simon made a mock salute to Hyroc before turning and heading off. The rest of the group followed. Hyroc began yelling after the group as loud as he could. The boys continued on their way, showing no signs of reaction toward his sounds. He watched the torchlight fade until it vanished completely, leaving him alone in the darkness. He yelled for what felt like hours, until all hope of anyone hearing him had been exhausted. Hot tears dripped out of his eyes toward the ground and his breathing began shuddering. No one could hear him. He would be out in the cold night until morning at the earliest.

He now missed Marcus more than ever. Marcus would have never let something this horrible happen to anyone at the school. This place had felt so much better while he was around. Now Hyroc was starting to hate it. It didn't feel like his home anymore. Why did everything have to change? Nothing ever seemed to work out for him. Everything seemed bent on preventing him from being happy. Why....

A cold pinprick materialized on the bottom of his foot, followed by a second and a third. Hyroc's breathing instantly returned to normal and his tears almost completely stopped welling up from his eyes. More pinpricks struck his skin. Dread washed over him; those pinpricks were raindrops; it was starting to rain. He couldn't spend an entire night outside in the rain in nothing but his breeches, he would freeze to death before morning! His teeth began to chatter. He needed to get down and he needed get down fast.

He tried sitting up to grab the rope. Despite a determined effort, he didn't have the strength to do so. He racked his brain for another way out of this situation, but his mind was muddled and he found it difficult to think. The memory of climbing the apple tree flashed into his mind. If he could grab a hold of the tree's trunk, he might be able to walk his hands up to the branch the rope rested on, haul himself onto it, and untie it from his feet. Then he could simply climb down. He reached out with one hand as far as he could toward the outline of the tree's trunk in front of him. His fingers touched only air.

The trunk seemed just barely beyond his reach. He began throwing both his arms from side to side and started swinging. After an agonizing length of time where every second he got wetter and colder, the tips of his fingers bushed something rough. Then a few swings later, he was barely able to grasp the tree bark with the ends of his claws. His hand felt leaded and with the added pull of the rope in the opposite direction, he barely maintained his tenuous hold. Grasping the trunk with the claws on his other hand, he pulled himself closer to the tree allowing for a more solid grip. He carefully walked both hands up the trunk and across the branch the rope hung on. He then started pulling himself up onto the wet branch. His arms burned severely and tiny slivers of wood dug into his fingertips and up underneath his claws. Straining every muscle in his body, he fought through the escalating pain and managed to pull his upper body onto the branch. Using the natural downward pull of the rope, he swung his legs on top as well. He lay there panting until the temporary warmth of exertion faded and the returning wet chill spurned him to work at untying the rope.

His fingers felt like blocks of ice and they were clumsy and slow at working the knot free. Slivers protruded from his fingers, stinging as they caught on the rope fibers. Slowly he undid the knot, letting the rope slip off his feet. After getting into a more stable position with his back against the trunk, he eagerly removed the rope from his snout. He sat there a moment working some of the soreness out of his jaw then carefully lowered one foot to the part of the trunk below his branch, digging his foot claws into it. He tested his footing with a stepping motion. His footing held and he put his other foot on the trunk, followed by his hand. When he shifted his weight to grab with his other hand, his numb fingers slipped. For a frightening moment, he thought he would fall, but his claws caught on the bark. The sudden stop nearly tore them from their beds in his fingers and toes. The muscles in his arms screamed with an angry burning pain. Once his breathing slowed from the shock, he continued down the tree. He made it a foot from the base, but with his remaining strength now depleted, he fell. A dull pain permeated his leg as he landed, though he barely noticed it through the euphoria of finally making it down the tree. Fighting through the pain of using his arms, he clambered to his feet. A faint point of light out of the corner of his eye caught his attention. Turning toward the light, he froze in place with terror as he saw two eyes peering at him out of the darkness. He locked his gaze with the watching eyes for a startling moment, then regained enough of his wits to turn and hurriedly limp toward the front door of the school.

He fumbled at the door handle with his numb fingers, envisioning whatever creature those eyes belonged to was creeping up behind him. He entered the building, slamming the door shut behind him. The normally cold floor felt warm under his feet as he stood there panting with his back pressed against the door. Dreading something was about to come crashing through it, while he simultaneously fought the urge to immediately collapse onto the floor for warmth, he made his way to the teachers sleeping quarters, leaving behind a trail of wet footprints as he went. He wasn't going to give those boys a second chance at harming him. He entered the common room that connected the hallway containing the teacher's rooms. The room was empty and faint embers glowed in the fireplace. He made his way into the adjoining hallway. After counting the doors, which was a strangely difficult task for him despite his countless hours of work in his arithmetic class, he located the fourth door on the right-hand side and knocked on it.

"Who's there?" June's voice answered groggily.

Hyroc's teeth were chattering so badly he was unsure if he could even speak coherently so he knocked again. He heard a quiet sigh. "I'm coming," she said in a grumpy tone. "But if this is some prank, I swear I'll —" the door opened. June's hair was unkempt, her eyes bleary; she wore a white nightgown and held a freshly lit candle in one hand. She stared down at Hyroc with an uncomprehending expression, then her eyes widened with alarm. "What happened!" she exclaimed. She rushed back into the room, yanked the blanket off her bed and wrapped it around him. The soft feel of the warm blanket was an extraordinary sensation. June hurriedly led him into the common room, where she quickly reignited the dying fire with a tinderbox. "Sit over here by the fire," she said, gently leading him closer to the fireplace. He was still sopping wet but the warmth of the fire helped subdue his discomfort. June shook a brass teakettle from a nearby table and set it on a hook in the fireplace. Hyroc began to doze in the overwhelming warmth and comfort.

The shriek of the kettle brought him back to consciousness. June prepared a cup of tea and handed it to him. "Drink this." Without hesitation, he took a big gulp of the hot liquid.

June pulled a chair close to him. She settled into it throwing her robe lower over her legs. "Now, tell me *what happened.*"

Hyroc took another sip of tea, cleared his throat, and with a sigh recounted the disturbing events that had led him to her door.

"That is unacceptable behavior," June exclaimed, shaking her head angrily when he had finished. "Winter isn't far-off; you could have easily frozen to death out there in the rain! I don't care what you look like, it's no excuse to hang you out like a line of dirty laundry. You got lucky they hung you close enough to the tree, but you may not be so fortunate in the future and who knows what they might think to do to you next time. In the morning, we'll bring this barbaric misbehavior to the headmaster's attention; this cannot be tolerated." June stood and he handed her the now empty cup. "You'll be spending the rest of the night in my room where I can keep an eye on you." Hyroc nodded gratefully. That was what he expected her to say. He knew she would protect him. "I'll send someone to get your clothes from your dorm in the morning. But before either of us can go to bed, I need to do something about those slivers."

Hyroc bowed his head and shrugged unenthusiastically.

Hyroc seated himself at the table in the dining hall. The few hours of sleep he had gotten in June's room had done little to alleviate his fatigue. His arms hurt more now than they had during his escape from the tree and many other aches had appeared all over his body. He rested his head on the table's smooth wooden surface and closed his eyes. He opened them at the sound of student's voices. Through bleary eyes, he watched the ever-increasing throng of students file into the dining hall. He sat up with a start when he spotted Simon enter the room. The head prefect stopped, staring at Hyroc with a subtle amount of surprise mixed with contempt. Although unnerved by the prefect's presence, Hyroc knew he was safe for the moment with June watching him from the teachers table. He gave Simon a challenging glare, daring him to try doing anything while June was watching. Simon smirked and continued on his way. Thomas entered the room. Hyroc narrowed his eyes angrily at his friend as the boy made his way over to him.

"Where were you?" Hyroc asked acidly.

Thomas shrugged apologetically. "I – I'm really sorry," he said. "I was asleep."

"How could you have slept through *that*?" All the commotion should have woken everyone in the dorm.

"It was the middle of the night," Thomas retorted. "And I didn't know you were gone until I got up this morning and heard some of the older boys bragging about what they did to you. If I had known somebody had done that to you, I would've gotten a teacher."

Thomas sounded sincere and his explanation seemed to make some of Hyroc's anger abate. With a sigh Hyroc said," *I guess* I can forgive you for that." Thomas nodded thankfully. "But I'm not going to be climbing trees for a while," Hyroc said, rotating his arm."

"You should take this to the headmaster?"

Hyroc glanced over at Simon who sat at the other end of the table. "Yeah, right after breakfast."

"Good, I don't want those *fat headed jerks* getting away with this."

"I want that more than you," Hyroc said smirking.

"There's something we need to talk to you about headmaster," June said to the headmaster after breakfast, as he came to the door leading into his office.

"Of course," the headmaster said, suspiciously eyeing Hyroc who stood at her side. He opened the door. "After you." The headmaster offered the two of them a seat before sitting down behind his desk. "What brings you to my office this morning?"

"Well it appears a number of your students, including the head prefect, took part in something despicable," June said, turning toward Hyroc. "Hyroc please tell the headmaster what happened."

Hyroc nodded and related the events of the night for a second time.

"Is that everything," the headmaster said when Hyroc had finished, his face impassive.

"Yes headmaster," Hyroc replied confidently, emboldened by the knowledge those boys were going to be punished for what they had done to him.

"Very well," he said as he stood. "If you'll excuse me for a moment, we can get this all sorted out shortly." The headmaster left the room and returned with Simon. The Prefect and Hyroc locked their eyes on one another as he walked over to the desk. "Simon it appears we have a bit of an issue," the headmaster said, re-seating himself at his desk.

"What kind of an issue headmaster?" Simon said innocently.

You know exactly what kind of an issue, Hyroc thought darkly.

"I don't much like to beat around the bush, so I'll get right to it. Hyroc here says you hung him in a tree last night while it was raining. Is this true?"

"Absolutely not," Simon scoffed sounding offended. "I was in my bunk sleeping the entire night just like the other students."

"Well then we have a problem." He turned toward Hyroc. "I don't take kindly to liars wasting my time."

"I'm not lying," Hyroc replied taken aback, warmth seeping into his face. "I told you the *truth*!" He would never lie about something like this. The headmaster should have known from his good behavior with all his teachers.

"He came to my door sopping wet and nearly frozen to death." June intoned angrily. "Are you saying he did that to himself? He may be different, but I know he's as right in the head as any other student."

"No, but I find it odd this happened less than a week after my arrival."

"What are you implying?" June said frowning.

He steepled his fingers. "Prefects are responsible for a large portion of the well-being of the younger students; sometimes this even includes disciplining them. And because of this, they are often held in a place of loathing by those same students. Hyroc here has probably found himself on the receiving end of such discipline by Simon. And with my arrival — someone who is unfamiliar with any past disciplinary events taking place in the school – he thought this an opportune moment for retribution on his discipliner."

Hyroc shot the headmaster a look of shocked disbelief. Everything he had just said was wrong and half of it didn't make any sense. Was it even possible for anyone to have such complicated thoughts?

June flushed. "You *can't* be serious."

"I'm afraid I'm quite serious," the headmaster said calmly. "I had a look at the trees before I got Simon and I found no rope near any of them. So where is the proof of this deed taking place?" June affixed a withering gaze on the headmaster but remained quiet. "If you cannot offer me any tangible proof I'll have no choice but to dismiss this whole thing out of hand." June sighed and gave Hyroc a regretful look. The headmaster nodded. "Simon you may go."

"Thank you, headmaster," Simon said, turning to leave. As he walked passed Hyroc he smiled malevolently. Hyroc felt a sudden surge of anger at the knowing arrogance in Simon's expression. He wanted to wipe the look right off his face and for the Prefect to be punished for what he had done. It infuriated him that after his long night of misery the headmaster thought he was lying and his tormentor would escape justice and be allowed to do it again. There had to be something he could use against Simon, something the headmaster would believe. The memory of Simon holding up his necklace popped into Hyroc's mind. Through his mind's eye, he watched the Prefect stick the necklace in his pocket. Thievery was a serious offense, especially for the head prefect. Hyroc smirked darkly at Simon. If he couldn't get Simon for hanging him from a tree, maybe he could get him for stealing his necklace. It would be hard to say he was lying when the head prefect had his necklace.

"Check his pocket." Hyroc said.

"Hold up Simon," the headmaster said. Simon turned around, a flash of apprehension appearing in his eyes. "Think very carefully about what you are about to say, *boy*. I've been extremely forgiving thus far, but my patience is running thin. If this is another one of your lies, *there will be consequences.*"

The headmaster's words give Hyroc pause, but the look on Simon's face solidified his resolve. "When they hung me in the tree, my necklace fell off," Hyroc said. "And I saw Simon put it in his pocket."

"I did no such thing, Headmaster. Are we finished listening to this, I have duties to attend to."

"Just turn out your pockets so we can get this waste of time over with and I can teach him about his poor choices." Simon hesitated and the headmaster frowned at him. "Turn out *your* pockets," the headmaster said more forcibly. Reluctantly Simon turned out his pocket. Hyroc saw a glint of silver, and in a quick movement, the prefect tried to hide it in his sleeve. "What was *that*?" the headmaster said. Simon responded with a confused look. "I just saw something fall into your sleeve." The headmaster stood and made his way over to Simon. Reaching into the prefect's sleeve, he pulled out Hyroc's necklace. The headmaster studied it, examining both sides."

"That's a family heirloom," Simon said hastily.

"Is that so?" The headmaster held the necklace in front of Simon's face. "Is that why it has *his* name on it?" he growled. Simon opened his mouth to speak and the headmaster slapped him hard in the face. The strike turned Simon's head and a bead of blood trickled out of his nose. The headmaster's face turned crimson as he spoke. "I will not tolerate thieves in this school! You have shamed your position and you have broken *my trust*." The headmaster thrust a finger toward the door. "Get your things and get out of this school," the headmaster said, shuddering with anger.

"But –"

"GET OUT!"

Simon turned and hurried out of the room. Hyroc felt an upwelling of pride as he watched the disgraced prefect rushing out of the room. The headmaster stared at the door long after Simon had disappeared into the hall. Eventually he turned back toward Hyroc, his face a lighter shade of red, and handed him the necklace. He took a deep breath and said, "thank you for bringing this to my attention Miss Burk. Now if you please, I have work to get to. And if Simon causes any more problems please inform the groundskeeper, he'll take care of it." June and Hyroc stood, thanked the headmaster for his time and left.

Hyroc snuck out of the school as soon as June left his side and went to the tree where he had been hung. He studied it a moment, remembering the night's unpleasant events, before climbing over the wall. Walking along the mossy stonework, he scrutinized the ground for any signs of the creature he had seen. He found no footprints and not so much as a bent blade of grass or trampled leaf. *Did I imagine those eyes?* The nearby fluttering of wings drew his attention to one of the school's trees. Perched on a branch, he saw a large black raven with what looked to be three silvery teardrop shaped markings on its neck arranged in an interlocking swirl. The raven stared at him a moment before making a strange "poot" sound and flying off. Hyroc watched the bird until it disappeared from view over the treetops.

CHAPTER 11

Jousting Tournament

H yroc lay on the cool grass of the boarding school's lawn, watching the blue cloud dotted void above as he absentmindedly tossed around the green stone Thomas had given him. It had been six years since his escape from the tree Simon had hung him from, and he was now fifteen years old. The dismissal of the head prefect had freed him from the boy's torment but with Marcus' death and the loss of the protection he offered as headmaster, Hyroc's bully problem suddenly got considerably worse.

One day, shortly after Simon's dismissal, a group of older boys cornered Hyroc and beat him. After this, he tried staying within sight of a teacher. This too proved problematic. Whenever a bully attacked him, most of the teachers seemed to pay no attention to his situation and did little or nothing to break up the fight. At this point, Thomas started staying with him between classes. Thomas hoped his presence would deter the bullies because he noticed fights between any other students were quickly taken care of. The bullying stopped as soon as he started doing this, but the reprieve didn't last long. A few days later, the bullies waited until the two of them were out of sight of a teacher then they simply beat the two of them. This beating then put an unexpected strain on their friendship. Thomas suddenly stopped accompanying Hyroc between classes. When Hyroc asked his friend about this, he found that the fight was the first time Thomas had ever been purposely hurt by another boy and he was afraid of it happening again. Subduing a surge of anger at his friend for deciding to abandon him, Hyroc understood Thomas' fear and reluctantly resigned himself to taking care of the problem himself. After Thomas' attempt at a solution, Hyroc decided to try staying within sight of June. The bullies never heckled him while she was watching, but unfortunately, her duties as a teacher prevented her from keeping an eye on him all the time. Like what had happened with Thomas' plan, they ambushed him when she wasn't looking. The cause of the resulting bruises never escaped her notice when she talked with him; there just wasn't much she could do short of removing him from the school and locking him up in the house. That seemed crueler than anything his bullies had done to him, so, frustratingly, he had to endure the torment. Knowing this, she gave him the only help she could offer.

"What they're doing is wrong," she had said, not doing much to hide her anger toward the bullies and the teachers. "I can't protect you from them; I wish I could. I know this probably goes against everything Marcus or I ever taught you, but you need to fight. I don't want you to sit there and take it, you need to hurt them back, make them feel some of the pain they made you feel. Then they'll start to wonder if it's really a good idea to mess with you. Never start a fight but always finish one. It's up to you now."

Despite the resolve her words imparted upon him, he still received a bad beating during his next altercation, but he had managed to get one or two hits on his attackers. Those strikes had done something to him. Though he hurt and had received a black eye, he was strangely unaffected by the depression and hopelessness he usually experienced after a beating. He actually felt good about what he had done. He hadn't let them have their way with him, he had fought back. The beatings continued without him having much success fending off his bullies, but with each fight he figured more about the ways those boys attacked him. Bit by bit, the fights slowly began shifting in his favor. Then one day, something happened that seemed impossible to him, he won. He was bruised and hurting, but he had won!

His euphoria evaporated when a teacher dragged him to the headmaster's office. He tried to explain he was not the one who started the fight, but the headmaster refused to believe him. The ordeal ended with two strikes from the paddle and a stern warning about future fights. After this, Hyroc learned to take the beatings despite the fact he could win most of them whenever a teacher was watching, and only defend himself when they weren't. He then discovered if he only hit a bully in places covered with clothing, they would avoid showing the resulting bruises to a teacher. Once it became apparent to the other students he was not such an easy target, his bully problem dropped off sharply, with insults being the preferred way of striking out at him.

Everything seemed to be getting better for him, up until a few months after his thirteenth birthday. Then things changed – along with many things all boys inevitably experience. He began taking on a more beastly appearance and slowly lost the appearance of the cute creature some of the more tolerant people saw him as. Beyond June and Thomas, everyone seemed more cautious, avoided eye contact and gave him a much wider berth if they dared walking past him at all. They acted as if they now thought he was suddenly more dangerous and would lash out at anyone with the slightest provocation. Then no one even dared to lob an insult his direction. Though grateful for this particular change, the abruptness of it all was somewhat disconcerting. His whole life had revolved around tolerating this unavoidable fact, and now it was just gone. But like everything else in his strange life, he acclimated to it.

A person's shadow appeared over Hyroc. Catching the stone, he turned his head to see Thomas. They were the same age but Hyroc had grown the taller of the two.

Hyroc stuck the stone in his pocket and rose to his feet. "Did you get it?" he said eagerly.

Thomas gave their surroundings a quick glance. "Yep," Thomas said, reaching beneath his jacket. He withdrew a snouted dark blue mask crudely resembling a wolf's face.

Hyroc gave his friend a toothy grin. "So, people are really going to be wearing these there?"

HYROC

Thomas nodded happily. "No one's going to think anything when they see you. Well, at least as long as they don't look too close."

"I'll just make sure to keep my hood up."

"Good idea," Thomas agreed. "Are you ready to go?" Hyroc nodded. He had been ready for the last hour. "I think most of the teachers have already left, but the groundskeeper is seeing the other boys off at the gate, so you won't be able to go out that way."

"Didn't think I would be able to anyway, I was just going to go over the wall and into the trees."

Thomas gave him a mildly concerned look. "Just be careful of feral dogs."

Hyroc gave him a flat look. His friend didn't need to remind him about them. "I know; I'll be sticking to the edge of the woods and from what I've heard the dogs usually avoid going there." He paused, his expression turning concerned. "Are you sure this is such a good idea? I mean, won't somebody notice I'm not here? I really don't want to get into trouble over this. The headmaster already hates me."

"If they really didn't want you to leave, don't you think the headmaster would have sent somebody to make sure you didn't? Other than making sure you're not hurting people or breaking the rules, none of the teachers – except June of course – seem to care what you're doing. So as long as no one recognizes you at the tournament, they won't even know you left."

Hyroc studied Thomas' face thoughtfully considering the merits of his plan. Now that he thought about it, besides reprimanding him or offering him up for punishment, the teachers did seem to lack a sense of responsibility for him in any other regard. *Would any of them care enough to come looking for me if they couldn't find me at the school?*

"Alright," Hyroc said after a long moment of deliberation. It seemed a good plan. "So where should we meet?"

Thomas smiled broadly. "You know that old tree on the hill beside the road on your way to town?"

Hyroc thought a moment, then nodding said, "I think I know what you're talking about."

"Okay, I'll meet you there."

Hyroc collected his hooded jacket from the now empty dorm, and careful not to be seen by the few remaining teachers walking the halls, slipped back outside. Donning his jacket, he made his way around the wall at the back of the school and into the concealment of the thicket beyond. From there he headed in the direction of the meeting place.

"Did anyone see you leave?" Thomas said as Hyroc came up to him. Hyroc shook his head. "Good." Thomas donned his mask.

Hyroc pulled his hood as far up over his head as he could to give his snout some concealment and the two of them made their way toward the tournament grounds.

The tournament grounds were on the western shore of a river running near the town, in a flat field just beyond any farmland. A large orange banner stretched between two tall poles staked on either side of a grassy path, marking the entrance. Thick groupings of faded white tents filled the immediate area behind the poles on both sides of the path, but their numbers thinned as they drew closer to the tournament field. The clamor of eager voices filled the air as patrons streamed through the entrance. Hyroc rechecked his hood and making sure to keep his head as low as possible, Thomas and he entered the stream of bodies. Hyroc relaxed after a few tense moments when he spotted people wearing the wolf masks and nobody seemed to take notice of his unusual features. Through the wide entrance flaps of the surrounding tents he passed, he saw a variety of tournament paraphernalia. At the center of the tents, the path widened into a circular court where all around its edges food was being prepared and the air was stuffed with a myriad of delicious aromas. Hyroc stopped to take in the smells teasing his nose, before continuing through to the tournament grounds.

"I sure hope Deroth gets this?" Thomas said, as the two of them searched for a decently concealed spot to watch from.

"Yeah, I'd hate for pompous pretty boy Alrich to win," Hyroc said. He really did not like that man, he reminded him too much of Simon.

Thomas nodded in agreement. "Let's just hope that arm injury Deroth got from his horse throwing a shoe doesn't affect him too much."

"It would be very annoying if one little incident cost him the tournament."

"But I think he's still pretty solid in the saddle even with a hurt arm." Thomas pointed to an empty spot shaded by a tree. "That looks like a good spot over there." Hyroc nodded his acknowledgment and the two of them walked over to it. Thomas clapped Hyroc on the shoulder when they arrived. "I'm going to go get some of those roasted nuts I saw when we came in. Make sure no one steals my spot." Hyroc smiled half mockingly as he nodded. "Thanks."

"Did I miss anything?" Thomas asked upon his return, sticking a small caramel colored nut in his mouth.

"No but I think it's about to start," Hyroc replied. He reached into Thomas' bag of nuts and popped one into his mouth.

Four horns sounded from the other end of the tournament field and everyone quieted. A man garbed in rust red and yellow clothing, with a dark brown cap that sported a single eagle feather, stepped into the middle of the field. "Welcome!" the man shouted, throwing his arms out in a wide welcoming gesture. "I present to you the brave and honorable men who courageously sought entry into this great tournament. I present to you Earl Gale of the Green Hills." A bearded man clad in shining silver plate mail, road atop a sandy brown horse into the tournament field, holding a green and white lance. A chorus of cheering accompanied his arrival. With an enthusiastic yell, Gale thrust his lance into the air, then spurred his horse toward the middle of the field. "I now present to you Lord Alrich." A tall thin faced man with immaculate blond hair, clad in armor so perfectly polished Hyroc had to squint when he looked upon it. He held a white lance with a strip of light blue coiling around the shaft and he rode a pony of pure white. Cheers followed Alrich's arrival, but a chorus of booing – which included Thomas – quickly drowned them out. Alrich lifted his lance above his head, glowering at a nearby group of onlookers, then road over to Gale. "Baron Deroth, or as some have come to know him, The Lancer Wolf." the Herald continued. Baron Deroth was a muscular man, with brown hair, a scar running from the middle of his stubble-covered chin and under his jaw at an angle. His armor had a slightly imposing dark tint to it and raven feathers adorned the top of his helm. He rode a black stallion and his lance was of a dark blue, with two strips of red on either side of the shaft. The crowd broke out into cheering the moment he entered the field. With a mighty cry, Deroth thrust his lance into the air. Everyone wearing a wolf mask cheered energetically.

"You call *that* a welcome," Deroth shouted. "I know you can do better than that!" He thrust his lance skyward once again and a deafening roar erupted from the crowd. With a pleased nod, Deroth trotted his horse over to join the other two. Alrich scowled at the new arrival, but Deroth returned the glare with a smile.

The Herald continued naming names, until every contestant was on the field. "Good luck to you all," the Harold said pleasantly. "Now let this tournament, begin!" The contestants trotted their horses in a circuit around the field before exiting.

A few minutes later two contestants with closed face guards on their helmets reentered the field, taking up positions on opposite ends of the field, with a wooden pole running between them. A flag bearer strode out between the two men. "Ready?" the flag bearer shouted. The two competitors nodded. The flag bearer waved his flag in front of him and quickly moved from the center of the field as the two men's horses thundered toward each other. The clamorous smash of shattering wood sounded as a lance contacted the other rider, throwing him from the saddle. A round of cheers followed the announcement of the victor.

Hyroc spent the next two hours watching lances shatter, horses scream out in alarm and armored men noisily falling to the ground. Then Deroth emerged onto the field. When Deroth charged his opponent, he held the lace too low and at an angle where it would merely glance off his opponent's armor. Hyroc watched with dismay as the lance bounced harmlessly off the opposing rider's armor and Deroth took a hit to the chest. Deroth barely managed to remain in the saddle and once or twice, it seemed he would fall. After a short reprieve for the acquirement of a new lance, the two competitors charged once again. Deroth held his lance high enough for a proper strike, knocking his opponent to the ground while at the same time remaining in his own saddle.

Unfortunately, about an hour later, Deroth lost against none other than Alrich. As Hyroc turned toward Thomas to vent his irritation at the turn of events, he got a start when he saw the headmaster and three ministry officials standing off to Thomas' left.

"I can't believe he lost to –" Thomas exclaimed angrily.

"*The headmaster's right there*," Hyroc said, through clenched teeth as he stared at the headmaster.

The color drained from Thomas' face as he stole a glance in the direction Hyroc was looking. "Go, get out of here," Thomas said, frantically flinging his arms toward Hyroc. Hyroc darted behind the tree they had been sheltering under just as he heard the headmaster say Thomas' name. Hyroc crouched down peering around the tree's trunk, watching the headmaster walk over to Thomas. After a brief exchange of pleasantries, the headmaster politely guided Thomas over to meet the group of ministry officials. Thomas turned toward Hyroc and mouthed the words; "get out." Unwilling to risk another encounter with the boarding school's staff or someone worse, he carefully wound his way back out of the tournament grounds, heading directly back to the schools.

He got another start when a hand touched him on the shoulder as he hung his jacket back up in the still vacant boy's dorm. Spinning around, he found June standing behind him. He took a deep breath, relaxing a little.

"I need to talk to you about something," she said.

"I'm in trouble aren't I," Hyroc said dejectedly, knowing the headmaster or another teacher watching the tournament must have seen him.

She looked puzzled. "You're not in trouble. Why did you think that?"

"I always seem to get blamed for everything."

She sighed. "No, you're not in trouble. And I honestly don't care you snuck off to watch the tournament."

Hyroc stared at her startled, then silently chided himself for revealing so much with his initial reaction. If he had done that with anyone else he would be in a lot more trouble right now. "W – what makes you think that?" he said sheepishly, though he suspected it was pointless to even pretend otherwise.

June smirked, folding her arms. "Well, I've been looking for you for the last hour and it wasn't hard to figure out where you had gone when I couldn't find you or your jacket."

Hyroc smiled nervously. Her logic seemed sound. "So, what did you want to talk to me about?"

"Not here, the other boys will probably be heading back here soon and it's a conversation best held privately." Hyroc nodded, following June from the dorm into the vacant teacher's common room. The two of them seated themselves in front of the fireplace with their chairs facing each other. "I think I found you work."

"Work?" Hyroc said confused. That was something he hadn't given much thought. He wasn't really expecting anyone to have the slightest desire to give him a job.

"Well, it's an apprenticeship. I've been talking to a friend of mine and he's agreed to take you."

"What will I be doing with him?"

"Rune carving." Hyroc frowned. "Don't give me that look, would you rather I found you an apprenticeship with a records keeper instead?"

Hyroc shrugged. No, the latter sounded a lot worse. "How much does he pay?"

"Five Flecks every two weeks, including room and board." Hyroc's frown deepened. Five was hardly anything at all. "I know, I know, it's not much, but it's a start."

"When does he want me to begin?"

"Somewhere around midway through the summer."

"Well, at least I'll be able to annoy Thomas when I start making money before him."

June frowned. "Hyroc, you won't be coming back to the school when you take the job."

"What?"

"It's an apprenticeship; you'll have very little time for anything other than learning your skill for quite a while and there's not much more you can learn from being here. Besides, Thomas will be leaving soon anyway, so —"

"*What do you mean* Thomas is leaving soon?" Hyroc interrupted, looking surprised. He couldn't have heard her correctly. That didn't make any sense.

June looked at him perplexed. "Didn't he tell you, his father is coming to pick him up the day after tomorrow?"

"No, he didn't say anything about *that*." How could his friend have forgotten to tell him something so monumentally important?

"Well, as far as I know, he only found out about it a few days ago and maybe he just didn't get around to telling you yet."

News this big didn't exactly seem like something to procrastinate about telling. What was Thomas doing keeping it from him?

"Was he the one who encouraged you to sneak off to watch the tournament?"

Hyroc nodded. "And I nearly got caught," he said sharply. "The headmaster and some ministry officials almost saw me there."

"And is that when you decided to come back to the school?"

"Pretty much."

June nodded. "Well there you go; he was probably going to tell you after the tournament, but your encounter with the headmaster prevented him from doing so."

"I guess," Hyroc said with half agreement. Her explanation seemed a little too convenient. "But still, why didn't he just tell me this when he found out?"

"He might've been scared, I'm sure you understand what that's like." Hyroc shrugged. He wished he wasn't so familiar with it. "Saying goodbye to a friend isn't as easy as it might seem." Hyroc stared at the floor, suddenly unable to find any fault in his friend's behavior to speak about. June put her hand on his shoulder. "You shouldn't be mad at him for what he did. I know this is hard but this is just another part of growing up, unfortunately.

Hyroc sighed angrily, but deep down, even though he hated to admit it to himself, she was right. *I can't stay here forever* Hyroc thought grudgingly.

CHAPTER 12

Departure

Hyroc stepped through the front door of the boarding school, making his way toward the open gate. The sun was sinking low toward the horizon and the shadows were beginning to lengthen as dusk approached. At the gate, he found Thomas standing beside two small bags of belongings.

"I'm sorry I didn't tell you sooner," Thomas said, as Hyroc came up to him.

Hyroc waved dismissively. "Don't worry about it," he said. "I figured you meant to."

Thomas nodded thankfully. "I was going to tell you after the tournament, but that didn't quite work out."

"Yep," Hyroc agreed. "But it could have been a lot worse."

"That's for sure."

"Still, I wish I could've seen Gale best Alrich."

Thomas nodded. The outline of a horse-drawn carriage slid into view not far away. Thomas and Hyroc shrugged at the sight; the time for the dreaded goodbye had arrived.

"And there's my dad," Thomas said. "I guess this is it then."

"Yep."

Thomas smiled. "I think it's funny I thought you were an enchanted animal when we became friends."

Hyroc smirked back at him. "Yeah, you asked some pretty weird questions."

"Well, I was only nine." His eyes flicked toward the carriage as it came to a stop in front of the gate and the humor faded from his expression. "I guess this is where we have to say bye."

Hyroc sighed. "You've been a good friend."

"You've been a good friend too."

The carriage driver dismounted and a thin man with a black cap on his head stepped out of the carriage, speaking as he did so. "Thomas, get in its time to go."

"Yes father," Thomas said. "Bye Hyroc."

"Bye."

Thomas walked over to the carriage and his father helped him inside. When he was done, the man turned a piercing glare on Hyroc. "So you're the one who drug my son into all those fights," Thomas' father said acidly. Hyroc narrowed his eyes at the man, but said nothing. He had learned long ago arguing with such people, no matter how wrong they were, was pointless. "I don't know why anyone would ever allow something so violent to be around children. At least now, my son will be free of you." Still shaking his head, the man climbed inside the carriage, closing the door behind him. The carriage driver finished loading Thomas' luggage and climbed back into his seat. With a whip of the reins, the horse began trotting off. Thomas stuck his hand out the window and waved. Hyroc waved back, saying goodbye to the only friend he had ever known.

CHAPTER 13

Childhood's End

Hyroc sat at the table in the dining hall, absentmindedly picking at his lunch. It was some sort of stew, or at least, that's what he thought it was. The composition of the school meals was always hard to identify. He knew he would miss Thomas, but there were things he hadn't expected his friend's departure to reveal. Beyond June offering advice, he hadn't spoken to another person. He hadn't realized ever since Marcus' death; Thomas and his aunt were practically the only people he ever had a conversation with. This knowledge had existed in the back of his mind, but with Thomas around, it seemed far away and irrelevant. Now there wasn't anything to divert his attention from the harsh reality. The school had suddenly lost what little comfort it possessed. It didn't feel like his home anymore, it felt like some place he had just arrived at and he wasn't welcome there.

Glancing from side to side, he noticed his half of the table was unoccupied. For as long as he could remember, at the table a gap had always existed between him and the nearest student, but over the course of the last few days, it seemed to widen considerably. With a dejected sigh, he dropped his spoon back into the bowl, got up from the table and walked out the door.

From the dining hall, he made his way to the nearest door that led outside. A group of younger boys stopped talking abruptly and began staring distrustfully at him when he came through the door. Shrugging off their behavior, he headed for the apple tree. At the tree, he began taking off his shoes, preparing to climb the tree. He stopped himself.

Pushing his shoes back on, he walked over to the wall behind the tree. Leaning over its stony top, he gazed intently at the trees beyond. The subtle rustle of leaves from a breeze almost seemed to make the trees call to him. He wanted to climb over the wall, feel the cool mottled shade beneath those trees, and permanently leave the school behind. The only thing that stopped him was June. If he ran away he would leave all the misery of the school behind, but he would also be leaving her. He had grown quite attached to her in the time since Marcus' passing. She cared about him and always did whatever she could to protect him. Even though she had been able to do little toward her goal, it made him feel good she had tried. She had made his world seem not quite so bleak, like there was something for him to look forward to.

After everything she had done for him, abandoning her seemed a dishonorable reward for her efforts. He could endure this misery a little longer, for her. It was the least he could do. He would be leaving her soon for work, but it was what she wanted for him and he had no desire to disrupt what she had done. After that, then he would go. Where, he wasn't sure, but he would figure something out. Maybe then, he could find answers about his past.

Nodding to himself, he stood up and made his way back over to the school. He began walking along the walls of the structure with no clear purpose in mind, letting its exterior guide the course of his feet. Students lounging with their backs against the building quickly moved out of his path when they noticed him coming. Trying his best not to notice, Hyroc continued on his way. Passed the front door of the school, he stopped when he noticed two boys his age standing near one of the school's trees. He couldn't quite make out what one of the boys looked like, but he recognized the other as Henry. Henry had once asked Hyroc if he could borrow the salt from his table. It wasn't much of anything really, but the request was more interaction a student beyond Thomas had offered for some time. Maybe he could somehow make the boy his friend, or at the very least, someone to talk to.

As Hyroc approached, he noticed some books strewn across the root riddled ground. Henry bent down and picked up a book. The second boy did the same. Then with one of the books in hand, the boy threw it at Henry. The book slammed into the boy's chest, knocking him onto his back. Hyroc felt his hands clench into a fist. Though none of the students dared heckle him anymore, it still bothered him to see some of the other boys getting bullied.

"Hey," someone yelled. It took Hyroc a second to realize he was the one who had said it. The second boy looked toward Hyroc with a suddenly surprised expression on his face. Now Hyroc recognized the boy to be Eric. From the few times Hyroc had happened to run into Eric, the boy seemed extremely cocky, as he never refrained from letting Hyroc know how much he wasn't afraid of him, along with a complement of insults directed at his mother. None of the other students dared talk to Hyroc, let alone insult him directly to his face, but for some reason Eric didn't seem to take any notice of this. He was either the bravest boy in town or the dumbest.

"What do you want?" Eric said irritably. "Shouldn't you be out chewing on a rat or something?" Rolling his eyes, Hyroc continued over to Henry. The boy looked surprised at his approach and doubly so when Hyroc picked up one of the books and offered it to him. Tentatively, the boy accepted the book. "Hey," Eric said. Ignoring Eric, Hyroc offered another book to Henry. "HEY, I'm talking to you," Eric yelled.

Hyroc turned toward the boy. "You've had your fun, now back off."

Eric grinned ruefully. "I'm not going to listen to a monster like you. If you want me to back off, then make me, I'm not scared of you." Shaking his head, Hyroc returned to helping Henry, but still kept Eric in his peripheral vision, ready to react if the boy should take a swing at him. "Hey, don't you turn your back on me, coward." Hyroc stiffened a little at the challenge to his honor but repressing the urge to show the boy how much of a coward he wasn't, he continued helping Henry. "You had better turn around and face me, coward." Hyroc continued ignoring him. "Alright, you asked for this!"

Eric lurched forward as he swung his fist at Hyroc. Fully aware of the oncoming strike and expecting it, Hyroc easily sidestepped it. The bully stumbled to a stop. As the boy turned, using his fist, Hyroc nailed him hard in the face. The boy jerked backward from the strike, careening toward the ground. As he plummeted, one of his legs slid into a small space beneath a protruding tree root. The space held the leg straight, preventing it from bending with the rest of the boy's body as he fell and with a sickening snap, something broken when he hit the ground. The boy gasped, his face turning ghostly white. Hyroc felt a knot form in his stomach as what he had just done came crashing down on him.

Someone yelled from behind him and Miss Duncan rushed over to the boy on the ground. "H – He," Hyroc stuttered, as an incoherent frenzy of thoughts prevented him from forming an explanation of what had happened.

"I knew your savage nature would appear one day," Miss Duncan said with grim satisfaction. She turned a hateful glare on him. A cold sinking feeling crept over Hyroc as he looked at her. "None of them would believe me about you, but now they will see just how wrong they were. Nothing good can ever come from a creature of darkness."

"He threw the first punch, *he started it*," Hyroc said, when he was able to speak properly

"Your lies hold no sway with me!" she snapped back

Hyroc turned his eyes toward Henry. "You saw what happened," he said to the boy. "Tell her!" The boy answered his request with a dumbfounded stare. "Tell her, please!" Hyroc took a step toward the boy and the boy recoiled as if bracing for something painful. A crowd had begun to form in a loose semicircle behind Miss Duncan. Hyroc turned toward them and took a step in their direction. The nearest students pulled away from him.

Miss Duncan waved a prefect over to her. "Tell the headmaster," she said to the prefect. "That one of the students has been badly injured." She sharply indicated Hyroc with her chin "*And that Hyroc assaulted him –*"

"It was an accident," Hyroc pleaded. He hadn't meant for that to happen. It was truly an accident. Why would none of them believe him?

"– and The Ministry needs to be notified immediately," she said, continuing to pay no heed whatsoever to his words. "He'll understand. Now go." The prefect nodded, and with a quick glance in Hyroc's direction, hurried off toward the front door of the school. She turned a withering gaze on Hyroc. "Your time here has ended and your savagery will finally be extinguished."

Hyroc swept his eyes through the crowd of students. They were all staring at him. He could feel every one of their eyes boring into him. Being watched had always bothered him, but this felt different, this felt worse, like something dangerous, something he needed to escape from. A growing wave of panic began gnawing at him beneath their unwavering gazes. The only thing he could think about was running, getting out of sight, putting something, anything, between him and their eyes. Hyroc turned away from the crowd and bolted toward the wall. Heart hammering, he scrambled over the stonework, dashing into the cool shadows of the trees beyond. Leaf laden branches slapped against his face as he darted between the trunks. He ran until he was gasping, stopping to rest beside a rotting stump.

He sat with his back against the trunk and covered his face with his hands. He yelled out in a mixture of sorrow and anger as the full weight of his predicament pressed down on him. With one stupid mistake he had destroyed everything in his life. He knew better than to help another student when it came to bullying. Everything would still be fine if he had just stayed out of it. Eric would have only given Henry a few bruises, nothing to cause any lasting pain. Now because of his reckless behavior, not only had he seemed to prove Miss Duncan correct, but now The Ministry was after him. If they caught him, they would kill him. They couldn't come after him before, but that was because he had never given them a reason to, until he had broken the leg of another student. Accidental or not, a broken bone was a serious injury. If there was any doubt in people's minds about him being dangerous, he had just eliminated it with a single punch. He had lost everything, it was completely his fault and there was nothing he could do to fix it. Pain and a frigid feeling racked him and his eyes began to glisten with hot tears. His life was over!

A stream of determination shot through him. He shook his head, and wiped his eyes. *Now is not the time for this*, he thought. *What's done is done. I need to focus on what's happening right now. The Ministry is after me and I will not lay down and die. Those bullies couldn't break me and I'm not going to let The Ministry have their way either. I can never go back to the boarding school but I was looking forward to leaving it behind anyway. I need to figure out what I'm going to do fast because it won't be much longer before The Ministry is out looking for me. Running is my only option. To where I don't know; I can figure that out later, right now I need to focus on getting away.* The image of the Burk family house appeared in his mind. *I could probably find everything I need at the house.* He shook his head ruefully; the thought of stealing from one of the few people to ever care for him was abhorrent. But then he began to wonder if Marcus or June would risk his safety for some easily replaced items. Deciding they would not, Hyroc stood and began navigating toward the Burk homestead.

He studied the building from a stand of trees behind the garden for any signs of life. June boarded at the school during the school year, but during which time she left the house in the care of a housekeeper. There weren't any signs of activity in or around the house he could see. Either the housekeeper was away on errands or had yet to arrive for the day, he couldn't quite remember how the arrangement actually worked. Glancing over at a nearby tree, he saw a raven perched on a branch staring at him. He thought he saw silver markings on either side of the bird's neck. He shook his head, turning his attention back toward the house, he had more important things to think about, the light was only catching the bird's feathers just right. Cautiously he crept toward the back door and opened it. Silently stepping through the threshold, he saw faintly glowing embers in the hearth, some freshly dirtied dishes, and the fading odor of something cooked not long ago. He listened for a long moment for any sounds of movement, but hearing none, he headed upstairs in search of proper travel clothing.

He stopped in front of Marcus' room. The last time he had dared enter it was after the funeral. Taking a deep breath, he walked into the room. It was almost as he remembered leaving it. Pushing aside a flood of memories, he walked over to the room's closet in search of clothes. He found a belt, dark gray jerkin to go over a white tunic and black pants, along with a long light green hooded cloak and some dusty leather hunting boots. Dressing out of his school uniform, he donned the pilfered clothing. He retrieved an old hunting knife that had begun to rust at its base from the corner of the closet and secured it onto his belt. As he turned to leave, his foot bumped against something beneath the bed causing him to stumble. Looking toward the thing he had almost tripped over, he spotted a long wooden box. A stab of longing struck him; the box contained Marcus' bow. He slid the box out from under the bed then carefully opened it. Marcus' cherry wood hunting bow lay within, covered in a thin layer of dust. Hyroc reached for it but stayed his hand. It didn't seem right for him to take something so dear to the man that had raised him. He closed the box and put it back in its place. He walked across the hall and into his own room. He gazed fondly at the box containing the small bow he had called his own during happier times. Pushing down the upwelling of memories, he stuck the courage stone Thomas had given him into his pocket, along with the wooden bear. It seemed childish to take the figure, but for some reason he couldn't bring himself to leave it behind. He stopped at the door and looked back into the room a long moment, before heading down the stairs, never expecting to see it again.

Returning to the kitchen, he began shoving food into a knapsack he had taken from a hook near the front door. He got a start when a voice said his name. Heart racing, he wheeled around to see June standing in the doorway connecting the living room to the kitchen.

"What's going on?" June said calmly.

"I got into a fight," Hyroc said, a sudden spike of fear forcing the words out of him. "I don't even know how it happened. It didn't make any sense. All I did was – was hit him – and then he fell – and – and – and then his leg –" Hyroc squeezed his eyes shut. "It was an accident, I didn't mean for that to happen!"

"Hyroc," June interrupted, her eyes considerate and gentle. "I understand."

Hyroc opened his eyes and gave her a puzzled look. "You do?" That was not what he was expecting her to say.

"Yes, you hurt someone and you're running away because The Ministry is after you. I always knew a day like this would come."

Hyroc's puzzlement deepened. "You did?" He wished he would have known.

She nodded. "You worked hard at your studies, but I could tell your heart was never truly in it. I knew you would never have accepted the life of a scholar. It's simply not who you are. And deep down I think he knew this too." She paused, her expression thoughtful and sad. "You'll probably want something a little bigger than that worn-out knapsack." She stepped out of view toward the door beneath the stairs and when she returned, she tossed a pack to Hyroc. Hyroc caught it, shooting her a baffled look.

"You're not going to try to talk me out of it?" he said confused. This didn't exactly seem like something she would encourage him to do.

"No, I happen to think what you're doing is the only way for you to stay safe. This is probably the first place they'll come looking for you, so I suggest you focus on getting your provisions into that pack instead of wasting time talking with me." Hyroc nodded and did as instructed. Her logic seemed pretty sound. "I'll be right back." She returned with a water skin, pair of gloves, a coat, and a roll of heavy twine." Hyroc accepted the supplies, but stopped and stared at the heavy twine roll.

"What's this for?" he said, holding it up.

She gave him a half-humored smile. "Remember when you were younger and you got that insane idea you wanted to try trapping." Hyroc nodded, smiling fondly. "Well, I thought when you get settled into a safe place maybe you can start trapping and maybe you can make some money off it. But beyond that, it's not a bad idea to have some with you." Hyroc nodded thankfully. June pulled a coin pouch off her belt and handed it to him. "There's not much in there, but it should be enough to be of some use if –" she trailed off. Even without the rest of her statement, Hyroc understood she meant if anyone would even accept money from him. She pointed to a box beside the hearth. "Grab that tinderbox and little wood hatchet over there by the hearth then go ahead and get that water skin filled."

Hyroc grabbed both items and headed out to the well in the garden. When he reentered the kitchen, he began double-checking he had everything he might need.

"Oh, I almost forgot," June said. "There's something else." She left the room, returning with the buckskin tube Marcus had used to house his bow and a quiver full of arrows. Another stab of longing struck Hyroc. June set the quiver down beside her and ran her hand thoughtfully across the buckskin tube. She was quiet a moment before speaking. "I know he would have wanted you to have this," she said. She looked up at him with misting eyes and held the tube out to him with both hands. Reverently, he accepted it.

"If you're careful, you probably have enough food in your pack to last you for close to a week. But you can stretch it out longer if you supplement your provisions with anything you manage to hunt. I know you've only hunted fowl, but if you can down a duck on the wing I don't think a rabbit will give you much trouble. I think it's about the same." She pulled a bowl and a small bag from the table, holding them out to him. "What's in that bag is for emergencies," she said, as Hyroc stuck them in his pack. "It's filled with cold-flour; all you have to do is add water to it. I know it won't be the most enticing meal you've ever had, but it'll get you by in a pinch. Be careful about using the roads, that's where they'll probably be looking for you, and avoid making a fire until you're at least a few days out. By that time, The Ministry should lose interest in you. Do you know where you'll be going?" Hyroc shook his head. "Okay that's probably good, it'll save me from having to lie when they come here looking for you. I put a map in one of the pockets of that pack, so you can figure out where to go later." She paused a moment staring at Hyroc thoughtfully.

Her expression saddened. "I wish there was another way, you've done nothing to deserve any of this. You shouldn't have to run, you've done nothing but try to be a good boy. Maybe if I had paid more attention, if I had – if I had been more like *him*, then maybe you wouldn't be in this situation."

"I don't blame you for this," Hyroc said, his words sincere. "This wasn't your fault; none of it was. I know you did your best to help me." Hyroc took a breath to help subdue his emotions. "It was more than anyone else had ever done. You and Marcus were the only kind of family I ever knew and you were the closest thing to a –"

June embraced him, stifling his words. "And you were the closest thing to a son, I ever had." Hyroc felt tears welling up in his eyes. June released her grip and sniffling, she took a step back. "It doesn't seem right for you to do this alone. But the road is no place for a foolish schoolteacher such as myself and I fear I would only slow you down. Marcus wouldn't have hesitated, but unfortunately, though I would like to think so, I'm not nearly as adventurous as he was. I would try hiding you, but if The Ministry found out about that, my life would be forfeit. You must understand, I do not care about my own safety, but anyone associated with me, including my students, would be in danger."

Nodding, Hyroc said. "I understand." He hated it, but he understood. More lives than just his own were at risk. He had learned about enough witch hunts that had started out that way to understand her reasoning.

June made a coughing noise at his words. "Of course you do. Anyone who thinks you're a monster is a damned fool. You've got a good heart. Maybe if I can teach my students properly, make them understand, I'll be able to prevent this from happening to anyone else. And I will have words with Miss Duncan about this, many, many words." Hyroc smiled a little at the thought of the woman finally being put in her place after all the years of torment he had endured from her.

June wiped away her tears and her face suddenly became serious, more serious than he had ever seen. "Don't you ever come back here," she said in a voice so stern that it startled Hyroc. "There's nothing left for you here. This place stopped being your home a long time ago. I don't want you to come back for Marcus, Thomas, and definitely not for me, *you got that*. Forget you ever knew us or that we ever existed. Get as far away from this place as you can. Once you step foot out that door, I want you to keep walking and I don't want you to turn back."

Tears were reappearing in her eyes and her whole body trembled as she spoke. "I need you to promise you will do this."

"I promise," Hyroc said, though a part of him screamed for him not to. It was what she wanted. She nodded, struggling to maintain her composure. "Thank you for everything June." In a reluctant movement, he turned away and walked through the door out into the garden. He stopped at the gate as he heard June weeping. He was just about to turn back toward the house when he heard June yell out, "NEVER TURN BACK." He wanted to turn around and defy her words but he forced himself to take a step through the gate, followed by another and another. The road was his home now.

CHAPTER 14

Keller and the two men under his command rode there horses hard down the dirt path in front of them. The day he had been expecting had arrived. The Hyroc creature had injured one of the students at the school. No amount of past value from the association with a dead man or bias could keep him from his goal. He was going to kill that creature and it would never again pose a danger to another person.

The men slowed their horses as they came up to a house. Quickly dismounting, all three drew swords. Spreading out, they darted around the house in search of their target. The creature knew this house and this was the likeliest place it would take refuge. Keller moved around the back of the house toward what looked to be a garden. He felt a surge of excitement when he saw the shape of a person within. Disappointment immediately followed when he realized it wasn't the creature, it was a normal person and a woman. The woman rose to her feet in a startled fashion dropping a hand spade as she took notice of him.

"Who are you, what are you doing here?" she demanded.

Keller raised his hand in a placating fashion and lowered his blade. Just then the other men came around the building. In the same fashion, he indicated that the woman was not their target.

"The creature's not around the house," one man said.

Keller suddenly recognized the woman. Her name was June, Marcus' sister and she worked at the school. But she also was the last remaining person caring for the Hyroc creature. As disturbing as that thought was.

"Your name is June if I'm not mistaken," Keller said calmly.

"Yes, but who –" she trailed off as recognition entered her expression. "Keller. You are not welcome here. Get out! All of you!"

"I'm sorry Miss Burk we can't do that. We have orders to find it." He turned his attention to the two men. "Search the house." The two men nodded and moved inside the house. He returned his attention to June. "And this is the likeliest place it would've gone."

June folded her arms. "If you're looking for Hyroc I haven't seen him and I suggest you look at the school. He's probably heading for his class right now."

Keller shook his head dismissively. He could tell she wasn't being entirely truthful. She knew something about where it had gone. "I have witnesses that suggest otherwise. And they say he broke a boy's leg and then fled." Even under the best of circumstances a broken leg was a seriously debilitating injury. Even she would have a hard time rationalizing such an occurrence.

She sighed, her façade melting away. "I'm sure it was an accident; he would never do something like that intentionally."

"He broke a student's leg! The boy he harmed will be in a lot of pain until it heals and he won't be able to walk for some time. That's hardly something that could be chalked up as an accident. And if he's capable of doing that who knows what else he could do?"

"You have not changed one bit Keller. You are still as blind as you were when we first found him. Even after all of those tests, you refused to believe you had made a mistake. Why can you not understand he is not so different from the rest of us. All he has ever wanted was to do good."

"Because he should not have even been allowed to exist!" Keller retorted. "You think that by giving it books to read and teaching it how to put on a polite face you have mastered its evil tendencies. When all you have done is trick yourself into thinking you are safe around it. And then when the blackness of its heart manifests you are unable to accept the truth about what you have done."

June laughed humorlessly. "If you were interested in *truth* you would not have been haunting his steps all these years; you would have understood by now what existed in his heart was nothing to be feared."

"And what of the reports of him fighting with the other students at the school. None have been definitively confirmed, but we both know they occurred. That should be proof enough that it is in his nature to do harm to others."

"It was not his choices that led to those fights. Those boys chose to go after him and to harm him. You didn't see the pain in his eyes and the confusion as he tried to understand why. And I did the only thing I knew would help him. I told him to fight, to cause them pain, to make them never want to do anything to him ever again."

"You did what!" Keller said, his voice laced with disbelief. It seemed absurd someone in charge of the safety of children could rationalize such actions. Was she truly so naïve to think she had made the correct decision? She was far more dangerous than he had ever suspected. "You mean to tell me you wanted it to do those things?"

"I never wanted him to do that, no, but the only other option I had was to sit there and let him suffer. And I know of no parent that – "

Just then the two men exited the house.

"It's not here," one man said.

"This debate can serve no purpose any longer," Keller said in an icy tone. He had heard enough of her madness, "*Where is it?*"

"I don't know."

"I know your lying to me; I can have you arrested for that."

"Then go right ahead, but I wonder how your superiors would look upon such an action. Not too kindly I would suspect."

Keller glowered at her. She was right, beyond empty threats, there wasn't much he could do to her without damaging his position in The Ministry. Even if she was completely without reason.

"I'll ask you once more, where is it?"

"I told you I don't know, and even if I did, I wouldn't tell you."

Keller shook his head in disbelief. This had been a complete waste of time. He wasn't going to get anything useful out of her.

"Let's go," Keller snapped.

When the three men reached the main road, they stopped. Keller reached into his saddlebag and retrieved a map. He began a thorough examination of the area around the school and the house. The main road ran between both structures. The surrounding area was rough enough to slow the creature's progress, so it would have stuck to the road wherever possible. Since it wouldn't have gone toward town, it's course seemed pretty obvious. It was on foot so it couldn't have gotten far even with a head start.

"Okay, I want you two to follow the main road west all the way to Rivermark," Keller said. "Kill the thing on sight if you see it, and be careful, we don't know how dangerous it is. I'll head back into town to assemble a search party."

"Yes sir," the two men said in unison. They snapped the reins of their horses and charged off down the road.

Keller turned his horse in the opposite direction. That creature's days were now numbered. It was only a matter of time before he found it and it breathed its last breath.

• • •

CHAPTER 15

The Lonely Road

Hyroc pushed aside the spindly branches of a bush in front of him to peer at the trail beyond. He swept his eyes up and down the path to see if there was anyone within sight. Finding nobody, he walked through the underbrush. Farther to his right up the trail, he saw the distant roofs of the boarding school. He knew venturing so close to it wasn't the smartest thing for him to do, but he had to do it regardless. There was one last thing he needed to do. Pulling his eyes from the structure that had been his home mere hours ago, he headed in the opposite direction down the trail. The murmur of a stream whispered through the air as he approached a pile of rocks marking his mother's grave. Crouching down, he brushed away an accumulation of dead leaves from the stones. He felt a pang of sadness as he looked upon them. She was his mother and he didn't even know the sound of her voice or her name. All he knew was she loved him and had died to protect him.

And even with her sacrifice his story had nearly ended along with hers. He was very fortunate a man such as Marcus had stumbled upon him. If it had been anyone else, he would have been killed immediately and that would've been it. And even with Marcus possessing such a demeanor, his life would have been snuffed out by The Ministry once they found out about his existence. Luckily Marcus was favored by The Ministry through long years of service with them and his reputation offered him protection. Because of this, The Ministry was reluctant to take any actions against him. So long as no one got hurt. But one punch had nullified the stipulation. Now, none of that mattered.

Wiping away a tear, he rose to his feet. He walked over to a rose bush and used his knife to cut off a flower. Reverently, he deposited the red flower upon his mother's grave.

"I have to go now," Hyroc whispered to the stones. "And I won't be coming back." He paused a long moment. "I just wanted to say thank you, for everything you did for me. I know you loved me. I just – I just wish I knew what you were running from." He took a breath to subdue an upwelling of emotions. "But I know one day, I'll find out." He took a deep breath. "Goodbye and I love you, mother." He stood and walked across the stone bridge spanning the stream, heading into the trees beyond.

Staying far enough within the thicket to remain out of sight but still close enough for him to see the trail in front of him, he followed it. The path gently curved through the trees before running onto a wide area of open ground. Toward the middle of this, the trail connected to the road leading to and from Forna. As the road led west away from town, it arced off toward the thicket Hyroc stood in and disappeared from view behind it. Past the road intersection, at the end of the open area, grew another thicket. Hyroc couldn't see its end, but it led east away from Forna and it seemed he could follow it for the rest of the day without encountering another opening. There was just the problem of getting to it. There was a lot of open ground for him to cover. Other than grass and some knee-high shrubs, he would be exposed if he tried to cross over to it. He could continue following the thicket he stood in, though he would be following the road if he did so and that was exactly what June had warned him against. Then if he happened to run into an even worse spot, he would have to turn back. By now, The Ministry was aware of what he had done and was organizing to find him. Coming back would be more dangerous and by then it might be impossible for him to cross through this opening unnoticed. The safest option was to do it now.

Taking a step out of the thicket, he glanced around. Nobody was in sight. He took a breath and started across. He froze three steps later when he thought he heard the sound of a horse snorting. Listening closely, he could hear the sound of hooves and it was getting louder. Someone was coming! He bolted back into the thicket. He ran as far as he dared before getting behind a tree. Slowly, he looked around it. The shapes of two men on horses came into view at the tree line. Hyroc yanked his head back behind the trunk.

"I thought I saw something," one of the men said.

There was a long pause before the second man spoke. "You sure, I'm not seeing anything," he said skeptically.

There was another pause. "I don't know, maybe I just saw what I wanted to see," the first man said.

"I would assume that thing isn't stupid enough to stick this close to town. It would've ran straight for the wilderness and it's got a few hours start on us." The man paused. "The road would be quicker, just like what Keller said, so I say if we ride hard along it, we'll catch him before sundown."

"Alright."

With a snap of the reins, the men rode off. Hyroc breathed a sigh of relief. He waited until the sound of the horses had died away before venturing out to the tree line. Tentatively, he stepped into the opening to have a look. The area was clear. Working up his courage, he started running toward the thicket as fast as he could. Every second spent out in the open felt like he was one second closer to being discovered. His legs seemed to move agonizingly slow as if he were running through mud. Hours seemed to pass before he reached his destination. He stopped just beyond the trees concealment to catch his breath. Stealing a glance across the opening, he was relieved to see there still wasn't anybody there. He had done it. When his breathing returned to normal, he took one final farewell glance at the school and toward his home before continuing on his way.

As the fading orange light of dusk shone through the trees, he had yet to spot the end of the thicket. It was what he had hoped for. He didn't stop walking until he was fully enveloped by the night. He slipped off his pack and settled down into the crook of a tree with his back against its trunk. Reaching into his pack, he felt around inside until he found what felt like a loaf of bread. After having his fill, he put the loaf back. He covered himself with his cloak and closed his eyes to sleep.

Everything seemed fine at first, but he quickly became aware of how uncomfortable the tree and ground beneath him felt. Keeping his eyes closed, he repositioned. No matter what position he tried to sleep in, there always seemed to be a rock or something hard in one inconvenient place or another. It didn't take long before he yearned for the plush comfort of his bunk. An aggravating length of time passed, before he found a position comfortable enough for him to ignore it. Then the night seemed to close in around him when he closed his eyes. He felt a tremendous sense of vulnerability as if there was something unseen in the darkness creeping up on him. Listening closely to his surroundings for a few long minutes, all he heard was the distant hoot of an owl.

He sighed irritably. He needed to get some sleep and he was too busy being scared of the dark. Only children were scared of the dark. In all of the stories he had read, none of those characters were ever scared of the dark. It seemed ridiculous he should either, he could see better at night than anybody else. If anything, that should make it bother him less not more! How was he going to get anywhere if he couldn't sleep at night? He might be able to make it through the next day without being too fatigued, but not much longer. He needed to find a way through this!

He reached into his pocket, withdrawing the green courage stone. He ran his thumb over its cool smooth surface and onto the etching at its center. The memory of his escape from the tree he had been hung from flowed through his mind. He had been scared then; more scared than he ever remembered being and he had gotten through it. In comparison, this was nothing; all he had to do was fall asleep.

He smiled, nodding determinedly down at the stone. There wasn't anything out there for him to be afraid of. It was just him, the trees, an owl, and probably some squirrels. He closed his eyes and eventually floated off to sleep.

As he ate his breakfast, he removed the map from one of his pack's side pockets. He frowned when he rolled it open; discovering the thicket he had entered wasn't even shown nor were any of the familiar landmarks around the town. Thankfully, the road leading into Forna was. All he had to do was figure out where he had crossed it and then he would know about where he was in relation to it. He put his finger on Forna and ran it north how far he guessed the boarding school was from town. From the boarding school he continued north where his mother grave should be, out to the road. When his finger found the road, he moved it east to where he should be within the thicket. Looking to the southeast of his presumed location, he spotted a river. And if he remembered correctly, to his north lay plains. On the plains, he would be as exposed as he was on the road crossing. Barely a day away from Forna, he was still uncomfortable with the idea of going where there wasn't anything to hide behind. If he followed the river, there seemed a higher chance of things to conceal him. It wasn't ideal, but he knew he really didn't have a choice in the matter. He had to get away from the town as fast as he could no matter what he encountered. Once he was a day or two out, just as June had said, he should be safe. Maybe then, he would have time to figure out an actual destination.

Nodding to himself, he rolled up the map and packed everything up. He resumed his easterly march through the trees. The trees began to thin as the coolness of morning burned away into the warmth of noon. Then he arrived at the edge of the thicket. Beyond, to the north and east, was the expected plain and it stretched all the way to the horizon. Following the edge of the thicket, he turned south. The thicket terminated not long afterward and the river came into view. At the tree line, Hyroc swept his eyes through his surroundings before making for the river. The ground dropped a little near the shore and as he had hoped, the plants here were high enough for him to crouch down into and have a decent chance of being hidden from any onlookers.

For the rest of the day: the river maintained a relatively straight easterly course as it meandered across the flat plain. When night arrived, Hyroc settled down to sleep away from the river at a small angular bolder. The darkness would keep him hidden until morning. He put his back against the flattest part of the bolder and attempted to sleep. In place of the disconcerting sensation of vulnerability, appeared an empty lonely feeling. This was the farthest he had ever been from home. He suddenly missed everything about it. He missed the woody scent of his room, sleeping beneath warm wool covers, crackling of fresh wood in the fireplace, the relaxing murmur of the stream where he caught fish, but most of all, he missed June. She was someone he could go to with his problems. Her words were often the only source of comfort he could find. She always seemed to have a solution. Then whenever a situation arose she couldn't help with, she got frustrated. For some reason, seeing her being frustrated always made him feel a little better. It reminded him someone wasn't happy with how he was being treated; that someone cared about him. Now, he had left it all behind.

He suddenly wanted all of it back. He didn't care what the consequences would be, he wanted to jump up and take off running back toward his home. Then the words "forget we ever existed," chimed in his mind. "I need you to promise you will do this." Hyroc felt a stab of cold shoot through him. There was no going back. All that mattered now was getting away.

Hyroc leaned back against the bolder. Above, stars shone brightly through the indifferent black void of the sky. For a moment, he was seven years old again, sitting outside of the garden, staring up at the twinkling pinpricks of light as Marcus pointed out the constellations. Hyroc found himself using his eyes to trace the familiar lines between stars. Marcus had once explained when someone died their spirit went into the sky, becoming stars, and from there they watched over their loved ones, alongside the Hallowed Knights. His relationship with the deified knights was a strange and confusing one. They were said to proclaim things such as stealing, murder and other such harmful behaviors were intolerable acts and punishment would follow the perpetrator. And they were also said to protect the virtuous, along with helping them in their times of need. But at the same time, they were also said to smite evil hearted people and things of darkness. Often, he wondered if the latter applied to him. Pretty much everybody thought he was evil and it did seem like sadness and misfortune followed him. Though Marcus nor June seemed to think so. "They judge you by what's in your heart," Marcus had said. "Not by what's on the outside. There's nothing you have to fear from them." And assuming that smiting meant something a lot worse than what he had gone through, Marcus' words seemed more than a simple attempt to make him feel better. He stared up at the glittering spots wondering if Marcus and his mother were watching him at this very moment. The thought was comforting and seemed to lessen the lonely sensation. He yawned and a sudden wave of weariness struck him. Offering the urge to sleep little resistance, his eyes grew heavy and he slowly went to sleep.

The following day, Hyroc continued along the river. Afternoon came and went with barely a change in its course. As the day began to wax toward dusk, the air took on an unpleasant smell like rotting autumn leaves. Then the river bent off toward the south. Moving along the shore, the smell steadily grew in strength. The ground began to soften and stagnant patches of water began appearing in his path. Soon, the isolated patches merged into a web work of thin waterways. When he stepped into one, his foot sank deep enough for the dirty water to flow over the tops of his boots. He stepped back onto dry ground and dumped out his boots. Looking further ahead, the waterways seemed to widen as they headed off toward a swath of swampy land. The swampy area ran beside the river for as far as he could see. If he continued forward, he would likely be walking through waist high water and his food would get soaked. From the unpleasant smell permeating the air, he could only assume all his provisions would get ruined. This wasn't a good place to pass through. He slipped his boots back on and began retracing his steps. When he reached the swamp's edge, he headed north, moving away from the river. He hoped he was now far enough from Forna to safely do so.

When he stopped at dusk, the only thing of interest he found was a lonely clump of thistle growing out of the side of an indent in the ground. He laid down where he seemed most shielded from the wind.

The next morning, a gray sky greeted him. Shortly after eating his breakfast, it began to rain. Hyroc sighed angrily when he saw nothing to shelter beneath. Aggravated, he pulled his hood up and continued onward. As the day went on the rain only got worse. It was still raining hard when dusk arrived. He bowed his head and groaned. He would be sleeping in the rain, if it were even possible for him to sleep at all. The deluge continued well into the night. The rains had slowed when he awoke in the morning. It surprised him he had even managed to fall asleep. Then almost in what seemed mockery, the storm returned to its previous intensity. Then the wind started blowing, driving the cold rain sideways into his face. Just as he began to dread spending another cold miserable night in the rain, the downpour ceased and he saw spots of empty sky above.

When he eventually settled down for the night, he was glad to find a concentration of bushes with woody branches. Four days out from Forna, he expected he was far enough away to safely make a fire. The branches of the bushes wouldn't make a very good fire, but he really didn't care. It would give him warmth. Using his wood hatchet, he chopped off the thickest branches he could find and made a pile. Kneeling down beside it, he used his tinderbox to get a fire going. The sparks fell on the wood, but nothing happened. Perplexed, he scratched the back of his head and tried again. The wood still didn't take a flame when the sparks fell. After several more attempts, he realized the wood was too wet to light. Groaning out in frustration, he smacked the ground with his hand. A sudden bolt of heat shot through his hand. The pile of wood burst into a blue flame. Staring baffled, he watched the flame turn from blue, to green, to orange. With a disturbed look scrawled across his face, he held his hand out in front of him and turned it over, searching for anything that might explain what had just happened. His hand looked and felt exactly as it always had. He shook his head. *I must be more tired than I thought. I need to get some sleep before I imagine something really strange.* Forcing the memory of what he thought he saw out of his mind, Hyroc went to sleep.

In the morning he saw strips of grey clouds stretched across the sky, but they were far enough apart rain seemed unlikely. The day passed with barely any noticeable change in the surrounding terrain. Hyroc's ceaseless footsteps were the only thing that told him he was even moving. Then as the sunlight began its shift toward dusk, two structures came into view. Placing one hand over his eyes to shield out the sun, he saw what appeared to be a farmstead with a house and barn. He breathed a small sigh of relief at the sight of the barn. Maybe tonight he wouldn't be sleeping outside. He would be sleeping in a barn and it would smell like a barn, but at least he would have walls to keep out the wind and a roof over his head. He just needed to make sure he left before anyone saw him. The only thing that might prevent him from going there was if there was a dog. A dog would start its irritating barking the moment he got near and everyone within earshot would know he was there. From the way everyone treated him in Forna he didn't expect any better of a reception from anyone out here. They would still think he was some monster. And it wasn't difficult to imagine what they would do to a monster. The safest option would be to wait until dark before attempting to enter the barn. Even if the farm had a dog, when it started barking the people that lived there wouldn't be able to see him. And when he moved off no one would be the wiser.

Hyroc moved a little closer to the farm before settling down behind a patch of bushes to wait until dark. When night arrived, he warily made his way toward the barn. As he drew near to the structure, after every step he listened carefully for any sounds of barking. He reached the barn without any sounds of alarm breaking the silence. Breathing a sigh of relief, he crept around the back of the barn until he came across a back door.

A single cow startled him when it lowed at him as he stepped through the threshold. The beast studied him with large lazy eyes, then deciding it was in no danger from him, turned back to staring at the boards of its stall gate. Letting out a breath, he began gathering some of the barn's unfettered hay into a bed. He sighed happily when he dropped onto it. It seemed impossible bare hay could ever be so comfortable.

When he sat up to eat his dinner, he heard a small meow. Turning his head, he saw a group of kittens wandering toward him. He held his hand out and the group cautiously sniffed the ends of his fingers. After a long moment of sniffing, the kittens moved on to investigating the rest of him. Hyroc petted the only two kittens interested in his attention, before picking up a long piece of straw and playfully poking at them. The two kittens swatted fiercely at the hay. Hyroc played with them until one yanked the piece from his hand. He pulled his pack closer to find something for dinner. When he opened it, he was dismayed to see how little food he had remaining. The last two nights had been so miserable he had forgotten to check on the amount of food he had. Beyond the bag of cold-flour, he only had two more days left with his provisions. He shrugged unhappily. He had enough money to buy more, but only if anyone he bought from would actually tolerate his presence without trying to kill him, and that seemed extremely improbable. He wondered if he was ever going to be able to use his money. Hunting or stealing food seemed about his only two options. Stealing was of course wrong and he would only ever consider it in a dire emergency so he had only one choice.

He ate his dinner and making sure his pack was closed tightly to avoid the kittens getting into it, he laid down to sleep. As he stared at the ceiling, trying to slow his thoughts, eerie shafts of moonlight appeared through a hole near the barn's rafters. He studied the silver light then reached into his pack and removed the map. This seemed as good of a time as any to figure out where he was going. Similarly to what he had done in the thicket outside of Forna, he guessed his position. If he was correct, there was a town nearby named Flatwood. The town didn't mean anything to him it was just another thing he needed to avoid. Moving his eyes past Flatwood to the north, the plains turned to forest. He glanced toward his pack, thinking of the heavy twine within. June had suggested he use it for trapping and a forested area would be best. Continuing north through the forest, he spotted what looked to be a small village named Elswood at the foot of a loan mountain. The village sat on the outskirts of the kingdom at the edge of the wilderness. The remoteness of the town would likely prevent The Ministry from having a hold there – if the things he had been able to gather from some of the school's library books he had read regarding outskirt- settlements held true – and it was far enough away they probably wouldn't come looking for him there.

He marked the town with a piece of straw then moved his gaze back to his current location. To the east, lay more plains and it ran for a considerable distance before encountering forest. The forest stretched all the way to the coast near the edge of the map and the only place he saw was a dot labeled Garathol. Whatever that place was, he didn't have the supplies to reach it, so he moved his eyes back. A large swath of plain also lay to the west, but no towns or villages were nearby, just a hilly spot. North seemed the best option, he just needed to get past the town. He brushed the hay from the map, rolled it back up and placed it in his pack.

When he got into a more comfortable position to sleep in, the kittens clambered on top of him. He scratched the closest kitten under its chin and it began rumbling happily.

"Do you think I'm a monster?" Hyroc said to the kitten. It stared at him with sleepy eyes then lowered its head onto its paws and went to sleep. Hyroc smiled as he shook his head. "Well at least you don't bark." After giving each member of the group some attention, the kittens laid down on or beside him. Blanketed by their warmth, he quickly drifted off to sleep.

The shrieking morning call of a rooster woke Hyroc. Knowing the arrival of the barn's owner was not far behind, he pushed a sleeping kitten off his chest. The kitten yowled in protest, digging its claws into his cloak. After dislodging the snagged feline, he collected his things and left the barn, quietly closing the backdoor behind him. Using a stand of scrubby brushes behind the barn as cover, he made his way behind an incline. He stopped to eat his breakfast while taking another look at his map. Farther to the east lay a river. Following it north with his finger it eventually flowed around the eastern side of the town like Forna's river. Farms would undoubtedly line the sides of the river close to the town, so unless he wanted to get soaked swimming across the river, east was out of the question. Looking to the west, he found a road running toward the town. He would need to cross it to get around the town. He felt some apprehension at the thought, but he knew at this point, there was little chance of running into anyone from The Ministry. Or at least he hoped not.

Re-placing the map, he made his way around the farm until he found a path that should lead to the road. Keeping an eye out for people, he made his way down it. When he arrived at the road, he followed it until the angular structures of the town came into view. Just as he had expected, numerous buildings lay near the river. He sighed. It would be so much easier if he could go there to buy some food. He wondered if he was ever going to taste anything baked once his provisions ran out. Shaking his head gloomily, he left the road and started navigating around the town.

Short lumpy grass covered hills came up in front of him, along with sporadic groupings of trees and bushes. By the time dusk arrived, he had about made it past the town. Close to when he was about to stop, he spotted a rabbit foraging at a grassy knoll. In the fading light, he silently slipped off his pack, strung his bow, and crept into position for a shot. He nocked his arrow and let it fly. It whistled through the air, catching the unsuspecting hare between the shoulders. The hare collapsed without a sound. Hyroc breathed a sigh of relief. Hitting things on the ground apparently was about the same as shooting ducks. At the carcass, he bled and gutted the hare the way he remembered seeing Marcus do it to the garden thief years ago. After collecting his pack, he stuck his kill on a spit made from alder branches and got a fire going on the side of the hill facing away from town. When it was done cooking, he eagerly bit into the meat. He ate as much as he could nibble off the rabbit, then a piece of bread before settling down for the night.

The morning sky arrived with a wavy film of white clouds and a front of thicker ones coming in from the west. A breeze carried a hint of the familiar scents of a town. Hyroc felt a pang of loneliness as the memories of his home in Forna washed over him. He quickly pushed them aside. That wasn't his home anymore. He stamped out his fire and resumed his journey north. Coming over the rise of one hill, in the distance he saw the edge of a vast forest. He smiled at the sight. Once he reach those trees, he would be safe from The Ministry. Then somewhere within, he would make a new home.

As he stood there, he became aware of movement off toward the northern edge of the town. Looking toward it, he got a start when he saw a crowd gathered around a large tree. He quickly backpedaled behind the top of the hill. Glancing ahead, he was dismayed to see a gap in the hills directly in front of the crowd. If he tried moving through it he would be seen. He would have to wait for them to leave. With nothing else to do, he settled into a more comfortable position to see what the crowd was doing. Beneath the tree, he saw a woman sitting atop a horse with a rope around her neck. Several members of the crowd were waving their arms angrily through the air. They were clearly unhappy with the woman. Hyroc suddenly realized they were going to hang her; she was a witch.

A man standing beside the woman at the tree slapped the horse on its rear. The horse jerked in alarm and took off running. The noose went taught and the woman was pulled off the horse's back by her neck. Hyroc felt sick as he watched. For an instant he saw Marcus' lifeless body lying in the bed at the boarding school. Hyroc knew, this was probably what would have happened to him if The Ministry had found him. That was what June was protecting him from. She knew it would be hard on him, but making him leave was the only choice she had if he was to have any chance of staying safe. And his safety was the most important thing to her. That was the only reason she could make such a choice.

The crowd began to disperse back toward town, leaving the woman's body behind. Hyroc waited until they were gone, before running through the gap in the hills. The woman getting yanked off the horse appeared repeatedly in his mind's eye. Eventually the images faded enough for him to concentrate on his surroundings. In front of him lay a small clear stream. He took a deep breath. Checking his water skin, it felt about half empty. Crouching down at the water's edge, he began filling the skin. A sloshing noise caught his attention. Looking in the direction of the sound, he froze when he saw a young girl on the opposite shore, filling a container with water. Quietly he slung the skin over his shoulder and slowly rose to his feet. Then the girl looked up at him.

CHAPTER 16

Witch Hunters

The girl looked at Hyroc, then she returned her gaze to the container she held within the stream. Hyroc wondered anxiously if she had actually noticed him, but an instant later, she sharply looked up at him again. Her eyes began to widen into the familiar look of alarm people usually showed when they saw him for the first time. Making sure he avoided exposing his teeth with what he would have intended as a friendly smile, he waved at her. She stared at him without moving as the color drained from her face. Hyroc knew what she was about to do. "Please don't scream," Hyroc pleaded in a calm voice. The girl screamed, bolting in the direction of a grouping of buildings. Hyroc chided himself for blindly walking up to the stream. He splashed through it to the other side and broke into a run. It would be mere minutes before the girl informed someone of his presence. Then not long afterward, people would be out searching for him. Out on the flat open terrain it wouldn't be hard for someone to spot him. His only chance was to make it to the forest ahead of him. If he reached it, he would be able to lose any pursuers.

Glancing over his shoulder toward the structures several minutes later, he didn't see anybody pursuing him. By now, he figured the girl had led someone to the stream. He was running out of time and the edge of the forest was still a fair distance away. He resumed his run, forcing every bit of strength out of his legs. They quickly began to burn from the exertion, but he fought through the discomfort, knowing every second brought him closer to safety. His progress felt too slow and that someone from the town would overtake him any second.

Then to his astonishment, he reached the edge of the trees. Most of them consisted of pines, with some birches and cottonwoods mixed in. He leaned against the closest tree, his breaths coming in deep gaspes. He had never pushed himself so hard in his life, not even when he fought his bullies. All he wanted to do now was collapse where he stood and take a nap, but he knew he couldn't, not yet. He looked back toward town, taking a long drought from his water skin. There still wasn't anybody there, but he didn't fool himself into thinking there wasn't somebody out there he couldn't see. Off to his right, a narrow road wound its way from the town and into the forest. It would be safer to stay clear of it, but he feared getting lost in the woods, though some part of him wondered if that would be such a bad thing. There wouldn't be anybody to hurt him and it seemed unlikely he would have to worry about ever being found. It was a tempting option, though. He couldn't stand the thought of how lonely he would be. After all the bad things people had done to him, he still wanted to be around them. He wondered if it was just him holding on to the hope he might run it someone who didn't think he was a monster. Not everyone had, Marcus, June, Thomas and the nice lady in the kitchen were proof of that. He just had no expectations of finding anyone like them ever again. In the end, he might not have a choice. He pushed the thought aside. Reaching Elswood was the only thing he needed to think about for the time being. When he reached it, then he would see what fate had in store for him.

He pushed himself upright and headed into the trees, angling toward the road where it entered the forest. When it came into view again, he followed along it through the trees, staying only close enough to keep it in view. The rest of the day passed slowly without him seeing any signs of pursuers. Amongst the trees, darkness came suddenly and Hyroc barely noticed its onset in time to make camp while he still had light. Kindling was plentiful here and it wasn't hard for him to get a fire going. Reaching into his pack, he was dismayed to see his provisions were nearly exhausted. He had enough for his breakfast the following morning. After that, all he had was the sack of tasteless cold-flour.

Sleep proved more elusive than he had expected. Strange sounds filled the night and he thought he could hear things moving through the trees. Then a shiver ran down his back when he heard the distant cry of a wolf. Nearby, a rabbit let loose a shrill death shriek. Hyroc added more wood to the fire. The fire eagerly devoured the fresh kindling, flaring brightly. Hyroc strung his bow and moved as close to the fire as he could endure.

The night seemed to stretch on endlessly, then suddenly he found himself waking up in the morning. He breathed a sigh of relief, stretched and settled in to eat what remained of his fresh supplies. As he did so, he gazed unenthusiastically at the sack of cold-flour. The unappetizing substance was all he had left and soon even it would be gone. Not bothering to unstring his bow, he held it at his side as he resumed following the road. If anything moved, he had to be ready to shoot it. Wild game would be the only thing keeping him from starving to death.

Mourning faded to noon and he found himself reaching into his pack for something to eat. He sighed bitterly when his hand found only an empty pack. Hunger pangs began gnawing at him a few hours later. He resisted the urge to start in on his cold-flour; he could wait until dinner. Trying to take his mind off his hunger, he scaled a tree to have a look at his surroundings. Everything around him seemed much the same, with rises dotting the terrain. Off toward the north he saw the bluish gray triangular shape of Wolf Paw Mountain. He smiled at the sight. That was where his new home lay, hopefully. Feeling a little better, he descended back to the ground and continued his journey. As the sunlight began fading to the orange glow of dusk, he spooked a wood grouse foraging at the base of a cottonwood. The bird took flight, moving skyward at a shallow angle. Hyroc immediately nocked an arrow and let it fly. The arrow struck the fowl in the chest and it plummeted to the ground.

Hyroc carried his prize over to a small gap in the trees, where he plucked, gutted and cooked it. Biting into the hot meat, he was grateful he was spared the cold-flour for at least one more meal. Done eating, he wiped the grease from his lips, then disposed of what little remained of his meal into a nearby stream before settling in for the night. The sounds didn't bother him as much, and beyond the occasional noise waking him, he slept relatively well.

A strange smell roused him from his sleep. With his eyes still closed, he absentmindedly sniffed. He recognized the smell as that belonging to a dog. He snapped his eyes open and was startled to see a muscular man in front of him leaning on the head of a two-handed ax. Left of him, another man stood holding the leash of a fearsome looking black and brown tracking dog. A twig snapped behind Hyroc. Turning his head slightly, he saw a third man approaching from behind with a bow and nocked arrow. Hyroc slowly got to his feet.

The man with the ax stood up straight. "No need for you to stand," the man said in a gravelly voice. "You can run but you won't get away." The man indicated the tracking hound with his hand. "If you get lucky, *you might* be able to lose *us*, but not that beast over there; he'll find you no matter what you do. So why don't you make this easy on yourself and just accept your fate."

"He's an ugly wretch isn't he," the man with the bow said in a disgusted tone. "I don't much blame that girl for being afraid now that I've seen him with my own eyes." The man with the ax raised one hand toward the man with the bow, signaling for him to be quiet. Then he grabbed his ax handle with both hands, holding it at the ready. Hyroc had no disillusion these men were going to kill him. Luckily, he was quite familiar with an effective strategy for dealing with such situations. He took a breath to calm himself and bolted. With a curse, the man with the ax yelled for the bowman to shoot. Hyroc heard the fluttering of wings and the cries of an angry sounding bird. The bowman swore. Stealing a look over his shoulder, Hyroc saw a large black raven attacking the man with the bow. The man swatted the bird out of the way and loosed his arrow. Hyroc yelped as the arrow whistled toward him. He felt a sharp pain in the edge of his ear as the arrow clipped it. Distracted by the pain, Hyroc tripped over a root, losing his balance and falling. Before he could get back to his feet, the dog was on him. He rolled onto his back and barely managed to grab the dog by its collar before it could sink its teeth into his throat. White spittle spattered on his face from the dog's snapping jaws that hovered mere inches from his face. Hyroc grabbed a rock and smashed it into the side of the dog's head. The beast yelped, pulling away. He kicked it under the chin, knocking it onto its side. He attempted to get to his feet yet again, but a hard kick to the ribs sent him back down.

"That's my dog, you filthy wretch!" the man bellowed. Just as he drew a sword hanging from his belt, a deafening roar erupted from a patch of foliage. Both the man and Hyroc instinctively looked toward the sound. A massive white bear slammed into the man with the bow, knocking him onto his back. The man yelled out in terror as the bear tore into his neck. There was a loud crunch and the man's screams cut short. The tracking dog barked furiously at the bear. With a curse, the man with the sword drew a throwing ax and hurled it at the bear. The bear sidestepped the ax and the projectile thunked harmlessly into the trunk of a tree. Hyroc gaped at the bear in terrified amazement. The man with the ax stepped back beside the one with the sword. Then the bear charged them.

The man with the ax raised his weapon above his head to strike the approaching beast. When he brought the blade down, the bear turned its head so it caught the wooden shaft in its jaws. With a swipe of its massive paw, the bear broke the ax head off. Before the man could react, the bear slammed its paw into the side of his head. There was a snapping crunch as the man's neck broke. The man with the sword cursed in a frantic tone as he stabbed at the bear's neck. The bear ducked out of the way of the strike and was on the man before he could make a second attempt. The man screamed, but just as with the bowman, his screams abruptly ceased with the disturbing sound of breaking bone.

Its head dripping blood, the bear then roared at the still barking dog. The dog whimpered and with its tail between its legs, bolted. Once the dog had disappeared into the brush, the bear turned its attention on Hyroc. He knew he should run, but his legs would not obey. He closed his eyes as he waited to feel the bear's teeth ripping through his flesh. He heard the rustling of leaves, followed by an eerie silence. When he finally worked up enough courage to open his eyes, the bear was gone. A trail of bloody paw prints led off into the bushes where the beast had first emerged. When Hyroc's legs allowed movement once again, he dashed to his pack.

He rapidly donned his things and took off at a dead run toward the road. Everything around him merged into a green and brown blur. He couldn't think about anything, all that mattered was he keep moving. He had to get away, he wasn't safe. Wasn't safe from that – from that *thing*. He emerged onto the road and nearly ran headfirst into a big brown, long faced animal. The animal let out a startled scream as it reared up on its two back legs. It flung its two front legs forward, catching Hyroc in the chest with the edge of a hoof. He was thrown onto his back, knocking the air out of him. A frightening moment of breathlessness passed before he gasped. His head felt suddenly clearer and he was able to think again. The three men's brutal deaths assailed his mind. For a moment it was all he could think about, but he forced the memory aside.

Focusing on the animal that had kicked him, he realized it was a horse. It was tied to the trunk of a pine, and a few steps to one side of it, there were two more. These horses must have belonged to the three men. All three horses stared at him warily. Riding a horse could cut days of his journey; unfortunately, he knew they wouldn't let him ride them. When he was seven, Marcus had rented a pony so he could teach him how to ride. The lesson had gone fine up until the point Marcus tried to get Hyroc on the horse. The horse began bucking wildly, throwing Hyroc from its back and the animal nearly stomped on him. Marcus tried repeatedly, with the same result, but to Hyroc's relief, eventually gave up. Pretty much for as long as Hyroc could remember, every horse he had ever come near had looked like it wanted to kick him to death. So, he didn't ride horses.

He saw a saddlebag on the horse. It seemed reasonable to think there was something he might be able to use in there. And the horse might let him get close enough to look inside if he was careful. While talking calmly to the horse, he slowly approached the saddlebag. The horse watched him warily but didn't move to attack him. Peering inside the bag, he found it stocked with a few days' worth of provisions. If he took the food then he should have enough to make it to Elswood. It wouldn't be stealing either because the people it was intended for wouldn't be eating it. Everything would go to waste if he didn't. He felt suddenly sick as he remembered what it had looked like to see what was left of the three men. Fighting through the urge to retch, he began shoving the food into his pack as fast as he could. As he did so, he noticed his hands were trembling. He closed his fists tightly and opened them again, repeating the process four times. The trembling subsided a little. He sighed as he resumed his pilfering. Now wasn't the time to worry about his handshaking.

Along with the food, he found a coin pouch and added its contents to his own. He wasn't sure how useful the coins would be, but it seemed irresponsible to leave behind something potentially valuable. Their owners had no more use for them. Moving on to the next horse, he found an extra quiver of arrows and a short sword. He calmly talked to the horse as he had done with the first until it let him touch it. Except for seven of the arrows in the quiver, most were no different than his own. Five were made of a high-quality steel and looked like they were designed to pierce armor. The remaining two had heads of silver. He remembered reading about the use of silver in fighting shadow demons and guessed these were specifically made to kill evil things. He didn't expect to need anything like them in Elswood, but he could probably sell the heads; if anybody would let him. He stuck the five steel arrows, two silver ones and as many of the regular arrows as would fit into his quiver.

He studied the sword thoughtfully. It might come in handy against wolves or dogs. His bow would work fine against either from a distance, but if they got close, he would be in trouble. He smiled at the idea of having it. From the first time he had seen a sword, he had always wanted one. He carefully pulled the sword and its belt from the horse. Once the blade was secured to his waist, he moved on to the last horse. This horse seemed much more nervous at his approach and began bucking the moment he got close. Lurching backward out of the way of a flying hoof, he decided there wasn't anything on the horse worth the risk of getting kicked. Besides, he felt he had spent too much time with the horses. He was still dangerously close to the site of the bear attack and that beast wouldn't be far away.

He glanced over at the ropes tied around the necks of the horses. It might be some time before anyone came this way again. Tied to a tree, the horses couldn't find food and they would starve to death if something didn't get to them first. It would be cruel of him to leave their lives to chance; they hadn't done anything to him. The three of them still might not survive, but at least they had a chance if they were untied. He pulled the sword from its sheath and was a little surprised by its shape. The blade was rectangular with a rounded end and appeared to be a Falchion. When he swung it; it almost had the same feel as his wood hatchet. He waved the sword through the air a few more times before cutting the ropes on the horses. The horses stared at him a long moment before starting to move around. Duty done, he sheathed his blade and turned toward the road to leave.

A bolt of fear shot through him when he saw the white bear standing right in front of him. With a surprised yell, he drew the sword. Then suddenly there wasn't anything in front of him. Heart racing, he swept his eyes through his surroundings. Other than the horses, there weren't any creatures in sight. He nudged the side of his head with the fist of his free hand. It was just a memory, what he had seen wasn't real. He didn't have time to waste worrying about what had happened, he needed to put as much distance between him and the kill site as quickly as possible. After taking several deep breaths to calm his nerves, he returned the sword to its sheath. His hand was still shaking as he did so. He hoped the trembling would go away eventually; it would make accurately shooting a bow difficult. When he was relaxed enough, he continued up the road.

With nothing to focus his mind on, the memory of the attack appeared repeatedly in his mind's eye. The ferocity of the attack was not what bothered him the most; it was the bear's behavior. The efficiency with which it killed those men was extremely disturbing. From what he understood about animals, nothing kills like that except people. Then there was the fact it disarmed one of the men before killing him and it dodged a thrown ax and ducked a sword stroke. An animal shouldn't have known to do so. Maybe it was a witch in the form of a bear. That could explain why the beast had acted so strangely, but those kinds of witches were usually half-mad and nearly incapable of rational thoughts. It seemed unlikely they would be in the correct mindset to dodge any kind of attack. There was also the fact it didn't kill him. If it tore those men to pieces, it should have done the same to him. He forced a vivid image of the kill site from his mind. That bear would have had an easier time with him, so why did it leave him alone? Maybe it was saving him for later he thought unpleasantly. The thought made him glance nervously through his surroundings. There still wasn't any sign of the bear. Maybe it was as simple as he had gotten lucky. No matter what the bear might have been, he was alive because of it. He had seen something horrible, but he was still alive, he just needed to make sure he stayed that way. Spending the night in a tree would probably be a good idea.

CHAPTER 17

A Place on the Mountain

Hyroc was shocked awake when one of the branches from the spruce tree he had taken shelter underneath for the night, released its glistening coating of ice-cold morning dew on his head. Using one of his sleeves, he dried the top of his head as best he could. He removed the mostly empty bag of cold-flour from his pack, dumping a meager amount into a waiting bowl. The provisions he had taken off the horses had run out a little under a week ago and for the last four days, beyond the occasional rabbit or wood grouse, this tasteless meal was his main source of food. As he cinched the bag shut, he felt strangely relieved to see only enough flour for one more serving. At least he wouldn't be eating much more of it. Though that was about the only good thing about it running out. After replacing the bag into his pack, he used his water skin to pour water over the grain in the bowl. He scooped up a spoonful of his gruel, turned the spoon sideways; letting the watered-down slop splatter back into the bowl.

When he finished choking down his breakfast, he donned his things before making his way through the thickly clustered pine trees surrounding his campsite, over to the road beyond. Cautiously, he looked up and down the rock-riddled path. At the end of it lay the village of Elswood.

This was his destination but beyond getting here, he hadn't put much thought into what to do once he actually arrived. About the only thing he had figured out was he could trap here. That seemed such a stupid thing to do, go somewhere and have practically no idea what to do when he got there. He knew better than to hope for a friendly welcome from the villagers, let alone a warm place to sleep. They would probably attack him on sight for fear he was some sort of forest monster. No one thus far had reacted toward him any better. He still wondered what he was expecting to find here when it was likely anyone he encountered would think he meant them harm. He couldn't make his home in such a place. He was liable to end up dead if he tried. Those witch hunters didn't even think twice about killing him. It disturbed him how lightly they had treated the task of ending his life. They looked at him as if he were less than a rabid animal in need of killing. The safest option would still be for him to venture out into the wilderness where there wouldn't be any people. Nobody wanted him around them. He was a monster and nothing he did could change that. Why was it so difficult for him to accept this? Was he hoping things would be better here? Treated as if he were a normal person. There was only one option open to him. He hated the thought of how isolated he would be out in the wilderness all by himself but it probably was his only choice. Maybe if he ventured into the village, had something bad happen, maybe he could convince himself to leave these ridiculous hopes behind.

He saw nobody on the road. Warily, he started walking in the direction of the village. Not long afterward, he heard voices. Looking through the trees at a bend in the road, he saw the shapes of two men heading his way. He felt a surge of anxiety as the memory of the three men who had tried to kill him flashed through his mind. Heart racing, he bolted off into the cover of the trees. The two men passed without showing any signs of seeing him.

He waited for them to disappear from view before making his way back to the road. As he did so, he noticed a slight partying in the undergrowth where a trail might have been once. Looking in the direction the trail led, he saw the rocky peak of Wolf Paw Mountain above the treetops. From the higher elevation of the mountain's slopes, he could probably get a good view of the village and maybe spot any waiting dangers. If he saw any buildings marked with Ministry insignias, he would know for a surety he couldn't enter the village. And so, he started following the trail.

Farther down the path, he could make out the shimmering surface of a lake. He smiled at the disc of water. Heartened by the prospect of having fish for dinner he left the trail to have a better look. A delicious odor floated over to him as he drew close to the shore. The trees began to clear and through them, he caught sight of someone at the water's edge.

Backtracking into better concealment, he snuck through the trees to get a closer look at them. The person turned out to be a girl cleaning clothes in the lake water. She wore a dark blue dress with a scarf covering golden blonde hair. She seemed a couple years older than he was with rather pleasing features; or at least what he thought was pleasing because he didn't exactly have much personal experience with it. He was then startled to see a hound emerge from the shade of a tree near the girl and it began moving toward him. It issued a warning bark in his direction. The girl turned to look at what the dog was barking at. Hyroc immediately dropped to the ground, nearly plunging the end of his snout into a spiky patch of Devil's club. Through the foliage, he saw the girl moving toward the dog and the hound woofed. Speaking to the mutt in a calm reassuring voice, she began stroking its back. A man, Hyroc assumed was the girl's father, came walking over to her from further up the lake shore. He was a tall, broad-shouldered man with black hair and a short mildly unkempt beard. The two of them exchanged a few brief words then both walked off. The dog remained where it was, continuing its woofing. Grabbing a rock, Hyroc nailed the dog in the head with it. The mutt let out a pain-laden whine as it ran away. Hyroc rose to his feet, following the father and daughter from a safe distance.

They stopped at a cabin situated in the middle of a large grassy clearing surrounded by pine trees. In front of the cabin was a small vegetable garden with green sprouts dotting the soil. Hyroc felt a stab of longing as he looked at the garden, remembering the home he had been forced to leave behind. Pushing the thought away, he continued his examination of the cabin. To the right of the structure at a woodpile was a boy with jet-black hair who looked to be about fifteen chopping wood, while a younger boy with brownish hair – who was maybe ten – gathered the chopped wood. To the left of the cabin, there was a small fenced off area with a goat and donkey milling around inside. Behind that, he could see the light-colored shapes of chickens outside of a small coop and the edge of what looked to be a barn. Farther to the left of the pen, a gray-haired man was smoking meat on a rack.

The girl opened the cabin door, disappearing inside. The girl's father made his way toward the woodpile. The man called out to one of the boys. The smallest boy set down his load of firewood and joined his father. The two of them walked behind the cabin to a wooden rack and two tables with a gutted deer carcass on one and some small fur-bearing animals lying on the other. Then past this, was a storage shed.

The father and son started skinning the deer carcass. Watching the two of them work, Hyroc wondered how this would affect the way they acted toward him. They hunted animals for their furs and he was covered in fur, so they might see him as nothing more than a walking, teenage boy sized animal pelt. There was also the matter of the family's children. People were always more cautious around him when they had children with them and they would often lash out at him if he got close. This might make these people especially hazardous. He would need to make sure he avoided them. He watched the family a little longer before sneaking through the bushes back to the trail.

The trail wound its way through the forest, steadily drawing nearer to the mountain. When Hyroc began contemplating heading back to the road, the trail entered an oval shaped valley between two uneven rises jutting away from the mountain. Close to the middle of the valley, beside the rightmost rise sat a small cabin beneath a large spruce tree. A stream snaked its way into the valley around the left rise, forming a bend close to the cabin, before flowing back out. Behind the cabin, lay the foot of the mountain. The ground sloped gradually upward onto the mountain before angling upward sharply. The sharp rise continued all the way up to the peak where there was still a swath of snow.

From the concealment of a tree on the outskirts of the valley, Hyroc scrutinized the cabin and its surroundings. He saw no smoke rising from the chimney. Testing the air with his nose, the only thing he could smell was pine needles and sap; it appeared empty. Making sure to stay shadowed as much as possible, he moved closer. The cabin had smooth wood logs for its walls, supporting a slanted moss-covered roof with a stone chimney, a single window, and a small porch in front of its loan door.

Judging from the amount of overgrowth he saw around the structure, it seemed no one had lived here for many years. He smiled at his luck. Something had finally gone right for him! Despite the cabin's dilapidated appearance, the fact it was empty made it an incredible find. Even if he had to avoid the villagers, he could definitely live here. It seemed far enough from the other cabin and the village for him to go unnoticed. Looking toward the chimney, he realized the spruce was closed enough for its branches to break up any smoke flowing skyward; substantially reducing the risk of someone knowing he was here if he used the fireplace. He still needed to deal with the issue of the village eventually, but he could hold off until he at least recovered from his journey.

Walking to the door of the cabin, he saw a board nailed across it. The presence of a barred door on the cabin was somewhat alarming because it seemed whoever had sealed the door shut, was trying to keep something in. Hyroc shook his head dismissively; the previous owner probably nailed it shut to keep animals out and for some reason never returned. His flight from Forna was just making him paranoid. Besides, after spending several nights in the rain, it would take more than some rusty nails to prevent him from sleeping with a roof over his head.

He slipped the side of his wood hatchet's blade under one nail head. Slowly working his ax up and down, the nail began to come out of the wood. The first nail fell from the door, followed by the remaining ones in likewise fashion.

He set the board aside and opened the door. It released a loud groaning creek as it was pushed open. The sweet smell of cedar greeted him as he entered the cabin. On the wall opposite the door was a small gray stone fireplace. Dust covered cookware hung from the stonework and there was a cooking pot within. To the right of the fireplace lay an empty bed frame, with a small cedar chest at its foot. On the opposite end of the structure, a stool sat beneath a table with a cobweb covered cup, bowl and spoon on top of it. Above the table, a line of three coat hooks stretched across the wall, ending just before a cabinet tucked away in the corner.

Movement on the porch and a grunting sort of wheezing noise caught Hyroc's attention. Turning toward the moving thing, he saw a porcupine shuffling away for him. He didn't know how good it would taste, but he had read somewhere about people eating them and it would save him from another dinner of cold-flour. He rushed over to the fleeing animal, plunging his hunting knife into its head. The unfortunate creature twitched twice before going limp. "Sorry little guy," Hyroc said apologetically. "But you're made of meat and I don't want to have watery-mush-grain for dinner another night if I can help it."

He skinned and gutted the porcupine away from the cabin, taking care not to get one of the spines shoved into his fingers as he did so. He hung the carcass on a tree branch while he collected firewood. Once he got a fire going in the fireplace, he stuck the porcupine on a spit and began cooking it. Smoke quickly filled the cabin. Eyes watering, he ran outside with the porcupine in hand. When his vision cleared, atop the chimney he saw the wiry shape of a bird's nest hampering the upward evacuation of the smoke. Grumbling, Hyroc staked the spit into the ground and climbed atop the roof via a moldering stack of old firewood against the side of the cabin. When he removed the nest, smoke flowed freely from the chimney. Then when the smoke had cleared, he resumed cooking his lunch.

He hungrily took a bite. The meat was gamy and the flavor was how he thought a rotting mulch pile might taste. After his almost enjoyable meal, he removed his bow from its buckskin tube and strung it. Slinging his quiver onto his back, he headed for the mountain slopes to have a look at his surroundings. When he reached what seemed an appropriate height, he set his equipment against the base of a tall tree, slipped his boots off, and climbed it. Surrounding him as far as he could see was a lumpy verdant mat, laced with rivers and streams. Looking out toward Elswood, he saw small farms running along the main road and other homesteads dotting the landscape around the village. The village itself was a cluster of a surprisingly sparse number of buildings arranged in a rough circle. The smallness of the village was somewhat surprising, but at the same time, he remembered this smallness was part of why he had come here. At this distance it was hard to make out details but he saw nothing indicative of The Ministry anywhere within sight. He would have to get a closer look to be positive. After taking note of some spots to investigate, he climbed back down the tree, heading off in search of his dinner.

When he returned to the cabin as the dusk sun neared the horizon, he had only managed to kill two squirrels. While his dinner cooked, he opened the cedar chest. Inside he found rotting pieces of parchment, shards of a shattered glass ink well and some moth-eaten rags. He cleaned out the chest outside, keeping only the rags. As he turned back toward the cabin, he saw a raven on a tree branch and it looked like it had silver markings on its neck. That couldn't be this same bird he had seen when he was leaving Forna. He hadn't even seen birds until he had entered the forest. There wasn't any reason for the bird to have followed him. This had to be another bird, nothing more. The light was probably hitting its feathers just right so it looked like it had silver markings. He had seen that a few times when he hunted ducks.

After returning the chest to the foot of the bed, he moved on to the closet. Other than a dusty knapsack, the only thing he found within was a clump of cobwebs. Sweeping the cobwebs aside, he removed the knapsack, dusted it off then hung it on one of the coat hooks. By the time he had done so, his dinner was ready. Seating himself at the table with his meal, he removed the wooden bear carving from his pocket and set it in the middle of the table. If this was going to be his home, he needed it to feel like one. He readjusted the carving, nodded his satisfaction, then started eating.

Before settling in for the night, he made sure the cabin's door was secure; he didn't want to wake up in the middle of the night to a hungry wolf staring at him. He brushed a brown wood spider from the dusty bed frame; placing the bag of grain at the head of the bed as a makeshift pillow. It was a sad imitation of his feather stuffed pillow at the boarding school, but it was better than nothing. In a few weeks' time he figured he would probably have killed enough fowl to stuff a pillow full of feathers. He slipped his cloak off, using it as a blanket when he laid down on the bed.

As he lay there staring up at the dancing orange shadows cast across the ceiling by the fire, the familiar empty feeling started gnawing at him. His thoughts turned to his only friend Thomas. He smiled as he remembered the mischief the two of them had gotten into throughout their friendship. Though he suspected nothing they had done was very disobedient. Hyroc wished he could talk to him. He heard June's voice say in a wispy voice, "Forget about us. You made a promise." He sighed, forcing his friend from his mind. His thoughts turned to a different solution to his feelings of forlorn, a pet.

Dogs were obviously out of the question. They only ever bit or barked at him. Maybe a cat would make a good pet. No, cats are solitary grump-balls who only come to people when *they want to*. A falcon, would be an interesting pet. One of those might not be much use for companionship, but they can hunt small game. Having something with such abilities could save countless arrows that would otherwise be damaged or lost trying to hunt rabbits. The only problem he could see with a falcon was he had absolutely no idea how to go about training one. And falconry didn't exactly seem like something he could figure out on his own.

As he lay there going through the merits and demerits of every pet he could think of, his eyes grew heavy. He fought in vain to stay awake a little bit longer to decide on a companion, but weariness quickly overcame his will to remain awake. His eyes closed and he gently drifted off to sleep.

CHAPTER 18

Mountain Huntress

Hyroc woke well past dawn. His neck ached from the awkward position the bag of grain he had used as a pillow forced him to lay in. When he sat up, his neck popped and his back felt stiff. With a groan, he rubbed his neck as he slid his legs over the side of the bed, resting his bare feet on the cold dust speckled wooden floor. Lowering his hand, he put his boots on.

His stomach growled as he got to his feet. He looked at the bag of grain hungrily, but tore his eyes away from it, remembering how much he hated eating its contents and decided it served a much better purpose as an uncomfortable pillow. Pulling open the cabin's door, he shivered as an unexpected wave of frigid morning mountain air flooded the cabin. As he stepped into the bright rays of sunlight, he sneezed three times. Once the fit passed, he made his way to the stream in search of his breakfast.

Along the shore, he found small patches of wild alpine strawberries and wild raspberries. After eating as many ripe berries as he could find, he stripped down, hanging his clothing on the branch of a tree. He had gone without a proper bath since before he left the boarding school, and he was starting to notice his own stink. He tested the water with his foot and was dismayed by how cold it felt. Taking a breath, he stepped into the stream. When the initial shock of submerging half his body in cool water faded, he waded out into the deepest part of the stream. Wanting to spend as little time in there as possible, he quickly washed and got out. Using the cloak as a towel, he dried himself, feeling the pleasant sensation of cleanliness.

Now dressed, he dipped his hands into the river, spending the next few minutes scrubby off as much grime as he could from his clothing. Satisfied, he filled his water skin then returned to the cabin. He hung his cloak on a branch to dry, strung his bow, collected the quiver, retrieved the length of heavy twine from his pack and headed out in search of trapping spots.

Toward the back of the valley, winding its way onto the mountain slope, he found an animal trail he believed rabbits used. He set a spring snare using a tall sapling growing at the edge of the trail. He had learned how to make this type of snare when he had happened across an old book on trapping in the school's library.

The trail disappeared at a stand of birch trees shortly after running onto the rise of the mountain. From here, he headed toward the eastern side of the mountain as straight as the terrain would allow. He arrived at the edge of a ravine filled with boulders. Picking his way down into the ravine, he found numerous animal prints and other such indications of game frequently traveling through it. He set a snare between two boulders in what seemed the most traveled part of the ravine.

Halfway through the process of setting his snare, he felt the disconcerting sensation of being watched. Scanning the upper parts of the terrain, he saw nothing. Right when he was about to disregard the feeling, he spotted a reddish brown mountain lion crouched on a bush-covered ledge, at the left topmost side of the ravine. Letting go of his half-made trap, Hyroc nocked an arrow and took aim. Time seemed to stop as the two of them locked eyes on each other. This was the first time he had seen a mountain lion outside of drawings. Everything he had read about them described the big cats as extremely dangerous and often unpredictable. They moved silently at night and by the time anybody knew they were nearby, it was already too late.

Even with that threatening image in mind, he had to admit the big cat possessed a strange kind of beauty. Or maybe he just admired it for its frightening ability to kill prey. In that, the two of them weren't so different. The big cat stood, causing Hyroc to tense as it did so, and to his relief slinked off. He watched the cat disappear into the trees over the lip of the ravine. His gaze lingered there long after it had left and he had relaxed enough to turn his attention back to the trap. He rapidly finished the trap, keeping a close eye out for the mountain lion, and hurried out of the ravine.

Warily heading away from the ravine to the flatter ground surrounding the base of the mountain, he found another game trail cutting through a clearing with a dark orange brackish pool of stagnant mosquito-water. He set another regular snare here then continued east away from the mountain for a short distance longer before encountering a creek; animal tracks lining its shore of gray sand. Following the tracks, he found a trap spot in a patch of brush near the base of a spruce tree beside an indent in the shore. From the creek, he made a wide northward arc back toward the mountain. He set one final snare at a rabbit trail running through a large opening beneath the rotting remains of a fallen tree. Figuring he had spent enough time creating traps for one day, he stuck the remaining twine in his pocket and made his way back to the creek to hunt.

Searching along the creek's shore, he found what he thought were fresh deer tracks heading south. He had spooked deer on his way to Elswood, but this was the first time he had actually thought to try hunting one. There was little difference between the size of the fowl and the rabbits he had seen, thus making a duck hunting bow effective in either case, but deer were far larger than any of those. Did his bow have enough power to effectively down one? Reaching into his quiver, he carefully removed one of the high quality steel arrows he had recovered from the dead witch hunters. If it was meant for piercing armor then it should make short work of a deer even if his bow was lacking in force. If he managed to kill the deer, he wouldn't have to worry about food for a while. There was just the problem of how to butcher it. His experience with fowl and rabbits probably wouldn't help him much toward figuring out what to do. He pushed the thought from his mind. He was getting ahead of himself. He hadn't even found it. If things worked out, *then* he could worry about that.

Holding his bow at the ready, he began following the deer prints. The tracks led along the shore then reentered the forest. After what felt like hours, he eventually found a lone doe munching on some greenery. Fitting the steel arrow to the bowstring, he carefully took aim. *If this doesn't do the trick, I doubt anything else I own will.* Suddenly the light-colored shape of a mountain lion burst out of the bushes, pouncing on the deer. The big cat buried its teeth into the back of the deer's neck, at the base of the skull. The deer struggled for a moment against its attacker before collapsing onto the ground. As soon as the deer hit the ground, the cat finished it off with several vicious bites to the neck.

Hyroc watched the cat dispatch its prey with a mixture of fascination and loathing. He recognized the mountain lion as the same animal he had encountered earlier in the ravine. It was tempted to kill the cat and take the deer for himself, but killing it for hunting like he was, seemed distasteful. The cat grabbed the deer by the neck and looked right at him. He thought the cat was mocking him. Then it vanished into the bushes with its prize.

Having run into the cat twice in one day, he figured it might be a good idea to follow it to its lair. Maybe he could figure out where it hunted and avoid another deer-stealing incident or something much more painful.

After letting the deer-thief get a head start, Hyroc began following the cat's tracks back up the mountain. They led him to a steep incline covered in birch trees and a brown and yellow blanket of dead leaves littered the ground. Cresting the top of the incline, he saw a rocky clearing dominated by a jagged cliff face. The mountain lion's tracks led up toward a rounded ramp of rock projecting from the ground, with a small cave entrance at its top. He cautiously snuck over to the entrance to peer inside. The cave ran a short way inside the cliff and the ceiling was so low he would have to crawl if he was crazy enough to enter.

The mountain lion lay in the middle of the cave devouring his stolen kill. To his surprise, he saw two speckled cubs gnawing curiously on a bloodstained rib protruding from the deer carcass. She was a mother. Hyroc felt a tremendous stab of guilt at having even considered killing her. If he had done so, he would have also killed her cubs. Berating himself, he backed away from the cave. Distracted by his thoughts, he stepped wrong and his foot landed on a dry twig. A loud snap erupted from the twig as it broke in half, sending a resounding echo through the cave. The mountain lion looked in his direction. Her entire body went rigid, and with ears flat against her head, she snarled savagely, exposing every one of her razor-sharp flesh rending teeth. Hyroc's stomach clenched with the fear he was about to incur imminent blood loss. Making a frantic retreat, he managed to reach the bottom of the rock ramp before she was out of the cave. The big cat growled at him with a fury in her eyes that made his dealings with Miss Duncan look pleasant by comparison.

He took off down the incline as fast as his legs would carry him, his heart hammering away uncomfortably within his chest. He ran until his breaths came in deep gasps and he was sure the mountain lion was not pursuing. Resting his back against a springy cluster of pine tree branches, he caught his breath. *That was too close!*

Once his mind allowed coherent thought again, he resumed hunting. He spooked a wood grouse, the bird instantly taking flight. Almost instinctively, he took aim and simultaneously loosed an arrow. The arrow whizzed through the air, striking the fowl and sending it plummeting to the ground. He rushed protectively over to the grouse's lifeless body; he was not about to lose this meal to another opportunistic animal. He plucked and gutted the bird before making his way back to the cabin to cook his prize.

When the bird had finished cooking, he hungrily sank his teeth into it before it had properly cooled. The delicious taste of hot meat flooded his mouth and he was so hungry he barely even noticed the burning sensation on his tongue. His only regret when he finished was there wasn't more.

Belly full, finally, he removed the fishing line from his pack and used a sturdy branch from the spruce beside the cabin to fashion a fishing pole. He then spent the rest of the day fishing in the nearby stream, managing to land a decent sized trout.

As Hyroc stared up at the ceiling of the cabin trying to force himself to sleep, he absentmindedly removed his necklace. He held the trinket in front of him, its silvery metallic surface, orange in the glare of the fire. He lazily studied the bear on the front. Then turned it around to look at the fox, badger, and claw symbol etched into its surface, trying to figure out the enigma of what each might represent. Other than speculating these were symbols used to describe someone's personality in times long past, Marcus was never able to give a satisfying answer to any of Hyroc's questions regarding them.

Foxes were smart cunning creatures and Hyroc thought he was smart. He was unsure what badgers represent but he had heard somewhere it was bravery. He liked to think of himself as being brave, but long ago he had learned going unnoticed was a far more comfortable option, which to his dismay seemed a somewhat cowardly lifestyle, making him question the accuracy of such thoughts. Bears represented strength, and even though he greatly admired them, if he truly possessed strength like a bear, he would not have been beaten so often. Just as with the badger, the bear too seemed out of place. Then there was the claw symbol. It didn't appear to belong to any animal anyone in Forna had ever heard of and Marcus was unable to give a sensible theory about its possible meaning.

What if this necklace is somebody else's? The thought sent a cold shiver down his back, as the few things in his life he thought were unshakable would be thrown into question. He pushed the thought out of his mind before it could take root and blossom into a black tree of despair. The idea was too painful for him to even consider.

"It's just a necklace, nothing more," he said aloud, squeezing his eyes shut. He repeated the statement several times in a quiet chant, and put the necklace back on.

CHAPTER 19

Deer Rabbit

Beams of morning sunlight streamed between the branches of the trees as Hyroc trudged toward the back of the valley to check the spring snare. A bolt of excitement shot through him when he saw the sapling standing upright and there was something dangling from it. He had hoped he would catch something with it but he hadn't really expected to on his first attempt. At the trap, he found a rabbit hanging helplessly in the air; at least he thought it was a rabbit. The rabbit was brown with white spots and two small antlers protruded from its head. Unsure if sleep was clouding his vision, Hyroc rubbed his eyes. The creature's appearance remained unchanged. He pushed one of his claws into the side of his snout to see if he was dreaming. Pain was supposed to reveal that. It hurt so, no, he was awake. Shaking his head, feeling as if a small part of his world just stopped making sense, he unsheathed his knife and stabbed the rabbit in the head. When it was dead, he moved a few yards away to slit its throat. A stream of blood spattered onto the ground before slowing to a few red drips. He gave the rabbit a hard shake, tied it to his belt, then reset the trap.

The rest of his snares were empty. When he finished with the last one, he made his way to the incline leading to the cliff face where the mountain lion's lair was. He knew this was not one of his best ideas, but he saw a good spot to set a snare when he was up here yesterday. Keeping a close watch on his surroundings, he made a final trap using the last of his heavy twine. He hoped he wouldn't end up catching the big cat or any of her cubs putting a trap here.

Once finished at the incline he made his way back to the cabin. Making sure to preserve the animal hide, he got to work skinning and gutting the strange rabbit. While the rabbit cooked in his fireplace, he studied the fresh hide, trying to figure out what he could do with it. Selling it in town would be the obvious option, but letting the villagers see him still seemed like a terrible idea. He didn't need to rush into a potentially hazardous experience, he could wait a little longer. Since selling the hide was out of the question, he knew he needed to figure out a way to use it or any future hides he obtained. He was confident he could figure out how to utilize any he got, but from experience he knew the hides would eventually rot and he had no idea how to prevent that.

Thinking back to the family of hunters, he remembered the father and son skinning animals. Much of their clothing looked homemade, which must mean they had a way to preserve those hides. Maybe sometime he would go see what the family did with their animal hides. By now, the rabbit had finished cooking. Biting into the meat when it had cooled, it had the same gamey texture as rabbit but it tasted strangely like the venison he had occasionally had for dinner in Forna. After lunch, he headed out to hunt. Whatever he needed to do with the hide, he knew it could wait for a while; food was a more pressing concern.

From the cabin, he made his way to the creek where he had found deer tracks the day before. Following along the shore he headed in the opposite direction as yesterday. After about an hour of walking, he settled down in the shade beneath a birch tree to rest his feet. As he sat there listening to the relaxing murmur of the creek, he caught sight of a weasel poking its head out of a hole in the tree's trunk above him. With his nearly disastrous encounter with the big cat still looming in his mind, he welcomed the presence of this small creature.

Slowly he reached into his pocket, removing a piece of meat from his leftover deer rabbit and held it up to his beady-eyed guest. Cautiously, the weasel took it before dashing down the tree and off into the forest. The weasel reappeared a few minutes later. Hyroc put a tiny piece of meat in his palm, resting his upturned hand on the ground in front of him. The weasel came over to his hand, tentatively sniffing; recoiling several times as it slowly drew closer. Once the weasel had a hold of the meat, it ran a short distance away before stopping to eat its prize.

Hyroc put another piece of meat in his hand. Having downed the meat scraps, the weasel stood up on its hind legs to sniff the air. It dropped back on all fours, coming toward his hand without showing much trepidation. The weasel touched the end of his fingers with its nose and pulled back. Hyroc remained motionless as the weasel leaned forward toward his hand again. It snapped up the meat then surprised him by dashed up his arm. The weasel jerkily worked its way to the top of his head. Hyroc felt a tickle on one of his ears as the animal sniffed it. Without warning, it sank its needle-sharp teeth into his ear. He yelled out in pain as he threw his hand at the top of his head. Startled, the mischievous creature leapt from his head and disappeared back into the tree. Touching his ear, Hyroc was irritated to see a globule of blood on the tips of his fingers.

Not wanting to risk another ambush by the evil weasel, he ventured to the opposite shore of the creek via a rocky crossing not far from where he was attacked. He found some yarrow on the edge of some trees ringing a hill. He cut off the yarrow's white flowers and held them on his ear. As he stood there waiting for the plant to stop the bleeding, he noticed a rabbit lying at the base of the hill to his right. He gently let go of the yarrow, which was now delicately stuck in place by congealing blood, and silently nocked an arrow. Right before he let it fly, he realized the rabbit wasn't moving or breathing, it looked dead.

As he cautiously walked over to the dead rabbit, he saw a strange silvery moss covering its back legs. When he touched the moss, it stuck to his hand, pulling uncomfortably on his fur. He had never heard of this kind of moss. When he grabbed the rabbit by the midsection, it was squishy like someone had filled a water skin full of cheese curds and a whitish pink substance began oozing out of every orifice. Startled, Hyroc dropped the rabbit. The carcass hit the ground with a wet slap. As he resisted the urge to be sick – he got the eerie feeling something was watching him. Grabbing a hold of the hilt of his sword, he scanned the surrounding terrain. He saw nothing but the disturbing feeling remained. Stealing a glance at the rabbit-curd-sack, he realized he had probably scared off whatever was feeding on the rabbit and it was probably watching him right now. It seemed wise to avoid incurring the wrath of whatever could do this to a rabbit. While keeping an eye out, he unsheathed his knife to cut off a piece of the moss. He was a little surprised how tough it was; it was harder than cutting through the heavy twine he made his snares out of. Moving his knife in a sawing motion across its surface, the moss began to come apart more easily. After a few more tense seconds, he cut a chunk off. Sticking it in his pocket, he hurriedly left the area the way he had come, listening for any sound of pursuit.

At the edge of the ring of trees, he stole a glance at the rabbit to see if he could spot the thing that was feeding on it. The rabbit carcass was missing, but he caught a glimpse of a dark shape disappearing behind the rise of the hill. The shape moved in a disturbing manner, as if it had more than four legs. Disturbed, he decided fishing for the rest of the day at the cabin was a great idea and made his way back to the cabin with his hand on his sword hilt the entire way.

CHAPTER 20

Two Brothers

O ver the following days, Hyroc settled into a routine of checking his traps in the morning and then spending the rest of the day hunting. He saw the mountain cat he shared the mountain with watching him from a distance on numerous occasions as he performed his daily chores. The sightings made him wary, as he knew she was probably trying to figure out if he would make a tasty meal. Despite his fears, she always seemed to keep her distance and avoided wandering near the areas where he set his traps. He in turn was careful to stay away from any of her hunting grounds and kept himself from cresting the rise leading to her cave. Slowly he lost some of his distrust toward her, giving her the name Huntress, but he never forgot she could kill him if she were so inclined. Still, as she was the closest thing to company he had had since leaving Forna, he felt an odd sort of attachment to her.

One day, just after checking his traps, which had frustratingly remained empty since the deer rabbit, he came across deer tracks within the ravine. They led him off the mountain, into the forest below. After tracking the animal for most of the day, he found a small doe. The deer stood in a gap between the trees, facing away from him with a single pine covered in thickly clumped branches at its back. He crept toward the tree, keeping its trunk between him and his quarry. Peeking through the branches, he nocked one of the steel arrows. He silently lined up his shot through a space between two branches.

Another arrow whistled through the air from his right, striking the deer in the chest. The deer took two steps before collapsing onto the ground. Hyroc lurched back, dropping down behind the cover of the tree's bottom branches as two boys came into view. He recognized them as the two boys from the family of hunters. The older boy carried a bow and wore a leather quiver on his back, while the younger one only carried a single sheathed hunting knife on his belt. Hyroc watched helplessly as the two boys approached the dead deer to claim it as their own. He hated the happy looks on their faces; those feelings should have been his. He was so close to killing the deer. It didn't belong to them!

He very much wanted to contest the fact this was his deer, but that seemed like a very bad idea. He could only imagine how they would react if he showed himself. The oldest boy was liable to put an arrow in him the moment he came into view. Then even if he managed to survive the encounter, everyone in the village would know he was here. It would be better to stay hidden until the two of them left with his stolen kill and resume hunting.

"Donovan, I thought I saw something," Hyroc heard the youngest boy say. He felt a surge of dread at the words. For an instant, he saw himself getting skinned, his head mounted on a wall. His heart pounded away inside his chest as he frantically looked for an escape route.

"There's no one here," the oldest boy said in an annoyed tone. "If this was someone else's game, they would've come out and said so by now."

Peeking through the branches, Hyroc saw the younger boy step closer to his brother as he pointed at the tree he was sheltering behind. "Do you think it was that monster?"

The oldest boy sighed, "I already told you it's not real, grandpa was just telling you that story to frighten you into behaving. You know how he is."

"But when I was in town with mother the other day I overheard Harold say something about people's animals going missing."

"Father told me livestock get lost in these woods all the time or taken by wolves. It's unfortunate but there's nothing unusual about it, it just happens. You know this area as well as I do; I wouldn't worry about anything happening to either of us. But we should be more worried about *Jägerin* smelling this kill, she hunts down here sometimes. So, you need to help me skin this carcass because I don't want to get between her and a meal." The youngest boy stared at Hyroc's tree a moment longer, before turning toward the carcass.

Hyroc was somewhat disturbed by mention of a monster and people's animals were disappearing. His thoughts turned to the shadowed thing he had seen at the hill with the dead rabbit. Could it have been the monster the boy was talking about? He felt a cold shiver run up his back at the thought. His luck couldn't possibly be that bad. How could he have found the one place on his map where there were actually monsters. He shook his head. No, it was like what the older boy said, it was just a story to make the younger one behave. Adults said things like that to young children all the time. Why would this place be any different? It was just a story. There wasn't a monster. But then what killed the rabbit? He stiffened a little, but pushed the thought aside. He had more important things to worry about for the time being.

The oldest boy drew his knife and slit the deer's throat, releasing a steady stream of blood from its neck. Preoccupied with the carcass, the two boys were no longer looking in Hyroc's direction. He saw his chance to escape, but realized this was also an opportunity to see how to properly deal with a deer carcass. Though he could probably figure it out on his own, it would make the process much easier if he watched someone do it.

At least I could get something useful out of losing my deer, again.

Settling into a more comfortable position, he attentively watched the two boys work. By now, the blood had almost stopped flowing. Starting at the deer's rear end, the oldest boy cut down along the belly, continuing up through the chest, stopping at the chin. Then he and the youngest boy began removing the innards. Once finished, the two of them made a cut down the inside of each leg. Then they made a circular cut above the hooves. After the legs, starting at the belly, they began cutting the hide free of the carcass, slowly working their way up to the neck. At the base of the skull, they simply pulled the remaining dermis off the head like a fleshy sock. The oldest boy draped the hide over a branch with the fleshy side out, removed a hatchet from his belt, chopped off two long limbs and several branches from a tree. Using the limbs as a base, the two boys set the branches across them, forming what appeared to be a ladder, then they tied it together with twine. The oldest boy rolled the skinless deer onto their sled, and the youngest boy set the hide alongside the carcass. After tying a length of rope to the ladder, the two boys grabbed a hold of it and started dragging the ladder away.

At least now, Hyroc had some idea of what to do with any deer he killed. He waited until he was sure the two boys were out of earshot, before stretching his legs and resuming his hunt. On his way back up to the mountain he managed to kill a grouse and then a deer rabbit before dark. As he picked his way across the mountain slopes with the animals dangling from his belt, out of the corner of his eye he caught sight of a dark shape moving through the trees below him. Turning his head in the direction of the shape, he saw nothing. Cupping a hand over his eyes to block out the setting sun, he studied the spot where he thought the shape had been. He started when he heard the distant shriek of a dying rabbit behind him. Wheeling around, his hand flying to the hilt of his sword, he saw Huntress farther up the mountain holding a lifeless rabbit in her jaws. She stopped to look at him. He relaxed slightly as she slinked off toward her lair. When he turned back to look at the spot below him, he froze as he saw a shadowed shape through a gap between the trunks of the trees. A shiver ran up his back when it felt as if many eyes were suddenly watching him. He blinked and the shape was gone, but the feeling remained. Worried, he rapidly made his way back to his cabin. It seemed his luck might be *that* bad

CHAPTER 21

Skittering Shadow

When Hyroc opened the cabin's door, enormous raindrops and an ugly dark gray sunless sky greeted his eyes. It looked like his day was going to be one of cold wet misery. Reluctant to feel the soggy embrace of the deluge, he waited for about an hour for a break in the storm. After the time had passed, the weather seemed no better. Loathing purposely going out in this, he pulled his jerkin tight, donned his cloak, put the hood up, and collected his gear before heading out into the downpour.

When he reached his nearest trap, it was empty. On his way to the next trap at the ravine, he was pleased to see the rain starting to let up. Then it slowed to a sprinkle and the sun managed to poke through a tiny opening in the clouds. The reprieve caused some of the birds hiding in their shelters amongst the trees to start twittering to one another.

Sometime before noon, he had checked all his other traps; he just needed to do the one near Huntress's lair. The sky began to darken once more when he reached the incline running up to her lair and the raindrops grew more frequent. Soon it seemed he would be returned to the discomfort of getting soaked. His trap was also empty. He sighed irritably; if he wanted to get something to eat today, it looked like he had to either fish or hunt in the rain. The fishing would be better in the rain and he might be able to find a tree to sit beneath while he did so, so he would fish.

As he turned to leave, he noticed rabbit bones littering the ground. It seemed strange as he had yet to catch anything in the vicinity. Then he spotted the paw prints of a large cat. That was why his trap had always come up empty here, he had actually been catching things, but Huntress had been stealing from it. He shrugged dejectedly; feeling stupid for thinking this wouldn't happen so close to her lair. It would be hard for her not to notice helpless prey over here. Admitting defeat, he began disassembling his trap to find a better spot for it.

He had just started when he heard the soft cooing of a wood grouse. Looking in the direction of the sound, he saw the fowl sheltering beneath a spruce tree. Quietly, he put the trap down and nocked an arrow. He took a step forward to get a better shot but the grouse fluttered out of view behind the concealment of a tree farther up the incline. He studied the top of the incline a long moment, then cautiously made his way up it. The bird was still way away from Huntress' cave. He spooked the grouse yet again and it disappeared over the top of the incline. Fighting his growing trepidation, he warily peeked over the rim. He saw the grouse amongst a patch of bushes growing along the stony prominence of the cliff face. Those bushes were dangerously close to the stone ramp leading up to the cave. The bird was so close! Getting it would save him a lot of work and he needed every bit of meat he could find. It seemed risky to pass up this opportunity. Because if he didn't catch anything today, he might be going hungry tonight.

If he was quick about it, he might be able to get the grouse before Huntress even knew he was there. He swept his eyes through the area. She wasn't anywhere he could see. He nodded determinedly to himself. It would only be for a second. He lined up his shot, letting his arrow fly. The arrow struck the fowl dead center. Taking a deep breath to stoke his courage, he hurried over to recover the bird. As he reached down to pick it up, he became aware that the forest had gone eerily quiet, like there was a much worse storm coming. He gave the sky a quick glance; but it seemed the same as it was a moment ago.

He froze, immediately forgetting about the grouse, as he heard the terrifying sound of a mountain cat's growl emanate from the cave. The growling intensified, growing in both volume and threat. That was all the encouraging to leave he needed. As he hurriedly turned to leave, he heard something rustling through the bushes near the cave. Stealing a terrified glance in the direction of the rustling, he glimpsed a black shape dashing into the cave. The shape moved in an unnerving fashion, making the hair on the back of his neck stand on end. It seemed as if it were walking on more than four legs. Suddenly, Huntress roared, making his back itch with sweat. A cacophony of ferocious noises erupted from inside the cave. Hyroc tried not to imagine what was going on inside its confines. Then everything went deathly quiet, except for an unnerving scraping noise from inside the cave.

He nocked an arrow and took aim at the entrance of the cave while backing away toward the incline. Whatever could kill an animal as powerful as a mountain lion, he had no intentions to meet it. He had taken one step when he heard the shuffling of an unbelievable amount of feet from within the cave. A small light brown streak shot out of the cave. He instantly lost track of the streak as an enormous black spider the size of a large dog, shuffled out of the cave. The spider's body was black with flecks of iridescent reds and purples, covered in many thick bristly hairs, and eight branching legs, each ending in a single curved claw. Multiple soulless orb-like eyes adorned the top of its head. Below these was a mouth with two large hooked fangs, dripping a dark yellow-brown substance.

Hyroc yelled out in a mixture of surprise and absolute horror. The spider abandoned its pursuit of the streak, turning toward him. A shiver ran up his spine and his blood ran cold as he met its gaze. Without even thinking, he took aim and loosed his arrow.

His arrow found its mark right in one of the creatures' eyes. The eye ruptured releasing a torrent of black oily blood. The spider let out an earsplitting hissing screech, which seemed to suck all warmth out of the world, then it charged. Before it could get close, Hyroc nailed it with a second arrow. It let out another horrendous screech before slumping to the ground dead.

He spotted another spider shape above him, running along the vertical cliff face to his left. This one seemed larger than the one he had just killed. He hastily nocked another arrow and let it fly. Hands unsteadied by fear, he missed. His arrow struck the cliff face, splintering to pieces. Just as he had another arrow in hand, the spider wheeled around, and leapt off the cliff face at him. The spider crashed into him, slamming him onto his back. He felt an unbearable burning pain in his right shoulder as if a hot knife had been driven into his flesh as one of the spider's fangs stabbed its way into the muscle.

The spider pulled its head back, causing the single fang in his shoulder to rip loose. His vision flashed red and he screamed out in pain. As the spider slammed its fangs down again, fighting through the pain, Hyroc wedged both his feet underneath its body. He barely managed to hold back the strike; the deadly dripping fangs hovered mere inches from his body. Using two of its back legs as leverage, the spider pushed toward him harder. It took nearly all his strength to continue holding the fangs back. The spider started tearing at his face with its clawed feet. He turned his head out of the way to keep his eyes from being ripped out. He pulled his knife out and drove it into one of the spider's eyes. The spider opened its mouth, revealing numerous pointed black teeth, and screeched out in pain. The sound was almost deafening this close to its mouth. The creature fell to the ground, scratching at the knife with one of its legs. Hyroc scrambled out from underneath the spider, jumping to his feet.

No sooner had he drawn his sword than the spider recovered from the pain and lunged at him. He gave the creature a hard downward stroke with his sword. The sword strike slammed the spider into the ground, cutting an enormous gash across its head. It howled out in pain. He frantically gave the spider another strike. The creature's legs twitched a few times before they stopped moving altogether.

He gave the spider's body a jab with his boot, but it gave no response; it was dead. He took several deep breaths before slipping his hand under his jerkin to examine the wound on his shoulder. It was a big circular puncture, and a steady stream of blood was running down his arm. He cut a chunk of cloth from his undershirt, and bound the wound with it.

As he did this, he suddenly felt fatigued and dizzy. The sudden onset caused him to fall forward and he barely caught himself with his outstretched arms. He shook his head to clear it away, but that had no effect. Then he noticed a dark yellow-brown substance mixed with his blood on the tips of his fingers. An overwhelming bolt of fear shot through him when he realized the substance was probably some sort of venom and he had been poisoned.

He needed to find help! The only people he had any hope of reaching was the family of hunters. They would think he was a monster, but if he didn't do something he would die anyway. When he stood, everything began to spin and he lost his balance, falling onto his back. He tried to get to his feet. His limbs felt unbearably heavy and he lacked the strength to move them. His vision began to blur, the edges of his vision darkening. Terror crept into his mind as he realized with despair he was going to die. After everything he had gone through, this was how he was going to die. *I'm sorry June I couldn't keep my promise.* As he slipped into darkness, he thought he saw a large white shape walking on all fours, trudging toward him.

CHAPTER 22

Ursa

When Hyroc opened his eyes, he saw light filtering through the needle covered branches of a spruce tree he was laying beneath. A bitter acrid taste hung in the back of his throat and he felt weak. It seemed strange he had decided to sleep outside when he had a cabin. He sat bolt upright when the terrifying memory of the spider attack poured into his mind. A sharp pain shot through his shoulder and he felt the painful cracking and popping of a scab. Sweeping his eyes around, he saw to his right lay the bottom of the incline that led to what used to be Huntress' cave. He even saw his partially disassembled trap on it. This wasn't where he had lost consciousness. The only logical explanation was someone had moved him. He was of course grateful no matter how out of place it seemed. He just didn't think anyone who saw him would think of treating him in such a considerate manner.

Lowering his gaze, he was confused to see a blanket of soft green moss laid across him. *Why would somebody use a mat of moss to cover me with instead of a regular blanket or a coat?* Pulling his other arm out from under the blanket, he reached up to feel the spot on his shoulder where the pain had emanated. A thin layer of what felt like yarrow coated the rough surface of an enormous scab. Turning his gaze skyward, he saw only a few elongated dirty white clouds dotting the sky. It seemed unusual such a heavy rainstorm would have dissipated within the day.

A cawing noise drew his attention to a tree at the bottom of the incline. Perched on a branch he saw a raven with silvery markings on either side of its neck, watching him. It had to be the same bird he had seen when he first arrived at the cabin. Having seen its markings three times, the chances they were caused by the sun seemed extremely unlikely. Was it scavenging the guts from the animals he killed? That seemed a reasonable explanation but something about the silvery markings on the bird's neck gave him the feeling this might not be an ordinary bird.

He heard the sound of something moving through the foliage to his right. Snapping his head toward the sound, he was horrified to see the white bear that had killed the three witch hunters emerging from the undergrowth, with a plant in its mouth.

Hyroc flew out from under the moss blanket to his feet. Just as he reached for his sword, everything around him began to spin, causing him to lose his balance. He caught himself with an outstretched arm in time to prevent his face from plowing into the ground. A sudden fatigue engulfed his body followed by an overwhelming nauseous causing him to start dry retching. The two symptoms were so debilitating it prevented him from making any kind of meaningful movements toward obeying the overpowering urge to run.

The bear dropped the plant on the ground next to him. He saw the mangled remains of the three men's bodies flash through his mind's eye. No matter how hard he willed his body to move, he remained doubled over on the ground. He was going to die!

"You should not have tried standing yet," the bear said in what sounded like a woman's voice. "You're still suffering the aftereffects of the spider venom."

Between a heave Hyroc stared at the bear flabbergasted; it was speaking! He then noticed a silver necklace chain around the bear's neck with a translucent twisted ruby spike attached to it. Wrapped around each ankle, the bear had a band of silver decorated with wavy etchings. On its shoulders and hips, it had dark blue swirly markings.

The bear sat on the ground beside him, using its large paw to slide the plant it had dropped closer to him. "When the sickness passes, eat this; it will help."

Hyroc continued to stare at the bear; not only was it talking, it was offering him medicine. He heaved two more times before the nausea subsided. Falling into a sitting position, he wiped his mouth on his sleeve, continuing to stare at the bear in astonishment. *This has to be a dream.* He pushed one of his claws into the side of his snout.

"No, you're not dreaming," the bear said, sounding slightly amused.

"You – you can talk?" Hyroc stammered.

The bear regarded him curiously. "Yes."

"*You're a witch.*"

The bear narrowed her eyes. "I'm affronted you would even consider calling me *that*," she said coolly. "The Ministry ignorantly uses such terms to describe every kind of magic as evil regardless of its purpose. Very few kinds of magic can be considered as evil; it is the caster who determines what purpose their magic will be used for. They understood this at their beginning, but they are now far too busy convicting the bakers of apple dumplings of witchcraft to see the true dangers of this world. You for one would be in a far worse condition if I had not healed you; can you call that evil hmm?"

Hyroc stared at the bear in bewilderment a long moment trying to make sense of its words before speaking again. "You – you healed me?"

"That is what I just said, is it not? I do not make a habit of telling falsehoods."

He gave the bear a blank look. Witches who altered their bodies to look like an animal were not known for their stable demeanor or logical lines of reasoning, let alone something so kind as healing others. She obviously wasn't a type of witch he was familiar with, but that didn't mean much since many classes of witches shared similar traits. Just because a witch seemed reasonable in one regard didn't mean they were in others. They might only know how to trick people into believing their intentions were good. And many times, once someone did, they would regret it very quickly. The only question was, why was this witch bothering to trick him? She had a clear advantage over him with her being a powerful bear and him severely weakened by spider venom. Why not just do whatever she planned and be done with it, there wasn't a whole lot he could do about it. Maybe he was missing something. If he could figure out what that something was, he might be able to play it to his advantage. And get out of this alive.

"Not to sound ungrateful," Hyroc probed, trying to sound as polite as possible. "I really am grateful, but why did you do that for me?"

"Because you are my charge and I am your protector."

"Protector?" Hyroc thought back to when the bear had attacked those men. If she was protecting him killing those men seemed a reasonable explanation for her actions. But why? What was she getting out of keeping him safe? "Wait, so you killed those three men to protect me?"

"Of course," she said as if nothing could be plainer.

It seemed a little risky, but challenging her claim might be the fastest way for him to learn something of her plan. So long as she didn't rip his head off. "If you're truly my protector, then why was that the first time I had ever seen you? There were plenty of instances where I needed protecting when I was in Forna."

"You only became my charge after the man who adopted you passed. But to answer your question, I'm only supposed to make my presence known if the life of my charge is threatened, as it was with those three men and the spiders, or until it's favorable to do so."

Hyroc gave her a confused look. That wasn't remotely close to what he was expecting her to say. That couldn't have been the truth. This was about something else. As far as he knew – beyond maybe the Hallowed Knights – there weren't protectors roaming the world and intervening whenever someone's life was in danger. "What about the night the prefect and his toadies hung me –" Hyroc paused, remembering the eyes he saw watching him in the dark. "That was you I saw that night wasn't it?"

"It was."

Hyroc flung his hand through the air, accidentally letting some of his dredged-up emotions free. "I nearly froze to death that night! Why didn't you help me then if I'm under your protection?"

"I saw no need to intervene and if I recall correctly you got yourself out of that situation without any help. Overcoming difficulties makes one stronger."

Hyroc gave her a questioning look. Her words almost sounded like something Marcus might have said. "Maybe, but I've had plenty of difficulties to overcome, I don't think helping me with one would have done any harm." Though he suspected that might have done a lot of harm.

The bear snorted in annoyance. "You lived, that's all that matters." She indicated the plant in front of Hyroc with her paw. "Unless you require further proof of the validity of my good intentions, eat some of the leaves, you'll feel better."

Hyroc studied the bear thoughtfully. This whole situation still didn't make any sense, but he had run out of things to question, and she didn't seem like she wanted to hurt him. And he didn't think a psychotic witch could even pretend to sound so reassuring. Maybe she meant every word she said.

Without taking his eyes off her, he tentatively grabbed the plant. After making sure the leafy parts didn't have thorns, he stuck one in his mouth. A cooling sensation spread through his mouth as he chewed, and when he swallowed, it helped settle his churning stomach.

The bear shook her head indignantly. "You'll need to take more than just one leaf or it's not going to do you much good."

Deciding the plant wasn't poisonous, he put a handful of the leaves into his mouth. A much stronger cooling sensation spread through his mouth and his stomach started to feel much better.

"Feel better?" Hyroc nodded, hoping he wasn't about to turn into a toad or something else slimy. "See, I'm not going to hurt you."

"I'm still not entirely convinced, for all I know you like your prey healthy before you kill it."

The bear snorted. "That's ridiculous, sick prey is easier to catch. If I wanted to harm you, don't you think I would have by now?"

Hyroc gave her a perplexed look. That same thought had been playing around in the back of his mind. He couldn't really think of another reason for her to hold back. "How did you know I needed you? Did someone send you?"

She turned her head to look at the raven still perched on the branch. "See that bird up there? His name is Shimmer." The raven fluttered its wings at Hyroc in what oddly seemed a greeting. "He helps me keep an eye on you from a distance. Whenever he sees something that could be dangerous to you, he comes and tells me of it. Then I decide how to deal with it."

"That's why I've only ever seen him when something bad happened."

"Precisely. I can sense when you're in danger but not specifically what's threatening you. Shimmer just gives me a better idea of what's going on."

Her story was steadily making more sense. Maybe there truly wasn't anything else going on with her. "Okay so, you're my protector, and you're obviously not a witch, so what are you then?"

"I am a Guardian."

"What do you guard?"

"Right now, I'm guarding you, but along with that, we keep things in balance and fight darkness wherever it appears."

"So, you're not some enchanted animal."

"Of course not," she said in an amused tone.

Hyroc grabbed a hold of the silver disc of his necklace and held it away from his neck toward the bear. "Do you know what these symbols mean?"

"Ah, I was wondering when you'd get around to asking me that. Give it here," she said, holding out her paw.

Hyroc slipped his necklace off, hanging it on the end of her paw. She lifted the necklace up to her eyes. She studied each side, showing more interest with something on the back, then she returned it. "You obviously know the name on the front is your first name and the one on the back is your last or family name. But tell me what you know about the symbols?"

"I assume the fox means intelligence, I think the badger means bravery, but I have no idea about the claw symbol, and the bear doesn't make any sense."

The bear gave him a puzzled look. "Why doesn't the bear symbol make sense?"

Hyroc scratched the back of his head. "Because bears represent strength and I wasn't exactly the toughest kid in the school."

"Wrong kind of strength." She slammed her paw into the ground, startling Hyroc with the force of the impact. "*That* is physical strength, and yes, bears mostly represent that, but they also represent strength here," she lightly touched the side of her head with her paw. "And here," she said, before touching her chest where her heart was. "Body, mind, and heart. What else does a bear represent?"

"Isn't that about it?"

The bear exhaled in what sounded like a sigh. "What do mother bears do?"

Hyroc thought a moment before saying, "Protect their cubs?"

"Correct."

"But that's what *female* bears do. From what I've heard, the males usually eat cubs instead of protecting them? So wouldn't that mean I'd have to be a girl for that quality to apply to me?"

"No, male bears fight other males to protect a female they want to mate with. It's not quite the same thing when it comes to people – most of the time – so don't take it too literally, but you understand my meaning. Strength, resilience, and protection are the three main things a bear represents."

"Okay I think the bear makes more sense now, but I don't understand the badger."

"Why do you say that?"

"Because I don't exactly see myself as a brave person. I know I'm definitely not a coward, but I'm far from brave. Back at the boarding school, I spent most of my time running or hiding in trees from bullies rather than facing them."

"That doesn't make you a coward, you may have ran and hid, but in the end you refused to let them beat you down and you decided to fight back.

"Only when they cornered me."

"That's not what matters. They pushed you down, you got right back up, and pushed back. Have you ever seen the way a badger defends a carcass? I've seen them chase off black bears, wolves, and mountain lions, who are three or even four times their size. That's not so dissimilar to what you did." Hyroc nodded in thankful acceptance. At least she had said something good about him.

She paused. "The fox symbol; well, I wouldn't necessarily say it means intelligence, but yes they are clever creatures. Most people consider them cunning and sly, but that really doesn't describe you. Instead of barreling headlong into a chicken coop, the way a wolf or a bear might, they often hang back and watch, looking for an opening." Hyroc smiled a little; that seemed to be what he often did.

"The claw symbol," she continued. "The Mark of the Dragon Hunter."

Hyroc perked up. That sounded promising "Dragon hunter, what does that mean?"

"It's the symbol of a great hunter. In every culture – if you don't already know – the killing of a dragon is the greatest achievement anyone may accomplish, because they are one of the hardest creatures to fell. It's unsurprising the man who adopted you or any of his colleagues were unable to identify the symbol; it is very old and very rare. You should be honored to have it." Awe washed over Hyroc and he gained a sudden feeling of worth.

"Now, explain to me what possessed you to get close to a cave when you knew full well a dangerous predator resided inside?"

Hyroc gave her a surprised look, caught off guard by the sudden change in subject. "I was hunting."

The bear shook her head. "The fact you were putting yourself in direct competition with a predator, *especially one with cubs*, by hunting a tiny meat bird just outside the cave is a kind of idiocy I have not heard the likes of for a long time. If those spiders hadn't shown up and killed her, she would have severally injured you instead. But fortunately for you, you're still breathing despite your stupidity. And that spider bite will serve you as a reminder to think twice before you do anything like that again. You can't expect to crack open a bee hive and not get stung."

"Don't get mad at me for *that*!" Hyroc snapped. "I needed food and you haven't exactly been much of a help."

"You almost died because of that mistake," she growled. "Do not shift the blame onto me when you were the one solely responsible for a poor decision."

"Alright fine." It seemed somewhat perilous to continue disagreeing with a large bear. "It was stupid I went up there and I'll make sure I don't do it again."

"That would be wise."

There was a long pause. "Where did those things come from anyway, I've never heard of spiders that big?" Or talking bears that weren't witches.

"They normally stick to thickly forested areas where there's plenty of shade and places with caves; they don't have much love for sunlight. And normally they hunt in groups of three or four. Since you only ran into two of them, I would assume those two were just a rogue pair."

"So there shouldn't be any more of them?"

"No, I wouldn't expect so." Hyroc nodded, feeling a little more relieved. "We've talked enough; I need to get you to the shelter of your wooden den to rest. Try getting to your feet."

Using the branch of a tree as support Hyroc slowly pulled himself to his feet. He got dizzy and stumbled, making the bear take a quick step toward him in what seemed preparation to catch him, but he remained standing.

"There's something I'd like to take care of first," he said, steadying himself. "Help me get up to the mountain lion's lair at the top of that incline."

"I already took care of that for you."

Hyroc gave her a surprised look. "You buried her and her cub?"

The bear nodded, "Shimmer told me about the way you acted around her and I figured that's what you would have done if you were able."

"You should have waited," Hyroc said downtrodden. She was just an animal but they were neighbors of sorts and burying her felt like his duty.

"Be glad I didn't, you would not have liked what you would have seen."

Hyroc cocked an eyebrow. "What is that supposed to mean? I hunt animals; I know what death looks like."

"Not like this you don't. Spiders kill with venom and that venom breaks down the flesh and sinew of their prey."

Hyroc paused, a disgusting thought suddenly entered his mind. "Are you saying that – that their bodies melted?"

"Basically." Hyroc felt nauseous again envisioning that. "Like I said, 'be glad I didn't.'" Lowering her head, the bear used her jaws to pick up the plant she had made Hyroc eat and offered it to him. He stuck another handful of leaves in his mouth. He accepted the rest of the plant from her, then she started leading him back toward his cabin.

"Why hasn't what happened to the mountain lion happened to me?" Hyroc said, as they walked.

"You have to be dead for the venom to affect you that way. A small dose weakens you; a moderate amount knocks you unconscious, and a large amount usually kills you. You got a fairly large dose, but it was still not enough to kill you out right. But over the course of that day you would not have survived if not for my intervention."

"What do you mean 'that day'? How long was I out?"

"Nearly a full day."

Hyroc gave her a startled look. "That explains why the rainstorm seemed to have vanished so quickly. Does size make a difference with the venom?"

"Yes, the bigger you are the more resilient you are to its effects so more is required and the opposite if you're smaller."

Hyroc fished around in his pocket, withdrawing the piece of sticky moss he had taken from the rabbit. "Do you know what this is?" he said, holding it out in front of her. "I found it on what I think was a spider kill?"

"It's spider silk. They usually wrap their victims in it and drag them to a safe place to eat them.

Hyroc frowned. "That must be disturbing."

"Extremely."

When Hyroc laid down on his bed, he was amazed by how much the short journey to his cabin had drained his strength. The bear headed off and he quickly dozed. He awoke to the sound of heavy clawed feet walking on his porch. Not fully awake, in a confused flurry, he sat up grabbing the hilt of his sword. He relaxed when he saw the white bear dropping several green stocks of a different plant inside his cabin's door.

"You should be able to keep these down," the bear said. "You're lucky these are still in season."

"What are they?"

"Cow parsnips, but you have to get them while they don't put your tongue to sleep." She paused. "Returning to what I was saying, only eat a little at a time, make sure you peel them first, and drink plenty of water. When you wake in the morning most of the affects you experienced today will have subsided, and your appetite should return. But be careful with that arm, it will be some time before the wound properly heals. Shimmer and I will be keeping a much closer eye on you from now on. If you need something, mark the trunk of the birch tree on the other side of the stream at the western side of the valley with animal blood. But make sure you only do it over something important, otherwise you'll make me grumpy and if you know anything about bears, you won't want that." Hyroc nodded his acknowledgment. Pulling her head from his cabin's doorway, she turned to leave.

"Wait, what's your name," Hyroc called out.

The bear turned her head back toward him. "My name is Ursa." With that, she left.

Hyroc stared at the opposite wall of the cabin trying to make sense of his day. Today was definitely something new for him. He had found out giant horrifying spiders existed and he had never had dinner given to him by a talking death bear. *What was this place?*

CHAPTER 23

An Unexpected Friend

A shaft of warm morning sunlight roused Hyroc from his sleep as it slowly crept across his face. Rubbing the sleep from his eyes, he groggily sat up. He grimaced as a dull throbbing pain radiated through his right shoulder and partway down his upper arm as he put weight on it. Then he became aware of an intense itching underneath the massive scab. Resisting the strong temptation to scratch his shoulder raw, he gingerly put on his boots and got off the bed. Dizziness came over him as he stood, but it soon passed. He stared at the cow parsnips laid in front of the fireplace. Though he felt substantially better than he had yesterday, the mere idea of eating food made him feel a little sick. As unappealing as it seemed, he knew he still needed to eat something. Pushing through his reluctance, he grabbed a parsnip and took a small bite. It didn't make him want to throw up when he swallowed, so he took another bite. Then much of his remaining sick feelings disappeared.

After breakfast, he donned his bow and quiver. Coming through the front door, he spotted Shimmer watching the cabin from a tree branch. He regarded the large black bird thoughtfully a moment, before going to the streambed to fill his water skin. From there he made his way toward the mountain to check his traps.

To his dismay, all were empty. When he had finished with the last trap, convincing himself the spiders were no longer at the cliff face, he cautiously made his way to the incline leading to it. From a safe distance, he watched the area for any sign of the spiders. He got a start when a shadow passed over the ground in front of him. Focusing on the shadow, it was in the shape of a bird. Above him, he saw a circling black bird. It was Shimmer, again. He swiped his arm angrily through the air. "Get out of here," Hyroc yelled at the bird. "You just startled me." That was the last thing he needed in a place where he had nearly died days before. He received an angry squawk in return and Shimmer made no move to stop circling. With a sigh, Hyroc began warily reassembling his trap. Since Huntress was dead, there wasn't any reason for him to move his trap. He couldn't help being a little sad at that fact. It had actually been kind of fun trying to figure out how to avoid her. Now their game had ended.

Still feeling some effects from the spider venom sickness, he was in no mood for wondering around for hours hunting and decided to fish in the stream next to his cabin instead. About an hour in, he caught a small trout. After dispatching the fish with a quick stab through the brain, he gutted it, laying its innards on the ground beside him to use as bait. He turned away from the innards to move his pole closer, but when he turned back to bait his hook, the piece he had set aside to use first was missing. He raised his leg to see if he had accidentally sat on it. There wasn't anything beneath him. Shaking his head in puzzlement, he baited his hook with another piece and cast his line.

Shimmer alighted on the branch of a tree on the other side of the stream then began preening his wings. The bird suddenly stopped, making a bobbing motion with his head as if he were looking at something. Glancing behind him, Hyroc caught sight of a small slender shape darting into the underbrush. Moving his eyes to his bait, he saw another piece had vanished. Then where the shape had disappeared, he saw a weasel peeking at him through the foliage. He recognized it as the same weasel that had bitten his ear at the creek. He sighed irritably as he set down his pole and stood. Grabbing his bow, he fitted an arrow to the bowstring and started backing away from his pile of bait. When he was about ten paces from the fish, the weasel tentatively stepped out of its hiding place. Drawing the bowstring back, Hyroc eagerly waited for the weasel to move farther away from cover so he could put a sharpening shaft through the beady-eyed miscreant. The weasel took a few more steps forward, then stopped to test the air. That was all Hyroc needed. The light brown, speckled shape of a cat exploded out of the bush onto the weasel. With a quick bite to the neck, the cat dispatched its prey.

A bolt of fear shot through Hyroc seeing the cat was a speckled mountain lion cub. Heart pounding, he held his bow at the ready as he rapidly scanned the surrounding forest, searching for any signs of the cub's mother. Seeing none, he backed away from the cub, listening intently for any sound of her approach. When he was a comfortable distance away, not wanting to leave his pole, he impatiently waited for the kitten's mother to arrive and retrieve it.

Several minutes passed, but the cub's mother never appeared. It seemed strange a cub this young would be so far from its mother. Had it been abandoned? It dawned on him the cub might have been the blur he saw escaping from those spiders. He waited until he was certain his assumption was correct, before slowly making his way back over to his fishing pole. When he got close, the cub raised its head and made a growling noise at him. Hyroc froze, looking around to see if there was a furious adult cat tearing toward him. To his relief, he didn't.

He stood there looking at the cub and the cub returned his gaze. Neither one of them had parents, siblings or anyone that cared if they died, or at least, not anymore. The cub was a survivor like him. It didn't simply lie down and die. It had escaped its fate. The odds were stacked against it, but it was determined to live. The two of them were not so different. He had been looking for a companion to make his seclusion more bearable ever since he arrived at the cabin. Maybe now he had found one.

There was just the issue with the cub being a mountain lion. The kitten was about the size of a house cat but Hyroc knew that would eventually change. Maybe he could train it. Even dogs could be trained. That's what he had heard anyway. Why couldn't he do the same with the cub? Ursa could probably help him; if what she had said wasn't a lie. Even if his plan proved impossible and he had to eventually release the cub when it grew up, he would still have a companion until such time.

Hyroc crouched down and started patting the ground, while calling the cub over to him in his most inviting voice. The cub simply stared at him without moving. Hyroc rolled his eyes in irritation at himself. He wasn't dealing with a house cat, it wouldn't come to him no matter how much he called. Fishing around in his pocked, he withdrew a tiny dry piece of three-day old grouse meat and offered it to the cub. The cub let out an initial growl, but stayed were it was. It watched Hyroc's outstretched hand a moment, then made its way over to him. The cat tentatively sniffed his hand then the pro-offered meat. Once it seemed sure he posed no danger, it snatched the meat out of his hand.

With the cub distracted downing the snack, Hyroc reached over to stroke its back. As soon as his hand touched the kittens' fur, it wheeled around, sinking its needle sharp teeth into his flesh. Hyroc yelled out in pain, making the cub bolt away from him. The cub turned around and hissed. Hyroc stuck the bleeding part of his hand into his mouth.

"Maybe I should name you after that weasel," Hyroc said coolly. The cub's ears went flat against its head and it hissed again. Hyroc smirked at the response. "How does Tom sound?" The cub's ears remained in the same position and he growled. It seemed the cub hated the name. Lucky would probably be a good name, since the cub was obviously lucky to have survived that spider attack. But the more he thought about it, the name Lucky seemed to be a favorite for owners of three-legged or one-eyed dogs and it was asking for trouble. He should probably use something less accident-prone. Especially with the luck he'd been having lately. He wondered about naming the cub Thomas. No, naming it after his only friend at the boarding school seemed an unacceptably strange thing to do, and would only serve as a depressing reminder. The name Kit popped into his head. A kit was the name for a fox cub, if his memory served right. That might work because the cub seemed smart like a fox.

"How does Kit sound?" The cub's ears returned to their normal position and although still glaring, he appeared pleased with the name. "Then Kit it is." Hyroc paused thoughtfully. "But before I take you home I need to catch some more fish, otherwise the two of us will be going to bed hungry." The cub stared at him blankly a moment, then walked back over to the weasel and resumed eating it. "And thank you for killing that little monster."

By the time dusk arrived, he had caught three more fish.

"Okay Kit, we should probably get headed home," Hyroc said, after tying his fishing line around his catch. Kit lay beside the bloody remains of the weasel fast asleep. Hyroc tapped a rock with the bottom of his fishing pole, waking Kit. "Come on, wake up, you can go back to sleep when we get to the cabin." He indicated its direction with his eyes. "It's just over there."

Kit stayed where he was and stared at him. With a shrug, Hyroc set down his fish and using his knife, sliced off a strip of meat from one right above the tail. After cutting the meat strip into pieces, he stuck them in his pocket, leaving one in his hand. He held his hand out and started calling Kit. The cub's eyes focused on the meat chunk. Kit studied Hyroc's hand then cautiously walked over and snapped up the treat. Hyroc took several steps back, pulled another piece from his pocket. In likewise manner, the cub ate the new piece of meat. This time when Hyroc walked away, the cub followed.

"That's a good boy," Hyroc said, before picking his fish back up. With only the use of an occasional incentive, the cub trailed him all the way to the cabin.

As Hyroc waited for the fish to cook, Kit wondered over to the deer-rabbit hide, sniffed it, and began gnawing on it.

"HEY!" Hyroc yelled, rushing over and snatching it away for him. With his ears flat against his head, Kit growled. Ignoring his protest, Hyroc examined the damage to the hide. Other than a chew mark, the hide seemed unscathed but the hair was starting to fall off and it had the beginnings of a rancid decaying smell to it. It was starting to rot. Hyroc sighed. "Never mind, it's yours," he said, tossing the decomposing hide to Kit, who happily tore into it. "It's useless now."

Although displeasing, its loss was not much of a setback, though any other hides he got would suffer the same fate. He needed to figure out how to prevent the hides from rotting; otherwise, he could never use them. His thoughts turned back to the family of hunters. He could probably figure it out by watching them like he had done with the two boys skinning their deer. Food wasn't much of an issue for a day or two, so he could devote at least that much time to watching them without worry.

"You know what Kit," Hyroc said, looking toward the cub. "I think it might be time for me to start paying closer attention to my neighbors."

CHAPTER 24

Lost Goat

Upon waking, Hyroc was relieved to no longer feel sick, but his shoulder was still very itchy and seemed even sorer than it had been the day before. With a yawn, he swung his feet over the side of his bed. He got a start as he reached for his boots when something with claws grabbed his bare foot. Quickly lifting his leg, he saw a light brown paw sticking out from under his bed. Smiling, he grabbed a boot and playfully poked the paw with the end of it. The paw began batting at the attacking footwear. After a moment, he lifted the boot then put it on. Setting the now protected foot down, the paw resumed clawing at it. Hyroc put the other boot on and was careful not to step on the paw as he stood. Stepping over to the fireplace, he used his tinderbox to get a fire going. He retrieved an already cooked slice of fish from the table and began to eat it. Kit emerged from beneath the bed, staring hungrily at the slice of fish.

"Oh, I'm sorry, I almost forgot about you," Hyroc said apologetically. It had been a while since he had needed to consider another living thing. A stab of longing and worry struck him when he suddenly thought of June. What had happened to her since he left? Had The Ministry arrested her? It was a serious offense to be associated with a witch. And people in those situations would often be tortured for information and a confession. The mere thought of June being in pain because of him sent a shiver down his back. Then he remembered his promise. He hated that promise, but he had made it and needed to keep it. It was what she wanted. No matter what had happened to her, it was what she wanted.

Forcing his thoughts from her, he cut another piece of fish and tossed it on the floor in front of the cub. Kit dove on it the instant it made contact with the wood. Hyroc regarded the cub fondly. The two of them was what he needed to concentrate on. This was what was important.

When Kit had finished eating, he wandered back beneath the bed and laid down. By the time Hyroc had donned his hunting gear the cub was already asleep. He felt a measure of relief at this. He hadn't quite figured out what to do with Kit while he checked his traps, but it seemed today he didn't need to. Moving quietly, he headed out the door, closing it behind him.

All of his traps were empty, again. Returning to the cabin, he opened the door to find everything that had been on the table strewn across the floor and Kit was lying on top of it wide-awake. With an annoyed sigh, Hyroc grabbed Kit by the scruff of the neck and set him on the floor. After picking everything up, he led Kit to a tree in front of the cabin. He tied a small piece of twine left over from making his traps around the tree's trunk. While Kit was distracted sniffing a plant, he pulled a smaller loop around the cat's neck. Kit bit at the rope and struggled vigorously to get free. Once he realized he could not, he began yowling for help. Hyroc tossed him a large piece of fish. Kit instantly stopped making noise, content to bite his treat. Hyroc hoped by the time Kit finished eating, he would have forgotten about the twine collar. Hyroc didn't like the idea of leaving Kit all alone, but it seemed a terrible idea to bring a mountain lion cub with him to watch the family of hunters. He hadn't seen any predators or signs dangerous things ventured into the valley and he reassured himself nothing bad was going to happen while he was gone.

He headed down the trail that had led him to his cabin. When he reached the end where it met the road, he warily looked for anyone coming his way. Seeing no one, he quickly crossed it and headed into the trees on the other side. When he could barely make out the road's flattened surface, he started in the direction of the hunter's cabin. Nearby, on the other side of the road, he found a well-worn trail leading off to the cabin. He continued walking until he was sure he had moved past every structure around the cabin before crossing the road. As the back of the cabin and shed came into view, he was disappointed to find the two skinning-tables were empty and no one was working here. He carefully moved through the trees to see if anyone was out in front of the cabin. The girl and a woman – Hyroc assumed was her mother because she seemed older and both shared hair color and similar features – were working in the garden. On the porch, the older man and ten-year-old boy were both sharpening arrowheads. The oldest boy and the father were nowhere to be seen.

He watched the four of them for another hour, hoping someone would start working on an animal hide. When no one did, figuring today was just a bad day, he headed off to try scouting the village for a tannery. Further down the road toward the village, farms came into view on either side of the road. People were working in the fields, and with much of the forest cleared away here; it seemed unlikely he could sneak past unseen. He thought about finding a way to circumvent the farmsteads but decided against it and headed home to fish; getting food was more useful right now.

The next day, thinking he might have more luck in the morning, he opted to check the other cabin first thing after breakfast. Taking the same route as yesterday, he arrived at the cabin. He watched the girl milk their goat then feed their chickens. The father and oldest son were still absent and no one worked out back yet again. The only explanation Hyroc could think of was the two of them must be out hunting.

He picked his way around the eastern side of the lake then on to the mountain to check his traps. He was ecstatic to find a regular hare in one of his traps. After he had skinned the carcass, he remembered with great frustration he still had no way to preserve the pelt.

Three days later, the family members he had been waiting for finally returned. They had a big dark brown hide that had the shape of a very large deer and a mountain of meat. He watched in anticipation as they headed over to the work area behind the cabin with the hide. After giving the hide a quick look over, they washed it in the lake before bringing it to the shed. The boy and father disappeared inside. Hyroc couldn't get a good view of what they were doing. He faintly heard what sounded like liquid sloshing around inside of something. The son emerged from the shed and carried a smaller and much lighter colored hide over to a wooden rack.

The father then came out of the shed holding a strange, curved blade, with handles on both ends. Using the blade, he began scraping off the hair of the hide on the rack with surprising ease. The father did this for a time then the son took over, and they did this until the hide had been scraped clean. They returned to the shed causing more sloshing noises then exited it without the hide. The son closed the door and the two of them went inside the cabin.

Hyroc covered his face with his hands groaning in frustration; after all this time spent watching them, he was still no closer to figuring out how to preserve any of his hides. *How could this possibly be so difficult?* Taking a deep breath, he subdued his aggravation by assuming his answers would be inside the shed. But the only way to find those answers was to sneak into the shed at night. He smirked a little. *That at least shouldn't be a problem.*

He waited long after dark when he thought everyone should be sleeping before approaching the door to the shed. The door was secured shut with a wooden board fed through two U-shaped door handles. He slowly lifted the board from the handles, careful not to make any sound. As he opened the door, he cringed when it made a frighteningly loud creaking noise. He anxiously watched the cabin, waiting for someone to come out to check the shed. When no one eventually did, taking a relieved breath, he slipped inside the shed.

Within, he saw numerous tools hung on or propped against the walls and two upright wooden barrels. It was obvious the sloshing noises had come from the barrels. When he pulled the lid off one barrel, he saw some kind of liquid. It smelled of damp burnt wood and musky wet fur. He was about to put a finger in the liquid, when he began to wonder if touching an unknown substance was a good idea. Maybe the liquid in one of these barrels did something to make scraping hides easier. If that was the case, then he probably shouldn't touch it. He put the lid back on and moved on to the second barrel.

When he pulled the lid off this one, his was struck by a pungent and extremely unpleasant odor. He coughed, burying his nose in the crook of his elbow. That was the only disadvantage of having a more sensitive sniffer. Along with smelling food and other pleasant things better than a normal person could, foul odors were also stronger. He quickly reached over with his other arm and put the lid back on.

He had seen what was in the barrels, but he was clueless to the composition of either liquid and knew nothing of their purposes beyond, *they seemed important.* The father and son would know but talking to them seemed suicidal and he doubted they would reveal the secrets of their trade even if he were a normal person. Unless he could glean some sort of answer from observing the family further, any future hides he obtained would rot. Trying not to think about his gloomy situation, he slipped back out of the shed and quietly made his way back to his cabin

When he arrived at his usual hiding spot the next day, the father and oldest son were having an argument in front of the open door to the shed. A bolt of dread shot through Hyroc when he realized he had forgotten to close the door and replace the board last night. He hoped the father merely thought his son had not closed the door and not that someone had snuck into it. As he nervously watched the two of them argue he saw the daughter walk over to them with a concerned look on her face. When she attempted to speak to her father, he was so entrenched into the argument he paid no attention to her.

After a few more attempts, she waved her arm at them in frustration and stormed off toward the open gate of their pen. When she arrived, she began studying something on the ground. She followed an imaginary line with her finger, eventually pointing toward the forest behind the cabin. Then she started toward the spot where she had pointed. Curious as to what she was doing, he silently followed.

When she reached the forest's edge, she began calling out "Grettle," like she was calling someone's name. She said the name twice more before heading into the trees, repeating the name as she walked. Shortly after entering the forest, he heard the bleating of a goat and the girl headed toward it. Hyroc nodded to himself in comprehension. Their goat must have wandered off.

The girl found the goat in a treeless spot munching on dandelions. Hyroc was about to head back toward the shed when the forest suddenly went silent. Feeling a surge of apprehension, he scanned his surroundings uneasily and saw the outline of a single wolf at the edge of the open spot. It looked gaunt as if it might have been starving. The girl was in serious danger. He could probably kill the wolf with an arrow, but that would surely give away his presence. Simply leaving was another option; it was doubtful the malnourished wolf could kill her. She just might get a few minor bites.

He felt a stab of guilt at the thought of what he was considering. This was a wolf; wolves kill people. How could he live with himself if she died and he could have stopped that? But she would see him! The last time somebody had seen him he had almost died. He felt a surge of fear as the memory surfaced. She would tell somebody about him, he would lose everything he had gained and would be risking his life. The lonely wilderness would become his home. He was suddenly struck by an inspiring thought. He didn't necessarily have to kill the wolf to keep her out of harm's way, he just needed to alert the girl to the presence of the wolf. So long as she didn't panic and run, she should be able to grab the goat and safely walk away.

Hyroc picked up a rock and chucked it behind the goat. It landed with a satisfying thud. When the girl looked in the direction of the rock, her eyes focused on the wolf. Slowly she got to her feet and began calmly but hastily leading the goat away by the collar, keeping an eye on the wolf. Relief swept over Hyroc. He shook his head in humored disbelief at the simplicity of his solution. All he had to do was throw a rock. That was it. He was still dangerously close to a wolf though, but once the girl was out of sight he could safely kill it.

Suddenly the goat scented the wolf and bolted, causing the wolf to break into a run. The girl lost her footing as the unexpected yank on her hand knocked her off balance. As soon as she tripped, the wolf fixated on her. Hyroc swore, nocked an arrow and loosed it at the wolf. The wolf yelped as the arrow burrowed into its side, before collapsing into a heap.

The girl drew a knife from a sheath on her belt, then froze looking confused. Turning her head, she looked directly at him. She stared at him with frightened bewilderment then got to her feet and took off running toward the cabin. Hyroc felt a cold sinking feeling as he watched her go. What had he just done? She had seen him! He rushed to the wolf and with a straining effort hoisted it over his shoulders. If he got rid of the wolf's body there would be no evidence of his intervention. Maybe without it, nobody would believe her story and he would still have a place to live. If not then – he pushed the thought aside; he would deal with that if the time came. Taking off into the forest, he ran for as long as he could carry the wolf, before hiding its body beneath a pine tree with thickly clumped branches scraping the ground. After recovering his arrow from the carcass, he rushed off in the direction of his cabin.

CHAPTER **25**

Unexpected Outcome

Flinging open the door to his cabin Hyroc rushed inside. He frantically stuffed the remainder of the meat left over from a grouse he had killed the night before into his pack, along with all of his belongings. Donning his pack, he hurried back outside, closing the door behind him. He untied a startled Kit from the tree and picked him up. The cub yowled in protest as Hyroc carried him toward the back of the valley. Moving on to the mountain slopes a short distance past his first trap – which was empty – he found a spot beneath a spruce where he could observe the valley, and see if anyone came to his cabin. He expected that would be the first place anyone looking for him might stumble across. Maybe without all of his things inside someone searching the structure would still think it was abandoned. If they didn't notice the board on the door was missing or that the inside looked like it had been cleaned. He knew better than to hope for such a slim chance to turn into an actuality.

Fearing a fire would give away his presence, he spent a cold night underneath the spruce with Kit as his only source of warmth. By noon the next day, no one had come. If he needed to run, he knew he would need every ounce of meat he could find, which meant his traps still needed checking. He detested the idea of taking his eyes off his cabin for fear he would miss someone's approach, but if he didn't his situation could become that much worse. When he removed the piece of twine he had been using to tie Kit to the tree from his pocket; he began to wonder if leaving the cub alone so close to a trap was such a good idea. Anything caught in it could attract a predator and there was a good chance it would scent Kit. If his companion got killed, he would be alone again. He might lose his mind if that happened. Checking traps was hardly a difficult task and since any game would be snared, it didn't matter if Kit spooked anything. Hunting could be a problem though, but he could deal with that later.

"Come on Kit," Hyroc said, replacing the twine in his pocket. "I need to check my traps."

Kit stared back at him curiously. Hyroc walked away and Kit eagerly followed after him. The trap in the ravine was empty and from there, he made his way to the incline. This trap was also empty. As he moved away from it, he noticed Kit staring at the top of the incline and his nose was twitching like he smelled something. Hyroc sniffed; he smelled nothing out of the ordinary. Kit became suddenly excited and ran up the incline. Hyroc rushed after him, yelling his name. The cub disappeared over the top of the incline. The memory of the spider attack flashed through Hyroc's mind, forcing him to stop. His shoulder began to throb and a frigid dread engulfed him. He knew the spiders were dead, but at the same time, he felt as if his eight legged assailants were just over the rise, waiting to sink their fangs into his neck. "Kit," Hyroc called out in a fear-laden voice. He shook his head trying to clear his mind. *The spiders are dead, why do I feel like this? Ursa told me there won't be any more.* Remembering the she bear's words about how brave he was; he took a deep breath. His body seemed to warm and a portion of his fear melted away. Fighting through the remnants of his trepidation, he forced himself to walk over the top of the incline. If her words could have that effect on him, it seemed even more doubtful she was actually a witch.

Everything he saw looked much as he remembered it the first time he had seen it, but the surrounding area seemed brighter and more inviting. The idea of another savage attack in this place seemed absurd. To the left of the cave lay a pile of rocks arranged in what appeared to be a grave. He felt a pang of sadness when he saw it, knowing Huntress and her other cub lay within. Even though she was a dangerous predator capable of killing him, he still felt an attachment to her. It seemed all he ever did was visit the graves of anyone or anything he got attached to. He saw Kit disappear into the cave and followed after him. Inside he found the cub standing in the middle of the cave near some moldering deer bones. Kit yowled, his tiny voice echoing through the space as he called out for his mother and sibling. Sadness welled up within Hyroc and he felt moisture forming in his eyes as he thought of his own mother. She too had been protecting him and she had died in the process. But just like Kit, he could make no sense of it all. Kit yowled again; unable to understand why the cave was empty.

"They're gone," Hyroc said, sadness clear in his voice. Kit looked back at him with large confused eyes. Kit yowled once more and wandered over to him. Reaching down Hyroc scratched him behind the ears. "It's just the two of us now. But don't worry I'll make it work, I always have." He walked away from the cave and after a moment's hesitation, Kit followed. Stopping at Huntress's grave Hyroc said, "I'll take care of him," before heading off to the next trap.

He only found a rabbit caught in the snare beneath the fallen tree at the end of his route. Kit's eyes fixed on the trapped creature, his body tensing. He crouched, then began stalking his quarry causing Hyroc to smile. Hyroc watched Kit for a few moments longer before grasping the rabbit by the back of its neck and removing the snare from its leg. Away from the trap, he slit the rabbit's throat and when the last drops of crimson fell from its neck, he got to work gutting the carcass – not bothering with the pelt. He gave the heart and liver to Kit, who after some investigation snapped it up. After cooking and eating the rabbit, the two of them returned to the observation point.

For the rest of that day, no one came by his cabin. The next morning, thinking he might have missed someone coming by while he had been out checking traps, he reluctantly tied Kit to a tree and headed to his cabin to look for footprints. When he arrived, other than some prints from a foraging rabbit and some bird tracks, it appeared no one had come by at all. He waited until the next morning before he was convinced the girl's family had not believed her and that he could safely move back into his cabin.

Two days after returning to his cabin no one had come and he was happy to find a rabbit caught in his snare at the ravine and the clearing with the dirty pool. Though he knew it was pointless to do so, he skinned them anyway. It didn't hurt to practice in case he ever figured out how to preserve them. After he and Kit had eaten their fill of the meat, they made their way toward the creek. Moving around a patch of thickly clumped pine trees on their way there, Hyroc started when he came face-to-face with the girl from the family of hunters. The two of them yelled out in mirrored surprise. Heart pounding, he darted behind a tree, scooping up Kit as he ran. They had found him! They were slower at it than he had anticipated, but they had found him. There was nothing for it now, he had to run! It would be hard out in the wilderness, but at least with Kit it wouldn't be so lonely. He just needed to figure out how to....

"Wait, don't go," the girl called out to him in a gentle voice. The tone of her voice caught him off guard; she sounded – she sounded kind and it reminded him of June. "I just want to talk."

Talk, she wanted to talk, *to him*. Most people didn't want him anywhere near them, let alone talk to him. Her behavior made him wondered if she had actually had enough time to take notice of his features. If so, then showing his face now would definitely be a bad idea. He just needed to figure out how to get away from her without letting her see his face. A far more frightening explanation rammed its way into his mind. What if this was a trap and her father and brother were waiting to shoot him in the head with an arrow the moment he stepped out from behind the tree? Cold dread engulfed him as the gravity of the situation took hold. Smacking the back of his head against the trunk of the tree, he berated himself for not paying more attention to his surroundings. *I should have seen her coming long before she ever saw me.* He shook his head. *I can feel stupid about this later. The father and son – or someone from The Ministry; I still haven't ruled that out yet – are probably circling around at this very moment to get a clear shot at me. I need to get Kit and I out of here!* Several yards in front of him, he saw another stand of trees growing beside a hollow. If he took off toward it at a dead run, he should get there before the father or son had a chance to take a shot at him.

"You don't need to be afraid, I'm alone and you have my word I'm not planning to hurt you," the girl said, as Hyroc prepared to run. "Please come out."

He paused mid-step. She sounded sincere, like she meant every word of what she was saying. He suddenly felt a strange desire to stay despite a screaming urge to flee. Listening carefully to his surroundings, he heard no sounds of movement. Looking from side to side, he saw no rustling of the foliage that would give away the presence of somebody moving through it. Above he saw Shimmer circling his position. If Ursa's claims held true then she probably knew about the danger he was heading for long before he ever encountered it. It seemed she wouldn't be that far away from him and she should have come to his rescue by now. Maybe the girl was telling the truth. Maybe she was alone.

"If I come out, you'll just run away," Hyroc said.

There was a pause. "I've already seen your face," the girl said calmly.

"Then why aren't you afraid?" Hyroc said, trying to keep the surprise from his voice. People were always afraid of him. Why wouldn't she be?

"Well, I was a little when I first saw you; right after you killed that wolf. But on my way back to tell my family what happened, I began to wonder if you really meant me any harm. Why else would you have killed that wolf? So, after thinking it over, I decided to go back and try thanking you. You did after all keep me from getting hurt. But when I got there, both you and the wolf were gone."

Her story sounded believable but was any of it actually true? For all he knew she was trying to get him to come out from behind the tree so someone could more easily shoot him. Deceit was a tactic he wouldn't put passed a group of witch hunters. All that mattered to them was getting their target. Just because Ursa wasn't there didn't mean he wasn't in danger. She might have been further away than he had thought. "How do I know this isn't some kind of trick?" Hyroc called back to the girl

There was a longer pause. "I've never been known as a trickster. I promise you I came alone and I'm not going to hurt you."

Hyroc wanted to believe her but it seemed too good to be true she was telling the truth. No one wanted to be around him, why would she? Her words had to be a trap. She never mentioned what she did after she couldn't find him. Maybe he could catch her in a lie, then he would know for certain she was untrustworthy. "You didn't say what you did after you couldn't find me."

There was another pause. "Well, it didn't seem like a good idea to tell anyone about what I had seen and without the wolf's body I doubt I would have been believed."

He couldn't detect any hints of deception in her words, but what she said didn't make any sense. Why wouldn't she tell anyone what she had seen? Nearly being attacked by a wolf and seeing a strange creature in the forest both seemed things to tell another person about whether or not anyone would believe them. She had to have told someone about him. Maybe the adults wouldn't have believed her but her oldest brother probably did. The boy was a hunter and that's how the girl had found him.

"If you didn't tell anyone about me, then who helped you find me?"

There was a long pause. He smiled ruefully, he had caught her now. "Nobody helped me, I tracked you by myself." Hyroc shook his head, that was exactly what somebody who was lying would say to keep their lie from being found out. He had her. "That creek nearby," the girl continued. "Seemed a good place to start because animals usually gather near sources of water and after seeing the way you killed that wolf, I figured you might hunt here."

He stared down at the ground thoughtfully. He actually hadn't considered that when he set his trap at the creek, he was just using the water there because it helped make a chokepoint. She spoke confidently as if she actually knew from experience what she was talking about. That was also puzzling. June never hunted ducks with him and he had never heard a story where girls hunted. He couldn't really think of a reason why they shouldn't, it just seemed they never did. Had everything she said been the truth?

"You hunt?" Hyroc said.

"Well, my father was expecting a boy first but when he got me, he had to change his plans. He taught me everything about it. I don't do it as much now but every once in a while, I join in on a hunt." She paused then spoke in a humored tone. "I still shoot better than my oldest brother, Donovan. It kind of annoys him." She paused again. "I'd really like you to come out from behind the tree so we can talk face-to-face."

Everything she said sounded sincere and he couldn't find anything suspicious with what she said. It seemed impossible that he had found another understanding person. Could he actually have a conversation with someone? It seemed like another life since he had had such a luxury. Keeping his head flush against the tree's trunk, he cautiously poked his head around it to have a look. The girl only seemed slightly unsettled by his outward appearance, but it wasn't enough to bother him. She held a basket containing what looked to be bread and some pieces of cheese. If she was planning to hurt him, it seemed odd to do so while holding a basket brimming with gifts. He carefully scanned the surrounding forest and could find no signs of anyone waiting to shoot him. It seemed the girl was indeed telling the truth. Pulling his head back behind the tree, he set Kit at its base. "Stay here," he whispered to Kit, before stepping out from behind the tree.

"I brought you something," the girl said, holding the basket out to him.

Hyroc stared at the pro-offered basket a long moment, before sweeping his eyes through his surroundings and warily walking toward her. Tentatively he reached over to accept it. Taking a step back, he set the basket down and slowly started putting its contents in his knapsack, intermittently glancing at her as he did so.

"I know it's not much," she said. "But it's the least I could do to thank you after what you did for me." She lowered herself into a crouch so the two of them were at the same eye level. "My name's Elsa.

He gave her a thoughtful look then said, "My name's Hyroc."

"It's nice to meet you, Hyroc," she said, making sure she pronounced his name properly.

Then to his dismay, Kit yowled and wandered out from behind the tree toward him. An instant later, Elsa's eyes widened in alarm. "That's a mountain lion cub!" she yelled, jumping to her feet. "If the mother –"

"It's all right, he doesn't have a mother. She was killed by –" he paused, wondering if nightmarishly huge spiders were common around the mountain. He had seen only two of them and for the time being decided it probably best to avoid mentioning them. "She was killed."

Elsa stared at him without speaking a long moment. "You – you adopted him?" Hyroc nodded. Her eyes lit with admiration. "I knew I was right about you," she said smiling. Avoiding a sharp-toothed smile in return, he nodded happily. "Would it be all right if I held him?"

"I don't see why not, just umm – be careful of his claws they're sharp."

Elsa walked over to Kit and held out her hand. Kit cautiously stepped forward, sniffing the ends of her fingers. As soon as he finished taking in her scent, Elsa scooped him into her arms. Yowling in alarm, he began squirming to get free. He instantly went limp when Elsa started scratching behind his ears. He appeared to enjoy the scratching, but at the same time, he seemed to detest the fact he was being held.

"Does he have a name?"

"Kit."

"Kit?" she said, then nodded approvingly. "It's a good name."

"Thank – thank you."

She hesitated before saying, "Are you a forest spirit?"

Hyroc gave her a strange look. "I'm not a forest spirit." Whatever those were supposed to be.

"You're not? I heard they were furry creatures that live in the forest and sometimes they help people who are in trouble."

Hyroc shook his head. His life would've been a lot easier if people saw him as something so benign.

"If you're not a forest spirit, then what are you? If you don't mind my asking"

Hyroc sighed, staring down at the pine needle littered ground. "I wish I knew."

A sad look came into her eyes. "You never knew your parents?" He shook his head. She put a reassuring hand on his shoulder, which gave him a start. She pulled her hand back, giving him an apologetic look. "I'm so sorry to hear that." An awkwardly long moment of silence passed between them. "Were you adopted?" Hyroc nodded. "Did you run away?"

"Yes, but not from him – my foster father I mean – he was one of the few people that treated me like I was worth something."

A sorrowful comprehending look came into her eyes. For a moment, the look in her eyes reminded him of how June looked when she was displeased with how he was being treated. "Why is it that you are here alone?"

Hyroc took a deep breath. "He died when I was nine."

"I'm sorry."

Another awkward silence descended between them. Elsa eventually broke it by asking, "Where do you live?" Hyroc gazed at her, wondering if telling her that was a good idea. "Don't worry, I won't tell anyone," she said, lifting her hand in a reassuring manner, realizing the reason for his reluctance.

After a moment's deliberation, he eventually said. "In an abandoned cabin near the foot of the mountain." With his hand, he indicated the general direction from where they were."

She gave him an alarmed look. "You must be extremely brave to live in that place."

"Why would I need to be brave to live there?" Hyroc said concerned. Her words didn't sound very reassuring.

"Because a witch once lived there."

He stared at her in horror. People already thought he was some type of monster, and if they found out he lived in a cabin where the previous owner was a witch, they would definitely be hostile toward him.

"What did this witch do exactly?" Hyroc said, hoping the witch had not done anything too serious; if such a thing were even possible.

Elsa looked thoughtful a moment. "From what I've heard, bodies went missing from the graveyard. Then shortly after that, bodies began getting out of their graves and started walking around and trying to kill people." Elsa shivered with disgust. "Then the witch was found out and killed."

Hyroc slumped and covered his face with his hands. Necromancers were one of the most hated of witches solely because they reanimated the dead. He knew how incredibly painful burying someone was, but then having that loved one reanimated into a mindless monster, was most people's worst nightmare. Anyone caught practicing necromancy was usually killed on the spot and their bodies burned. Anyone with half a brain would figure out he was definitely not a necromancer, but the mere association coupled with his appearance, would make people far from understanding.

He put his hands down, turning his attention back to Elsa. "You cannot tell anyone about me or where I live."

"I already guessed that, you don't have to worry about me telling anyone. My lips are sealed."

"Thank you," Hyroc said, taking a deep breath.

"But if no one can know that you're here why did you come here in the first place?"

"I wasn't thinking that far ahead, I just needed a place far away and this was the best place for that."

"You won't be able to stay hidden out here forever."

Hyroc sighed. "I know; I just – I just need time to figure out what to do."

"You should also stay away from our cabin. My father thought he saw someone lurking through the forest behind the shed the other day."

He gave her an alarmed look. Speaking hastily, he said, "I was only trying to see how they tanned animal hides; I don't know how."

"Were you what got into the shed then?"

"Yes, but I didn't take anything, I just looked at what was in the barrels, that's all, I promise."

"That explains the argument between Donovan and my father."

He scratched the back of his head nervously. "I umm – forgot to put the board back on the door when I left."

"You shouldn't sneak around our home anymore or anyone's home for that matter."

"I won't, unless it's a dire emergency."

"Thank you, I would hate for you –" she indicated Kit with her eyes "– or your friend to get hurt."

Hyroc paused as a thought entered his mind. "Do you know what that liquid in those barrels your family keeps in the shed is used for or how to make it?"

"I don't work with the hides, my father and brothers do that. But I could try and find out for you."

"It's very important that I know how to do that myself."

"I understand. Where should I meet you when I find out?"

He stared up at the sky thoughtfully a moment before answering. "Along the shore there is a lone tree where I have a trap set." He pointed in the direction of the trap; Elsa followed his finger with her eyes. "I check it almost every day before noon. You can meet me there; just make sure you're not followed."

She nodded. "It may be a few days before I'm able to meet you again. But I don't know how long I can help you without someone getting suspicious and figuring out what I'm doing."

"I know; I'll figure something out by then." Elsa nodded; set Kit on the ground and picked up the now empty basket. "It was nice to meet you, Hyroc."

"And it was nice to meet you, Elsa."

"I hope you enjoy the bread and cheese." He nodded thankfully. "I'll see you in a few days then."

"I'll be here."

"Good day."

"Good day."

She nodded, then headed off. He watched her until she disappeared from view. He breathed a sigh of relief and gave Kit a disbelieving look. "I think I might have just made a friend," he said.

CHAPTER 26

A Better Spot

From the shore of the creek, Hyroc looked down into the calmly flowing water at his feet, spots of shimmering sunlight glowing brightly across its gently flowing surface. His distorted reflection gazed back at him, reminding him of how inescapably different he looked from a normal person. He understood why people feared him. His features didn't exactly give him the appearance of something non-threatening. He probably reminded most people of a wolf. It made sense they wouldn't want something that looked like that around them. For all they knew, he looked upon them as a meal. He pushed the thought aside; there wasn't much point in dwelling on something he couldn't change.

Lifting his gaze to the other shore, he did his best to gauge the depth of the water. Save for catching a single deer rabbit at the back of the valley, all his traps had been empty. The trap he had set at the incline had yet to capture anything and with his reprieve from hunting the girl named Elsa had given him with her gift of food, this seemed a perfect opportunity to scout for an alternate trap site. His encounter with her the day before felt like a dream. If not for her gift, he might not still believe it had actually happened. Both the bread and cheese tasted amazing. He never remembered feeling so thankful to eat either one. It was starting to get a little tiresome eating nothing but meat and whatever berries he managed to find. But above everything else, he was actually able to speak to somebody. He hadn't done that since his parting words with June. It seemed years had passed since then. He felt a pang of sadness at the memory of her face. He forced it from his mind.

He stood at a shallow part of the creek he had crossed through a few times while hunting during those days he was observing Elsa's family. He remembered seeing some promising areas on the other side and those seemed the best places to start. Carefully he walked out into the cool water. He grimaced when he reached the deepest part of the crossing as water cascaded into his boots, soaking his feet as it had during every crossing. The soggy sensation reminded him he needed to roll up the bottoms of his leggings and walk barefoot across the creek. With a long sigh, he continued to the opposite shore. Once on dry land, he removed his boots and waterlogged socks, before dumping the water out. *I really need to stop doing this*, he thought bitterly to himself. He shook the bottom of his damp pant legs to shed some of the soaked in water then put his bare feet in his boots. After ringing his socks out as best he could, he slung them over his shoulder to dry as he continued searching for trap spots.

Away from the creek, where the brush began to form, he found what appeared to be the faint line of an animal trail leading off into the trees. Following the trail, it steadily became more defined and easier to see the thicker the plant growth it ran through became. After walking a short distance, he found what looked to be the nexus point where numerous tendrils split off from the main path. Most of the surrounding foliage seemed somewhat flimsy and insubstantial, which did not necessarily guarantee any animal bigger than a mouse traveling through here would use the trail. Looking farther ahead, he saw a closely grouped line of pine trees with a gap toward the middle where the trail cut through. The line of trees was no easy obstacle to pass through. Setting a trap there would vastly increase his odds of catching something. On his approach to the gap, he saw a tiny oval shaped clearing dotted with dandelions on the other side.

He froze when he saw something brown and furry lying in the clearing. Drawing his bow, he silently crept closer. He felt a thrill of excitement when the thing resolved into the shape of a deer. If he got a deer, he would be free of the fear of going hungry for quite a while and would have more time to focus on other important things. As he walked up behind a tree on the right side of the gap to take a shot, he realized the deer was lying on its side. Focusing on the animal, he saw what looked to be an arrow wound in its side. Its chest did not move with breath; it was dead. He wondered if a hunter had wounded it, the deer had gotten away, then succumbed to its injury sometime later. If that were the case, those same hunters may still be looking for it. He listened intently to his surroundings for several minutes, but other than the knocking of a distant woodpecker and the sound of leaves being rustled by a mild breeze, all was quiet. He began to entertain the thought of dragging the carcass away or cutting the back haunches off before the hunters found it. It was risky, but the reward seemed well worth it. Smiling at his good fortune, he lowered his bow and made his way toward the deer.

As he approached, he noticed a pile of leaves directly in the middle of his path. For some reason they felt out of place to him though he was unsure why it should, leaf litter was obviously common in the forest. He studied the pile and found nothing dangerous poking out from under it. He shook his head. *Those hunters might arrive at any moment, I don't have time for this, they're just leaves.* At the edge of the leaves, he cautiously put his foot on it.

Other than a dry crackle under his boot, nothing happened. He smiled. *Just like I thought, nothing.* He had taken two more steps when he felt his foot push against what felt like a taut rope. A snap sounded nearby and the resistance suddenly disappeared. Then the dark shape of a net exploded out of the ground beneath his feet, closing in around him like a flower blooming in reverse, and he was violently yanked into the air. When the world settled only one thought entered his mind, *get out*! Fighting through a wave of panic threatening to consume him, he frantically unsheathed his knife and started cutting the net. He had nearly sliced all the way through the side when a sudden sense of weightlessness came over his body as he plummeted to the ground. The impact knocked the breath from his lungs and pulsing black spots appeared in his vision. A flare of terror struck when he was unable to take a breath, but after what felt like an eternity, he finally gasped.

Just as he started getting to his feet, a disabling weight appeared at the center of his back shoving him back to the ground. Before he could try throwing the weight off, two hands grabbed both his arms, pulling them behind him at a painful angle. He struggled desperately to free himself but it only caused the weight to press down on him even harder. His hands were pulled together and he felt the roughness of a rope close around them. Once the rope was secured, his sword was removed from his belt. He was then rolled onto his back and roughly sat up on his knees with his hands resting in an uncomfortable position behind his back. He looked up at the man who had subdued him as he tossed his things aside and stepped back. The man wore a green tinged leather-hunting jerkin with its hood shadowing the main features of his face, and the feathered ends of arrows stuck up from behind his shoulder from a quiver on his back. A large hunting knife scabbard hung on a simple brown leather belt at his waist, holding up a pair of slightly darker patched leggings, and on his feet, he wore a pair of supple boots. The man studied him with hidden eyes, then turned his head away and made a waving motion at something. With that slight turn, the sunlight illuminated his face enough for Hyroc to recognize him as Elsa's father. Hyroc strained a glance in the direction Elsa's father waved and saw the oldest son emerge from the tree line with a bow held at the ready. The brother was dressed much the same as his father, but his clothes seemed fresher and less worn.

"So, you're the little *sneak* who's been prowling around our home," Elsa's father said coolly. "Thought we would make an easy mark eh? Well, we weren't so easy after all were we now. We don't take too kindly to thievery around here. I found your tracks all over and then my son over there found where you dumped that wolf you pouched." Elsa's father paused, smiling mockingly. "It wasn't nearly as light as you thought it was hmm."

"I'm not a thief," Hyroc retorted. "I never stole anything and I didn't poach that wolf."

"You didn't steal anything *yet*, but to me, catching someone before they can steal anything still makes them a thief. And if you didn't pouch that wolf, then why did you kill it?"

"It was going to attack your daughter, so I killed it."

"Now I know you're a liar and a thief."

"I'm not lying!"

Elsa's father shook his head dismissively. "If *my* daughter had been attacked by that wolf, she would have told us. And I trust her a whole lot more than you."

"She didn't tell you, because – because she didn't want you to find me."

"I think I've heard enough of your nonsense. Donovan, why don't you take his mask off so we can have a good look at his face?"

Narrowing his eyes, Hyroc gave Elsa's father a strange confused look. "I'm not wearing a mask," he said. That was the first time anyone had accused him of that.

"Think we're being smart, are we?" Elsa's father said, shaking his head in annoyance. "I don't have the patience for any more games."

Donovan reached over and gave one of Hyroc's ears a hard yank. Hyroc grimaced as his ear popped and the rest of his head turned. Donovan frowned, stepped behind him, pulled back the collar of his jerkin, and began running a finger across the base of his neck, searching for something.

"Umm, I can't find the end of it," Donovan said in a puzzled tone.

"It should be right there at the base of his neck."

"I know that's where it *should be*," Donovan said in an irritated tone. "But I'm telling you, it's *not* there."

"Let me see," Elsa's father said, walking over.

Hyroc considered running at that moment, but with his hands bound, he doubted he would get far and without his bow, escape seemed somewhat pointless. He looked up to see Shimmer circling the clearing. Besides, all he needed to do was wait for Ursa to show up and everything would be okay. He envisioned her crashing through the forest as she rushed to his aid. She hadn't done that yesterday but he presumed that was because he wasn't actually in any danger. Now he was.

Elsa's father ran his finger across the base of Hyroc's neck as Donovan had done. "What kind of a mask is this? Is it glued on? It almost looks as if –" There was a long pause. A shiver ran up Hyroc's back; he knew what they were realizing.

"What is he? Is he a witch?" Donovan said in a clearly shocked voice.

Else's father was quite a moment. "Well, whatever he is, we need to take him to the village elders, they'll know what to do. Let's get him on his feet." They stood Hyroc on his feet in a less than gentle manner. "If you try anything I'll put a knife in your back, got it." Hyroc nodded his understanding.

Stepping in front of him, Elsa's father collected a coil of rope from beneath a nearby tree. After unwinding the rope, he made a loop at one end with a length trailing off. He put the loop over Hyroc's head and cinched it down. Grabbing hold of the length of rope, Elsa's father started leading him out of the clearing. Hyroc stole a quick glance in the direction of his cabin, worried what would happen to Kit, tied to a tree all alone. Sadness gripped him at the thought. *Ursa I need you, where are you?*

CHAPTER 27

A Puzzling Guest

Hyroc's legs ached as Elsa's father and Donovan continued leading him through the forest by the rope around his neck. He had walked about this same distance every day while checking his traps, but Elsa's father was forcing him to walk at a much faster pace than he was used to and after tripping several times, the journey was starting to take its toll on him.

"I need to take a break," Hyroc said.

"You'll get a break when we get where we're going," Elsa's father growled. "Keep moving."

Hyroc sighed irritably; he needed a break. If Elsa's father wouldn't give him one voluntarily, he would force that break out of him. He looked at the ground passing beneath his feet, it was devoid of protruding roots and green tufts of soft moss lay in the path before him. He smirked. *This looks like a good spot.* He purposely made his legs give out, careful not to hurt himself when he landed.

"Get back up," Donovan said stepping closer.

Turning his head Hyroc noticed Donovan's shin was within kicking distance. He had a strong temptation to exact some sort of revenge upon his captures, but that seemed a great way for him to get his ribs kicked in or worse.

"I told you, *I need a break*," Hyroc said indignantly. He sat up into the most comfortable position he could manage with bound hands. "And if you don't give me one, you can carry me the rest of the way."

Elsa's father glowered. "Fine, you've got two minutes and not a second more."

"Thank you," Hyroc said halfheartedly. As he sat there, he saw a flash of white fur in the trees in front of him. This was the third time he had seen the creature since he left the clearing where he had been captured. The only thing that made sense was Ursa following them. But he was becoming concerned she hadn't rescued him yet. Surely being captured by the two hunters was considered dangerous.

"I thought I saw something," Donovan said, looking in the direction Hyroc had seen Ursa.

"Where?" Elsa's father said, walking over to him.

"Just over there," Donovan said, indicating the general area of his sighting.

"What color was it?"

"It looked white."

"Probably just a coyote or lynx following us hoping we'll drop something it can eat." He turned back toward Hyroc. "Okay, that's long enough, back on your feet." Hyroc shrugged and arduously got to his feet.

The lakeshore came into view and not long afterward, the three of them arrived at the cabin. Almost as soon as they entered the clearing, a cacophony of excited barking sounds filled the air as the families' dog came rushing over. The hound gave its masters a quick greeting before moving on to Hyroc. Catching his scent, the dog became more agitated and began to growl.

Elsa's father led Hyroc over to the fence post of the pen where their goat and a donkey lazily munched on a mouthful of feed. On the porch, the older man sat smoking a pipe on a stool with his back against the side of the cabin. Donovan's younger brother sat nearby with a whetstone in one hand and an unsheathed knife in the other, curiously watching their approach. Elsa's father unbound Hyroc's hands, retying them to the post in an even more uncomfortable position behind his back.

"Curtis," Elsa's father called out to the youngest boy, as he finished securing Hyroc's hands. After slipping his knife back into its sheath and setting the whetstone on the porch, Curtis made his way over, never taking his eyes off Hyroc's face. "I need you to go into town and tell Harold we found something *unusual* in the forest and he should get here as fast as he can. And to bring a few others who can keep their mouths shut." Slowly turning his attention from Hyroc, Curtis nodded and headed off toward town at a quick pace.

"Oh you're back," Elsa said, as she stepped outside the house. Hyroc snapped his head in her direction, a wave of relief washing over him. She could explain everything. "Mother wants –" she stopped talking the moment she saw Hyroc, her eyes widening in shock.

"Elsa!" Hyroc called out.

"Hyroc!" she said in alarm.

Her father, brother and the older man snapped their attention to her with dumbfounded looks on their faces. "*How do you know his name?*" Her father and brother said simultaneously.

She paused. "Well…because…he…told it to me," she said tentatively.

"He *what*," her father exclaimed, his face flushing. "You'd better explain yourself *right now young lady*!"

Elsa hurriedly recounted the events of the morning of the wolf attack, how Hyroc killed it, her search for him, and then their meeting.

"You're telling me you knew about *him* this whole time *and you never told anyone*," Elsa's father said, as she finished her account.

"I didn't tell *you* –" she angrily indicated Hyroc with her hand "– because I knew *this* was how you would react."

"That's not your place to decide! You've put everyone in this family in danger"

"If he wanted to hurt *me* or any of *us* why did he save me from that wolf?"

Else's father squeezed his eyes shut, pinching the bridge of his nose between his index finger and thumb. He thrust a finger at the open door of the cabin. "Go back inside, and stay there, I'll deal with you later."

"But –"

He opened his eyes, affixing a fiery gaze on her. "Now," he growled. She bowed her head a little and after giving Hyroc a worried glance, stormed back into the cabin. "Donovan, you too." Donavan obeyed without question. "She's going to put me in an early grave," Elsa's father grumbled to himself almost too quiet for Hyroc to hear.

He turned his attention back on Hyroc, giving him a severe look that made him stiffen in alarm. "You're going to tell me everything right now! And if I think for one instant that you're lying, *I swear I'll use your skin to make a blanket for our goat.* What did you want *with my daughter?*"

"Nothing," Hyroc said. Elsa's father furrowed his eyebrows in a look of deepening mistrust. The back of Hyroc's head prickled as the horrifying image of being skinned alive appeared in his mind.

"*Then why were you sneaking around our cabin?*"

"I – I was trying to see how you tan hides."

"You expect me to believe such a ridiculous lie," Elsa's father scoffed. "That goat's going to be warm tonight."

"I don't know how to do it myself," Hyroc quickly added. "And I – and I thought I could learn it by watching you and your family. But I swear *that's all* I was doing, sir. I never took anything."

Elsa's father raised an eyebrow giving Hyroc a strange look. "Give me one good reason why I should believe that's what you were really doing?"

"I –" he slumped his head down "– I can't," he said gloomily.

"Why did you kill that wolf?"

Hyroc looked back up at him. "It was going to attack her – your daughter – and I killed it. That's what you're supposed to do when you see someone in danger isn't it? Keep them from getting hurt?"

Elsa's father hesitated, a deeply puzzled expression coming over his face, then said, "Yes. Why did you come to this place?"

Hyroc shrugged. "This looked like a good place for – for trapping."

"Trapping?" Elsa's father said in a surprised tone. Hyroc nodded. "For food?"

"Mostly that, but also for the hides…if I can figure out how to keep them from rotting."

"What were you going to do with those hides?"

Hyroc sighed. "I was hoping to maybe sell them until I figured out what I was going to use them for."

Elsa's father gave him another even more confused look. "You were going to *sell them?*"

"Yes."

"Then why hasn't anyone seen you in town if that was what you wanted?"

Hyroc bowed his head. "I – I was afraid someone would try and – try and kill me."

"If you felt that way, then why would you come here?"

"I didn't think that far ahead and my only other option was the wilderness."

"Isn't that where you came from?" Hyroc shook his head. "Then where did you come from?" Hyroc opened his mouth to answer, but quickly closed it, returning his gaze to the ground, causing Elsa's father to frown. He watched Hyroc for an uncomfortable length of time before asking, "Where do you live?"

Hyroc grimaced. That was the one thing he hoped to avoid answering. Though it seemed doubtful letting the man know such a thing would really make much of a difference at this point. After a long moment's contemplation, Hyroc reluctantly said, "in a cabin I found in a valley at the foot of the mountain." He indicated the general direction with his chin. The expression on the face of Elsa's father hardened. Hyroc began to wonder if he had actually made the correct choice.

After a long pause Elsa's father said, "Why did you go there?"

"Well, when I first arrived here, I found a trail leading off from the road into the trees. I followed it and – and that's how I found that cabin." Else's father studied his face impassively. After an uncomfortable and worrying length of time under his gaze, Elsa's father turned, heading off toward the cabin.

Hyroc slammed the back of his head against the fencepost in frustration. He berated himself for not trying harder to make Elsa's father believe he was not some evil creature and he had failed. It felt as if a cold pit of despair had opened beneath him and he was plummeting uncontrollably into its lightless depths. Suddenly, he saw the image of Kit's face materialize in his mind. The look in the cub's eyes seemed to be saying, "If you give up, I die too." Hyroc shook his head, throwing off some of the weight he felt trying to crush him. *I won't abandon you*! He felt a surge of anger toward Ursa. Everything she had said was clearly a lie. And he had started to believe her. She had no intention of helping him or she would have done it by now. He had squandered numerous opportunities to escape waiting for her to rescue him. If he was going to find a way out of this mess he would have to do it himself. He couldn't count on anybody else's help and he was done expecting it.

• • •

CHAPTER 28

More Than It Seems

Svald strode through the door of his family's cabin. Dull orange embers glowed across a thin layer of gray ash within the cabin's fireplace, which was made from smooth river stones, near the center of the wall opposite the door. Toward the left wall was a large bed big enough for an entire family to sleep in, with both the head and footboards made from polished spruce boughs. Then at the opposite end of the cabin lay the kitchen. At the center of which stood a circular wooden table ringed with chairs and running across the wall were shelves with glass jars filled with medicinal forest plants. His eldest son, Donovan, sat at the table and standing beside the bed was his wife Helen folding clothes.

Two days back Svald found the footprints of someone unfamiliar around his home. It was apparent whoever they belonged to was a thief, because no one in the village would ever sneak around someone's home, unless they intended to take something. Thievery was rare around the village, but it did still happen from time to time. Then Donovan found the remains of a dead wolf not far from their home. The carcass was too far-gone for anything useful and it infuriated him someone could kill a wolf then leave a perfectly good pelt to rot on the body. There was absolutely no excuse for such a wasteful behavior.

And whoever was responsible was also threatening his family's lives by leaving the animal's body so close to their home where it could attract a predator. That fact above all else made him want to apprehend the perpetrator as soon as possible.

Before the sun had risen this morning, starting at the wolf carcass, Donovan and he had followed the thief's faded tracks toward the mountain. Near the mountain's foot, a short distance from a creek, the two of them found a choke point where it seemed likely the thief would pass through again. Using a large net concealed under a bed of leaves, and a small deer carcass as bait, because he assumed it would be hard for the thief to pass up a free meal, they set up a trap and waited for the thief to fall into it. And a few hours later the thief had done just that. Then right after subduing him, Svald's world turned upside down when he discovered the thief was not what he was expecting.

The thief looked normal enough from a distance, but up close Svald realized beneath the person's clothing was fur and his head resembled what appeared to be a wolverine. Svald wondered what kind of person would wear such a mask and stick so much animal fur beneath their clothing during the summer. His wonder quickly turned to shock when it became apparent everything was attached.

Memories of the necromancer, memories he wished forgotten, from ten years ago reentered the forefront of his mind. He remembered vividly the nightmarish scenes of bodies – some of which belonged to people he once knew – walking around trying to strangle anyone they came across. He had grown up hearing stories of witches and forest monster's, and he had sometimes seen strange things while out hunting, but he had never really believed any of them until that day. Once the initial chaos caused by the arrival of the walking corpses abated, the villagers got themselves organized to fight off the dead. When they had finished with their grim task, they found and killed the person responsible. Anyone capable of such a terrible deed deserved no pity.

The thief he had captured was obviously some unnatural thing; there could be no other explanation for its appearance. After what the village went through ten years ago, he knew killing him was the safest option. But he felt an awful wrongness toward the very thought.

There was something strange about the way the thief spoke; it almost reminded him of his son Donovan. Killing him oddly felt akin to killing a child and he could not bring himself to do it. Confused, he decided to bring the thief back with him and turn him over to the village elders. They would be able to better judge what should be done; he was out of his depth.

Then when the three of them arrived back at his home, to his astonishment, he learned from his daughter Elsa that not only did she know about the thief, she had actually met him days earlier. He was furious at her for not telling him. Keeping the thief's presence a secret was bad enough, but merely being associated with such an aberration, she ran the risk of being exiled from the village. With his little girl's future hanging in the balance, he needed to try and preempt any troubles headed her way so he attempted to glean whatever answers he could from the thief. The following conversation with the thief only served to deepen his confusion. The thief explained he was sneaking around their home in order to learn how to tan animal hides. Svald assumed the thief was lying, but he could find no trace of a lie in the thief's words. If what the thief said was the truth, it was hardly what he expected a bloodthirsty monster to want to do. That was basically what he and his family were doing. With his mind reeling, he entered the cabin to try and make sense of what the thief had said.

Using his thumb, Svald pointed over his shoulder through the door at the furry creature he had captured, who was apparently named Hyroc. "Donavan, keep an eye on –" he waved his hand, searching for an appropriate word for describing the Hyroc creature "– on – on *our catch*. I made sure I tied up his hands good but I don't want him getting away while my back's turned."

Donovan gave him a reluctant look, then said, "all right," and headed out the door.

Svald swept his eyes around the cabin, suddenly noticing his daughter was nowhere to be seen. "Helen, *where's Elsa?*" he said, anger seeping into his voice. "*I told her to stay in the cabin.*"

Helen turned her head toward him with a pair of pants folded around one of her arms. "I sent her out to put Grettle in the barn,"

Helen said, neatly setting the disentangled pants on the bed. She made her way over to him "And I told her to stay there until one of us comes out to get her. That way the two of us could talk, alone."

Svald nodded his understanding. "I suppose she already told you about what happened," he said, glancing out the door.

"Bits and pieces; she seemed very upset with you."

"That doesn't surprise me. She doesn't understand I'm trying to prevent her foolishness from hurting her. If anyone finds out she knew about that *thing*, she could be implicated in all of this."

"I know." Helen looked out the door, watching the Hyroc creature. "He looks scared," she said, sounding somewhat puzzled.

Svald turned, joining his gaze with hers. There indeed looked to be a tremendous amount of fear in the Hyroc creature's eyes. He was unsurprised; it should be scared, it had been captured. Whatever powers it held whilst going unnoticed, he and his son had robbed the creature of them, it had plenty to be scared of. But even as he thought that, something about the Hyroc creature made the thought seem callous. As if he had wished harm upon someone's child. Puzzled why he should feel bad about making the Hyroc creature afraid, he pushed the feeling from his mind. This creature was a danger to the village, there was nothing wrong with eliminating danger.

"I would too if I were in its position," Svald said.

"I see you found a new pet," Walter said, entering the cabin with his pipe in hand.

Svald smirked wishing the Hyroc creature was just an animal, that would at least make the whole situation simple. He knew how to deal with animals, not whatever he and his son had found this morning.

Walter shook his head ruefully. "Creatures like *that* need to be put down like a rabid dog. They're just not natural."

"A rabid dog?" Helen said indignantly. "We might not know what it is but I haven't seen anything about him that suggests he's crazed, have you?"

Walter cocked eyebrow at her. "Does it really matter?"

"Of course it matters!"

Walter waved his hand dismissively. "Bah, there's only one way to deal with things like that."

Helen's expression hardened. "There will be *no* killing here as long as I have anything to say about it."

Walter shook his head in disbelief. "That's no better than what it deserves."

"Walter, get out!" Walter gave her a shocked almost hurt look.

"Fine, my advice obviously isn't wanted here; even though I know I'm right." Walter turned and headed for the door.

"And I swear if anything happens to him while he's here, I'll smother you in your sleep." Walter paused a moment, before continuing out the door. Svald smiled at her, repressing a laugh. Helen gave him an unamused glare. "What are you smiling at? You were about as helpful as a pine cone."

"You had it handled just fine," Svald said. "There really wasn't anything for me to say."

"A likely excuse coming from you."

Svald's smile broadened. He leaned over and kissed her on the side of her face. Helen smiled, now showing only a hint of annoyance at her husband. She returned her gaze back out the door.

"Do you know how old he is?" she said.

Almost without thinking, Svald began studying the Hyroc creature more closely trying to discern the answer. His eyes slowly wandered over to Donovan who sat nearby on the edge of the porch. Shifting his gaze back to the Hyroc creature, he noticed it was slightly smaller than his son. It reminded him of the size difference between two boys separated by only a few years of age, but something about the difference was troubling. He wondered why such a trivial detail about the Hyroc creature would feel that way to him, if anything it made the creature easier to deal with. He remembered how the creature had sounded when it spoke. Its voice wasn't as deep as he had expected, and he thought he caught it cracking at times. It became apparent the creature possessed many of the same characteristics as a normal teenager. If that were true, then he had essentially captured a scared child. He shook his head. That couldn't be what he was seeing. He knew practically nothing about witches and from what little he had been able to gather, they were never quite what they appeared to be. For all he knew, this *thing* was playing some sort of trick on his eyes. Something to make him show pity toward it. He had to focus. This thing was dangerous and it needed to be dealt with accordingly. His family was not safe so long as it remained here.

"He doesn't seem like he should be that old," Helen said. "Does he?"

"No he doesn't," Svald said, shaking his head slowly.

She paused. "He looks like he hasn't been eating very well."

Svald felt a twinge of guilt cut through his determination as he remembered hours ago he had used a deer to bait the trap that inevitably captured Hyroc. For some strange reason, the fact the Hyroc creature may be starving put a bitter taste in his mouth. He forced the impression from his mind. That was just another one of its tricks.

He walked over to the kitchen table where the creature's things lay and removed one of the arrows from the quiver. Maybe its equipment would reveal something about its intentions. Shallow chips in the wood ran the length of the shaft and the feathers were split and bent in places. He knew the marks were caused by the arrow skipping off objects; he had often seen the same thing on his own arrows while hunting small game.

"He's been hunting rabbits," Svald said, setting the arrow down on the table. Helen turned from the door, walking over to join him at the table. "There's lots of them up near the mountain where we captured him. But you can't to live off those alone." Helen began examining the arrow he had been looking at.

Svald unsheathed the creature's hunting knife, examined the blade a moment and slipped it back into its scabbard. Next, he picked up the bow. It was a beautiful hunting tool, made from a rich cherry wood, and he couldn't help wishing his own looked half as nice. Other than a few scuff marks where the arrow shafts had rubbed against the wood, it seemed very well cared for. This level of care was not what he expected a depraved creature to be capable of. Carefully, he set the bow back down.

"This doesn't feel right," Helen said, setting the arrow down and turning toward him. "I feel like we're looking at this whole thing wrong. If he meant anyone harm, why would he save Elsa from that wolf?"

The wolf attack was the strangest details of the whole situation. In none of the stories Svald had heard, was the forest monsters ever depicted saving people. In fact, they usually devoured or dismembered anyone they came across and were always something in need of killing by a brave soul, not something to be helped. He wanted the attack to be untrue; a lie would be easier to deal with. An unplanned wolf killing accounted for the dead wolf and a wish to remain hidden explained the wasted carcass. And to further complicate the issue, if saving his daughter from the wolf was true, there was a chance so too was everything else it had said.

"That's for the elders to decide," Svald said.

"I know but –"

Donavan stuck his head in the door, interrupting Helen. "Harold's here," he said eagerly. Svald nodded and Donovan disappeared back outside.

"I just don't think he's done anything wrong," Helen said. "He kept Elsa from getting hurt, that has to mean something doesn't it?"

Svald shrugged. "Harold knows more about these kinds of things; let's see what he has to say about this. Maybe we're missing something he'll see."

"Maybe," she said agreeing, but the skepticism was clear in her voice.

Harold and three others stopped at the front door, staring in disbelief at the Hyroc creature. The three others whispered to one another in alarmed tones. Harold seemed unfazed almost curious. He was a tall broad-shouldered man, with black hair tinged by strips of gray.

"Harold," Svald called out in greeting. "Please come inside, we need to talk with you." Harold slowly turned away from the creature toward him. He said something to the three others who nodded in response, before heading inside the cabin.

Harold indicated the Hyroc creature with his hand as he came through the door. "I assume *that's* why I'm here."

"Yes, please sit," Svald said, indicating a chair at the table.

"How'd you come across *that?*"

Svald briefly explained the thief's tracks, how he had captured him up until the three of them arrived back at the home, leaving out the wolf carcass and his daughter's involvement.

"Well, I'm glad you brought this to my attention first," Harold said gratefully. "Wouldn't have done any good to cause a panic."

"Do you know what he is?" Svald said.

Harold scratched his chin thoughtfully. "There are some types of witches I've came across that he might be. How did he act when you captured him?"

"What do you mean?"

"Was he aggressive, any snarling, growling, roaring, biting, that sort of thing?"

"He struggled a little to get free, not that I can blame him much for that, but nothing like what you just described. Once I got him back here he answered a few questions."

"He can talk?" Harold said taken aback.

"Yeah, I was just as surprised when he did."

"Did he growl or slur his words, or speak in a manner that reminded you of animal noises?"

"No, nothing like that, he pretty much sounded the way we do now."

Harold rubbed his chin in contemplation. "You probably got a better look at him than I did just now, but how were his clothes when you found him? Were there any noticeable gashes in the material, were they dirty or have any large spots of dried blood."

"I saw nothing out of the ordinary with that."

"Did he stink?"

"Well, I didn't go out of my way to figure that one out," Svald said, repressing the urge to laugh. "But now that I think about it, he did have a little bit of a smell to him. It reminded me of that soggy fur smell you get from a wet dog, but it was subtle. Nothing like the stink you get from a bear."

"Did he walk hunched over or on all fours?"

"He walked like a normal person as far as I could tell."

Harold shrugged. "That doesn't match any of the kinds of witches I know about. Whenever they resemble an animal, like our friend out there does, it always affects more than their appearance. They act and sound like an animal, walking on all fours, dried blood all over their clothing from eating live prey, a stench from not bathing, and so on. They never lack any of those characteristics. Our friend must be something I've never seen before." He indicated the Hyroc creature's things. "Did you find those on it?"

"Yes."

Harold unsheathed the sword, turned the blade over, carefully examining it then slid it back into its scabbard; doing the same with the knife. When he looked through the quiver, he pulled out several arrows that appeared to be steel tipped and two with heads made of silver.

"This is for piercing armor," Harold said, holding up a steel tipped arrow. He set it down and picked up a silver tipped one. "And this is a Shadow Killer arrow."

"Shadow Killer?" Svald said.

"They're for killing undead creatures and what most people would call a shadow demon. I know for a fact these are not his, only witch hunters carry these."

"So he stole them?"

Harold nodded. "It wouldn't surprise me if he stole everything we see here. Has anything gone missing from around your house lately?"

"Nothing as far as I know."

"I haven't noticed anything either," Helen added.

Harold stared thoughtfully at the arrow. "It probably took the Shadow Killer's for the silver in their arrowheads, and that also tells me it's not a demon; they wouldn't even touch those." He set the arrow back down. "But it seems like it stole everything else because it thought it might need them."

"With all the bears and wolves around the mountain," Helen said. "I know I'd feel better with a sword."

Svald and Harold nodded.

"How long do you think it's been up there?" Harold said.

"As far as I can figure, less than a month," Svald said.

"If he hasn't stolen anything by now I doubt he's going to," Helen noted.

"Or he just doesn't have a reason to yet," Harold said.

"Or he knows it's wrong." Both Harold and Svald raised a questioning eyebrow at her.

"Wait, are you implying someone taught it that?"

She nodded. "Why else would he refrain from stealing from us, he's had plenty of opportunities to do so."

"Fear is an excellent motivation to avoid going near something dangerous."

"Then why would he save my daughter from a wolf?"

Svald cringed; he trusted Harold but he still wanted to keep the wolf a secret if he could.

"Wolf? What wolf?"

Svald sighed. It was out now. "Elsa told me she was attacked by a wolf," he said. He indicated the Hyroc creature with his hand. "And *he* killed it. We both know she would never make something like that up."

"I don't understand; if he was trying so hard to stay hidden, why kill a wolf right on your doorstep when there's nothing to gain from it, and risk being discovered."

"Because he knew it was the right thing to do," Helen said. "He wasn't thinking about himself. Does there need to be any other reason?"

"Morality is never a strong characteristic of these things and I find the creature's actions with the wolf baffling, but why was it hanging around your cabin in the first place? It must have wanted something."

"Well, when I talked to him, he told me he was trying to see how we tan our hides because he didn't know how to do it himself."

Harold gave him a bewildered look. "That has to be a lie; it has to be something else."

"Why is that so unbelievable?" Helen said. "He was scared of us, and he needed to learn something, so he watched us to learn that thing. It makes pretty good sense to me."

Harold shrugged. "Even if you're right and that's really what he was doing, I doubt the other elders will see it your way."

Helen's expression hardened. "So that's it, you're just going to let them decide his fate. He did something to help somebody – my daughter – and now you're going to pretend it never happened."

ADAM FREESTONE

"I never said I wasn't going to help him," Harold said indignantly. "I've seen plenty of people being wrongfully convicted of witchcraft. And from what the two of you have told me thus far about our friend out there, I don't think he's deserving of punishment. I will do my best to show the others there's a good chance he's not going to hurt anyone, but I cannot make any promises. In the end, it may not matter what I say. The rest of the village may not want him here at all. And after what happened the last time a situation like this arose, I wouldn't blame them."

Helen nodded, but her expression was still unhappy. Harold stood up from the chair as did everyone else. "Svald you should come with me, since you're the one who found him. The others will want you to explain your experience with the creature."

Svald nodded. "I'll be out in a moment," he said. Harold nodded and headed out the door.

"You have to help him," Helen said. "He protected our daughter, that's worth something. If he could do something selfless I know he must have a good heart. I think he deserves to stay."

"I'll try my best."

"For his sake you need to."

Svald kissed her on the cheek before heading outside after Harold.

With a movement of his chin, Harold indicated the three villagers he had brought with him. "I'll leave them here to keep an eye on our friend until the town elders decide what to do with him."

Svald nodded appreciatively at the thoughtfulness toward his family. "Donavan, Curtis," Svald called out to his boys, who promptly joined him. "I'll be back in a few hours. Keep your guard up, understood." Donavan and Curtis nodded their understanding. Then he and Harold headed off toward the road.

Harold wore a troubled look on his face as they walked. "You saw *it* too didn't you?" Svald said. "In his eyes."

Harold shrugged. "He looked like a damn scared kid," he said. His expression saddened. "And I – and I've only seen that once."

Svald nodded understandably. "When I talked with him earlier, a few times I thought I was scolding one of my kids. And he – he called me sir."

Harold gave him a strange look. "He addressed you as *sir?*"

"Yeah, I thought I was hearing things the first time he said it."

"So, now you're telling me he's also polite and respectful?" Harold shook his head in disbelief. "Your wife might have been onto something after all. This doesn't feel right, none of it."

"Then maybe we should try and make it right."

"You make that sound so easy."

"...I then sent my son Curtis to get Harold and once he arrived, we came to the village to notify everyone here," Svald said, finishing his account of his encounter with the Hyroc creature for the second time, making sure to leave out his daughter's involvement.

A large fireplace, with a stuffed boar's head mounted above the hearth, cast dancing orange shadows across the long center table and the tables scattered throughout the emptied Black Spruce Tavern. He, Harold, and four village elders sat gathered at the end of the center table, with a pint of beer in front of them.

There was a long pause. "So we have another witch," Anton said. He was a portly man, with a bald spot on the top of his head. Svald had always thought Anton was a little on the shaky side, but despite that, he usually had the best interests of his fellow villagers in mind.

"I wouldn't exactly call him a witch," Harold said.

"What else would you call that *thing*? You don't get that way on your own unless you're dabbling in something dark. We should notify The Ministry and let them deal with it."

Harold's expression hardened. "That is a terrible idea, Anton. If they find him here, sure they'll deal with him for us, but how do we know they'll stop there and won't think one of us was participating in whatever arts the creature was. Before we know it, we'll have people throwing accusations at each other for fear of being suspected. And it'll be all the more damning when they find out we said nothing about that little incident with the necromancer. I'm telling you, we're better off dealing with this ourselves."

"I agree with Harold," Yary, the owner of the tavern, said. Yary was a tall burly man, with black hair and a large bushy beard. "We dealt with that necromancer without anyone's help; we can deal with this creature."

"And that is why we have come together this day," Luna said. "What to do about our new arrival?"

Luna was a slender older woman with long strands of silvery gray hair falling down to her shoulders. Svald thought she was the wisest person in town, often coming up with solutions to problems no one had ever thought of.

"All right then, if we're going to deal with this ourselves," Anton said. "I think the best solution is to kill it and be done with it." Svald cringed at Anton's words. Hyroc had saved his daughter from a wolf, why did he deserve to die for keeping her from harm? But if he said anything about it, then they would know about his daughter's involvement. Was Hyroc's life more important than hers? No, he had an obligation to her. She would hate him for it, but he could handle that, he would remain silent, for her.

"I agree with Anton," Kipen said. Kipen was a skinny man with thinning hair. "This thing poses an obvious danger to the village."

"That seems the safest option," Yary said.

"I am in agreement," Luna said. "Harold, what say you?"

Harold shifted uncomfortably in his chair, unsure how to respond.

A trickle of doubt began creeping through Svald's mind. What if his decision had no bearing on his daughter's safety? What if she was safe regardless of his choices? In which case, he was allowing someone to be killed essentially because they did a good thing for another person. That didn't seem like justice. That was him letting fear drive his judgment. His daughter would never forgive him for that and frankly he would have a hard time living with himself. The guilt would never leave him and a part of himself, probably the best part of him, would wither and die. Just because he couldn't bring himself to tell the whole story. He would never be the same and what would it have all been for? No, he was making the wrong choice. If Hyroc had any evil intentions, he would've simply stood by and let his daughter be mauled.

And what was he worried about? Every one of the elders knew his daughter. They would never exile her from the village simply because of her involvement in all of this. They were all good, understanding people. He didn't have to worry about them making a decision to harm her. They would see the truth in all of this. She was safe. It wouldn't harm anyone to tell them. If he did that, no matter what they decided, his conscious would be clear. He took a long drought from his pint.

"Why does he deserve to die," Svald said, just as Harold opened his mouth to answer the question of the elders. "What has he done to deserve that?" Everyone in the room fixed their eyes on him in a mixture of odd expressions.

"Have you gone mad?" Anton said in bewilderment. "You've seen firsthand what that thing looks like, it is clearly something unnatural. Who knows what kind of depraved and sinister thoughts go through its mind? You're not seriously suggesting we let it stay are you?"

"Svald does have a point," Harold said. "Yes I agree his appearance is startling, but what has he done that is deserving of death?"

Luna turned to Svald. "You have spent the most time with the creature. When you captured it, did you find anything about the creature's actions when you captured it dangerous?"

"I can't say I wouldn't have reacted the same way as he, but when I talked to him he acted no different than you or I."

"How do you know it's not faking it?" Yary said. "What if that's just an act to get you to let it go free and as soon as you do it'll turn on you."

"I honestly don't think he'll do that."

"What makes you think you know what it may or may not do?" Anton said. "How can any of us know that?"

"What proof do you have to support your claim?" Luna said.

Svald took a deep breath. "There was more to that dead wolf than what I told you." Harold sighed. Everyone gave him a surprised look. "Our goat got out of its pen and wandered off into the woods. Elsa went after her and while getting the goat, she was attacked by a wolf. But before the wolf could hurt her, the creature killed it."

"The creature killed it?" Luna said, taken aback. "Why did you not bring this up sooner?"

Svald shrugged. "I was afraid for my little girl. I didn't want anything to happen to her because of this." Everyone nodded their understanding.

"It was obviously a trick," Anton said. "She got lucky, that's all."

"How can that possibly be a trick," Harold said. "I know firsthand these things never do that under *any* circumstances. The result is usually something grievous and often times, fatal. I've gone over the situation several times in my head already, and I can find no other reason for the creature's actions other than to protect her."

"Wait, are you saying it knows right from wrong?" Kipen said.

"There seems no other explanation."

"Are you now saying it isn't dangerous?" Anton said skeptically.

"I wouldn't say that," Svald said. "But he seems no more dangerous than any one hunter in the village."

"Okay, hold on, let's just say for a moment we let the creature stay," Kipen said. "What good will that do for any of us?"

"Well, when I talked with him, he said he was here for the pelts."

Anton made a disbelieving cough sound.

"Do you believe what he said to be the truth?" Luna said.

"I do; everything it said seems to fit." Luna nodded. "Anton, you're always running out of pelts to work with. And the way he killed that wolf, he could very well solve that problem for you. Would that not be worth him staying?"

Anton stabbed his index finger down on the table. "Perhaps, but I would not jeopardize the safety of my fellow villagers just to earn some extra coin," Anton said. "And if that were truly its intentions why hasn't it come into town to sell any of them?"

Svald gave him a flat look. He had thought the answer seemed pretty obvious. "Because he knew this was how we would react," he said, indicating everyone with his hand. "And now that I see it, I don't much blame him."

"What about the disappearing livestock? Surely you haven't forgotten about those."

"He arrived after those started up if I'm not mistaken," Svald said.

"Besides," Harold interrupted. "If he were responsible for those, why hasn't any of Svald's chickens gone missing? Or better yet, why didn't he try to steal their goat when it got out. His family is the closest home to him."

"What about the fact he lives in the very same cabin as the necromancer?"

"I found nothing of a dark nature in that cabin before we boarded it up," Harold said. "But disregarding who the past owner was, it makes perfect sense the creature would move into it. It's abandoned for one, it's on a fairly secluded part of the mountain and close to some decent hunting grounds. That sounds like a pretty good spot to go if you have no home."

"That makes a lot of sense to me if you put it that way," Yary said.

"Harold," Luna said. "You know more about these matters than any of us here. Do you honestly think it safe to allow this creature to stay?"

"I cannot say with absolute surety, but I believe so."

"And what of The Ministry?" Kipen said.

"We're too far from their power center for there to be much of a chance of their coming here." He gave Anton a suspicious look. "So long as no one tells them *it's here*."

"I trust your judgment, but what say the rest of you? Should we allow the creature to stay?" There was a long pause.

"I trust Svald and Harold," Yary said. "If they think it's a good idea I believe them."

"As do I," Kipen said.

Everyone turned their attention to Anton. "If that's what everyone wishes, I will not object," he said, a note of angered reluctance in his voice.

"Then it is settled, for the time being at least, the creature will be allowed to stay," Luna said.

Svald breathed a silent sigh of relief.

"But I'm sure everyone will agree with me when I say, this arrangement only stands if the creature does not become dangerous and if no objects of a dark nature are discovered in its possession."

"When we release the creature I will examine it, its belongings, and the cabin for any of those traces," Harold said.

"And I will leave it up to you and Svald to explain to our *guest* what will and will not be tolerated in this village."

"Agreed," Svald and Harold said.

"There is one more thing? Since the two of you vouched for the creature, should it turn dangerous both of you will be held accountable. Do the two of you accept this burden?"

Svald and Harold gave each other a quick uncertain glance, before saying, "I do."

"Very well. Does anyone have anything else they would like to say regarding this matter?" Luna paused, looking through the faces of all in attendance. "Then I now leave this matter to Svald and Harold. We're done here." With that, the rest of the town elders began filing out of the room.

Harold leaned over toward Svald with a smirk on his face. "Well we got what we wanted, or at least what your wife and daughter wanted." he said smugly. "Now what the hell do we do?"

• • •

CHAPTER 29

Crow nests

Hyroc focused on the tiny shape of a black spider crawling across the ground in front of him. Other than the families' hound coming over to growl at him, the tiny creature was the most interesting thing he had seen for a while. Shortly after Elsa's father had disappeared into the cabin, he found enough slack in the rope tying his wrists together for him to press the side of one claw into it and begin cutting through his restraints. He knew it would still take him an incredible length of time to cut through, but what choice did he have? They were going to kill him. The presence of guards clearly indicated they thought he was dangerous and there was only one way they would deal with something dangerous. It was just fortunate they were taking so long to decide what to do. Their indecision would give him the time he needed to cut his restraints. Then once he did that, he just had to wait for an opening and make a break for the tree line. He was confident he could out run those guarding him, but the dog was a problem. Outpacing the beast on open ground would be impossible. He had scared it off before by hitting it in the head with a rock so maybe that was all he needed to do. Sweeping his eyes across the ground, he found several stones that would work. He could snatch one up as he made for the tree line. The only thing wrong with his plan was it required him to leave behind his, bow, sword and knife. Save for the sword, the other two were of vital importance, but he saw no way to recover them without dying. And being dead seemed a considerable step backwards. Maybe in a few days after his escape, he could come back and get them.

When he got away from the men and the dog, he would make his way back up to the mountain and salvage as many of his traps as he could on his way to the cabin. Then he should have just enough time to get Kit, pack up his things and sneak off north toward the mountain. The wilderness would become his home. He was stupid for believing he could ever stay around people. They simply didn't want him anywhere near them no matter how honest his intentions were. The only exception had been Elsa. He felt no animosity toward her, he had actually liked her, though he wondered if that might have been because she was nice to him. His encounter with her made him think this whole thing could work out after all. Then reality came crashing down on him, shattering his deluded hope. He now knew it would never work. He couldn't trust anyone, not even his so-called guardian Ursa. Her inaction was proof of that. Why else would she leave him in such a dire predicament? For now on, he would rely only on himself and no one else. He just had to get out of his restraints.

The spider disappeared into a clump of grass. Hyroc searched for it a moment, before resuming staring absentmindedly at the ground, hoping some other creature would come along for him to look at.

Back and forth…
Back and forth…

The families' hound rose to its feet from where it lay on the cabin's porch and broke into a run, barking excitedly as it went. Following the dogs with his eyes, Hyroc felt a thrill of apprehension when he saw Elsa's father and the other man – Harold might have been his name – walking down the trail leading to the cabin. It was too soon! He needed more time to cut through the rope.

Chiding himself for not working faster when he had plenty of time, he desperately began cutting as fast as he could. The two men continued their approach, almost seeming to fly toward him. The three guards turned to greet the returning men. Everyone exchanged a few words, indicating Hyroc once or twice as they spoke.

Then to his relief, Else's father and the other man disappeared inside the cabin. He had a little more time. In a frighteningly short amount of time, they emerged through the door, making their way toward him. Dread engulfed him as he realized he wasn't going to make it. His plan had failed before he even had a chance to attempt it.

Elsa's father propped some things against a fence post and drew his knife. A cold shiver ran up Hyroc's back and every part of his mind screamed for him to run. He watched in horror, transfixed by the dull gray metal of the approaching blade. He closed his eyes; he didn't want to see what was about to happen. It now almost seemed better if the spider bite had done him in, he had at least been fighting then; instead, he was going to die tied to a fence, helpless as a newborn kitten. He hoped it was going to be quick and wouldn't hurt.

He felt a hand pull his up. His restraints grew tighter, then their pressure vanished altogether and he felt them being slipped off. Confused, he opened his eyes to see Elsa's father stand and step over to join the other man. He had an urge to break for the trees but something about the looks on the men's faces made him stay where he was. He didn't see fear, they almost seemed glad to see him, almost as if they wished to talk with him. That didn't make sense, why would they want to speak with him when they were here to kill him? Those witch hunters had shown no interest in any such thing. He wondered if it was a trick, though neither one of them seemed ready to draw a weapon. He rubbed his wrist as he stared at the two men, unsure how to react. Elsa's father looked at the rope in his hand and frowned at the frayed spot where Hyroc had been trying to cut through. Hyroc stared at the fray, which was barely a quarter of the way through the rope, and was gloomily surprised by his lack of progress

"You're free to go," the other man said.

Hyroc gave him a disbelieving look. Why would they simply let him go after going through all the hassle of capturing him? What was going on here? Was this some elaborate trick to get him to reveal something? Maybe if he played along he could use this opportunity to get his things back. It was worth a shot, but that game was really starting to aggravate him. It would be so much easier if people would simply tell him what they wanted.

Using his hand, Elsa's father indicated the things he had set against the fencepost. "All your things are right here," he said, in a slightly gentler tone than last he spoke.

Glancing in the indicated direction Hyroc saw his things. They knew he was dangerous, why would they give him his things back? Making him more threatening seemed an odd thing to do. Maybe they really weren't going to hurt him. He wanted to believe it, but part of him told him to be ready for an attack. At the first sign of trouble he would bolt and never turn back. Cautiously, he got to his feet ready to react, never taking his eyes off the men.

"My name's Svald, Svald Shackleton." Elsa's father said. He indicated the other man with his hand. "And this is Harold."

Hyroc stared at him puzzled, it almost sounded like they were introducing themselves to him. Why would they waste their time getting to know him if they were going to kill him? Could what they said be genuine?

Tentatively Hyroc said, "My – my name's Hyroc."

"Good to meet you, Hyroc," both men said.

"The town elders have decided to let you stay," Harold said, after a brief pause. Hyroc gave the two men a baffled look. Had he heard the man correctly, had he said he could stay? Did they really mean that? Would he be able to keep the cabin? What was going on! None of it made any sense. "But we have rules here. Foremost of all don't murder anyone." Hyroc raised an eyebrow wondering why they needed to tell him that, didn't everyone know that rule? "Stealing is another one," Harold said, affixing a sterner gaze on him. Hyroc smiled uncomfortably. Harold indicated his things. "We know none of those are yours."

"The bow is," Hyroc said without thinking. He cringed, realizing he had inadvertently admitted to stealing everything else.

Harold gave him a flat stare. "But so long as it wasn't from anyone in the village," he continued. "And since you likely have a use for them, you can keep them, with one exception." He reached into Hyroc's quiver, removing the two silver-headed arrows and dropping them on the ground. Hyroc silently sighed, he had meant to sell those, but he would gladly part with them if it meant he could stay. "If you break any of those two rules the deal is off, understood?"

Hyroc nodded. "Does this mean I can come into the village?" he asked hopefully.

"I believe it does, but I wouldn't expect a friendly welcome, let alone a hello." Hyroc nodded understandably; he expected nothing less. If he could go into the village without fear of being killed, everything else was nothing.

"I hope I don't find you sneaking around our home again," Svald said.

With a sigh Hyroc said, "You won't," he would figure out some other way to tan hides.

"Use the door next time."

Hyroc cocked an eyebrow. Why did they want him to use the door? Were they actually suggesting he could come ask them for things? Not that he really planned on doing so, it was just exciting it was an actual possibility. He had never been invited into someone's home before.

Out of the corner of his eye, he thought he saw Harold slip something into his hand. Glancing over, he noticed Harold had interlaced his fingers, holding his hands in front of his stomach, as if concealing something. Harold smiled back at him.

"My family dose most of its trapping from here, north to the river and we usually hunt to the East," Svald continued. "I don't think of myself as a stickler for trapping or hunting rights, if you accidentally wander into our area it's not a big deal, just don't make it into a habit, understood."

Hyroc nodded his understanding. He saw Harold steal a glance down into his hands. His expression turned to confusion, then it immediately vanished when he noticed Hyroc looking at him.

"Is everything understood?"

"It is," Hyroc said, returning his attention to Svald.

"Good. You probably have some things to get done, so let's get you home."

"Thank you." Hyroc walked over and began warily collecting his things, while at the same time keeping a close eye on Harold; he wanted to know what he was holding. After belting on his sword, he saw Harold put what looked like a small crystal ball in his pocket. Hyroc vaguely remembered Marcus saying something about that kind of object turning blue when it was used on him. It was called a Peering Orb if he remembered correctly. It was supposed to turn purple or black if it detected any trace of witchcraft on a person or object. It must have turned blue otherwise Svald and Harold wouldn't still be talking to him.

"Lead the way," Svald said, once Hyroc had finished getting his things together.

Feeling nervous showing them the way, he began leading them to his cabin. A crow squawked angrily, fluttering a short distance away as the group passed its perch on the fencepost. Hyroc had seen a crow standing on that fencepost ever since he was brought to the cabin. Looking up into the sky, he saw the dark shape of Shimmer circling overhead. Glancing back at the first crow on the fence, he saw it watching him intently. Something strange was happening with that crow, but Hyroc dared not mention it to the two men escorting him.

Very little was said during the trip back to his cabin. When they arrived the long shadows and cool light of dusk had settled on the mountain.

"This is it," Hyroc said, presenting his cabin.

"You're very fortunate to have found this," Svald said.

Hyroc nodded knowingly.

"You two stay here," Harold said, walking toward the cabin's door. "I need to check something before we can finalize the deal."

A sense of alarm crept into Hyroc's mind. What was Harold looking for? A bolt of fear shot through him when he realized Kit was tied to a tree near the cabin's front door. How would they react to him having a mountain lion cub? Hyroc stole a glance at the tree. Kit was nowhere to be seen. Repressing a surge of despair, he watched Harold pull the door open and step inside. What felt like hours passed before Harold walked back out.

"There's nothing here," Harold said.

"I didn't think there would be," Svald said. "But it's better to be safe than sorry."

Hyroc breathed a mild sigh of relief. "We'll let you get back to whatever you needed to do before dark," Svald said. "Just don't forget anything we said and we won't have any more problems." With that, the two men headed off.

The instant they were out of earshot, Hyroc rushed over to the tree he had tied Kit to. The twine that functioned as a collar looked like it had been cut. Kit must have finally managed to chew through it. Night was rapidly approaching and the night predators would soon be out and none of them would think twice about snapping up a mountain lion cub. Repressing a new feeling of urgency, he scoured the ground for tracks. He found none. "Kit," he called out. No response. He continued yelling as he frantically checked in and under every nearby tree. Hoping Kit had gone to drink from the stream; he quickly made his way over there. Looking up and down the shore, there was no sign of the cub.

"Kit," Hyroc yelled as loud as he could.

He heard a tiny, faint yowl. Doing his best to suppress a flood of excitement, he carefully listened. The yowl sounded again a little closer. "Kit," Hyroc called out, cautiously walking in the direction of the sound. Several paces later, he started, seeing Ursa come into view. Hanging limply from her mouth by the scruff of his neck, Hyroc saw Kit. "Kit, there you are," he yelled excitedly. Kit yowled pathetically. After a few more steps, Ursa lowered her head and dropped Kit. With a hiss, he bolted behind Hyroc, growling at the large white bear.

"I thought something had happened to you," Hyroc said scratching Kit behind the ears.

"It's fortunate," Ursa said. "I had enough time to get him away."

Hyroc narrowed his eyes, anger welling up within him. "I thought you were supposed to protect me!" he said acidly.

Ursa gave him a curious look. "Is that not what I have done for you?"

He gave her a baffled glare. "You could have gotten them to release me."

"What would that have accomplished, besides hurting two hunters that were doing what they thought best for their family? It turned out all right didn't it?"

"Yes, but what if they had decided to kill me instead?"

"Then I would have stopped them. I don't see what your complaint is? You still have your den, don't you?"

"Yes but –"

A flutter of movement in one of the trees beside Ursa caught his attention. Perched on a branch he saw Shimmer, but beside the raven stood half a dozen crows. Sweeping his eyes around the clearing, he saw still more crows perched amongst the trees, all of which were watching him.

"Are you making them do that?" Hyroc said, indicating the tree beside her.

"I'm not making them do anything, I'm asking them to."

Hyroc gave her a bewildered look. "You're *asking* them to watch me?"

"Yes, I made a deal with them and they accepted my terms." Hyroc stared at her strangely a long while, not quite sure how to respond. "In simplest of terms, I told them to watch you and if they did that, the mountain would be safer for their eggs and fledgling."

"How are you going the keep your end of the bargain, without killing every predator on the mountain?"

"I'm not going to keep it, you are."

Hyroc gave her a startled look. "WHAT! HOW AM I SUPOSED TO DO THAT? I might think of myself as a good hunter, but I know I'm not nearly good enough to do that."

"You've already done that," she said in an amused tone.

"I'm pretty sure I'd remember killing scores of dangerous animals single-handedly," he said indignantly. "About the best I've done is take out a few rabbits."

"Your mere presence makes the mountain safer for them." Hyroc raised a skeptical eyebrow at her. "By trapping and hunting around here you reduce the number of predators that prey on birds, thus making this area safer for their eggs and fledglings."

"But I haven't killed enough animals to make a difference, have I?"

"Not really, but birds are just like any other animal, they'll take whatever advantage they can get. A little safer may not seem like much of an improvement, but it is still an improvement nonetheless."

"Are they worried about you, I don't know, *eating them?*"

Ursa gave him a humored look. "I'm a bear, unless a bird is dumb enough to sit there and to let me eat it, I really don't have any hope of catching one and they know it. But also because I'm a bear, no other animal, except for maybe a weasel or a wolverine, will make a deal with me because I'm a danger to them."

"So, you told – I mean, asked them, to keep an eye on me?"

"Precisely, you couldn't see me but you never left my watch. Did you ever wonder why The Ministry never got to you after the man who adopted you died?" she said proudly. "They definitely tried." Hyroc gave her a puzzled look. "The Ministry requires far more parchment than most people realize. Whenever I discovered an order went through related to harming you and other such dangerous instructions, that order would mysteriously go missing from a curer's bag or someone's desk beside an open window. With the help of my feathered friends, the ones in the capital who wanted to get rid of you could never get their orders to the ones who took care of those things –"

Hyroc smiled mischievously, imagining a man in a long robe turning from his desk to grab a book from a nearby shelf, then turning back to find his parchment suddenly went missing.

"– And that woman who looked after you was able to take care of any problems that happened near you. That is, until the incident with that boy happened. There was nothing losing a few orders would do to remedy that situation. Anyway, the villagers would not have allowed you into the fold if I had shown up to rescue you. The birds were the safest option. Do you understand now?" Hyroc nodded as he reached down to scratch Kit, who was lightly biting his leg. "Just make sure you don't raid the nests of any birds on the mountain, unless your need is dire. Your friend knows not to as well." She paused, looking up into the sky. "It's getting late; the two of you need to eat."

With that, she turned, disappearing into the trees a moment later. Hyroc stood, looking down at Kit when she had gone. "Well, I think everything went a lot better than I had expected," he said casually. "I thought we were going to have to run." Kit yowled in what sounded almost like agreement. Hyroc smiled down at him. "But I think things are actually starting to look up." And it even felt safe for him to allow himself to believe it.

CHAPTER 30

An Unwanted Customer

Thin lines of rain streaked downward, disappearing silently into the ground as Hyroc stood beneath the spindly canopy of a birch tree. In front of him lay the first scattered buildings marking the eastern edge of Elswood. How his frightening encounter with Elsa's father had turned out still puzzled him. Elsa's father and brother were shocked by his features, treating him as if he were some terrible beast. Then hours later, when he had convinced himself coexisting with people was impossible, he was released and informed he could come into the village. Elsa's father obviously thought he was dangerous, why else would he restrain him and summon guards, not to mention threatening to turn him into a blanket. After such a strong reaction, it made no sense for them to simply let him go, least of all in such a polite manner. For as long as he could remember, when somebody feared him that fear never subsided, it often got worse. Maybe his actions with the wolf had somehow changed the mind of Elsa's father. He did seem suddenly conflicted when he learned of that. Whatever the reasons, he was thankful for how everything turned out, no matter how strange it seemed. Now he needed to figure out if what the two men told him regarding the village was actually true. It would make his life tremendously easier if it was. He really couldn't think of a reason why someone would deceive him with that.

He pulled his hood up as far over his face as it would go. He didn't know how many of the villagers actually knew about him, so it seemed a good idea to try and conceal at least some of his features on his first trip there. Maybe then, it wouldn't be as much of a shock for those people.

Reaching down, he untied the pelt of a deer rabbit hanging from his belt. He had caught the horned hare during the morning and despite having cleaned it as best he could, it still smelled of blood. He didn't fool himself into thinking the villagers would treat him any better than the townsfolk of Forna, but if he brought something to trade, maybe they wouldn't be as inclined to think he was a mindless monster. Trading seemed a very odd thing for a monster to do, unless it was for human skulls or something. Though, it still seemed prudent for him to bring his sword. Having it gave him a measure of confidence and if things did not go as he hoped, the villagers might think twice before trying to harm him.

After ensuring his sword was properly secured to his belt, with the deer-rabbit pelt in hand, he headed toward the village. The buildings grew steadily closer together as he walked down the muddy street path running between the structures. He lowered his head, turning away as he passed a group of three villagers gathered at the entrance of a side path between two homes, talking to one another. The group's conversation paused as they regarded him, but resumed once he was out of their sight. He felt an increasing number of eyes on him the farther he ventured into the village. The street path widened into a circular space with a well where a smaller path cut through at an angle forming what appeared to be the village center.

Across the space, he saw a building with a carved sign naming it the Black Spruce Tavern. The smell of freshly baked bread wafted over from somewhere to his right. Turning, he saw a bakery and the edge of a butcher shop. On the other side of the village center, opposite these two buildings, were what looked to be a mercantile, tailoring shop, and a third shop with what looked to be kitchen aids. To his immediate left, judging from a fur mounted on a rectangular rack inside the building, lay a furrier. That was the shop he was looking for.

Taking a deep breath, steeling his nerves for the shopkeeper's inevitable response, he walked inside. The shopkeeper, a portly man, with a woolen cap mostly covering a large bald spot on the top of his head, stood at a bench near the right wall of the shop with his back to the door. Hyroc anxiously waited inside the door for the man to take notice of him. The man did not turn; in fact, he didn't seem to have noticed he had a customer. Hyroc smiled to himself seeing how quiet hunting in the forest had made him. He opened his mouth to make his presence known, but wondered if that would startle the shopkeeper. The man would then be surprised again when he saw his face. Startling this man twice seemed a very bad way to introduce himself, so he stepped back and knocked on the door frame instead.

"Good afternoon," the man said kindly, setting something down on the bench and turning toward him. "I just finished a..." the man cut off mid-sentence, startled by Hyroc's face. Hyroc shrugged. Knowing it was coming still didn't make it feel any better. "Oh, *it's you*," the man said in a far less kind manner. Hyroc raised a puzzled eyebrow. The man almost sounded as if he already knew about him. That worried him a little. Had word of his presence already spread through the village? He expected that to happen in a few more days but not this fast. Now more eyes would be on him, people gawking to get a look at the strange thing venturing into their village. He quickly pushed his thoughts from that. They couldn't hurt him by looking at him. If people weren't trying to kill him, being stared at was nothing.

"I guess it was too much to hope for that you had left. What do you want?" he said acidly.

Hyroc held up the deer-rabbit pelt, eliciting a perplexed look from the shopkeeper. Unsure how exactly to phrase his query, he said, "I want to sell this."

The man's sighed, holding his hand out. "Let's get this over with," he said under his breath. Hyroc handed him the pelt. The man held it out in front of him, examining it with what seemed to be only a mild interest. "It's in surprisingly good condition; I'll give you five Flecks for it."

That seemed a reasonable amount. "Okay," Hyroc said. Reaching into his coin sack, the man removed the coins and warily dropped them into his hand, doing his best not to actually touch his hand. Without another word, the man walked backward to his bench without taking his eyes off him. Taking that as his cue to leave, Hyroc headed out the door.

He looked from the bakery and the three shops across from it. His hand drifted down to the bag of coins hanging from his belt. The bag only contained a small amount of coins, but it should still be enough for him to buy a few things. He needed twine to make more traps, a needle and thread would be nice for patching up his clothing, a proper ax for chopping wood, and it was probably a good idea to get a collar for Kit. The mercantile was the first one he headed for.

A tiny bell rang as he pushed the door open to enter the shop. The shopkeeper and two women standing together stared at him once his face came into view. He tried saying hello but the word caught in his throat, causing him to make a sound more like a burp. Mortified, he quickly turned from the three people and began looking through the shop's wares.

"That's the thing the Shackleton's found out near their place," one of the women said in a whisper.

"It's hideous," the other woman whispered in response. Hyroc felt warmth creeping through his face as he continued his search.

"I hear it drinks the blood of the animals it kills and sucks the marrow from their bones." He paused, caught off guard by the comment, though not entirely surprised by it. He was used to hearing uncomfortable details about the things he supposedly did. But it was still incredibly irritating.

"That's disgusting."

"Well, look at it, that shouldn't surprise you."

There was a pause. It felt as if their eyes were creeping over every inch of his body. "I thought it would be bigger."

"Let's just be glad it's not."

"Why on earth would the elders let *that* into the village?"

"Too much ale I suspect," the woman said with a laugh.

Hyroc found coils of heavy twine and wood axes at the back of the shop. Ready to be rid of the women's gossip, he grabbed the smallest coil of twine, a wood ax, then went to the shopkeeper. The women stopped whispering, taking a step back when they saw him approaching.

"How much for these?" Hyroc said, using his eyes to indicate the items in his arms.

As expected, the shopkeeper seemed even more disconcerted seeing his features up close. After an awkward moment of being stared at from an uncomfortably short distance, the shopkeeper said, "Eight Flecks for all that." Hyroc fished the appropriate amount out of his coin sack, laying it on the counter in front of the shopkeeper. The shopkeeper's eyes flickered down to the coins, then he resumed staring. Hyroc waited for the shopkeeper to indicate their transaction had ended. The shopkeeper continued to stare and seemed to become more nervous with every passing second. Hyroc looked from the two women to the shopkeeper. All three continued to stare. Hoping it was now okay for him to leave, he hurried out the door.

Next was the tailoring shop. Inside he found a slender older woman with long silvery gray hair down to her shoulders, working on a loom. She regarded him in a somewhat surprised manner, but seemed more curious than afraid. She looked at him as if he were some interesting bird she had never seen before. It was somewhat disconcerting being looked at that way, but it was much better than being awkwardly stared at. It reminded him of how the school cook had reacted upon their first encounter. Maybe the same sort of thing could happen with this woman eventually. Sweeping his eyes around the shop, he located the spools of sewing thread.

"It's five Flecks for every spool," the women said.

Hyroc walked over to her with the spool in hand and paid for it. "Where are your needles?" he asked politely. She pointed to a pincushion on a nearby shelf. He extricated a needle. "How much for this?"

"No charge, it's yours," she said with a smile. He gave her a surprised look, then felt a smile creep across his face in turn. He nodded gratefully. "Good day," she said, as he headed out the door.

From the tailor he made his way to the shop with the kitchenware's. Feeling a little better about his situation, he walked through the door. A brown-haired woman and a younger woman, who appeared to be her daughter, turned to greet him; both immediately gasped when they saw his face.

"HEATHEN!" the oldest woman yelled, lunging for a broom propped up against the back wall. Wielding the broom like a halberd, she rushed toward him.

"*WAIT, I'm just here to...*" Hyroc managed to call out before the hard part of the broom that held the bristly parts slammed into his face.

"OUT YOU HIDEOUS BEAST, OUT!" the woman yelled. Hyroc threw a hand up as the woman struck him again even harder. Turning to flee, he took another hit to the back of the head. "YOU WILL NOT TAKE MY DOUGHTER!" The woman got another three hits in on his head before he darted out the door. "YOU ARE NOT WELCOME HERE BEAST," the woman shouted from the door, brandishing her broom menacingly.

Every villager present in the square was staring at him with a myriad of interested expressions. With a frustrated sigh, he angrily rubbed the back of his head as he wandered down the nearest street path to escape the unwanted attention.

He hated people always staring at him and talking about him behind his back, but at least none of those caused him actual pain. Why had the first three shop owners treated him the way they did, while that woman tried to beat him senseless with a broom. "YOU WILL NOT TAKE MY DOUGHTER!" she had said. It was true nearly every parent lashed out at him if he got too close to their children. That usually involved nothing more harmful than some unkind words and a lot of shooing, never an attack. None of them ever made any indication they feared him stealing their children. Maybe his size frightened that woman. Maybe he was big enough to seem capable of whisking small children off into the woods. It wasn't a very reassuring thought. Reaching up, he began running his hand across his face which had gone from a throbbing sting to an uncomfortable hot sensation. He felt no noticeable difference in his features. If he looked scarier, what was there to do about it? He couldn't exactly get a new face, well at least not in any way he wished to explore. He could only make the best of it, as he had always done.

Tearing himself from his thoughts, he realized he was nearing the edge of the village. A pungent odor drifted on a light moisture-laden breeze. There was something familiar about that odor. Following the smell, he saw what looked to be a shop several yards from the last buildings of the village. The pain of the broom strikes flashed through his mind as he looked upon the building. Then the memory of the old woman's smile made him forget the pain for a moment. Not everyone in the village thought he was a monster. Elsa definitely didn't think he was. Taking a deep breath, he pushed his worries aside and walked over to the shop. Inside he found a variety of leather goods. A burly blond haired man entered the shop through an open backdoor. The man paused taking in Hyroc's features. He didn't seem alarmed, but there was mistrust in his eyes. His expression seemed to say, "take one step out of line and I'll make you pay for it."

"Do you have any collars, like umm, for a dog?" Hyroc said tentatively.

The man gave him a strange look. "I have a few," the man said in an unexpectedly deep voice. He walked over to a shelf behind a counter with a pair of leather gloves laid across its top, removing three dusty collars of different sizes. Unsure exactly how big Kit would get, Hyroc pointed to a medium-sized collar with a loop for attaching a leash.

"That'll be eight Flecks," the man said. Hyroc reached into his coin sack, pausing with dismay feeling only eight Flecks left. With an effort, he removed the last of its contents and set them on the counter. "Anything else?"

"No," he said with a quiet sigh.

"Pleasure doing business with you."

Unsure which part of the village this was in relation to his cabin, he reluctantly headed back toward the village center. Hopefully, everyone's interest in the broom incident had subsided by now. As he reentered the circular space, most of the earlier onlookers had left. The Tavern caught his attention. He remembered the teachers at the boarding school and even Marcus mentioning going to one in Forna.

It seemed an important place from the way they always talked about it, but beyond drinking beer, he had no idea what went on inside. Curiosity piqued, he headed inside to have a look. The inside smelled of what he assumed was beer, along with a few aromas somewhat more pleasant. Tables were scattered throughout the structure, with a long table toward the middle in front of a fireplace with a tusked boar's head mounted above. Behind a counter at the right wall stood a tall broad-shouldered man, with black hair and a bushy beard of a matching color, absentmindedly wiping down the flat wood in front of him with a cloth. Men in separate group's occupied tables scattered throughout the Tavern, all with a pint of beer in front of them. Beyond an initial glance, no one seemed to pay much heed to his entrance. Hyroc had to admit he was disappointed by what he saw, there didn't seem to be anything remotely interesting about this place.

Catching a snatch of a conversation between a group of men talking about hunting spots and some references to what other people were doing, he covertly slipped into the chair of a nearby table to listen with his back toward the men. As he listened, it slowly donned on him why it seemed people came here. There really wasn't anything special about the tavern, people came here to talk to friends and to find out what was going on around the village. This place might be useful after all.

The men said their goodbyes after a few minutes and dispersed, leaving behind their beer steins. Looking at the unattended steins, he wondered what beer tasted like. Every patron he saw had a stein and he could only assume they contained something tasty. Stealing a quick glance around, no one was looking in his direction. He snatched a half-full stein off the table. Heart pounding with the thrill of his theft, he darted over to a shaded corner, away from the tavern's occupants. Carefully tipping the stein to his mouth, he eagerly took a drink. He frowned. It actually wasn't close to something he wanted to drink. *Why was everyone drinking this? I've drank better tasting water than this.* Disappointed, he set down the stein and snuck out the door.

As he headed toward the street that led toward his cabin, he heard a familiar voice call his name. Turning, he saw Elsa waving as she made her way over to him with a basket in her arms. Nearly forgetting what the appropriate response was, he waved back after a long pause.

"I'm glad you're still here," she said relieved. "I was worried they had scared you off."

"It'll take a little more than that to scare me off," Hyroc said proudly. Though that wasn't anywhere close to the truth. Her father and brother had almost done so.

"I'm sorry for not coming to see you, but my father was angry with me for not telling him about you and he wouldn't let me leave the house until today."

He gave her a strange look. That hardly seemed something worth apologizing about. "Why are you sorry, it was only two days? It's not like you abandoned me for months."

"I know, but after what you went through, it seemed the kind thing to do."

He smiled gratefully. "Thank you; kindness isn't something I'm used to."

Elsa frowned sympathetically. "Mother, over here," she said, with a beckoning gesture towards somebody.

Looking in the director she had indicated, Hyroc saw Elsa's mother coming over to join them.

"I'm sorry about how we first met," Elsa's mother said, with a look of displeasure. "You must think we're terrible people. We thought – we thought you were something else."

"I understand," Hyroc said, reluctantly keeping his anger from appearing.

"I want to prove to you we're not as bad as you think. My name's Helen and though you probably already know her name, this is my daughter Elsa."

"I'm Hyroc."

"It's good to meet the one who saved my daughter, Hyroc."

"See, just like I told you he's like everyone else," Elsa said with a smile.

"Indeed he is," Elsa's mother agreed with a smile. She paused. "I have a wonderful idea, how would you like to come over for dinner tomorrow, love?"

Hyroc gave her a surprised look; no one had ever dared to invite him over for dinner. What was with this place? "You umm really want me to come into your umm home?"

"Of course we would. With us being neighbors and all, we should get to know each other properly and put the past behind us. It's the least my family can do after what you did for my daughter."

"I – I would like that."

"Great."

"You won't be disappointed by my mother's cooking," Elsa said beaming.

"Anyone's cooking is better than mine," Hyroc admitted. The only two recipes he seemed to know were burnt meat and dirt crusted meat.

"Well, it was nice meeting you, but we should be getting to our errands," Elsa's mother said kindly. "We look forward to having you over tomorrow night."

"As do I."

"Good day," Elsa and her mother said in turn, before heading off toward the shops. Hyroc headed home to put a collar on what would no doubt be a very upset mountain lion.

That night, he waited until Kit had dozed to put the collar on. It went around his neck easily enough but an instant later, the cub had slid the collar back off. Hyroc growled in frustration. As soon as he came in for another attempt, Kit growled angrily and started swatted at Hyroc with his razor-sharp claws. Hyroc backed away, put on his gloves and ran at the cub. Startled Kit, recoiled leaving an opening in his stance for Hyroc to immobilize him by seizing the scruff of his neck. He lightly placed a foot on Kit's back just to be sure, then put the collar back on. This time he made sure it was on tight enough.

He laughed triumphantly, releasing his grip on Kit. The infuriated cub flipped over onto his back, latched onto Hyroc's leg above the boot and began biting it savagely. Hyroc yelled out in pain and detached the cub's claws and teeth from his skin. With a hiss, Kit fell onto his side scratching at the collar. Looking down to examine the extent of his injury at a safe distance from his attacker, Hyroc found a tear in his leggings. He pulled his pant leg up. He didn't seem to be bleeding but the scratches were deep enough to hurt like he was. Kit struggled to get the collar off for a few minutes without any success. Once he realized it wasn't coming off, he flopped down on the floor glaring at Hyroc and began making a very irritated growling noise.

"Oh it's not that bad," Hyroc said.

Kit glared at him more severely, and the fiery look in his eyes seemed to say, "Then why don't you have one?"

"At least I didn't hit you in the head with a broom!" Hyroc said, reaching for the needle and thread.

CHAPTER 31

Stray Dog

The surface of the gently flowing stream was serenely smooth beside Hyroc as he knelt shirtless, scrubbing his jerkin with one of the old rags from the chest in his cabin. Kit lay sprawled out beneath the bristly skirt of a nearby tree half-asleep. He had exhausted himself by spending the previous night and most of the day unsuccessfully trying to get his collar off. Hyroc hoped this would be the last of Kit's defiance; he had not slept much because of the cub's incessant spasms to rid himself of the collar.

He wetted his rag in the stream. This was the first time he had been invited into someone's home and making sure his clothes were clean seemed an appropriate response to the occasion. It should help prove to the family he had a sense for cleanliness and wasn't some manner less thing. Marcus had always said, "If you don't want people to think you're no better than an animal, make sure your clothes are spotless."

Returning his gaze to his jerkin, he frowned, noticing a dried blood smear on its right side. It looked a few days old, making him wonder how long it had been there. Was it there when he ventured into the village? Maybe that's why the woman had reacted so violently. It might have made her think he just attacked somebody on his way to her shop. Then again, she was probably too preoccupied with his features and grabbing a broom to notice the blood. Regardless of the reason, it would only make him look unsightly at dinner with the Shackleton's. Luckily, after some hard scrubbing, the blood came off. The rest of the jerkin looked as clean as he was going to get it. Satisfied, he slipped it back on.

"Okay Kit, time to go," he said, rising to his feet. Other than an ear twitch, Kit remained asleep. Hyroc poked him with the end of his boot. Kit stretched his limbs absentmindedly then shoved his head under his paws without opening his eyes. "You can sleep when you get back to the cabin, now get up I've got to get going soon." Kit remained motionless. Rolling his eyes, Hyroc reached down and picked him up. Kit yowled in protest, giving him a scathing look. "Don't give me that look; you're the one who wouldn't get up." Kit began to growl, but made little effort to free himself. "Yeah, I can tell how much you want down," Hyroc said sarcastically.

He headed off toward his cabin with his unhappy passenger in his arms. As usual, he tied Kit to a tree outside his cabin, securing the twine to the small loop of leather on the collar. Using his back leg, Kit scratched at the collar. Hyroc smiled with relief when Kit's foot returned to the ground, he rested his chin on his paws, and closed his eyes. *I actually might be able to sleep tonight.* He frowned at the bite marks all over the twine. How much longer could it restrain the cub? He figured he should probably replace it with rope soon. With that thought in mind, he headed off toward the Shackleton's cabin.

He approached the cabin from the road, as it seemed the proper way to come to the cabin. The instant he entered the clearing, the family's hound made his presence known with a chorus of excited barks. It rushed up to him in a flurry and began growling. He stood his ground considering whether or not he should find a rock. "I'm sorry; I hit you with a rock," he said apologetically. "I won't do it again, just please let me by." The dog suddenly stopped growling, regarding him curiously. He gave the hound a strange look, surprised by its sudden change in behavior.

"Dilo, stop harassing our guest," Svald called out, as he stepped from behind the cabin. He made a stern sweeping motion with his arms as he drew close. "Come on *get*, you crazy mutt." The dog bounded off. "I hope she didn't bother you too much."

"No, she wasn't a bother," Hyroc said. "Not compared to how dogs usually react to me."

Svald looked thoughtful a moment. "I know we got off on the wrong foot with that whole incident the other day. It wasn't anything against you, I misunderstood the situation and was doing what I thought best for my family. I hope you understand that. And I'd like to put all that behind us and start over."

"I would too." Though he suspected forgetting about it would be a lot harder.

"I'm glad to hear that. Supper should be done soon; you can head inside if you want. We're finishing up a few chores while we wait and then we'll be right in."

Hyroc nodded, heading for the cabin door. On the porch, he saw the old man sitting on a stool.

"I warned my daughter about feeding strays," the old man said, without turning his head to look at him. "You feed them once and they'll just keep coming back for more. And they might seem tame, but as soon as you stop feeding them, they'll show you their true nature. And when they eventually do, there's only one way to deal with them."

Hyroc gave him a sideways look. Being called a stray was pleasant compared to most of the demeaning things people said to him. But he sometimes did feel like a stray no one wanted. He opened the door and stepped inside. Helen stood at the cabin's fireplace stirring the steaming contents of a tin soup pot hanging above the flames. Sweeping his eyes around, he took a moment to take in the cabin's interior. It was much nicer than his cabin. He couldn't help feeling a little envious about what he saw.

"I'm glad you could make it," Helen said, looking at him with a grateful smile. Hyroc nodded thankfully. She tapped the wooden spoon off on top of the pot. "Could you help me get this dished up so it can cool." He regarded her curiously then took a step toward her. She frowned and he felt a bolt of fear at her expression; *what had he done wrong?* "Take your boots off please," she said, indicating his feet. He looked down at his boots; feeling irritated something so simple had elicited such a response from him. These people weren't going to hurt him. They wouldn't have invited him into their home otherwise. He took his boots off, setting them by the door. Helen looked at his feet inquisitively before beckoning him over. "This one's yours," she said, filling a bowl and holding it out to him. Hesitantly, he accepted it. "You can sit wherever you want." He set his bowl on the opposite side of the table where he could see the other family members as they entered. Then in likewise manner, the two of them set a bowl out for the rest of the family. "Thank you," she said, gently squeezing his hand.

"You're welcome," Hyroc replied, looking at her hand. It seemed a strange thing for someone to do but it was comforting.

She let go, headed over to the door and stuck her head outside. "DINNER," she called out. Taking that as his cue to sit, Hyroc sat down at his bowl. One by one, the rest of the family filed in.

The old man frowned in mild surprise, seeing Hyroc seated at the table. "Well at least *it* has manners," the old man scoffed, as he settled into a chair. Helen glared at him.

"Before we eat," Helen said. "I'd like to introduce everyone. You've already met my husband, daughter and I." She indicated Elsa's oldest brother. "This is Donovan." Next, she indicated their youngest son, followed by the old man. "This is Curtis and Walter. Donavan, Curtis and Walter, this is Hyroc." Hyroc and the two boys acknowledge each other with a simple head nod, while Walter grumbled something inaudible under his breath, warranting another glare from Helen and Elsa, then everyone started eating.

Hyroc eagerly took a bite of his soup. He sighed happily louder than he had meant to at the taste of the hot food entering his mouth.

Helen smiled. "You like it?"

Embarrassed, he nodded sheepishly before taking another bite. He had almost forgotten how good even a mildly seasoned meal tasted.

"I hear you got into a bit of trouble with Carla yesterday," Walter said. "What did you do, threaten to eat her daughter?"

Hyroc regarded him inquiringly. "Is she the one who owns the shop with all the kitchen things?" he said after swallowing.

"That's her."

"She hit me in the face with a broom!" Donavan and Curtis began snickering, but immediately stopped when he looked in their direction.

"Don't mind her too much, she hasn't been the same since her oldest daughter went missing," Helen said.

Hyroc studied her thoughtfully. "What umm – what happened?"

Helen sighed. "We don't know, she went out one day to pick berries and never came back."

"Her father thought an animal had gotten her," Svald said. "But we never found any tracks heading off from where she had gone to. It was as if she just disappeared."

"Where did this happen?"

"Out past the western edge of the village, a ways from here. She's been the only person to up and vanished like that, but around fall last year, animals started going missing the same way. People would find the ground torn up a little as if the animal had been struggling with something, but then nothing. And if you're worried about us thinking it was you, don't. The town elders know you weren't responsible."

Well at least that was something good, but hearing about disappearance was disconcerting. What else could there possibly be here besides giant spiders? Asking Ursa about them later might be a good idea. He didn't want to have another nasty surprise. "I was just, curious."

"Like a fox in a hen house," Walter said under his breath.

"Would you like some more?" Helen said, indicating Hyroc's empty bowl.

"Yes – yes please," Hyroc said, holding his bowl out to her.

"Other than Carla, how'd everyone else treat you?" Svald said.

"Good I guess. But the lady who runs the tailoring shop was very nice to me."

Svald's eyes lit a little at that. "Oh Luna. Yeah, she's a sweet old woman. She's actually one of the people responsible for allowing you to stay."

Hyroc gave him a look of intrigue. It seemed reasonable someone who could treat him so kindly would play a part in that. "I'm very grateful she did," he said sincerely.

"So, you've been looking to tan hides."

Hyroc snapped his head in Svald's direction excitedly. "Yes – yes I am."

"Well, I can help you."

"You'll teach me?"

"Of course, you won't be able to use any of those pelts if you can't tan them. But I'm letting you know right now, this isn't a hand out; you'll need to give me something in exchange for my knowledge. And since you don't have anything I want – and frankly I wouldn't feel right taking anything from you in your current situation – so you'll pay me in work. Does that sound like a reasonable trade to you?"

Hyroc studied the man's face thoughtfully. He didn't like the idea of adding even more work to his days, but he needed the knowledge Svald possessed if he was going to make a living here. He didn't seem to have a choice in the matter.

"Okay, it's a deal."

"Good to hear."

Svald reached toward him with one hand. Hyroc stared at his hand trying to figure out how he was supposed to react to the gesture. Racking his brain, he remembered seeing people in Forna shaking hands. It was related to finalizing trades or something. Hesitantly he reached out with one hand, mindful of his claws and shook Svald's hand. Then he let go.

"When umm do we start?"

"We can start tomorrow if you like. I assume you check your traps in the morning?"

Hyroc nodded. "Yes."

"About when do you usually finish?"

"Before noon normally."

"Okay then I'll expect you sometime around noon tomorrow." He paused a long moment. "It's getting late; you should probably get headed home soon."

Hyroc finished off the rest of his bowl's contents, before standing. "Thank you for the meal," he said. "It was very good."

"Thank you for coming," Helen said. "If you should need anything, our door is always open."

After a quick goodbye to the rest of the family, with a full stomach, he headed off toward his cabin, feeling much happier than he had in a long time.

CHAPTER 32

Keller slammed his fist down on the map laid across the table in front of him unable to contain his anger any longer. For the better part of a month he had been searching for the Hyroc creature. That search had led him across the kingdom to this guard post near the western edge of the wilderness and he was still no closer to locating his quarry. His assumption that the creature would stick to the more easily traversable terrain of the roads had proven false. But even with his incorrect judgment, his target was on foot and with mounted men it was still only a matter of time until he found the creature. After a week with no sightings he was forced to broaden his search. At which point, the only logical destination for the creature was the western wilderness as it was the closest and least populated region near Forna. And after figuring out what seemed the most expedient path for the creature to do so, he and his men began searching every town it might have passed by. But they found no evidence it had gone that way, not so much as a whisper or even a rumor.

So where was it? How could it possibly be so masterful with evasion? He had known elite scouts that left more evidence of their presence. It seemed ridiculous that it could possibly be so good. Nothing about its time at the school should have prepared it in the least bit for such behavior. Maybe something about its creation had imparted it with these powers.

"How can there be no sign?" Keller said with a raised voice. "Are your men so incompetent?"

The captain before him showed a flicker of anger in his eyes but hid all other signs of emotions. "Sir," the captain said calmly. "I trained most of these men myself and I assure you they are quite competent. Most have tracked fugitives before; they understand how to hunt."

"Then why does all evidence indicate otherwise?"

"I don't know, sir."

Keller shook his head in irritation. No one seemed to know the answer to that question.

The captain was quiet a long moment. "But if I may, sir. We could be looking in the wrong place."

"Then where would you suggest we look?" Keller growled. He seriously doubted the man was more knowledgeable than he in such matters and any answer he gave would be wrong.

The man stepped over to the map. He studied it a quick moment before speaking. "We have not searched the northern towns."

Keller shook his head. "I already thought of that, those towns are too far out of the way and unless I thoroughly overestimated the creature's intelligence, it would have avoided those towns for a direct path to the wilderness."

"I understand that, sir. But we have no other leads."

"There is still plenty of ground to cover here," Keller snapped. "I know there is some sign of the creature that we're missing."

"Then may I at least send couriers to those locations, they will not diminish our search parties and they are fast enough to return with any information they find before the month is out."

Keller shook his head irritably. "Very well, you may send out riders. I suppose it prudent to do so."

"Thank you, sir."

"You are dismissed."

The captain saluted respectfully before exiting through the open flap of the command tent.

Keller shook his head irritably as he watched the man leave. The creature had to have come through this area, it was the only logical thing he could think of. Escape would be the only thing on its mind. Surely it wouldn't be thinking about finding a place to live. Keller cocked an eyebrow at the thought. Or was it? Was he thinking about this whole situation wrong? Was that why he couldn't find it? He was fixated on the wrong reasoning.

He turned his attention back toward the map, moving his gaze toward the northern towns. His eyes settled on Flatwood. It still seemed doubtful the creature would have gone anywhere near that town. It was still relatively close to Forna, the creature would have had to go out of its way to get there if it wished to escape into the wilderness. As he studied the town's location he noticed a small village further north, in the midst of the Elswood forest. The name was written so small it was hard for him to even see. He shook his head dismissively. If the creature went there, the villagers – people who dealt with dangerous forest animals on an almost daily basis – would kill it on sight. It wouldn't have gone there; and if it did, it was dead and he would have heard about it by now. No, it couldn't be there. The couriers would confirm this. The creature had to be close by. He was just missing something.

• • •

CHAPTER 33

Chores

"**. . . N**ow make sure you keep your knife at an angle and don't push in," Svald said. He stood in front of a hide he had helped Hyroc obtain the night before which was tacked onto a slanted board, using his knife to demonstrate what he meant. "Otherwise you might cut through and damage the hide. Right now, you're just removing the hair. This will take a few days so there's no need to get in a hurry, take it nice and slow."

Hyroc nodded, eagerly stepping up to the hide. Finally, he was learning about the thing that had eluded him for so long. After all this was finished, it seemed improbable any more of his hides would rot. He leaned forward and trying his best to copy Svald, carefully made a scraping motion with the side of his knife down the hide.

"A little bit more of an angle and not quite so hard." Hyroc adjusted his next scrape to what Svald said. "Yeah, keep doing it just like that." He picked up the long curved blade with handles on both ends Hyroc had seen once before and held it up. "Your hunting knife will work fine for this, but I'd recommend getting a fleshing knife like this when you can afford it. It makes scraping much easier." Hyroc nodded, returning his attention back to the hide.

"That's probably good enough for now," Svald said approvingly, little over an hour later. "Now take it down, roll it up and stick it in the shed.

Hyroc wiped the flat of his knife blade on his leggings before slipping it back into its sheath on his belt and taking care of the hide.

"I've done my part of our bargain, now it's your turn," Svald said. He indicated a pile of wood rounds lying beside an ax buried in a stump. "Head over and start getting those chopped." Hyroc quietly sighed dejectedly as he headed over to the chopping-stump. He had hoped Svald had forgotten about that part of their deal. But it was the price of learning what Svald had offered to teach.

Hyroc set the smallest wood round he could find on the stump. Lifting the ax, he brought the blade down as close to the center as he could. With a satisfying crack, the wood round split partway down the middle and another strike split it the rest of the way. He tossed the two pieces of wood off to the side before collecting another to chop. This round and the next two split easily, but the fourth was considerably larger, requiring several strikes to split. Hyroc ruffled the fur around his neck with his hand, letting the air dry the sweat forming on it. On the following round, the ax blade stopped, hitting a hard spot in the wood. Turning the round, he growled in mild irritation seeing a knot where the ax had stopped. He leaned forward and pushed on the back of the ax head with the palms of his hands, trying to drive the blade through the knot. No matter how hard he pushed, the ax wouldn't cut any further. Glowering, he extricated the blade. Looking around he found a small wooden mallet and a wedge propped against a tree. He stuck the wedge where he had split the wood and used the mallet to hammer it in. Each hit slowly drove the wedge through the hard knot, until the round split in half.

With a sigh of relief, he aired out his dampened neck with one hand and reached for his water skin with the other. To his dismay, the skin was empty. He chided himself for not refilling it earlier when he knew a day of work was ahead of him as he made his way toward the lakeshore. Coming around the back of the cabin, he saw Walter working with a smoking rack laden with deer meat. Curious, Hyroc walked over, stopping behind the old man. Smoking his meat or drying it would be another useful thing to know, especially if he got more than he or Kit could eat before it went bad.

"Are you just going to stand there and drool?" Walter said, without turning to face him. "Not that I expect *you* to do anything else when you see food, considering how I saw you eat the other night, but Svald expects to get some work out of you." He pointed toward the lake. "Go wash your hands; I don't want this meat getting covered in your hair, because I actually plan on eating some of it."

With an annoyed glare, Hyroc headed to the lake, washed his hands more thoroughly than was probably necessary just to spite the old man's assumptions he was filthy, and refilled his water skin before heading back. With a sideways look, Walter studied his hands and gave what appeared to be some form of approval. Reaching into a small sack lying beside the smoking rack, Walter removed a handful of salt.

"Grab a handful and rub it into the part of the meat not already salted." Walter demonstrated by rubbing his handful into a piece of meat. "Do it just like that, *and try not to drop any, it's not free* – unlike what you seem to think about the food here." Copying Walter, Hyroc grabbed a handful of salt and rubbed it into a piece of meat. Walter scrutinized the meat, but to Hyroc's mild surprise, he nodded his satisfaction. "Well, would you look at that, you can follow instructions." Walter smiled derisively. "Maybe *we can* train you for something useful after all." Then in a sarcastic over bearing voice he said, "Good boy," as if he were speaking to a pet. Rolling his eyes, Hyroc reached into the sack and started salting another piece of meat.

"There you are," Svald said, as he walked over to the smoking rack.

"I was helping Walter salt this meat," Hyroc said, indicating the older man with his eyes. He was going to be irritated if helping the man was something he shouldn't have done. He couldn't afford to go without learning how to tan a hide.

"Yeah, it looks like we might get some good work out of him," Walter replied. "I think you made a great deal with this one."

Svald nodded appreciatively. "Well thank you for that Hyroc." Hyroc breathed a silent sigh of relief. Everything was good. "Walter do you mind if I take him, we need to get some more work done on his hide before it gets any later?"

"I suppose that's fine, I was about done here anyway."

"Okay."

Hyroc brushed the salt from his hands, followed Svald to the hide and tacked it back up onto the stretching board. Then he began scraping it as he had done earlier.

"DINNER," Helen called out. Hyroc looked skyward and was surprised to see it was close to dusk. It hadn't felt like he was here long enough for it to be so late.

"You're already here," Svald said invitingly. "So you might as well stay for dinner."

Hyroc smiled gratefully. "I – I would like that."

"Good, we like having you."

"You do?" Hyroc said taken aback.

Svald smiled. "Of course we do, now come on I don't want to keep everyone waiting." Hyroc happily made his way to the cabin's door.

"Oh, what a surprise, he's still here," Walter said dryly, as Hyroc came into the kitchen. "He must have heard there's food in here." Helen frowned at Walter. "Try to leave some for the rest of us, if you don't mind."

Helen filled a bowl with stew and set it at an empty spot at the table. "How was your day?" she said conversationally.

Assuming the bowl was meant for him, Hyroc settled into that spot, watching for any signs of disapproval on Helen's face. "It was good." Helen nodded. Looking down to his bowl, he smiled seeing it nearly overflowing. He began shoveling the stew into his mouth. He then noticed Walter watching him rapidly devour his meal with an unsurprised look on his face. Hyroc forced himself to eat slower to prove to the old man he could. Other than Donovan and Elsa throwing joking insults at each other and Walter lobbing an annoying jibe his direction, the meal passed peacefully.

When he returned to his cabin, the towering spruce had enveloped the structure in its looming shadow. Kit yowled hungrily from the base of the tree he had been tied to. "I hear you," Hyroc said, as he walked over and undid Kit's leash. Yowling impatiently at an ever-increasing volume, the cub eagerly followed him inside the cabin. Hyroc cut a slice of venison from his portion of the deer he had been given and tossed it to the expectant cub. Kit immediately stopped making noise, content with tearing into the piece of meat. With his companions needs fulfilled, Hyroc stepped outside to try stealing a glance at the sun before it disappeared below the horizon. He was startled to see Ursa sitting beside the tree he tied Kit to, looking toward the red and orange strips cast across the sky by the setting sun.

"It's a nice sunset tonight," she said, without turning to look at him. "No clouds to disrupt our view."

"It is," Hyroc said, trying to calm his heart back to a normal rhythm. It was still alarming to suddenly see a big bear up close, even if it had no intentions of hurting him. Though the fact he hadn't noticed her coming was a bit disturbing.

She tipped her head to look at him. "I see those hunters have accepted you into their pack."

He nodded knowingly. "The father is teaching me how to tan hides. I just wish he didn't make me do so much work for it."

"Work is good; it makes you strong."

Hyroc looked at her thoughtfully. "I know, I just meant, it makes it hard for me to get everything done that I need to do."

"You're building bonds and that's important. You're less vulnerable with others than on your own. No such bonds can exist within the shadows, as it knows no light of companionship."

Hyroc narrowed his eyes at her in an odd expression. Only about the first half of what she had just said made any sense. "Why do you speak in riddles? I don't know what that means."

Ursa regarded him with an annoyingly expectant look in her eyes. "In time you will find the answer." She returned her gaze to the orange sliver of the vanishing sun. Hyroc sighed in muted frustration and watched the sun sink out of view.

The next day, after working on the hide, Svald made him clean out their fireplace. After the fireplace, he made him clean out and put clean bedding in both the chicken coop and barn. He hated the reek of both structures, but he suspected his heightened sense of smell made it all the more unpleasant. He kept his aggravation toward the work to himself; it was what he had to do and complaining about it wouldn't do anything beyond psyching him into disliking it even more. Then mercifully, he was returned to chopping wood the day after.

While splitting a particularly stubborn round, he noticed the family's youngest son Curtis watching him, and the boy looked as if he had a question burning in his mind.

"What?" Hyroc said, tossing the firewood into his pile and setting another on the chopping stump.

"What kind of animal are you?" Curtis said innocently. "Most people say you're a wolf."

Hyroc gave him a curious look. "What do you think I am?"

Curtis studied his face thoughtfully. "I thought you might be a bear when I first saw you, but up close you remind me of a wolverine; I helped my father skin one once." Hyroc nodded, centering the wood round on the stump. "He told me wolverines are really mean, but since you saved my sister from a wolf, you don't seem very mean."

"You really think so?"

Curtis nodded. "Bad things don't do things like that."

That was an encouraging comparison. With a thankful nod, Hyroc raised the ax over his head and brought it down on the wood round. It split all the way down the middle save for a tiny sliver of wood requiring a sharp twist of the ax to sever. "Most people think I'm really mean when I'm not."

Curtis smiled. "But my grandpa says wolverines are greedy, and that's why he says you eat the way you do."

Hyroc shook his head irritably. It didn't surprise him much the old man had said that. "Well, I hadn't been eating very well up until that first night your mother invited me over for dinner and I was really hungry then. I'm not a good cook and what your mother made tasted really good."

Curtis nodded comprehendingly. "That's a little like what my mother said about you." There was a pause. "Why were you scared of us?"

Hyroc sighed, turning his head to look at the boy. It seemed that subject was inevitable. "Well – a lot of people have tried to hurt me and I thought your family would do the same."

Curtis studied him thoughtfully. "We wouldn't hurt you."

Hyroc stared down at the ground. "I didn't know at the time."

"Do you miss your parents?"

Hyroc tightly squeezed his eyes shut. A flare of longing shot through him and June's face materialized in his mind. He opened his eyes, pushing her from his thoughts. It hurt too much to think about her. "So what animal do you think I am?" Hyroc said quickly, hoping to change the topic back to something more benign.

Curtis looked toward the sky in contemplation. "Well, I think you look like a wolverine."

Hyroc breathed a silent sigh of relief. Good. "Then I guess I'm a wolverine."

"A nice wolverine."

"A nice wolverine," Hyroc agreed. If only everyone else in the village could see him in such terms.

"Curtis stop bothering Hyroc," Donovan called out. "He's got work to do."

"I'm coming," Curtis yelled back. He returned his attention to Hyroc, speaking conversationally. "I've got to go, he'll keep yelling until I go. But I'll keep trying to figure out what you really are. Bye."

"Bye then," Hyroc said.

Curtis turned and headed off toward his brother. Hyroc watched him a moment before sticking another wood round on the stump.

The next day, he had removed all the hair from the hide.

"It looks good," Svald said, after a quick examination.

"So now what do I do?" Hyroc said.

"Go ahead and take it down, I'll be right back."

Svald turned and headed off toward the shed. Hyroc took the hairless hide down. Svald returned carrying the head of a deer in one hand and a wood ax in the other. Hyroc regarded the severed head ominously. What was that for?

"Why are you carrying a deer head?" Hyroc said.

Svald set the head on the ground and touched the top of it between the antlers with the back of the ax. "You see where I have the back of the ax?" Hyroc nodded warily. Where was this going? "I want you to hit that spot as hard as you can with the back of my ax."

Hyroc gave Svald a confounded look as he was handed the ax. "What are we doing this for?"

"How else are we supposed to get to its brains?"

Hyroc looked at him in bewilderment. *Did he just say brains?* "Why do you want the brains?"

"It's what we're going to use to tan the deer's hide."

"What do you mean *we're going to use its brains*? That can't be what's in the barrels stored in your shed."

"You're right, what's in those isn't made from brain."

"*Then why are we doing this?*"

Svald sighed in mild annoyance. "Because doing it the way I do it is not the best way for you to do it, at least not right now. I'm showing you the simplest and easiest way I know how to do this, which is with brains."

Hyroc sighed dejectedly. What had he gotten himself into?

"Now hit the deer's head between the antlers where I showed you."

Hyroc reluctantly lifted the ax, took a breath, and brought it down as hard as he could. The back of the ax struck with the sickening sound of breaking bone. "Just like that; two more hits should do it." Hyroc struck twice more, making a hole big enough to satisfy Svald. "Now set the hide fleshy side out beside the skull." Hyroc did that. "Now reach inside and scoop up a handful."

"You want me to WHAT," Hyroc said indignantly. He wanted him to – to touch what was in there? That was the most disgusting thing he had ever heard of.

"You heard me, reach inside and get a handful."

Hyroc gave him a pleading look, but the man's gaze did not waver. *Oh, no he's serious about this.* He rolled his sleeves up and after taking a deep breath, reached inside the deer's head. The brain had a repulsive gelatinous texture reminiscent of a cold undercooked egg, making him feel a little queasy. He took a long breath to try calming his stomach, then scooped up a handful of brain tissue.

"Now start smearing it over every inch of the hide." Hyroc brought his handful of brain-mush over to the hide. As soon as he felt the slimy gelatinous substance squish between his fingers when he pressed down, he tasted acid in the back of his throat. He flew to his feet and managed a few steps away from the hide before doubling over and retching.

"Feel better?" Svald said, trying to hide a smile.

"I – I umm think I'm good now."

"Are you sure about that?" Donovan said, as he came around the side of the cabin beaming. "You're not going to faint, are you?"

"No," Hyroc said defensively, a ting of warmth spreading across his face. Why did the other boy have to see him doing that? The one time he thought it safe to let his guard down. "The texture just – just struck me wrong."

"I'm sure."

An hour passed without another throwing up incident – though Hyroc came close twice – and only the occasional friendly, if not annoying, gibe from Donovan, before he had completely covered the hide in brains.

"The brains will set in overnight," Svald said. "And in the morning you'll need to work the hide. Just find something smooth to drape the hide over and start working it kind of like what you'd do when you're washing clothes. Don't use anything too rough or you might damage the hide and have to start over with a new one. Keep doing that for about an hour every morning until the hide is soft and pliable. And if everything goes right, you've got yourself some leather."

Hyroc nodded, glad there wasn't another step. What he had done thus far was more than enough. "Does that mean we're done," he said, wearily hopeful.

Svald smiled. "Yes, other than what I said, you're done." Hyroc quietly groaned with relief. "And you've paid off your debt to me; you don't owe me any more work."

"What do I do if I want to keep the hair on?"

"It's pretty much the same process; you just don't necessarily need to do this last step – it's just a good idea normally – or anything to take the hair off."

"Thank you for showing me this."

"You're very welcome.

CHAPTER 34

Friends

S cattered clouds dotted the pale azure sky and the air held the cool freshness of morning dew. Hyroc stood on the shore of the stream near his cabin where he normally fished. He studied a grouping of smooth boulders thoughtfully as he held the brain covered hide in his arms. It still seemed bizarre something as repulsive as smearing the contents of an animal's head on its own skin was necessary to tan hides. A shiver of revulsion ran through his body as he remembered in excruciating detail how the cold slimy brains had felt squishing between his fingers. If it had been warm it might not have been as bad. Then to compound the issue, he had thrown up in front of both Svald and Donovan. He felt embarrassed about displaying his weakness in front of another person when he wasn't actually sick. Now the two of them probably thought his senses were easily offended and he couldn't do anything mildly unpleasant without a relapse. He should have been able to handle the work without retching; he was stronger than that. And it stung Donovan had found such humor in that incident. He wished he hadn't taken the teasing without a single retort, there were so many things he should have said to shut the boy up.

He forced his thoughts away from what had happened, he couldn't change it. There were more important things he needed to focus on.

He knew he would eventually be feeling brains between his fingers again, but he was determined not to let it affect him when it happened.

Looking through the boulders, he found the smoothest one and draped the hide over it. Slowly, he drew the hide back-and-forth across its surface like he was trying to remove a stubborn patch of rabbit blood from his jerkin. As per Svald's instructions, he did this for his best estimate of an hour. He held the hide in front of him, looking for any signs of damage. Finding none, at least none he recognized, he folded one side experimentally. The hide still felt stiff.

He returned the hide to the inside of his cabin, then he headed off to check traps with Kit trailing him. The first trap through the fourth were empty. While he examined the trap beside the dirty pool, a robin alighted onto the ground searching for bugs. Kit entered a crouch and began creeping closer with his eyes firmly fixed on his target. Hyroc stopped his work, remaining motionless as the cub slowly drew closer to his prey. Kit stopped when he was within pouncing distance; a ripple ran from his shoulders to his rear end and he exploded into a run. The robin had unfurled its wings for flight when Kit threw himself on it. He dispatched the bird with two quick bites to the neck. Hyroc exhaled, suddenly realizing he was holding his breath in anticipation.

"You got it!" Hyroc called out excitedly. "Good boy." Kit glanced at Hyroc happily, before turning his attention back to savaging his felled quarry. Hyroc gave Kit a disturbed look as the dead bird's head flopping lifelessly from side to side as he played with it.

Knowing Kit would follow when he got far enough away, Hyroc headed off. Kit joined him moments later carrying the bird in his mouth. With a sigh, Hyroc continued on to the next trap, trying not to look at the clump of blood-smeared feathers Kit had in his mouth. The remaining traps were also empty. By the time he finished with the last trap, there wasn't much left of the bird for Kit to toy with. Kit gave him an annoyed and puzzled look.

"Don't look at me," Hyroc said humorously. "You're the one who tore it to pieces. But enough about the bird, it's time for us to head back."

Passing the creek shore south of his last trap, he stared longingly toward the other side. There was a good spot for a trap just across the creek, not far from where he stood, and he finally had time to set one. Unfortunately, he still needed to get Kit back to the cabin. It bothered him to be so close and leave, only to come back after wasting an hour or two he could have otherwise spent hunting. His situation would be more convenient if he didn't need to go back. He cocked an eyebrow as he wondered why he actually needed to go back.

When he had first found Kit, the cub was still walking in a wobbly crouch to maintain his balance and seemed to spend a good portion of his time sleeping. He was barely in any condition to accompany him to check traps. But he had grown some in that time, stood straighter, lost most of the wobble when he walked and seemed energetic and eager to explore his surroundings. He obviously knew the basic concepts of being stealthy, the dead robin was proof, so it seemed unlikely he would spook any game they came across. Besides, his presence would make hunting less lonely.

Hyroc looked down thoughtfully at Kit who was sniffing the sap-strewn trunk of a cottonwood. "How would you like to come hunting with me?" Kit paused, looking toward him absentmindedly, then returned to his investigation of the tree. Hyroc smiled, deciding that could count as a yes.

This time, he remembered to roll his leggings up before trudging out into the water carrying his boots. Halfway across, Kit loudly yowled out in distress. Turning around, he saw Kit at the edge of the shore cautiously putting a paw forward and pulling it back when it touched the water's surface. Hyroc gave him an understanding nod. He continued to the other shore, tossed his boots on dry land, and walked back to Kit. Kit seemed glad when he picked him up, but the moment he stepped into the water; the cub began squirming in fear, threatening to drag razor-sharp claws across his arms and chest.

"Kit stop!" Hyroc said sternly, struggling to maintain his hold. "I'm going to drop you if you don't." Instantly Kit stopped struggling. Hyroc gave him a bewildered look; he hadn't actually expected his words to do anything. Not wanting to risk his luck running out, resulting in much pain, he hurried through the creek. As soon as he stepped out of the water, Kit resumed squirming. He happily dropped him on the ground. After shedding some of the water by shaking his leg, he put his boots back on and unrolled his pants.

"Next time you're getting yourself across," Hyroc said irritably. He flicked some lingering moisture off his fingers at Kit. Kit recoiled, putting his ears sideways in displeasure. "You'd be swimming if you had clawed me." Kit growled in response.

Hyroc made his way up the small animal trail to the opening in the line of trees leading into the clearing where he had been captured. It seemed such a long time since that had happened. He remembered vividly the terror he felt when the net flew out of the ground and flung him into the air. In that moment he thought he was going to die, but some miracle of kindness from a complete stranger had saved him from what seemed an inescapable fate. He shook his head at what still seemed a strange and completely unexpected turn of events. After every frightening thing he experienced from the encounter, it had actually turned out good for him. He was prepared to make the wilderness his home and he was glad he didn't need to.

Putting his back to the clearing, he found the narrowest part of the trail where it ran through the space in the trees. Using the twine he had bought in the village, he began setting up a snare. Kit wandered over and began batting at a piece of twine he had made the mistake of dragging across the ground. He shooed him away, garnering a loathsome look from the cub. Kit tried killing his work materials once more before the trap was finished.

He caught movement out of the corner of his eye as did Kit. Turning in a slow practiced movement, he saw a brown hare on the other side of the clearing. Carefully, he strung his bow and crept into position to take a shot. Kit came crashing through a patch of brush; excitedly running at the rabbit. The hare dashed off, vanishing behind the branches of a tree. Kit continued forward for a few strides before stopping to stare at the spot where the rabbit had disappeared with a confounded look on his face.

Hyroc sighed, returning his arrow back to its quiver. "You have to be more careful. Otherwise –" he pointed toward where the rabbit had escaped "– that happens and you have to find another one. Come on, I'm sure we'll get the next one, if you're quiet."

When they eventually spotted another rabbit, right before Hyroc pulled the bowstring back; Kit once again spooked his target. He glared mournfully at the suddenly vacant patch of ground where the hare had been before growling in frustration. "KIT," Hyroc yelled pointedly. Kit snapped his attention to him with an innocently confused look in his eyes. "We're not going to have anything to eat tonight if you keep scaring everything off." He sighed and once his grudging feelings dissipated, he continued searching for food. He found nothing to hunt for the rest of the day. On the way back to the cabin, he rechecked his traps, hoping for something. To his relief, the trap at the bottom of the incline had caught a wild turkey.

Near the creek the next afternoon, Hyroc found another rabbit. He managed to shoot it before Kit could do anything to spook the long-eared creature.

"See," he said happily, as he removed his arrow from the rabbit. "That worked much better." He slit the rabbit's throat, and held it away from him by the back legs. He sighed as he looked at the hare. "I don't know about you, but I'm really getting tired of having rabbit all the time." Kit stared at him, and he took it as agreement. "I know we got a turkey yesterday but if we got a deer we won't have to worry about meat for a while. And I can finally try smoking some venison." He smiled derisively. "We haven't gotten anything big enough to even bother doing that with." By now, the blood had stopped dripping from the rabbit's neck. He tied the lifeless animal to his belt and left the clearing.

Although Kit's technique for being quiet while hunting had improved, to Hyroc's frustration, the cub still managed to spook something at least once a day for the next three. But every time this happened, Kit seemed to learn from his mistakes; doing something slightly different. Over the next week, the spooking incidents eventually ceased and Hyroc started being the only one scaring animals off as he got into position to shoot them.

Then shortly thereafter, the hide he had been working on seemed finished. He showed the hide to Svald to make sure and the man confirmed it was finished.

The following morning, when he stepped out of his cabin, he nearly fell on Donovan who was just walking up to the door to knock. Curtis stood behind his brother trying not to laugh aloud.

"That's one way to start the day," Donovan said with a smile.

"Sorry," Hyroc said, after regaining his balance. He regarded the two boys with a puzzled look. Beyond Svald and Harold, this was the first time anyone had dared visit his cabin. What did they want?

"That's okay, we're just —" Donavan paused looking down at Hyroc's feet. Following his gaze, Hyroc felt a bolt of fear shoot through him when he saw Kit standing beside him in full view of the two boys. He stomped his foot, irritably jerking his head back. Another secret was out!

Donovan pointed at Kit. "Is *that a mountain lion cub?*"

Hyroc bowed his head. "Yes," he said with a sigh. Kit growled, keeping his eyes fixed on Donovan.

"Dose my father know about that?"

"No."

Donovan regarded him thoughtfully then with a smile, said, "Don't worry; I'm not going to tell him."

Hyroc gave him a confounded look. Why wouldn't he tell his parents? A large predatory cat – even a cub – should be of some concern to them. "You're not? Aren't you worried about him killing your goat and donkey when he gets older?"

"A little, but as far as I know, mountain lions don't normally hunt during the day and we always keep Grettle and Packard locked up in our barn during the night. Besides, Dilo tells us if anything we need to be worried about comes near the cabin. So I don't think we really have anything to worry about from him for a while." Hyroc breathed a sigh of relief. "And well, you're the first person I've known that has *a pet mountain lion.*" Hyroc smiled appreciatively. "I've never actually seen one up close or dared to. What's his name?"

"It's Kit," Curtis answered.

Hyroc and Donovan rounded on him. "How do you know his name?" Hyroc demanded. How many others knew about this? Donovan's assurance really didn't mean anything if everyone already knew about Kit.

All remnants of a smile disappeared from Curtis' face. "umm… because…Elsa told it to me – *I wasn't going to tell anyone.*"

Hyroc breathed a sigh of relief. That was probably okay. As long as her little brother was the only person she told. But Donovan's reaction indicated even he didn't know, so it seemed reasonable no one else knew.

"That's good," Donovan said malevolently. He indicated Hyroc with a jerk of his head. "Because I'm sure Hyroc here doesn't want you telling anyone. And if you say anything to anyone, you'll have me to answer to. Got it?"

Curtis nodded.

There was a long pause. Donovan crouched down and extended his hand toward Kit then pulled it back. "Does he bite?"

"Not usually; mostly when he's hungry, but I fed him when I got up, so you should be safe."

Donovan nodded, cautiously reaching over to Kit. The cub sniffed his fingers inquisitively, before allowing him to scratch the top of his head. Curtis came closer, and in likewise fashion he pet Kit.

"So, umm – what are the two of you doing up here? Not that I mind. You two are the first actual company I've had since coming here. I'm just curious."

Donovan stood. "Oh, I found some deer tracks up by the river north of here and I was wondering if you'd like to try getting it with us. Our father's in the village running errands with our mother and sister, so we could use an extra bow. We'll split the kill with you."

Getting some venison would free up some time for him to get a few other things done. But he thought he caught glimpses of suspicion in Donovan's eyes. That made him wonder if there wasn't more going on here than it seemed. He doubted it was anything dangerous due to the casualness of their interaction. Maybe Donovan was trying to figure something out about him. Maybe he was trying to get a look at his demeanor for himself. And that might be a good thing. It could mean he was in some way curious about him. Curiosity was a lot better than out right fear. It meant his mind wasn't entirely made up about him. And he could see there wasn't anything he needed to worry about with him. He just needed to make a good impression.

"Yeah, I'll go," Hyroc said.

"I figured as much," Donovan replied.

"But I've still got to check my traps; I don't want to risk missing anything I might have caught."

Donovan studied him thoughtfully. "They're along the east side of the mountain, right?" Hyroc nodded. "Okay, you can check them on the way, the deer tracks are in that direction anyway."

"And I'll have to bring Kit." Donovan raised an eyebrow. Hyroc felt a surge of anxiety at the look. Was he asking too much? Had he already done something to damage Donovan's evolving opinion about him? "Don't worry he knows how to be quiet," Hyroc quickly interjected.

Donovan gave him an even stranger look. "Umm – I don't see why not; he's probably more useful when it comes to hunting that that mutt we have back at the cabin. But try not to take too long, I don't want to risk the trail going cold."

Hyroc breathed a silent sigh of relief. No damage done. "Thanks," he said, as he closed the door to his cabin. "I'll be quick."

Donovan nodded. "Lead the way."

The first trap at the back of the valley was empty.

"What have you been catching?" Donovan said conversationally, as Hyroc stood after looking his trap over.

"Mostly rabbits and those strange hares with the antlers."

Donovan and Curtis gave him a perplexed look. "Why are they strange? You didn't have those where you came from."

Hyroc returned their gazes with an equally disbelieving look. "No, back in Forna we only had *normal* rabbits." He gritted his teeth, realizing what he had just said. He didn't want anybody to know where he had come from. If they knew that they might figure out The Ministry was looking for him.

"You're from Forna?" Donovan said sounding surprised. Hyroc nodded, denying it now wouldn't be the least bit believable. Donovan was quiet a moment. "You came all the way from there, all by yourself?"

"Well, I really didn't have a choice and I –" he trailed off unwilling to admit June's part in his running away from there.

"Were you running away?" Curtis said.

Hyroc gave the two of them a severe look. "*I don't* want to talk about it," he said pointedly, a note of sadness entering his voice. He turned away and headed off toward the next trap. There were too many memories of what he had been forced to leave behind for him to talk about Forna anymore. An awkward silence descended between the three of them to and from the trap at the ravine.

"Isn't there a cave just over that rise?" Donovan said, as Hyroc knelt to reset the tripped but empty trap at the base of the incline. Hyroc nodded. "I hear Jägerin lives in a cave near here, I wonder if that's it."

"She not there anymore; she died after I got here."

"Do you know what got her?"

"Spi –" he sighed, barely managing to stave off a shiver. "I'm not sure," he lied. It still seemed risky to tell anyone in the village about those creatures. Donovan's eyebrows drew together in a look of subtle disbelief, but he nodded.

"Can we see the cave while we're here?" Curtis said.

Donovan sighed "I guess we could while Hyroc finishes with that trap," he said. "Nothing's moved in there since the mountain lion died right? I don't want to accidentally run into a den of wolves."

"I don't think so."

Donovan nodded, then the two of them made their way up the incline.

Hyroc had finished with his trap just after they disappeared over the top. He headed up to join them. They were both standing beside the mouth of the cave looking at the pile of stones marking Huntress' grave.

"Did you bury her?" Donovan said, as Hyroc came to them.

Telling them a white tattooed magical talking bear had actually done it seemed a great way to make them think he was crazy. And that wouldn't exactly help him. Hyroc shrugged. "I thought she deserved a proper burial," he admitted. It was true, he would have done it if Ursa hadn't for him, so he wasn't really lying.

Donovan and Curtis regarded him with intrigue.

"I heard she had cubs," Curtis said. "Do you know if any of them made it?"

Hyroc looked at Kit. "Only one," he said with an affectionate smirk.

When they came to the trap at the dirty pool of water, there was a rabbit caught in it. After dispatching it, Hyroc slit its throat and waited patiently for the blood to stop. Glancing over his shoulder, he saw Donovan and Curtis staring at him with odd expressions on their faces.

What had he just done to make them look at him that way? All he did was slit the rabbit's throat. It seemed absurd to think he could've done anything strange while doing so.

"Umm – Hyroc, what are you doing *that* for?" Donovan said.

Hyroc gave him a perplexed look. "I'm bleeding it," he said.

Donavan and Curtis looked at each other as if he had said something unheard of. "We've never bled rabbits." Donovan stepped over to him holding his hand out. "Let me show you something."

Hyroc slowly handed him the rabbit, curious as to what the boy was about to show him. Holding the lifeless rabbit by the hind legs Donovan dropped its head onto the ground. He pressed the heel of his boot firmly down on the head and gave a hard yank. With a disturbing sounding wet crunch, the rabbit's head, spine and its organs were ripped from its body. Hyroc felt mildly queasy but he was almost to fascinate with what he had witnessed to notice. Donovan handed him the headless carcass

"See, much easier," Donovan said happily. "Though you still need to clean out the inside."

Hyroc nodded thankfully as he examined the rabbit. After a moment he tied it to his belt.

"Can I see your sword?" Curtis said.

Hyroc regarded him a moment before saying, "I guess. Just be careful." With one hand, he slid his sword from its sheath and carefully offered Curtis the bottom of the hilt. "You got it?" Curtis nodded and

Hyroc slowly relinquished it to his grip. Curtis looked upon the blade with awe. His expression reminded Hyroc of the joy he felt the first time he had held a bow. He quickly shied away from that memory.

"Just don't cut your hand off," Donovan said. "Mother would kill me if anything like that happened to you." Curtis rolled his eyes, taking a few steps back. He swung the sword experimentally, then made a fast downward slash as if slaying an invisible monster. He then turned his attention to the thin stalk of a plant. It made a quiet snap as he sliced it in half.

"Okay you've seen it," Donovan said. "Now give it back to Hyroc so we can get going." Downtrodden, Curtis moved back toward Hyroc and gave the sword back to him.

The trap beside the creek was empty.

"I was wondering," Donovan said, shortly after they started toward the trap beneath the fallen tree. Hyroc looked at him inquiringly. "Those claws of yours – do they by chance help you climb trees?"

Hyroc nodded. "Yeah. I can get up where there aren't any branches to grab onto. It really comes in handy when someone wants to beat you up."

"You had bullies?" Donovan said sounding surprised.

Hyroc cocked an eyebrow. Why did that always seem surprising to people? He thought his appearance would make it obvious. "You seem surprised by that?"

"Yeah. No offense, but I wouldn't want to get in a fight with you – " he indicated Hyroc's hands with a head nod "– especially considering your claws, those don't exactly look dull."

Hyroc couldn't help smiling a little at that. Holding his hand up, he said, "I think a few of them discovered *that*."

Donovan gave a look of humored empathy. "Well, it seems you can hold your own in a fight."

"Do you shed?" Curtis said.

Hyroc raised an eyebrow, causing Donovan to snicker from seeing the look on his face. "I might," Hyroc said. He wasn't quite sure if he did or not, all he knew was he seemed to get very itchy during early spring.

Donovan smiled. "Maybe you can stuff something with your hair and use it as insulation during the winter." Hyroc rolled his eyes.

"Can you track by smell?" Curtis said.

"No, I can only smell things a little bit better than – than a normal person can."

"Can you see in the dark?"

"Yes, but I still can't hunt very long after dark."

"Do they glow?"

"When it's dark."

There was a pause. "What color–"

"Curtis enough questions," Donovan interrupted. "Stop impersonating a squawking magpie."

Curtis frowned. "*I'm not!*"

Not long afterward, they arrived at the next trap. It was empty. When Hyroc finished with it, he started heading in the direction of the crossing he used to get to his final trap.

"Where are you going?" Donovan said.

Hyroc turned around and pointed in the direction of the crossing. "There's a crossing back the way we came."

Donovan pointed in the opposite direction. "There's one our father showed us not far from here up that way. Its a lot shallower than the one I think you're talking about and I figure it'll be easier –" he used his hand to indicate Kit "– to get your cat across."

Hyroc knew about the other crossing but he had been purposely avoiding that area after he found the half liquefied spider kill. But he was reasonably confident even those spiders wouldn't attack a group of people even on the off chance there were any. He figured he could safely get away with remaining silent. He took a deep breath and said," alright. But I've got one more trap on the other side of the creek."

"Is that where we cap –" Donovan said, looking suddenly embarrassed. "– I mean, where we first *met* you."

Hyroc narrowed his eyes in annoyance. It was obvious what Donovan was implying. So obvious he wondered why Donovan even tried to hide it. "Yes, it's right about there."

"Yeah – yeah that's fine, it's still on our way."

Hyroc nodded.

At the crossing, he was still forced to carry Kit to the opposite shore, but other than a few drops of splashed up moisture, the water remained comfortably below the lip of his boots. From the crossing, they entered into the trees. Then they came to the hill where he had found the spider kill. As they walked up the hill, he constantly scanned their surroundings with his hand on the hilt of his sword ready to draw it in an instant.

Hyroc started slightly when Donovan said, "You okay?"

"I'm fine," Hyroc said, composing himself.

"You just seem, a little tense ever since we started up this hill. Did you run into something here?"

Without thinking, Hyroc started saying spider, but after the first two letters left his mouth, he realized what he was saying and for some reason said badger, causing him to say, "Spadger."

Donovan cocked an amused eyebrow. "Oh a *Spadger*," he said smiling. "I've never seen one of *those*. Are they dangerous?"

Hyroc rolled his eyes half humoredly. He had to admit that *was* kind of funny.

They traversed the area and turned in the direction of his final trap. In the trap, they found a squirrel. Donovan gave Hyroc some advice on how to properly skin it as he tied its carcass on his belt. From the final trap, they picked their way north until they reached the shore of a river.

Hyroc put a hand above his eyes to block out the sun, as he gauged the distance to the other shore. The river seemed to have a moderately strong current but if he needed to, it looked like he could swim across.

"Is there a way across," Hyroc asked.

Donovan stared off toward the opposite shore thoughtfully. "I think there's one a few miles back, past the mountain, but we usually only cross in the winter when everything's frozen over." Hyroc nodded and turned away, continuing along the river.

They stopped for lunch beside an outcropping of rocks jutting out into the river. Donovan shared some jerky with Hyroc that was flavored with some herb he had never tasted. Kit began nipping hungrily at Hyroc's ankles. Hyroc skinned the squirrel, and tossed Kit what was left. They waited for Kit to finish play-eating his meal before continuing on their way. Hours passed before they came across some fresh deer tracks. Donovan called for everyone to be quiet while he and Hyroc got their bows ready for use.

"You hear *that*, you need to be quiet," Hyroc said softly to Kit.

The tracks fallowed along the river, before sharply curving into the woods onto a game trail running southward. They spooked a wood grouse when they lost sight of the river, but Hyroc couldn't get a shot in time through the branches of the surrounding trees.

The tracks then turned east, leaving the trail and spiraling through a tiny clearing pockmarked with thorny raspberry bushes. From the clearing, the tracks wound through the forest into a muddy moss lined stream bed with only a trickle running through a low part at the middle.

After following the stream bed for a short time, over the rise of the leftmost edge, they saw a buck nosing through some undergrowth.

"Stay here," Hyroc whispered to Kit. Donovan did the same with Curtis.

Silently, Hyroc took to the foliage left of the stream, while Donovan took to the right, making sure to stay out of the deer's line of sight. Slowly the two of them crept into position. Hyroc got there first. In a smooth motion, he nocked an arrow and carefully lined his shot up. A twig snapped from Donovan's position. The deer wrenched its attention toward the sound, turning away from Hyroc, obscuring his shot to where he thought the heart was. It looked directly at Donovan. Hyroc staved off the sinking feeling that always proceeded watching his quarry disappear from view, keeping his eyes focused on his target. The deer wheeled away from Donovan to bolt off into the woods, re-exposing the side of its chest to Hyroc. He let his arrow fly. The deer's feet had lifted off the ground as it broke into a run when the arrow found its mark. The animal disappeared from view an instant later, but a crashing sound seconds later told them it had not escaped.

Donovan cheered as he crossed the streambed. His face was red with a mixture of frustration and embarrassment. "There was a *stupid* twig under a patch of pine needles," he said sounding relieved. "I'm glad we brought you." He clapped Hyroc on the shoulder. Hyroc beamed, feeling a warm flood of euphoria coursing through his body. Curtis made his way over to them with Kit plodding close behind.

"Did you get it?" Curtis asked excitedly.

"Yeah, we heard it fall over there in the trees," Donovan said, pointing in the direction it had fled.

After relieving the animal of its blood, they set to work gutting it.

"Can I umm – take the hide?" Hyroc said as he, Curtis, and Donovan began removing the deer's innards.

Donovan frowned, leaning back away from the carcass. "We gave you the last one," he said.

"I know, but I was going to try keeping the hair on this one to make something for me to sleep on. The bear wood of my bed frame isn't very comfortable "

Donovan sighed. "I suppose we would still be trying to hunt it down if you hadn't hit it. Yeah, I guess it's fair that you have the hide."

"Thank you."

"But next time you're waiting your turn." He smiled impishly. "And you're going to have to gut it and smear the brains on *all by yourself*. And please don't throw up this time."

Hyroc glared at him.

CHAPTER 35

Summer's End

A chill wind pulled at the edges of Hyroc's hood, nicking the end of his nose with its bite and sending billowing waves through his cloak. His fur kept most of the nipping wind away from his skin, but enough got through for him to be aware of its coolness. The sun's light shone a silvery gray through a layer of rainless clouds. It was mid fall and the deep greens of the leaves had begun their shift to yellow and orange. Winter was not for off. Its rapid approach worried Hyroc, he wondered if he would have enough food and if his clothing was enough to get him through those frigid months. In Forna, he only needed to spend short amounts of time outside when it got cold; he would have no such luxury in this place. When those days came, he would be spending most of his time outside in the snow.

He shook the thought from his mind, he had time before then and there was something requiring his immediate attention. He looked warily upon the threatening grin of the coyote standing before him caught in his trap beside the creek. Kit stood off to his left tensed for a fight, growling a deep warning. His coat had developed a deeper reddish hue and the spots speckling it had started to fade. Standing just short of Hyroc's waist, he was nearly the same size as the coyote. Hyroc regarded the animal a moment more before knocking an arrow.

He carefully aimed at the coyote's eye so he wouldn't damage the pelt and put an arrow through it. The animal shuddered and collapsed. Kit stopped growling, his body returning to a more relaxed posture.

Hyroc untied the coyote's foot and dragged the body away from the trap. He wasn't going to eat any of the animal's meat, he planned to use it to feed Kit. He skinned the carcass then gutted and butchered it, placing the meat inside his knapsack.

Shouldering the knapsack, he moved off. From there, he headed to the easier creek crossing Donovan had shown him. Growling and hissing, Kit beat him across the creek with a series of frantic jumps. Hyroc stopped at the hill. When he had subdued his trepidation about coming through this area and explored it more thoroughly two months ago, he had discovered a promising spot to put a trap at its base. It was empty now, but he had previously caught two squirrels in it.

Next, he checked the trap at the line of trees beside the clearing.

There was a crow caught in it and Kit prepared to pounce on it the moment he saw it. "No not this one," Hyroc said, putting a foot in front of Kit to break his focus. He didn't think this crow was one of Ursa's but he couldn't actually tell the difference so he tried his best to avoid killing any of them. The crow squawked a shriek and fluttered its wings at Hyroc's approach. "Don't yell at me," he snapped back at the bird. "I'm trying to let you go." The crow cocked its head, seeming to calm a little. Cautiously, he reached down to release the bird. When it was free of his snare, it eagerly flew off. Kit gave Hyroc an annoyed glare. "It was a crow! I don't think there's any meat on those anyway." Kit flicked his tail in what Hyroc thought was disagreement.

Returning to the cabin, Kit energetically scrambled up his favorite tree, perching on a thick limb halfway up. Hyroc laid a few pieces of coyote meat at its base, before passing his newly constructed smoking rack on his way inside the cabin. He flipped open the chest at the foot of the bed. Inside lay two oilskin wrappings, one containing smoked meat and the other with three strips of uncooked meat he used for feeding Kit. He added the meat from his knapsack to the oilskin of uncooked meat, shut the chest and went back outside.

Sliding into a sitting position, he put his back against the cabin's wall and held the coyote pelt in front of him trying to figure out what he could use it for. Selling it was the easiest choice, though bringing a pelt of unknown worth to Anton was unappealing. Anton accepted his pelts, but he didn't exactly seem to want anything else to do with him. Svald would be able to tell him what a coyote was worth, if they were worth anything. Throwing the pelt over his shoulder skin side out, he rose to his feet and started walking toward the lake.

At the lake shore, he heard a distance quack. Lifting his eyes, he saw ducks lounging around in the water at the other end of the lake. He saw the pond in Forna, the tall water grasses, reeds gently swaying in a breeze, and dragonflies zipping through the air as Marcus instructed him on how to properly set up a shot. "The key is to remain quiet," he had said. A pang of sadness stabbed at him and he pushed the memory aside, returning back to the lake shore.

When he arrived at the cabin, he found Helen out front wearing a coat as she stood beside a large basket. The two of them exchanged a quick greeting, punctuated by the sound of Dilo barking excitedly at him.

"Where's Svald?" Hyroc asked, glancing around.

"Oh, he took the boys out hunting this morning," Helen said. "He's trying to teach Curtis how to shoot game. They probably won't be back till tomorrow night. Is there something I can help you with?" Her eyes drifted over the coyote pelt.

Hyroc held the pelt up. "I got a coyote today, but I'm really not sure what to use it for."

Helen held her hand out. "Let me see it." He handed it to her. She gave the pelt a thorough look over. "Well, they're mostly considered a pest around here because they like to go after people's livestock and most folks don't even bother skinning them once they're dead."

That didn't sound promising. "Is it worth selling?"

She nodded. "Yeah, you'll probably get maybe ten Flecks from Anton for it." She paused, looking toward him thoughtfully. "Do you have a hat?"

"No, but I've got a hood on my cloak."

She frowned. "You're going to need a hat for the winter. That hood of yours won't do you much good when it gets cold. And that fuzz on your ears won't help you much either. *You need a hat.*" She indicated the pelt. "You should use this to make one." He nodded thankfully re-accepting the pelt.

"Okay, I'm ready to go," Elsa said, coming out the door of the cabin attired in the same fashion as her mother. She regarded Hyroc. "Hello, Hyroc."

Hyroc nodded a greeting. "Where are you going?"

"Oh, we're off to collect fireweed," Helen said. Her eyes lit slightly. "We could use another hand. There's a jar of jelly in it for you if you do."

Hyroc gave her an attentive look. "Umm, sure." He didn't have anything urgent to deal with for the day.

Helen smiled. "This way," she said.

She led them from the cabin across the trail leading to Hyroc's, to a gravelly hillock with a strip of purple fireweed running from one end to the top. Bee's buzzed throughout the strip, working their way from plant to plant.

"Okay, Hyroc," Helen said. "This is what I want you to do." She bent down, grabbing the base of a fireweed plant with one hand where the purple petals began. "First of all, make sure there are no bees on the plant, because this *will* make them very angry." She smiled. "And I don't expect I have to explain why you don't want to make them angry. Then pull your hand up like so." She moved her hand up the stalk stripping off the petals with her fingers. She then dumped the petals into the basket. "And that's all that's too it."

Hyroc nodded, moving over to a plant. He waited for a bee to finish its work before stripping the plant of petals.

"Hyroc you doing all right getting ready for winter?" Helen said.

"I think so," Hyroc said, brushing another handful of petals into the basket.

"You're making sure to stock up on meat." She ran her hand up the stalk of a plant.

Hyroc sighed. "I've been trying to."

Helen frowned. "You might want to do better than 'try,' winter isn't far off."

"I know but, I've been really busy."

"Then make *time* for it. You won't be very happy with yourself when you're going to bed hungry."

"But you're still going to help me if I need it?"

Helen sighed. "*We are*, but what if something happens and we don't have anything to give you. You'll starve, that's what'll happen. If we can help you, we will, but you need to do more of the work yourself." Hyroc nodded. "And how are you doing on firewood?"

Hyroc grimaced; collecting firewood hadn't seemed a high priority. He remained silent and avoided her eyes, hoping she wouldn't take his response as a no.

Helen's frown deepened. "*Don't go neglecting that either.* I know it might not seem important now but *you don't* want to be chopping firewood in the middle of a blizzard." Hyroc nodded somberly. Her expression softened. She put a hand on his shoulder. "I really don't mean to sound like a nag; I just worry about you is all."

"We all do," Elsa added.

Hyroc gave them an appreciative half smile. "You don't need to worry about me." People worrying about him was almost as aggravating as people thinking he was going to sink his teeth into them. He had spent weeks all by himself and he did just fine. It seemed absurd to think people could worry about him when he had done something like that.

She smiled. "I'm a mother and you're a boy who lives all alone, so yes, yes I do."

They returned to the cabin shortly before dusk after they had filled the baskets. Then Helen convinced Hyroc to stay for dinner.

The following day, Hyroc caught nothing in his traps, felled a small tree and spent the rest of the day chopping it into firewood. Then the day after, he only caught a single rabbit and killed a wild turkey while hunting. After working the coyote pelt the next morning, Donavan and Curtis showed up. Donovan held a sack filled with something heavy from the way it weighed down his arms. Kit climbed down from his perch, fixating on the sack.

"How'd your trip go?" Hyroc said.

"Good," Donovan said, gently pushing Kit's head away. "We got a moose."

"*Really*, you got a moose?" He wished he could get a moose.

Donovan nodded. "Pretty big one too. We almost ran out of room to carry all the meat." He indicated the sack as he held it out to Hyroc. "Some of it's in here. My mother told us to bring this up to you."

"Thank you," Hyroc said gleefully.

"This is kind of heavy. Where do you want it?"

"Oh, umm…set it on the table in there," Hyroc said, pushing the door open and cleaning a spot off on his table. Kit rushed after Donovan but Hyroc caught him by the collar before he crossed the threshold.

"Our mother wants you to smoke every bit of that meat and she says if you make a meal out of it before we have snow on the ground, she'll make you clean the barn for a month." Hyroc grimaced. Her orders were duly noted. "Oh, and she also told me to give you this." Donovan removed a wooden container from his pocket and held it out to him. "This is fireweed jelly."

Hyroc gratefully accepted the container. He opened it, dipped a finger in the purplish jelly and stuck it in his mouth. He smiled at the sweet taste.

"I killed a grouse," Curtis said gleefully.

"Is that your first?" Hyroc said, putting the lid back on the container. Curtis nodded happily.

Donovan ruffled his little brother's hair. "Yeah, this little goober can shoot now." There was a pause. "I wanted to ask you something."

"What?" Hyroc said.

"Well, I was wondering if you wanted to try getting some ducks with us tomorrow morning."

Hyroc gave him a stunned look, a wave of nostalgia washing over him. "Of course I would!"

Donovan grinned. "Good. Meet us at our cabin early tomorrow, and I mean earl, before the sunrises."

"I'll be there."

A faint line of rising sunlight illuminated the darkened sky, shadowing the clouds with black. Hyroc yawned as he Svald, Donovan, Curtis and their dog Dilo stood at the tree line, looking across an empty field littered with broken wheat stalks. Up until he had arrived here, Hyroc had thought the only places to hunt ducks were rivers, ponds and the edges of lakes. It had made perfect sense to him before now, ducks were waterfowl, and they lived near water. Svald had disturbed his simple logic by telling him this place was where they were going to hunt ducks. He still wondered if this was some misunderstanding, Marcus had always taken him to a pond, with water, not a freshly harvested farm field. There had to be a reason for that. Maybe this close to the wilderness the term duck actually referred to an entirely different type of bird? There were rabbits living in this area with antlers coming out of their heads, a talking bear, to say nothing of brain tanning, so it wouldn't be the weirdest thing to happen since he arrived at Elswood.

Donovan yawned.

"See, I told you those were contagious," Hyroc said dryly.

"They are *not*, we're just tired," Donovan said. "It's not like you coughed on me and made me sick."

Then Curtis yawned. He stamped his foot in annoyance.

Hyroc and the two other boys leaned forward turning their attention on Svald to see when he would yawn. Several minutes passed without a yawn. Svald met their gazes with a smirk on his face.

Donovan pointed at Svald. "*He didn't yawn*," he said triumphantly.

Hyroc paused thoughtfully. "How do you know he didn't start it?" He challenged.

Dilo stood, growing suddenly excited about something. Svald held his hand up, ending the debate. Everyone listened intently. Hyroc heard the faint gaggle of ducks. Svald cupped his hands together, blowing three bursts of air into them; making three noises sounding surprisingly like duck calls. Slowly, the quacking grew louder. Svald made the noise again. He drew his bow and dropped into a crouch. Hyroc and the other two did the same. A formation of ducks came into view over the treetops. The flock descended, landing in the middle of the field.

Hyroc cocked his head; apparently, they were indeed hunting ducks in a field. This seemed a lot more comfortable than slogging through cold knee high water to retrieve a kill. Why had Marcus only hunted at the pond, there were plenty of farms around Forna? He then wondered if it was because none of the farmers would allow him onto their land or if it would have given The Ministry an excuse to kill him. He pushed his pondering aside and returned his focus to the flock of ducks in front of him. He didn't need to worry about The Ministry anymore.

"Everyone ready," Svald said in a barely audible whisper. All four of them silently rose to their feet. "On three... one...two...three."

Simultaneously, the four of them let their arrows fly. Hyroc and Svald's arrows found their mark, but Donovan and Curtis missed. In a flutter of wings, the flock took flight. Hyroc rushed forward, loosing another arrow. His shot came close, but missed.

"Go get em," Svald said, sweeping his hand forward. Dilo eagerly took off running in the direction of the nearest duck. She picked it up in her jaws, brought it back and dropped it at Svald's feet. Then she headed off to collect the others. Hyroc studied the hound as she worked. He had no idea dogs were even capable of such useful things.

"Nice shot," Svald said. He turned his attention to Donavan and Curtis. "Don't get hung up on that, we just started, there'll be more. Go find your arrows before you forget where they landed. "

A long stretch of boredom passed before another flock landed in the field. Donovan and Svald got one each, while Curtis and Hyroc missed. Then Svald and Hyroc got one each from the next flock. On the following group, something made the fowl take to the air before anyone was ready, but with a lucky shot, Hyroc got one mid-flight. The momentum of the duck carried it close to the trees on the other side of the field.

"Nice shot," Svald commented excitedly. "I didn't think any of us were going to get anything from that flock." Hyroc nodded thankfully. "Go get it," Svald said to Dilo. The hound gave him an uncertain look, but remained where she stood. "Go get it," he repeated. Dilo still didn't move. He nudged her with his boot. "What's wrong with you girl, go get it." Svald shook his head in annoyance when she still didn't move. "Hyroc, I don't know what *she's* doing, so I guess you'll have to go get it." Hyroc nodded his understanding and made his way across the field to collect his prize.

When he was a few steps from the felled bird, the shriek of a dying rabbit sliced through the air. Startled, he looked in the direction of the disturbance. Peering between the trees, he felt a thrill of terror when he found the rabbit. A giant black spider stood over the rabbit with its enormous fangs buried in its flesh. His shoulder itched with pain as he struggled to nock an arrow. The spider pulled its bloodied fangs from the rabbit and turned its attention on him. His breath caught in his throat. The spider regarded him with its ebony eyes then used its mouth to grab one of the rabbit's back legs and drag it further into the shadows. Heart still hammering away in his chest, he scooped up the duck and ran back to join the rest of the group. He didn't care what they were going to think about him, he needed to tell them about the nightmarish creature.

"SVALD, SVALD," Hyroc yelled, as he came up to Svald, who was looking over the dead fowl.

Svald's happy expression sharpened into alarm. "What – *what wrong*," he called out.

Gasping, Hyroc pointed where he had seen the spider. "There's – there's – there's –" He couldn't seem to say what he wanted.

"There's a *what*? Take a deep breath."

Hyroc took a deep breath. "*There's a –*" A crash in the trees behind Svald cut him off, drawing everyone's attention. Kit came into view walking toward them. A new kind of fear took hold of Hyroc.

Dilo instantly started barking in alarm. Svald swore throwing his arms out and yelling menacing warnings at the cub. Kit paused, regarding Svald curiously. Still yelling, Svald nocked an arrow. Hyroc threw himself in front of Svald to block his shot. "GET OUT OF THE WAY HYROC," Svald roared.

"I can't," Hyroc said sternly.

Svald swore and lunged forward to throw him out of the way. Hyroc backpedaled out of reach. Svald stopped as Kit ran up beside Hyroc, with his teeth bared, ears flat against his head, and growling savagely.

"KIT STOP," Hyroc snapped. Kit covered his teeth, his ears rose and he stopped growling.

Svald looked from Kit to Hyroc in bewilderment.

"STOP!" Donavan and Curtis yelled as they came between their father and Kit. "That's *his pet*. Don't shoot."

"Pet?" Svald stated, focusing a stern gaze on Hyroc. Hyroc nodded, knowing he was about to be in trouble. Svald folded his arms, his expression darkening. He indicated Donovan and Curtis with a look. "The two of you go." Donavan and Curtis gave Hyroc a sympathetic look before they turned and walked off. "Why have I not heard of this?" The anger in his voice was clear."

Hyroc cringed. He was in for it now. "I was afraid you would kill him."

"Kill him? And why would I kill him, if he's your pet, hmm?"

Hyroc bit down. "To protect your livestock."

"And why's that?"

"Because… mountain lions… kill… livestock."

"Yes, mountain lions *kill* livestock. You might see why I'm upset with you," he said pointedly. "If you were one of my children, I'd give you a whipping for this, fortunately for you, you're not."

"I'm sorry, I –"

"I'm disappointed you kept this from me."

"I meant no harm; *please don't kill him*."

"I'm *not* going to *hurt* your pet," Svald said irritably.

"You're not?"

"No, killing somebody's pet needlessly isn't a decent thing to do." Hyroc breathed a sigh of relief. Svald's expression darkened further. "But don't go thinking you're off the hook, I'm not finished with you yet." Hyroc stiffened, bracing himself. "Right now, he's not much of a threat to anything much bigger than a house cat. But he won't be like that forever you know. If I catch him stalking around my home –" Svald paused "– I won't hesitate to protect my family. *Am I understood?*"

Hyroc nodded, avoiding eye contact.

"Good. Take your ducks, and you and *your pet* had better head on home before I change my mind." Svald stalked off.

Hyroc bowed his head guiltily as he collected his felled ducks and headed off with Kit. When he arrived at the cabin, Ursa was laying in the shade of Kit's tree. Hyroc grumbled to himself; he was in no mood to talk with her. Especially if everything she said was in riddles.

"What happened?" she said calmly. "It felt like you were in danger and then the feeling vanished."

Hyroc shrugged. "I saw a spider," he said scathingly. He glared at Kit. "Then *stupid* here got seen by Svald." Kit growled in response.

"I see. You should have known better than to think he would be content to spend his morning idle while you hunt."

"Well, he picked the worst possible moment to go exploring and he got me yelled at. And now Svald doesn't trust me."

"For the moment maybe, but it will pass soon enough. They will not abandon you over something so trivial. All you can do now is learn from your mistake and move forward." Her expression darkened slightly. "But you must still be careful; you can never come back from the shadowed tunnels." Hyroc glowered at her. He knew he should have expected nothing less of her. The darkness vanished from her face and she got to her feet. "You need not worry about that spider, it will not harm you." With that, she left, leaving Hyroc to wonder about the mysterious tunnels she had mentioned.

CHAPTER 36

Mischief

A damp orange leaf listed wildly from side to side as it drifted down from its branch, landing between Hyroc's ears while he sat beside the stream with his fishing pole anchored into the ground, waiting for a bite. He promptly brushed the leaf away. Reaching behind him, he picked up his coyote pelt, that with the help of Helen he had finished fashioning into a hat the day before. He thoughtfully regarded the folded skin of the coyote's face as its eyeless sockets gazed back at him then stuck it on his head. The fur wasn't as soft as he would have liked, but it still fit comfortably, covering his ears without folding the ends of them enough to be a bother. He had only needed to use the part of the pelt above the shoulders for the actual hat, but a considerable amount of the hide remained unused. Not wanting to waste any of it, he decided to keep the remainder attached and it hung halfway down his back.

He walked closer to the edge the stream. Leaning over the water's surface, he looked at his undulating reflection. He slowly turned his head from side to side. As far as he could tell, other than the unsightly part hanging off the back, it looked like a passable hat.

He turned toward Kit who lay at the tree line resting his head on his paws, lazily watching the fishing pole. "How does it look to you?"

Hyroc said. Kit lifted his head and yawned. Hyroc shrugged. "Yeah, I don't really like it either. But its –" his fishing bobber plunked down into the water. He jumped for the fishing pole. With two hard yanks, he pulled a small fish from the water. Smiling, he walked from the water's edge with his catch dangling from his line. He set the flailing fish down, reaching for his knife. Kit bounded forward and snatched the fish off the hook.

"HEY," Hyroc yelled, lunging forward to grab his catch. Kit dodged out of his reach, bolting for the trees with the stolen fish in his mouth. "GET BACK HERE WITH THAT" Hyroc dropped his pole and took off in pursuit. Kit was rapidly pulling ahead. A wrong turn around the trunk of a tree led him to a thickly grown alder he couldn't easily pass through. Kit bobbed his head from side to side, trying to figure out how to overcome the obstacle. His hesitation gave Hyroc just enough time to grab him by the tail before he could escape. Kit yowled out angrily. "HA, I GOT –" Kit wheeled around and clocked him upside the head with his paw. The force of the impact threw him off balance, skewing his hat over to one side of his head, and causing him to lose his grip. Kit scrambled up the nearest tree. Hyroc shook his head to focus his eyes and when the world stopped moving, he readjusted his hat. He glared up at Kit who was now happily eating the fish on the branch of the tree. "I'm the one who caught that you know," Hyroc said pointedly. Kit looked down at him while licking his chops. Hyroc sighed, got to his feet, brushed himself off and stormed back to the stream to try for another fish. And this time he was going to be more vigilant.

He landed another one not long afterward, but it was uselessly small. *Why couldn't Kit have stolen this one* he thought grudgingly. Knowing that turning the tiny fish into a meal would be more work than it was worth, he tossed it back into the stream. Too frustrated to try for another, he picked up his fishing pole and went back to his cabin. He propped the pole up beside the fireplace. From the cabinet, he retrieved a grain sack brimming with the feathers from all the ducks he had downed since arriving at the mountain. He set the sack outside the front door, settled down beside it, pushed any protruding feathers back in, threaded a needle and started sewing the opening shut. It was a pillow. He smiled excitedly as he worked, knowing tonight he would be resting much more comfortably. Halfway through closing the opening, he ran out of thread. He squeezed his eyes shut, annoyed with himself, wondering why he hadn't brought the entire spool out with him. He poked the needle in a crack in the wood around the doorway and went inside to retrieve the spool of thread.

When he came back outside, he was horrified to see Kit, holding the pillow between his paws and kicking it savagely with the claws of his back legs. "KIT NO," Hyroc bellowed, grabbing hold of the pillow. Refusing to let go, Kit bit into the fabric when Hyroc tried to wrench it from between his paws. Hyroc pulled even harder, causing Kit to respond in kind while growling. "LET GO – THAT'S – MY – PILLOW." Mustering all of his strength, he yanked on it as hard as he could. A loud ripping noise emanated from the pillow as its middle was torn open and it erupted into a cloud of feathers. Hyroc and Kit were thrown backward with the sudden release of tension.

Hyroc stared at the destroyed pillow in shock seeing its innards littering the ground and floating gently through the air. Kit bounded forward, batting at the descending feathers. Hyroc covered his face with his hands, rocking his head from side to side and moaned in frustration. After all the time and effort he had put into that pillow, this was his reward. Nothing ever seemed to be easy for him. He took a long deep breath before uncovering his face. He watched Kit play with a maelstrom of unpleasant feelings toward the cat swirling around inside his head. With a sigh, he got to his feet and walked over to assess the remnants of the pillow. Mourning it's passing wouldn't help him be more comfortable tonight. Seeming to sense his foul mood, Kit stopped his play, taking an uncertain step back. Hyroc smiled ruefully at his reaction. *Yeah, you'd better watch out.*

Picking up the pillow, he was dismayed – though not at all surprised – to see a large tear slashed across the middle, but it was still salvageable. He stuffed the feathers in his knapsack and set to work repairing the damage to the pillow, wary to keep it away from Kit.

It took him the rest of the day and part of the night to complete his task. He reverently placed the resurrected pillow on the head of his bed. He sighed happily when he laid down on it, as the plush cushion contoured to his head in its delightful embrace. Kit leapt up on the bed. Hyroc glared at him angrily. Kit countered with a look of supreme innocence. Hyroc couldn't maintain his anger toward that. He rolled his eyes. Maybe what his companion had done wasn't so bad. His pillow had still gotten finished. "Okay, I guess, I forgive you," he said with a reluctant sigh.

Hyroc leaned sideways in the yellow light of morning, trying to see around the trunk of a tree. "Kit," he called out. His first three traps were empty and he was just leaving the incline, when a small furry something darted into a bush ahead of him. Kit immediately disappeared into the foliage after it. "Come on; I need to get to the other traps." Hyroc shrugged, heading in the direction Kit had gone. "Kit get over here already." He caught movement in the shadows out of the corner of his eye. He turned in time to see Kit barreling toward him from around a tree before his feet were knocked out from under him. Startled, he sat bolt upright only for Kit to leap on him and knock him back down. Kit gripped his shoulder and neck with his paws then playfully nipped at his face. Hyroc cringed at the painful wet pinch of teeth. He grabbed Kit around the shoulders and threw him off. Kit fell on his back, but instantly righted himself, bounding back on top of him. Kit lightly nipped the side of his snout. He threw Kit off with an abrupt roll followed by a hard shove. Before Kit could recover, Hyroc threw himself at him and pinned him to the ground. Kit quickly wriggled out from his hold and lunged into his chest. Hyroc stuck his arms behind Kit's neck as he was thrown backwards, pulling the cat down with him. He realized he was laughing as the two of them hit the ground. A warm sense of joy washed over him. Kit backed out of his hold. Hyroc coughed as Kit bounded off his stomach sideways. He crouched; a ripple ran through the length of his body, then he took off back toward Hyroc. Hyroc threw an arm out toward the charging cat, causing Kit to veer away. He jumped to his feet and stood hunched forward with his arms extended, ready to intercept Kit's next charge. Kit regarded him through wild eyes as he lurched left. Hyroc leaned in the same direction to block him. Kit then lurched right. Hyroc countered by leaning that way. The two of them repeated the same moves twice more. Kit straightened his stance, giving Hyroc an annoyed look.

Hyroc patted the ground invitingly. "Come on, *get me*," he said excitedly. Kit regarded him before crouching and charging. He came at an angle to avoid the center of Hyroc's reach. Hyroc playfully jabbed Kit in the side, causing him to tumble forward as he lost his balance. Snickering, Hyroc poked his hand at Kit's belly. Kit swiped at his hand. Hyroc pulled his hand back. Coming in with the other, he ruffled the fur on Kit's unguarded side. Kit rolled onto his back and swatted at his other hand. Hyroc alternated between attacking hands until Kit bolted out of reach. He patted the ground to insight another charge. Kit charged, but ran past him. Hyroc ruffled the fur along Kit's back as he darted past. The big cat then abruptly wandered over to the shade of a tree and laid down, panting heavily.

Hyroc sat down beside him, resting his back against the same tree. "Yeah, I think that's enough for a while," he agreed breathlessly. Reaching over, he smoothed out a patch of disturbed fur on Kit's head. He drank several mouthfuls of water from his water skin. Kit regarded him with tired eyes. Hyroc looked at Kit thoughtfully, lowered the end of the water skin to his mouth and squeezed two squirts of water into it. Kit licked a few stray droplets from around his mouth. Hyroc felt a stinging pain on his face and the side of his neck. When he touched the spot on his face, he grimaced. Pulling his hand back, he saw a thin coating of blood on his fingers. He laughed, not entirely sure why the sight of his blood should be humorous.

Once rested, the two of them continued on their way through the traps. Other than a deer rabbit, they were all empty. Hyroc regarded the animal's small antlers curiously while he ate his lunch at the cabin. He pressed a finger experimentally onto the tip of the antler. It didn't cut into his finger, but it seemed somewhat sharp. He wondered if there was a use for them. Svald would probably know. He grimaced, remembering the yelling at Svald had given him. That had happened nearly a week ago and the mere thought of coming to him, made Hyroc nervous. He shook his head ruefully at himself. He felt like he was being immature about the whole situation. All Svald had done was give him a warning, a warning he had obeyed. Besides, the whole time Helen was helping him make his coyote hat, Svald hadn't acted like he was angry with him. It wasn't as if he had punched Elsa in the face or anything. If he had done that then he definitely would have something to be afraid of. All he had done was make a simple mistake and no one had gotten hurt because of it. Like Ursa had said, they wouldn't abandon him over something so small. There was nothing for him to be worried about.

As soon as he headed in the direction of the Shackleton cabin, he heard Kit's claws scraping down the trunk of the tree. He bowed his head in mild annoyance, turning to see Kit sauntering toward him. "No Kit," he said calmly. "I'm going to the Shackleton's; you can't come with me there." Kit regarded him curiously. "I won't be long." He took several steps and Kit continued toward him. He held his hand up sternly. "NO, *stay*." Kit took another step. "Stay!" Hyroc said more forcefully. "*I'll be right back*." Kit slowly sat. Hyroc continued on his way and to his relief, Kit remained where he was.

Helen, Elsa and Curtis were in the garden extricating the last of their vegetables from the soil. After exchanging greetings and dodging an inquiry from Helen about the scratches on his face, they directed him to the back of the cabin where Svald and Donovan were working on a hide.

He braced himself for the possibility of a reproach from Svald. The man showed no signs of remembering the scolding he had given. Relieved and feeling irritated at himself, he held up one of the deer rabbit antlers. "I was wondering if there's some use for these," he said.

Svald rubbed his chin thoughtfully. "I don't know much about using *those* antlers," he said. "But with deer antlers you can make spearheads if they're at just the right angle. Things like that and I've heard you can make some kind of medicine from grinding them up into powder, but beyond that –"

A cacophony of urgent barks echoed from the other side of the cabin, interrupting him. Hyroc felt a shiver of fear run up his back. He remembered Dilo making those same kinds of noises when she spotted Kit in the field. *He must've have followed me!* Svald and Donovan took off running in the direction of the sound. He took off in pursuit, desperately hoping he would get there first. The two of them beat him around the cabin. He heard Svald curse. A cold sinking feeling pulled in his gut. He came around the cabin, fearing he would see Kit's lifeless body lying on the ground with an arrow through his chest. Svald, Donovan and the rest of the family stood fixated on Kit with a mixture of odd expressions on their faces, as he and Dilo rolled together in a flurry of movement. Despite the frenzy of activity, Dilo and Kit's behaviors seemed strange for a fight. None of them had any visible injuries and they were showing an odd amount of restraint when it came to their attacks. There was something strangely familiar about the situation. He realized with amazement, Kit wasn't attacking the dog, he was playing with her.

Hyroc turned toward Svald. "Svald please don't –" he pleaded. Svald silenced him with a raised hand. When he turned, instead of seeing a look of fury on his face, Hyroc saw humored interest.

"I'm not going to hurt him," Svald said serenely. He indicated the playing animals with his hand. "Definitely not for *this*. What I said to you before still stands, but if he can behave himself, well, you're welcome to bring him over to play anytime."

Hyroc gave him a bewildered smile.

CHAPTER 37

Snowfall

Wing beats drummed ominously through the night air. Hyroc snapped his eyes up at the darkened sky, seeing only the silver disc of a full moon suspended in the blackness. He frantically scanned the void overhead for the creature with the wings. The wing beats grew steadily louder. Sweeping his eyes around, he saw he stood in the middle of a clearing surrounded by trees. This was a bad place for him to be. Here in the open, he was easy prey for the creature. He needed to get to the trees; their branches would protect him. He broke into a run. The wing beats grew even louder; the creature was very near. He reached the trees. The wing beats stopped. He took a deep relieved breath.

The sound of huge wings fluttered behind him. Turning, he saw an enormous hawk staring down its beak at him. He reached for an arrow but found none in his quiver. Going for his sword, he found it too was missing. He realized with horror there was nothing he could do against the bird. The hawk remained where it stood, watching him. Hyroc fearfully returned its gaze. It had blue eyes, but they had an unusual look to them. They had the thoughtful appearance that reminded him of a person, not an animal. He felt a strange familiarity with those eyes, as if he should know them.

"I never wanted this for you," the bird said sorrowfully, speaking softly in a woman's voice. Its voice was even more familiar than its eyes. Hyroc felt the brush of a memory in his mind, but it refused to come forth. Every time he tried reaching for it, it would slip from his grasp. "I'm sorry." The bird gave him a look of remorse and in the moonlight; he saw the glimmer of a tear rolling down the feathers below one eye.

"Who are you?" Hyroc said.

"You never knew me."

He felt a chill in the air. Everything blurred to blackness as he began to shiver. He instinctively reached over his shoulder to pull his blanket up. His hand grasped nothing. Opening his eyes, he saw the light colored shape of Kit on the floor coiled up in something brown he was chewing on. Slowly a fog hanging over his mind parted. His eyes widened with anger when he realized the brown something was the blanket he had made for his bed.

"GET OFF THAT!" Hyroc bellowed as he sat upright. Kit started, leaping from the blanket with an alarmed look in his eyes. Hyroc climbed out of his bed, groggily wrapped the blanket around himself and laid back down, facing away from Kit. Just as he began to warm, he heard the scrape of claws at the inside of his door. He glanced over his shoulder to see Kit scratching at the door to be let out. Grumbling, he squeezed his eyes shut and tightly pulled the blanket over his head. The scratching got even louder. He groaned. Uncovering his eyes, he saw from the amount of light filtering into the cabin, it was time for him to get up. With a shrug, he sat up. He yawned widely as he swung his legs over the side of his bed. After putting on his boots and hat, he opened the door. The end of his nose tingled as a burst of crisp morning air swept over his face. Kit bolted outside disappearing from view around the side of the door. Hyroc finished off some leftover duck for his breakfast before joining Kit outside in the cold air.

The sun shone unchallenged from the pale blue sky above. Leafless trees now dotted the surrounding area, and besides the evergreen trees, every plant drooped unhealthily beneath a thin coating of frost, their leaves an ugly brown or sickly yellow.

"Come on Kit," Hyroc said with another yawn, a short-lived mist drifting from his mouth as he spoke. "We need to get going." He started toward the back of the valley and Kit joined him moments later.

The first trap was empty. From the higher elevation where the trap sat, he noticed a thick mass of gray clouds off to the east. With the chill in the air, he had no disillusion those clouds carried snow. The icy grip of winter had finally arrived. He just hoped he was prepared for it and hadn't neglected anything important. The clouds seemed hours off, giving him enough time to check his traps and maybe get a few more wood rounds chopped before the storm hit.

The mountain was quiet as Kit and he made their way to the second trap. In the silence, Hyroc's thoughts wandered from one worry about his winter situation to another before eventually turning to his dream. His dreams rarely made any sense, and a giant talking eagle hardly seemed unusual in that regard, especially considering Ursa. But why did the bird seem so familiar? Everything always seemed familiar to him while in a dream and he never noticed how strange some things were until he woke. Somehow, this felt different. He almost felt as if he expected to see the bird waiting for him whenever he came around a tree. The feeling reminded him a little of the nightmares he had when he was much younger. Waking with a frightful start in the middle of the night, wrapping himself in his blankets; scared something was watching him from the dark recesses of his room. His dream had certainly started out like a nightmare, so maybe that's what it was. Except a sad predatory bird seemed an odd thing to have in a nightmare. It was absurd to think he had a terrible fear of tear shedding hawks.

He suddenly flung forward, losing his balance when something pulled his leg back. He caught himself with an outstretched arm on the cool surface of a boulder in front of him. Alarmed, he looked back at his leg. There was a loop of heavy twine wrapped around his ankle, trailing a line off toward a snare behind him. He glared at the snare, irritated someone was encroaching on his trapping grounds. There wasn't supposed to be anybody trapping this close to the mountain besides him.

Carefully stepping toward the snare's epicenter, he slackened the line. Reaching down to his ankle, he fed the twine back through the loop that enabled the trap to tighten around his foot, loosening the snare until it fell off. He looked around and was puzzled to see that he stood at the bottom of the ravine. Sweeping his eyes through his surroundings, he didn't see his trap anywhere, only the strangers trap. He took a few steps back. Warmth surged through his cheeks when he realized with embarrassment the trap he had stumbled into was his. He had walked right through it while he was obsessing over his dream. If there had been something caught in it he would have walked right over the top of it. It didn't take much thought for him to imagine the pain from making that mistake if the animal had sharp teeth. Looking over the lip of the ravine, he saw the tips of the storm clouds drawing ever closer. He needed to stop wasting time worrying about the strangeness of a dream and finish with his traps before the storm arrived. It was an odd dream nothing more.

None of his remaining traps had caught anything. When he returned to the cabin, the storm clouds dominated the sky, steadily casting their shadows over the mountain. After splitting two wood rounds, he felt a pinprick of something cold melt on the end of his snout. Lifting his eyes, he saw tiny specks of white drifting toward the ground. Soon the air became thick with large flakes of wet snow fluff. Deciding it was time to go inside; he made his way to the front door. He found Kit, excitedly batting at any falling flakes within reach. Hyroc smiled mischievously; knowing Kit probably wouldn't be so happy with what awaited him in the morning.

When Hyroc opened his door the following morning, he found a thick blanket of snow and clumps of sparkling white powder covering everything in sight. The cold air smelled fresh and clean. Stepping off the porch, the snow crunched delightfully under his boots. He liked the sound, but he couldn't stand snow when it squeaked. It made him feel like he was stepping on a white mat of squealing mice.

Kit stood at the edge of the snow just outside the door, looking at the white substance uncertainly. He experimentally put one paw forward into the snow, wrinkled his nose angrily, and pulled it back.

"Oh it's not that bad once you get used to it," Hyroc said. He started patting his leg, "Come on, we still have work to do."

Kit looked from the snow to Hyroc's face, before stepping out into the snow. He irritably shook the snow from his paws for his first couple of steps and bounded toward Hyroc. On his second leap, he fell face first into a snow-covered hole with only his hindquarters sticking out. Hyroc burst out laughing. Kit growled and in a flurry of movement exploded from the snow. Hyroc brushed any remaining snow from Kit's back. Kit shook, showering him with half melted snow. He threw a hand up to block the incoming slush. Kit took a tentative step forward, but once he saw the snow was solid, he continued exploring his surroundings until Hyroc was a fair distance toward the back of the valley.

Hyroc only found a white hare caught in the trap by the hill. He really didn't have any immediate use for the rabbit's pelt, so after lunch, he began his slog toward town to sell it. As he came to the road, he heard yelling off toward the Shackleton cabin. He headed toward the sound. When the clearing came into view, he saw Curtis, Elsa and Donavan running around and throwing snow at each other. He regarded them curiously as he came closer. The instant he opened his mouth to ask what they were doing, a ball of snow hit him in the face. Donovan tensed sympathetically, Elsa covered her mouth with both hands and Curtis burst into laughter. Now a little annoyed, Hyroc spit out a mouthful of slush and wiped his face off on the back of his glove.

"Oh sorry, I wasn't actually aiming at you," Donovan said with a laugh of embarrassment. With a primal yell from Curtis, he and Elsa started pelting Donovan with balls of snow as punishment. Donovan responded in kind and started throwing balls of snow back at them.

"What are you doing?" Hyroc said inquisitively.

The three of them stopped to give him a strange look. "What does it look like, we're having a snowball fight," Donovan said.

"Snowball fight?"

Donovan, Curtis and Elsa exchanged concerned glances with each other.

"Yeah," Donovan said. "Haven't you been in one before?" He shook his head. The three of them gaped at him in shock. Their reactions were starting to make him feel stupid for not knowing what they were talking about

"You've never been in a snowball fight?" Elsa said.

"No, the place I came from wasn't the sort of place you got to play games. And well –" he indicated his face with a subtle wave of his hand "– there weren't exactly a lot of people that wanted to play – with me." The three of them looked at him sympathetically.

"Would you like us to teach you?" Donovan volunteered.

Hyroc's eyes lit at that. "Sure, what do I do?"

"It's simple really." Donovan reached down and grabbed a handful of snow. "You pick up some snow like this." He began fashioning it into a ball. "Then…you… hit somebody with it!" Donovan threw the snowball and it hit Hyroc in the chest. He narrowed his eyes in annoyance. He didn't need to know anything about the game to know that was a cheap shot.

"Donovan!" Elsa yelled in outrage. "I can't believe you." She quickly fashioned a snowball and hit Donovan in the side of the head with it. Curtis smiled impishly before hitting Donovan with a snowball of his own. Donovan jumped back, made a snowball and hit Elsa with it.

Hyroc scooped up a handful of snow, packed it into a ball and threw it at Donovan as hard as he could. Donovan dodged out of the way of a snowball from Curtis, and Elsa was suddenly in the path of the one Hyroc had thrown. It splattered against the back of her head. Hyroc cringed. Elsa wheeled around with a stunned look on her face.

"Did you just," Elsa said pointedly.

Hyroc felt a tinge of warmth seep into his face. "No, no, I was aiming at Donovan," he said sheepishly.

"Well let's see how you like this!" Elsa made a snowball and hit him in the shoulder with it. Curtis did the same.

Hyroc put his arm up to block the incoming snowballs and used his other hand to grab a handful of snow. Without even bothering to make it into a ball, he threw his handful at Elsa. With an excited yelp, she jumped back.

Donovan nailed Curtis in the back with a snowball.

"HEY," Curtis yelled.

Donovan grinned. "You're the one who left yourself open," he said.

Curtis made a snowball and threw it at him. Donovan dodged out of the way, then took aim at Elsa. She narrowly avoided the incoming attack and retaliated with one of her own. Hyroc used this reprieve in their assault to make a snowball and hit Curtis with it.

Donovan thrust a finger at him. "That's my brother, you fiend!" he yelled with mock intensity before hitting Hyroc with a large snowball.

After this, the fight turned to chaos and the four of them were quickly covered in snow. While Hyroc fought back, he felt like he did the day Kit had savaged him with his play. He realized the feeling was enjoyment; he was having fun! It had been so long since he had been able to do something fun. He had almost forgotten fun even existed. This place was starting to feel like home, like he belonged here. Maybe winter wouldn't be so bad for him after all.

CHAPTER **38**

Winter Hunt

T he midday sun shone brightly between the snow-caked trees from a hole in a layer of light gray clouds. Hyroc, Donovan and Elsa followed tracks left by a deer's hoofed foot piercing through the white powder blanketing the frozen ground. The three of them had been tracking the animal since noon. Each print was getting sharper; lacking much of the distortion that occurred over time from snow collapsing into them. Kit plodded through the snow beside Hyroc, his large paws preventing him from sinking far into the cold powder. This was unfamiliar territory to either of them. The river north of his cabinet had solidly frozen over recently, and the deer tracks had led across.

This morning Hyroc had been pleasantly surprised to find Elsa and Donavan waiting for him outside his cabin. They invited him on a hunt. Curious to see Elsa's skills with her being the first girl he knew to hunt, he gladly accepted.

Kit stopped suddenly, raising his ears then veered away suddenly to investigate the lower branch of a tree. Hyroc stopped, eying Kit inquiringly. Kit pawed at the snow below the branch. He tensed as a tiny gray shape shot out of the snow. He lunged forward and struck the shape with a quick strike of the paw.

"What did you get?" Hyroc said, as he came over. Kit lowered his head and picked the shape up in his jaws. Hyroc saw a lifeless vole clasped between his teeth. He turned back toward Elsa and Donavan. "It's just a vole," he said in a hushed tone, before returning his attention back to Kit. "Good boy." A bright colored speck in the snow caught Hyroc's attention. He crouched down and brushed the snow from the speck, exposing a frozen rosehip. He remembered Helen telling him he could usually find rosehips that were still good to eat beneath the snow during winter. He stuck the rosehip and three more he uncovered in his pocket. The sun's light dimed as it disappeared behind the clouds, then sporadic snowflakes began descending from the sky. Hyroc stood. "Come on Kit, I think we're gaining on the deer."

Not long afterward Hyroc began to feel thirsty. But not wanting to go through the trouble of removing his water skin from the inside of his coat – where his body heat kept it from freezing – put a handful of snow in his mouth.

"You know, that'll kill you," Donovan said, keeping his voice low so as not to risk spooking their quarry. Hyroc shot him a startled look. Nobody had ever told him eating snow was deadly!

"No, it won't," Elsa said, taking notice of his expression. "What Donovan means is, snow is cold and if you eat it when your cold, then it might kill you because you'll freeze to death. So, no, a few handfuls won't hurt you." She swatted Donovan on the shoulder with her hand, eliciting a sly smile from her brother. Hyroc shook his head and feeling a little embarrassed toward his reaction, turned away, continuing to follow the tracks.

"Wol'dger," Hyroc heard a hushed voice say. He turned toward Elsa who stood a few steps off to his left. "Did you say something?" he said. She shook her head. With a shrug, he returned his attention to studying the deer tracks.

"I smell Wol'dger," the voice said again a few minutes later. Hyroc stopped, looking left. Donovan and Elsa were studying the snow in front of them intently. Elsa gave him an attentive look, followed by Donovan. "Who keeps saying things?" Hyroc said.

Donovan and Elsa gave each other a confused glance. "We didn't say anything," Donovan said. "Did you hear something?"

Hyroc felt a flood of anxiety. Was he hearing things? The last thing he needed was to start hearing voices. Being thought mad wouldn't help his situation with the villagers any. Maybe he had only thought he heard a voice? It could have been the wind, it did make some odd noises sometimes while blowing through the trees. The only problem was the wind wasn't blowing. That was a little disconcerting. Still, in his present company it might be best if he avoided acting like he was hearing voices, at least until he could talk to Ursa about it.

Hyroc shook his head and waved dismissively. "Never mind," he said, keeping the concern from his voice. "I'm probably just hearing Kit, he makes some weird noises sometimes when he's excited."

Donovan and Elsa nodded. "Or you might've heard an elk off in the distance," Elsa suggested. "They make some pretty unusual noises sometimes and how quiet it is out here doesn't help either."

"Yeah, it's nothing."

They nodded again. Hyroc breathed a silent sigh of relief. Then they resumed their march through the snow.

"Yes, our prey is near," the voice said. "We must move faster."

Resisting the urge to stop and risk alerting Elsa and Donavan to his behavior, Hyroc stole a glance through his surroundings. Nothing moved, but a feeling of unease slowly descended upon him and he felt as if they were being watched. He very much wanted to tell the other hunters, but if the voice was only in his head he might start looking crazed, so he said nothing. Besides, if there was something following them, he was certain the four of them could handle it.

As they came to a stand of trees, Kit suddenly stopped mid step, holding one paw in the air and ears pricked forward at the same time as Donovan suddenly threw his hand up. Donovan dropped into a crouch – Elsa and Hyroc doing the same – and he pointed toward the trees. Focusing on the indicated spot, Hyroc saw something knock a cascaded of snow from the branches of a tree ahead of them. All three of them readied an arrow and slowly crept toward the disturbance.

Through the trees, the back end of a small doe came into view. Mindful of every step, Hyroc moved around the snow-crusted skirt of a tree. His heart beating noticeably faster, he took a deep breath of icy air that made his nostrils tingle. Just as he lined up his shot, the deer raised its head sharply skyward and bolted. Drawing his bow string slack when the deer disappeared from sight, he blew out an exasperated breath. They almost had it. Turning toward Donovan and Elsa, he saw they wore similarly displeased expressions.

"What happened?" Donovan said, throwing his hand up angrily.

"No idea," Elsa said. "Maybe Kit spooked her?"

"Don't think so," Hyroc said. He pointed back toward Kit who was only a few steps away from where they had stopped, moving toward him. "He looks like he stayed back where we spotted the deer."

"Yeah, I don't think it was him either," Donovan said. "She kind of acted like –" he trailed off when they spotted something moving between the trees in front of them. The something resolved into the shape of a wolf.

"Is that a wolf?" Elsa whispered. "I think that probably explains it." An eager look came into her eyes as she gazed upon the animal. "Anton would pay a good amount for a wolf pelt, he's been trying to get his hands on one ever since it snowed."

Donavan and Hyroc nodded their agreement. "Yeah, getting a wolf would be proper compensation for it scaring off our deer," Donovan agreed. "Just need to make sure we kill it as cleanly as possible."

Elsa glanced from Hyroc to Donovan with a proud look in her eyes. "Well boys, that would mean me then, I can get it in the eye."

Hyroc couldn't help feeling a little deflated at her words and he even saw Donovan sigh. Debating their shooting abilities would take too much time and their voices might scare the wolf off, so neither wanted to disagree, or at least for the moment. They nodded reluctantly, garnering a taunting smile from Elsa.

She readied an arrow, waiting for a clear shot of the wolf. The wolf moved toward them. Before she could shoot, four more wolves came into view behind it. This wasn't just one wolf, it was an entire pack! This was something dangerous even for the three of them. Seeing this,

Elsa slowly let off on her bowstring, taking a few steps back toward Donovan and Hyroc.

"I didn't even hear them howl," Donovan said. "How did we stumble across a wolf pack?"

"Don't know," Elsa said. "Getting a pelt isn't worth risking someone getting mauled and who knows how they'll react toward Kit."

"Yeah, let's just scare them off," Hyroc suggested, remembering how he had once frightened off a pack of feral dogs. "As soon as they see we're not an easy target they'll leave us be."

Donovan and Elsa nodded their agreement. The three of them began yelling as threateningly as they could. Strangely, this had no effect on the wolves, they continued forward, seemingly oblivious to the cacophony of voices. But even more strangely, Hyroc noticed they had purple eyes. He had never seen or heard of eyes that color on an animal. Something about the color put him on edge. Then the wolves began arraying themselves in a neat line. The neatness of their formation seemed unnatural. As far as he knew animals were never neat. They should be behaving more chaotically and he expected there should be a lot more noise. They were quiet? Why were they so quiet? There was something frighteningly familiar about the silence. Something was wrong?

"Elsa, Donovan, something's not right," Hyroc said.

"Yeah, I'm starting to get that feeling too," Donovan said, a hint of apprehension entering his voice.

"They're not even reacting to us," Elsa noted. "And I've never seen ones with purple eyes. We should get out of here. Everybody back away slowly and don't put your back to them."

"Yes, the Wol'dger is here," Hyroc heard the voice say. Just then a bird's shadow passed over them. He glanced up to see Shimmer circling them. The sight of the raven sent a prickle of fear down his back. Shimmer seemed to frequently visit him when something bad was about to happen.

"Kill them!" the voice said, it's words full of ice.

All five wolves immediately broke into a run. Hyroc cursed, leveled an arrow at the nearest wolf and let it fly. The arrow struck the wolf in the head and it collapsed. An arrow from Donovan and Elsa killed two more in the center of the formation. The last wolf on the left darted toward Elsa and the other moved toward Hyroc.

Elsa dropped her bow, reaching for her knife on her belt. The wolf lunged into her before she could draw it, knocking her off her feet. Just as it tried to sink its teeth into her neck, Kit rent the air with a roar, tackling the wolf. The two of them tumbled into the snow, sending up a poof of snow when they landed. The wolf shook off the big cat, bounding sideways toward Elsa, its face covered in bleeding gashes. Elsa rushed over with her knife drawn and brought it up under the back of the wolf's chin, covering her hand with its blood. And an arrow from Donovan to its rib cage finished off the wolf.

Hyroc hastily knocked an arrow and shot the remaining wolf. It shuddered and collapsed. Three more wolves burst through the trees, two heading for Elsa Donovan and Kit, and the third peeling off to attack Hyroc. The wolf going after Hyroc, came in from the side and jumped at him. Hyroc dodged out of the way, barely avoiding his attacker slamming into him. He backpedaled, readying another arrow. There was a loud crack and the ground gave out beneath him. He was weightless for an instant before he came down on the side of a hill. Tumbling backwards, he came to a stop at the bottom.

Having lost his bow on his way down, he drew his sword. The wolf appeared over the lip of the hill and tore down the incline at a suicidal speed. It jumped at him again. Hyroc raised his blade and caught the wolf on the shoulder with a quick swing. The wolf lost its balance when it landed, going face first into the snow. Then to Hyroc's surprise, it clambered to its feet and started limping haggardly toward him, streaks of its blood staining the snow. Hyroc moved backwards half baffled by the wolf's determination to kill him. Even at a subdued pace he could prevent the injured animal from catching up to him. Then he became aware of frantic yelling from the top of the hill and loud growling noises. Feeling a surge of fear toward his companions, and a pang of sympathy for how much pain his wounded adversary must be feeling, Hyroc moved over and finished it off with a hard-downward stroke. When nothing else moved to attack him, breathing heavily, he quickly moved back to the hill.

"Wol'dger!" the voice said angrily, as Hyroc started trudging back up the incline.

The ferocity of the voice startled him, but even more startling, it sounded like the voice was coming from somewhere close. Tightening his grip on his sword, he glanced in the direction the sound was coming from. He found another wolf standing nearby. Only it wasn't a wolf. Its body was shaped like a wolf's but it was bigger, with sharply defined muscles on its limbs and their seemed to be a slight shimmering around it. A ridge of sharp grey spikes ran from the base of its head down to its tail. The tail had a thin coating of fur, with three bony protrusions at the end. Razor-sharp triangles of black teeth lined its open mouth. There was a purple glow emanating from the back of its mouth and its eye sockets contained burning embers of purple light.

Was this the thing that had been speaking to him? It didn't seem like it should be capable of speech. Instinctively he reached for an arrow, but instantly remembered he didn't have his bow. The creature started moving toward him in an accentuated arc. Hyroc turned with the creature to keep his front facing it.

"The covenant has not been completed," the voice said. The thing's mouth did not move, but somehow Hyroc knew it was speaking. "My task must be finished. The Wol'dger will not stop me."

"What task?" Hyroc said, surprising himself he had the nerve to even attempt speaking to this thing.

The creature stopped as if caught off guard and glared at him with its fiery eyes. "The sacrifice was committed and the command was given. The Wol'dger must die."

"Sacrifice? What sacrifice?"

"The sacrifice of flesh. *It was committed by he* and I must obey."

"Who is he? Who sent you?"

"The one that demands your death. The command was given."

"Why does he want to kill me?"

"Only death matters, death, death, I must obey. The covenant must be fulfilled. His command is my will. No escape. No escape for the Wol'dger. Only death!"

Before Hyroc could raise another question, the creature broke into a run. He dodged out of the way of its charge, whipping his head back when it tried to slash his face with its tail. The creature wheeled around and leapt at him. Unable to raise his sword in time, Hyroc threw his arm in front of him to take the brunt of the creature's attack. A hot sensation shot up his arm. The air shimmered blue in front of him and the creature flew off to his right as if it had glanced off something solid. The hot sensation faded from his limbs and the shimmer vanished.

The creature shook its head as it regained its footing. The instant it was standing it hurled itself into his chest, flinging him to the cold snowy ground. Hyroc grabbed the creature by the side of the neck, away from its spikes, and punched it in the head. Another surge of heat shot up his arm and into his hand. When his knuckles contacted the creature's skin, a small blue flame blossomed across its snout, snaking its way across its flesh in several directions. One tendril of fire ran up into the creature's eye, extinguishing the purple ember within. The creature wailed out in pain, it's cries sounding like a horrible mix of twisted metal and fire eagerly devouring wood as it lurched away.

"Wol'dger should not have their power!" the creature bellowed. "Wol'dger should be a weak, weak like beasts. Sacrifice was committed, the covenant has not been fulfilled. Cannot fail!"

Movement on the hill, and a deep guttural growl caught Hyroc's attention. Sparing a quick glance toward it, he saw Kit at the bottom of the hill with his hackles raised and eyes fixed firmly on the creature.

The creature snapped its attention to the mountain lion. "Covenant will be fulfilled, beast will assure death," the creature said, a disturbing amount of eagerness in its tone.

Kit loosed a long shrieking yelp of pain. Hyroc turned toward his companion. A bolt of cold shot through him when he saw Kit with his eyes closed tightly, thrashing his head from side to side and stumbling through the snow.

"Kit what's wrong, what's he doing to you?" Hyroc yelled. He turned back toward the creature. "What are you doing to him!"

"Beast will assure death," the creature said. "Covenant will be fulfilled."

Kit yelped even louder. "Fight it Kit, fight it!" Hyroc turned toward the creature and gave it a hard glare. "Stop it!" He gripped his sword tighter. "I said STOP." Hyroc raised his sword high above the creature. Two arrows whistled through the air, striking the creature in the midsection.

The creature growled out in pain. "Covenant must be —" its words were cut short when Hyroc lopped its head off. Instead of a torrent of blood rushing out of its neck, a purple smoke began issuing from where its head had been attached. The body fell over limply. The creature's head settled into the snow and its remaining eye slowly went out. Then the head and body began condensing into a pile of ash with a purplish hue.

Glancing toward the top of the hill, Hyroc saw Elsa and Donavan running haphazardly down its slope. Moving his gaze down, he saw Kit laying in the snow on his side. Fighting down a wave of dread, he rushed to the big cat. Kit was breathing rapidly and his eyes were closed. Hyroc kneeled down beside him and carefully pulled one eye open. Kit's eyes were their normal yellowish brown.

"You're okay buddy, you're okay," Hyroc said, wiping a tear from his eyes. "It's dead, you're safe now."

Elsa and Donavan reached the bottom of the hill. Their eyes darted from Kit to the two piles of ash where the creature had been with confounded expressions on their faces. Elsa opened her mouth to speak, but closed it, settling into a crouch beside Kit.

When Hyroc lifted his eyes from his companion, off in the trees he saw Ursa watching them, but the look in her eyes wasn't a happy one. She seemed thoroughly concerned about something, something beyond the danger of what he had just experienced and he felt a flash of apprehension as he wondered what that other something could be.